BLOOD CREED

BOOK TWO

REVELATIONS

BY
ERIC STILL

First and foremost, thank you for choosing to read Blood Creed Revelations. Within our endeavors to not forgo our humanity, it is important to recognize the things that aren't conducive to our own wellbeing. As such, below are the relevant themes that will be found within the book that you are to be advised of.

Trauma
Sexual Assault/Rape (referenced, not graphically depicted)
Suicidal Ideation
Depression
Loss of child
Torture
Imprisonment
Death of loved ones
Damaged parental relationship
Animal abuse
Violence (blood, death, etc.)
Racism

ISBN: Paperback: 978-1-965988-03-9

ISBN: Hardcover: 978-1-965988-04-6

ISBN: eBook: 978-1-965988-05-3

First printing 2025 by **Eric Still**

Book Cover and Chapter Decoration by **Anna-Mariya Georgieva**

Interior illustrations by **Philip Neumeister**

Map Frame and Structures by **Izzy C. Xavier**

Edited by **Maddi Leatherman**

Proofread by **Salman Azhar**

Author photo by **Dwight Taylor**

To my cat, Grim.

Through the subjugation you wrought when you took my heart, you have given me far more.

Runes of Sin

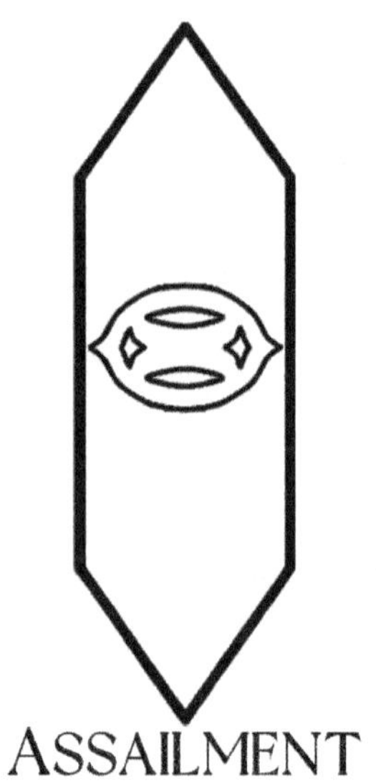

Assailment

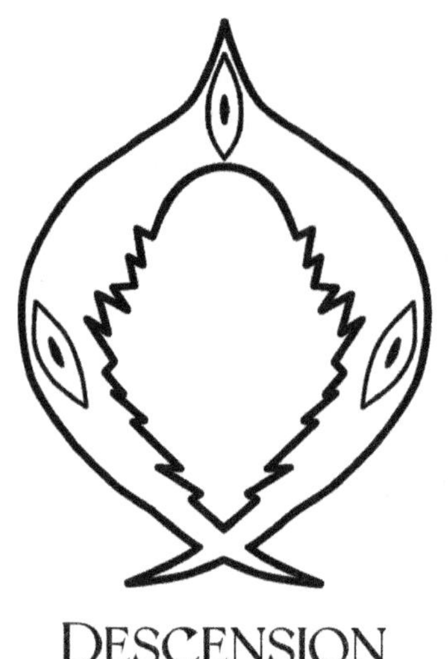

Descension

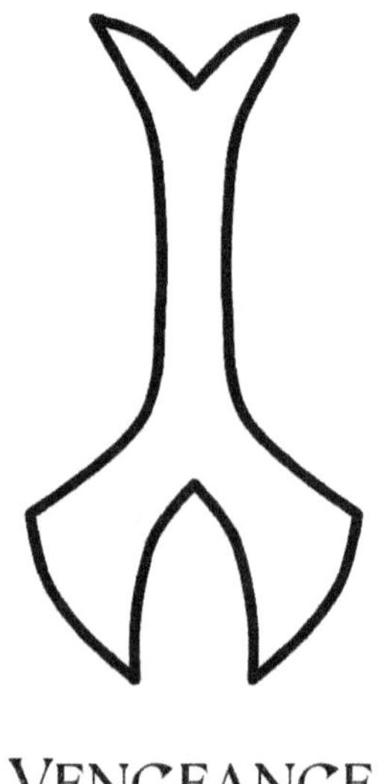

Vengeance

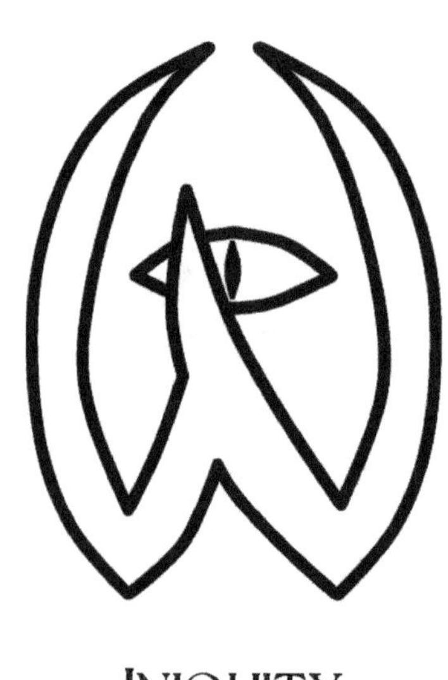

Iniquity

Runes of Virtue

PROTECTION

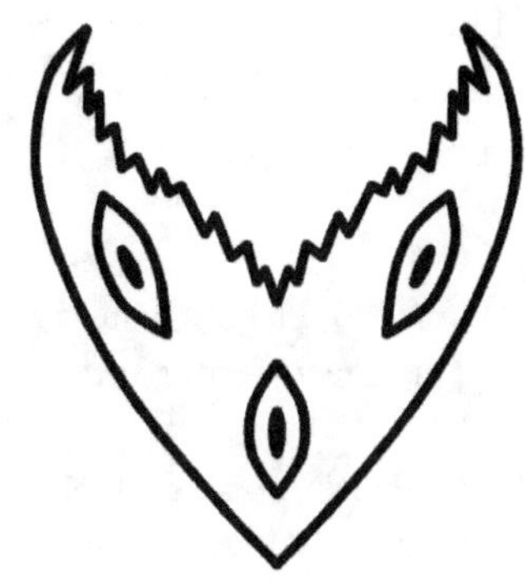

ASCENSION

BLOOD

ABSOLUTION

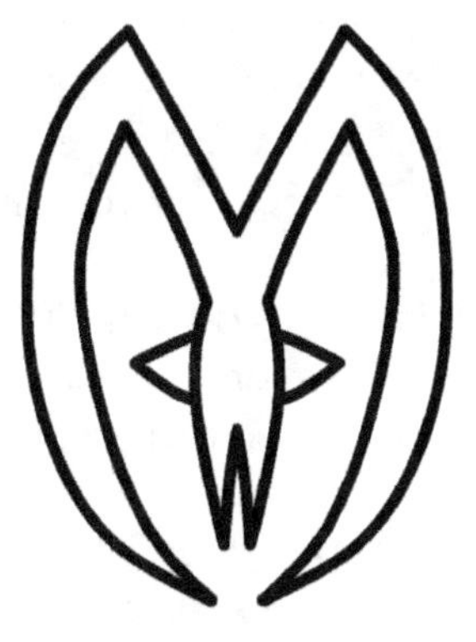

EQUITY

The Hunters is an international organization with thousands of personnel. While there are many bases and strongholds throughout the globe, the most indomitable is the Rosemary Fortress. One of the oldest but most renown of their bases, it has withstood the test of time and has proven to be impenetrable by demons that would seek to test its barrier. Nestled in the wilds of West Virginia, it spans over 400 square miles. The heart of the base is nestled between forests and snakes through an expansive valley with a larger river. There are several facilities on base that serve to both train hunters and cultivate the means with which they remain dominant in dealing with demonic threats.

TRAINING FIELD- A field in the northern section of the base that connects to both the Engineer Center and the valley. It serves as the focal point of training regimens.

ENGINEERING CENTER- The section of the base dedicated to technological innovation and tools squads with a location where they can formally congregate for equipment maintenance and strategic planning.

MESS HALL- The Mess Hall nourishes all personnel on base, where they are given a stipend for their meals should they choose to eat there.

HQ- The most fortified of buildings on base, serving as the facility where high-ranking personnel confer to direct operations.

COMMAND- The fortified hub of technological interfacing with squads and other bases around the globe. Command serves to consolidate intelligence and serve as a communication hub for all operations.

BARRACKS- The barracks are a large conglomerate of dwellings for both hunters, cadets, and their families who remain on base.

MEMORIAL STONES- A section of the base dedicated to the hunters that have fallen, either after a long career or in the line of duty. It is conveniently located across from the teleportation terminals for hunters to pay their respects prior to missions.

TELEPORTATION TERMINALS- The teleportation terminals are a marriage of technology and magic, allowing squads to teleport to a variety of locations without stressing their energy reserves.

AIRFIELD- The airfield features all airborne vehicles that the hunters use for getting across the base or providing a means of travel for operations requiring them. It also features large terminals for teleporting the vehicles to other bases and locations as necessary.

ROSEMARY FORTRESS
VALLEY SKY TRAM
VALLEY
TRAINING FIELDS
ENGINEERING CENTER
MESS HALL
HQ
W. BARRACKS
E. BARRACKS
W. FOREST
E. FOREST
COMMAND
TELEPORTATION TERMINALS
MEMORIAL STONES
AIRFIELD

Table of Contents

Prologue … 1

1. Revelations Within the Dark … 7

2. Embittered Reticence … 25

3. Vacant Vows … 59

4. Elations in the Cold … 87

5. Lament our Shadows … 121

6. All That is Taken … 143

7. Tormented Vagrant … 177

8. Indispensable Bonds … 207

9. Oath of Chains … 243

10. Near and Far … 277

11. Sins We Abhor … 295

12. Elegy of Sin and Sentiment … 329

13. Rondo of Emptiness … 353

14. Oblivion's Call … 379

15. Dance of Greed … 401

16. Evanescence of Condemnation … 433

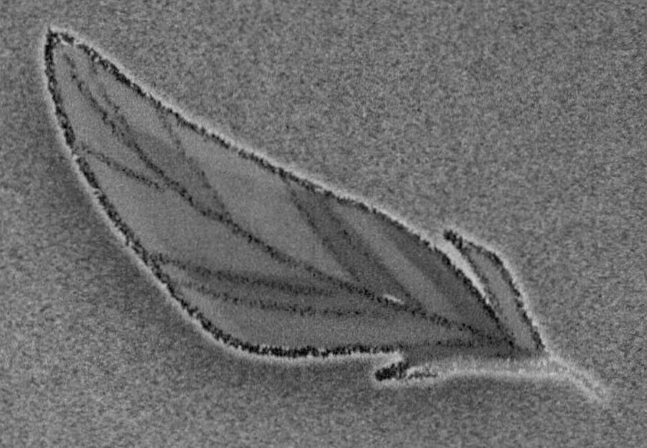

MANY TRUTHS ARE OBSCURED FROM EYES FORLORN, BUT WITHIN THE UMBRAGE OF SUCH TRIBULATIONS, THERE ARE MANY

REVELATIONS

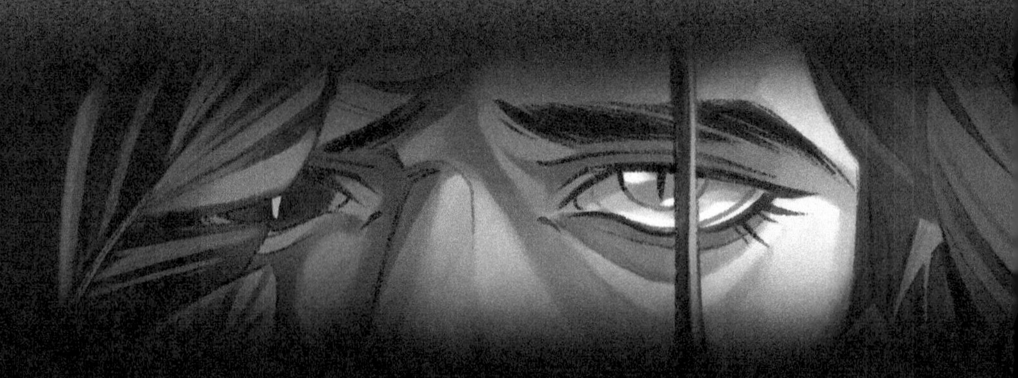

PROLOGUE

A LONE IN THE DARK, tears coursed from Eden's eyes. His cold
cheeks were saturated with warm tears—a paradoxical sensation
marred by their genesis. The chamber he occupied had never been comfortable, but now there was an irrevocable despair that swelled in his chest,
supplanting the cadence of his thrumming heart. With a heavy gasp, he
shakily exhaled, but it did little to relinquish the suffering.

The shackles bound to the clasps on his wrists stung with a fresh pain,
his thrashing moments prior having proved fruitless. Still, his right hand
remained clenched tightly. Within his blood-caked fingers was a single
frayed feather. Once of a brilliant, ethereal white sheen, its luster had since
faded and was stained red.

There was no reason to still cling to it; his fate was certain. But amid the
crackling grief that evanesced within him, rebellion flickered. His helplessness was challenged by this phantom sentiment, and the voice that haunted
him continued to boom. The cold fled from his body as the clashing ideals
roiled, but he failed to gather the strength to raise his head. Before him, the
impervious bars of his cell towered, and the empty maze of halls taunted
his fractured mind.

The brewing turmoil became kindling for that festering sentiment.
The voice he feared in the encroaching darkness breached once more, and
his tears soon burned. The air quaked, filling with a power unbecoming of
divinity, yet it promised liberty with its declaration.

Those tears became blood—glowing and insidious. It flowed from his eyes, sizzling against his icy skin and carving him. The cell sweltered, and all traces of the cold that once remained were incinerated. Weathered fingers dug into his palms. Yet the crackling power paled to the feather, no less brilliant than when it had come from *her* wings. And as the vengeful blood marked his form, it colored the once hueless feather with its vendetta. The light voice that had begged him to live was soon supplanted by the source of his rebellion. That darkness called to him once more—just as he would call to her. It was all that answered.

Would you allow them to continue to take?

Quietude cut through the thick air as Eden stood. The chains bolting him to the floor tugged but easily relented under the power that tore through them. No longer bound, the terrible power surged, and his eyes flared bright red. Within that eternal stretch, the pits of darkness expanded before Eden. In front of him, there was a single barbed chain that glowed. He reached out and grasped it, letting it sear into him like the bloody tears that marked him. Letting this pain ignite the kindled wrath, his voice swelled with energy and damned the pain of his existence.

"No."

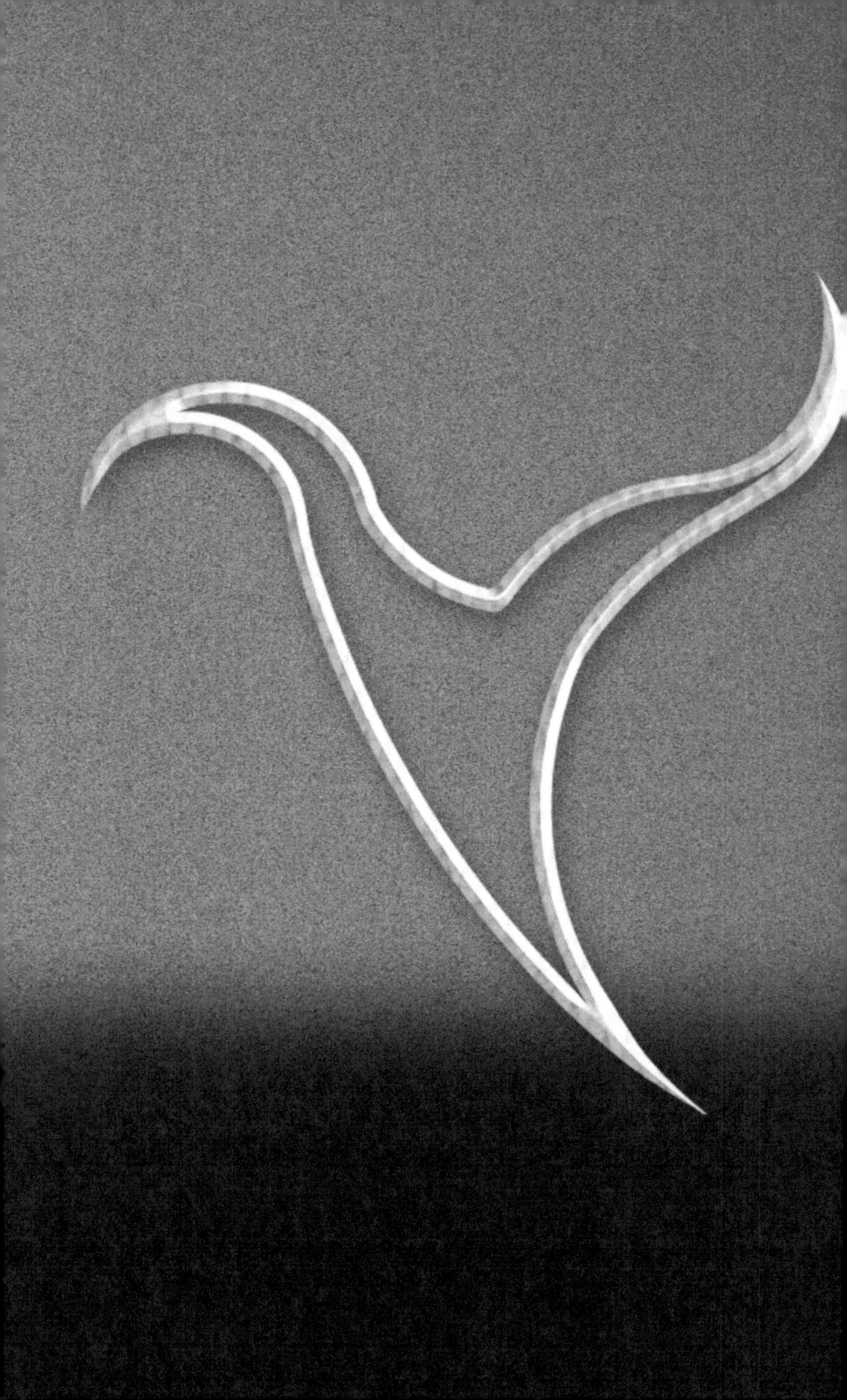

ONE

Revelations Within the Dark

DEMONS EXIST, and those that hunt them remain vigilant to challenge their dark ambitions. Yet sin would always exist, but what distinguished man from demon was a thin line that was easily blurred. Sentiment and sacrament alike were often tested in the growing harrows of all whom Ichor breathed life into, including the demons who were born with darkness sequestered in their souls. Such darkness, while inviting fear, also welcomed wonder from curious souls who would see its truths unfurl. Should this darkness consume, eyes of greed, deprived of grace, would see the world diminish before them to know its revelations. But before their endless want, a diminutive yet resilient sentiment remains: In the subjugation wrought by those who take, hope is found in that which is given.

Unsure of what Kendra would give, the forest and its looming horrors stretched before her. The limbo of shade danced with the swaying leaves as the wind roared in her ears. Quick-paced steps barraged the floor, crushing twigs and scattering dried leaves from beneath her boots. Those resolved, royal-blue eyes snapped from left to right, carefully scanning the trees as she dashed through the thick foliage.

"Path ahead of you is all clear. No demons or environmental hazards in the preliminary scan. Stay vigilant," Andrew's voice buzzed through her earpiece, and she reached up to touch it.

"Copy," Kendra replied, and she quickened her traversal of the terrain, more certain in her scouting of the forest. She inhaled deeply but detected nothing peculiar beyond the floral scent. Her squad had already covered ground at the eastern and western perimeters of the forest, and she was assigned to the northern section, which she intended to survey.

The reports leading into the mission only gave an approximation of where the missing hunters had last been detected by Command before going offline. By Jessica's speculation, a Fracti Alas Laboratory was likely. The infamous laboratories had been determined to be the source of innumerable dark experiments and scientific research. That was what Kendra knew, at least. But she was acutely aware that the Hunters had been seeking out the laboratories for generations but had never made significant progress.

The closer she drew to the heart of the forest, the more pronounced her heartbeat became, and she was suddenly on edge. She skidded to a stop and swiveled her head. Inhaling deeply, she carefully analyzed the subtleties within the surrounding scents. It was almost visual: specific flowers, the type of grass, the tree bark, and the native creatures. A family of birds hovered above her head, tucked quietly into their nest. Before her, she locked onto two unfamiliar scents, however faint they were. A trained demon could hide their energy signature, but their scent was almost always too harsh to disguise from her nose.

Kendra curled her fingers into a tight fist, and with a slow, controlled extension, she uncurled them to reveal sharp black claws where her nails had been. They crackled, and without warning, she lashed, sending a thin row of flames ahead of her. The air rippled, and several beady red eyes glared at her before zipping out of the path of her attack. She quickly drew her hand back, and the flames disappeared at her command so as to spare the flammable vegetation.

She glanced to where the beady eyes had gone, and slowly appearing from the veil of their illusory holding, two tall humanoid bird demons emerged. Draped in black feathers with lanky limbs, clawed digits, and large talons that stabbed the grass, the demons' gazes suggested an intelligence she'd avoid underestimating. They were well-trained, based on their camouflaging ability. That hypothesis proved itself quickly when they let out a low squawk, and two black spears appeared in their hands. Holding their gazes in the tense moment, Kendra touched her earpiece and spoke.

"Two vulcans on my twenty, both armed with spears. They can command illusions and summon objects."

"Copy that. Need backup?" her comrade Damion Rigs spoke.

Kendra carefully searched the energy signatures within the area, only parsing out the two foes before her along with her comrades in the far distance. She pondered her options for a moment, sizing up her opponents, but after a moment, a smirk carved across her face.

"Nah, I got this," Kendra replied. Lowering her hand, she inhaled deeply and manifested flames atop her palms. The moment was brief, but she covered the distance between them quickly, swiping upward to cut the spear of the vulcan. With the weapon halved, the vulcan leaped back, and Kendra turned her attention to the other as it brought its spear down toward her. In that decisive moment, Kendra snatched the handle of the spear and slammed her palm into the vulcan's chest. An explosion of fire consumed it, sending it back while it violently screeched.

The other vulcan hissed at her, blinking its several glaring eyes before it dropped its broken spear and shot into the air.

"It's fleeing to the sky!" Kendra called out over her radio, worried it might alert further defensive forces to their presence. Before she could leap into the air to hurl fire at it, a low whistle rang through the air with a pop. A bullet struck, and the vulcan fell through the trees. Crashing into the ground, it began squawking in what she presumed to be pained cursing—she didn't speak bird demon to know for sure.

"You're covered," Emily's voice chimed over the radio.

Kendra breathed a sigh of relief, slowly walking toward the flailing demon before touching her earpiece.

"Nice shot, Grayson," she complimented as she approached the demon. The gaping hole in its chest, while possibly fatal, hadn't immediately ended its life. Curiously, the more she peered into its eyes, the more depth she gleaned than she had initially presumed. Vulcans, while above-average intelligence of the feral variety, were still typically incapable of deeper levels of rationalization. Yet its eyes suggested otherwise.

"Please ... no," the vulcan said in a low, croaky voice.

Kendra paused, confounded. A feral demon, however trained it was, didn't speak, nor had she read about such a thing in the demon compendium when she was a cadet.

"What the ..." she spoke hesitantly, stopping in front of the vulcan. "You can talk?" In response, it raked the grass beneath it and choppily croaked,

"Please. I don't want to die." Choking, its large beak was ajar, and a long tongue flicked out.

Kendra clenched her right hand, flames spilling between her fingers as she glanced at it. The hairs on her neck stood on end, and her instincts screamed at her while she held its gaze, but something was off about the situation. The scent of vulcan, while weak, was in two places at once—in front of her—and above.

Kendra leaped back as a vulcan's talon plunged into the ground where she'd stood—an attack that could have cut through her barrier. Rebounding, Kendra leaped forward and slashed through the demon with flaming claws, the upper half of its body fizzling away. The injured vulcan in front of her kicked its long legs and scrambled backward. However, Kendra's hesitation had all but disappeared, and she hurled a wave of flames at it, burning it to nothing.

Breathing a heavy sigh, her fingers brushed along the gray fabric that hugged her arms. She took a moment to examine the state of her hunter suit before relaxing. As long as she released her flames in brief bursts, she found that the Kevlar didn't burn. The discipline with her powers ingrained into her by Zane helped, but the heat of the moment sometimes compromised her focus.

Tension fled her hands, along with her claws receding. The vulcans' guile was noteworthy, assuming the tactic was deliberate. It had certainly startled her, but she had learned to trust her nose, especially in earlier missions she had undertaken. This was another advantage she appreciated with her mutation. With exercised caution, she examined the scene once more before touching her earpiece.

"Hey ... uh, have you guys ever heard of a talking vulcan before? The one Grayson shot was definitely speaking just a moment ago."

"Vulcans speaking? It's ... not unheard of. Isn't well-documented, though," her comrade Bonnie Blair spoke over the radio.

"Guess I'm getting close then. If these labs live up to their reputation, we'll probably encounter all sorts of unusual shit."

"Captain Blackwell also encountered vulcans at the southern end of the forest, so they're definitely guarding something," Bonnie added.

Shortly after their communications, Kendra pushed the idea of the talking vulcan from her mind and resumed her trek through the forest. Eventually, she came to a cliff face that was caked in moss and foliage in an unusual way. Nature had an almost chaotic way of covering its landmarks, but this seemed more controlled and deliberate. To the untrained eye, it would easily be missed if one could make it that far, but the faint scent of chemicals and rusting metal didn't escape her. With vigilance, she began to search the perimeter for the source of the scent.

Soon, she found it. Hidden beneath a thick mesh of vines and moss, disguised among the lining foliage, there was an indentation. A swift wave of her hand was enough to burn away the façade that disguised the presumed entrance.

"I found a large metallic door. I think this is it," Kendra spoke, touching her earpiece as she warily eyed the door.

"Copy that," Eden spoke over the radio. "Ardent, Grayson, and Romero, you guys stay with Carter. The rest of Seraph Seven, converge on Mallory."

The squad gave their confirmations over the radio, but one voice spoke out in concern.

"Think it's a good idea for your bastion to stay behind during a breach?" their squadmate Alicia Romero questioned.

"More concerned about ambushes on our support camp than I am about the main squad. Stay with the others until I say otherwise," Eden replied.

"Aye-aye, Captain," Alicia sarcastically spoke. With Eden's command standing firm, the radio went silent.

Kendra folded her arms and kept a close eye on the entrance, waiting with anxious nerves as to what they would find within the lab upon breach. She had heard several stories about what had allegedly occurred within their confines, but she took some of the stories with a grain of salt. Even in the fantastical world that she still had trouble believing in at times, exaggerations were still plentiful in their organization.

Kendra still recalled the ghost stories her training platoon would tell at the end of the day. Her comrade Valeria Alma always recalled how she'd hear reverberating rattles whenever she did night watch in the Western Forest. Kendra understood why. The forests throughout the Rosemary Fortress, the Hunters' HQ, were spooky at night. Most of the remote regions of West Virginia were. Eventually, she had overheard Commander Rigs say to another commander that he'd play sounds in the forest at night to keep the cadets on their toes. She still teased Valeria about that.

With a low hum from above, Kendra looked to the sky. In a narrow clearing where she stood before the cliff face, a shadow loomed. A sturdy, redheaded woman with light, freckled skin and a stocky build slowly descended, connected to the base of a drone.

"Sup, Ken?" Bonnie spoke as the drone lowered her to the ground, and she landed before disconnecting from it. Bonnie interfaced with her hunter gauntlet, and the drone shot back into the sky.

"Ever think it's cheating to use those to get around?" Kendra inquired, causing Bonnie to scoff.

"Hardly cheating if I made the thing with half a year's salary. It's worth more than the legwork I'd put in trekking back to base on foot."

Kendra cocked an eyebrow.

"That's like a ... 3,000-mile hike through several countries," Kendra challenged.

"I said what I said," Bonnie spoke with a snort, placing her fists on her hips as she approached. "I may not be jogging marathons, but your girl can walk one. That's for damn sure."

"I don't doubt it, Bon-Bon," Kendra said, smirking as she heard rustling nearing them from the east. She smelled Damion before he emerged minutes later. A tall, lean man with mahogany-colored skin, shoulder-length black microlocs, and hazel eyes approached. The large shotgun strapped to his back swayed as he jogged over to Kendra and Bonnie, and he sighed lightly.

"Hey, BB, looks like the little sis of Seraph Seven is all grown up now—taking down vulcans all on her own!" Damion spoke after letting out a heavy breath from his journey across the forest.

"I've taken down stronger, Dame," Kendra sneered.

Damion gave her a skeptical look, folding his arms.

"What about the time that wraith snuck up on you?"

"You mean the *one* kind of demon I can't smell?"

"Gotta use more than your nose, Ken," Damion said, shrugging as he eyed the door, nodding to it.

"Well, my nose found the secret demon laboratory, so I think it's doing fine enough for now. Gives you something to do, anyway," Kendra challenged as Damion slapped her back.

"Yeah, yeah. Keep doing your thing, private," Damion sighed.

Kendra would have protested further, but she knew it was useless. Treating her like the runt of the squad was his teasing habit. Both she and Valeria were *young bloods*, but he especially insisted on keeping her ego in check.

With idle banter, the three waited for the others to arrive. Bonnie inspected the door, looking for the mechanism as to how it worked, and soon, both Yuki and Valeria arrived.

"Good to see you made it in one piece, V," Kendra greeted, offering a kind smile to Valeria.

Valeria was a short woman with light skin, black eyes framed by tactical goggles, and short, silky black hair tucked into a gray beanie. Valeria had trained alongside Kendra when they first became hunters, and they shared a special bond from the days they spent covered in sweat and dirt from the valley they were tempered in. She idly held her rifle up, but her demeanor was more relaxed than it suggested.

"Of course. Yuki had my six, and we're a pretty scary-looking duo," Valeria attested with a triumphant grin.

"Really? 'Cause if I were a demon, I'd eat you right up," Yuki teased, pinching Valeria's cheek before she swatted her hand away.

"Well, she's not wrong. You do have a pleasant scent ..."

"I'll make sure to douse myself with extra rosemary oil later," Valeria snapped defensively, slinging her rifle over her back before folding her arms.

Kendra sneered playfully before looking up at the cliff face, suddenly sensing Eden's energy at the top. She cocked an eyebrow, concerned that he might just jump down.

With a thud that seemed too soft, Eden landed in front of the squad, unperturbed. His long black coat rustled as he stood straight, and he adjusted Avenger's sheath as he eyed his squad. While they stood stiff with their attention on him, they couldn't hide the bewildered looks on their faces.

"Uh, Captain, wasn't that like ... a ten-meter drop?" Valeria tepidly asked.

"Twelve," Eden corrected, rolling his shoulders before turning to face the metallic door embedded into the cliff face.

"How did you even do that?" Kendra asked, exasperated.

"Precise energy control and conditioning," Eden spoke flatly, shaking his head. "I'm presuming none of you saw anybody enter or exit, so we don't know how the door works, right?" Eden questioned.

"Affirmative," Kendra spoke, shrugging in defeat as she sighed and joined Eden's side. "Bonnie didn't find any apparent technology that operates it, so it probably uses some kind of runes or incantation to open."

Eden glanced at Bonnie, who nodded to corroborate Kendra's claim.

"Then we'll need to breach it," he said.

Standing at attention, Valeria reached into the pouch strapped to her right leg.

"I have some thermite charges we can—"

"We'll refrain from wasting resources. Kendra, you're up," Eden said, nodding his head toward the door as Valeria pouted.

"Me?" Kendra gestured to herself, flashing a smug look at Damion before returning her attention to Eden and continuing, "But I'm only a private, Captain Blackwell."

Damion scoffed, tapping his temple with two fingers.

"That means you pick up the slack," Damion said, snorting.

"Mhm," Kendra dismissed, clicking her tongue. "Slacker," she mocked and approached the large metal door. Her claws flexed while sparks flickered on the tips. After a few moments of concentration, heat surged through her fingers as her flames danced across them, and she bared her teeth in preparation. With four swift slashes, her claws sliced through the metal, leaving a jagged diamond-shaped mark where she had scored the metal. Still glowing red-hot, she focused her energy into her right foot, twisted her body, then lunged forward and kicked the center, sending the chunk tumbling across the smooth stone floor.

Kendra took a deep breath, air rushing in to cool her lungs. The squad examined the empty hall within, and she took a step back, admiring her handiwork. With another exhale, her claws receded, and she repeatedly clenched her hands.

"Hall looks clear," Kendra called out, and Eden took to her side. The ordinary, cramped hall begged the infamy of the potential laboratory, but it could have been a purposeful ploy they remained wary of.

"Good work. I'll take point. Ken, watch the others' sixes. Assume ballista formation," Eden commanded, and the others walked past Kendra, giving silent nods of approval.

"I'll ease up on you. Don't want you to start fantasizing about making me sashimi," Damion whispered to her.

Kendra grinned, flashing her fangs at him.

"Too late," Kendra said, pushing him when he passed her. Once Bonnie was ahead of her, she followed her squad inside.

The hunters drew their weapons, keeping them trained carefully to fire whenever necessary, and Yuki, following beside Eden, hovered her saber in front of her. The formation within the cramped hall, while not as wide as it would usually be, placed the most vulnerable in the center. At the front were the captain and highest-ranking close-range hunter, both serving as *blades*. Behind them were the *cannons*, Valeria and Damion. In the middle would have been Alicia, their *bastion*, but instead, it was only their *engineer,* Bonnie. At the rear, Kendra treaded, serving as their lowest-ranking blade.

Seraph Seven was designated as an elite squad of demon hunters that Kendra had earned a spot in. It had taken nearly two years to condition her and several others into fully fledged demon hunters. Working with Eden was the outcome she had tirelessly trained toward. However stale he could be, he was her friend, and she got along well with the others as well.

The squad had carefully crossed the hall, reaching the end where a metal door waited. Pausing, Eden held his fist up as the squad readied their weapons. The door slid open, revealing a well-lit lobby containing a desk with two metal doors on either side of it. Behind the desk was a large demon man whose back was to the squad, but he slowly turned to face them when he heard the door open. Glimmering yellow irises eyed them warily, but then they widened in realization. He had been holding a soggy donut in one hand and a mug in the other, filled with what was presumably coffee. But with one sniff, Kendra knew it had been spiked with whiskey, causing her to scrunch her face in disgust at the combination.

"Hands, now," Yuki spoke out, drawing her pistol on the demon. He dropped his donut immediately, lips agape as he choked out in surprise.

Eden boldly approached the desk, grabbing the demon by his neck and yanking him over the desk. The coffee mug splattered on the floor, and the scent of whiskey and cheap coffee filled the lobby, prompting Kendra to pinch her nose.

"Blair," Eden called to Bonnie, and she jogged behind the desk to hack into the terminal. She got to work on the computer system, plugging in a device she pulled from her belt.

"Hunters ..." the demon man grumbled between his gasps before Eden placed him on his stomach. He then beckoned Kendra over and gestured to the man.

"On it," Kendra sighed out, approaching as she held her hand out toward the demon. "Religo," she spoke, and his arms snapped behind his back as his ankles bound together, constricted by orange rings of energy. "Couldn't you have done that?" Kendra questioned Eden.

"Good practice for you," Eden reminded, echoing one of the sentiments he'd spoken to her in their numerous training sessions.

"Right," Kendra muttered, then shot a look at the guard. "Whiskey? On the clock?" she chastised before turning her attention to Bonnie as she interacted with the terminal.

"Carter, do you copy?" Bonnie spoke, touching her earpiece.

"Copy," Andrew chirped over the radio.

"Things should be coming through the tunnel I opened. You receive access to their network yet?"

"Uh … yeah! I've got eyes on the facility." There was a moment's pause before he continued, "This is … Laboratory C-19. Weird naming scheme from the others we read about." Andrew went silent for a few moments to review the data. "Seems like it stretches quite a ways underground too. The elevator to the west of you guys should lead to the research center, and directly north of that, in the lower levels, is some kind of prisoner holding. There's only like twelve others I can see on the cameras there, and I've got a list of the employee IDs that have scanned in. I'll get to work on deactivating the security systems."

Eden carefully used his foot to roll the demon onto his back, then placed it atop the guard's chest threateningly.

"What security systems are ahead? We'll know shortly, so you might as well just tell me now," Eden imposed, meeting the ire-filled gaze of the guard. After a few seconds of stubborn silence, Eden's heel sunk down, causing the guard's eyes to bulge while he groaned.

"We got an alarm system and some biometric locks!" the guard sputtered out, and Eden removed his foot.

"You copy that, Carter?"

"Yeah … injecting the disarm command into their network. No way to override the locks, but I've engaged the manual door mechanisms. You're clear to move through the facility now," Andrew spoke, and Eden nodded to his squad, beckoning them to follow him.

"Grab Mister Whiskey Donut, and let's get a move on," Damion told Kendra as he and the rest of the squad circled to follow after Eden.

Kendra stared down at the guard and clicked her tongue, shaking her head before hoisting him onto her shoulder. Even with the discomfort touching the guard caused her, she followed silently and without complaint.

The next hallway was wider, allowing them some space as they walked, a reprieve from the claustrophobia Kendra abhorred. Reaching the door leading to the research center, she set the guard down temporarily in preparation for their next task.

When the squad entered, several vats with fleshy amalgamations suspended within them filled the white-tiled floor. They glimmered with an amber liquid that cast an orange hue. Above, the lights were dim, allowing the vats to be observed more clearly as the faint glow colored the room.

The scientists, umbra demons in formal wear and long black coats, were met with a rush of commands and physical handling from the squad. Between the Seraph Seven's three blades and the barrels of the others' guns aimed at them, the scientists were quickly subdued and restrained. Given the nature of how the incantation bound them, they couldn't channel energy effectively, rendering them immobile and mostly helpless.

The squad piled the scientists up in the center of the room, having swept to search for remaining employees. With a quick headcount, they knew they had detained all the demons who were accounted for in the intel provided by Andrew. Kendra returned to the entrance and snatched the demon guard by his legs. She haphazardly dragged him across the floor before tossing him onto the pile of demons, much to their displeasure when he landed on top of them. She snorted, returning her attention to the rest of the room while Valeria and Damion held the scientists at gunpoint, commanding them to remain still. While the bindings suppressed them, a powerful enough being could break them—assuming a bullet didn't end their life before they could.

Eden approached the demon scientists shortly after examining the room. The sharp taps of his footsteps caused them to tense, eyes agape as his fierce crimson gaze glowered in the dim chamber.

"Is Onaga here?" Eden asked, pensively watching their expressions to determine whether they'd be truthful or not, but they were quick to shake their heads.

"No, he's not …" one spoke, swallowing hard as he shifted his wrists.

"Then where is he? Where are the other laboratories?"

"Don't know," another began. "We're relegated to this facility and this facility alone. None of us are informed of the network or logistics between labs."

Eden went quiet, holding the scientist's gaze before he glanced at the several vats throughout the room.

"Which of you is in charge?" he asked. Following a pause, the oldest-looking scientist sighed.

"That would be me," the man croaked.

"What's in the vats?"

The scientist was quiet for several uncomfortable moments, prompting Eden to approach slowly.

"They're … chimeras. Synthesis between several kinds of demons," the scientist blurted out, shifting uncomfortably as he averted his gaze.

Eden was prepared to question further, but then Yuki touched his shoulder, garnering his attention. Her iridescent, pale eyes narrowed as she glanced to the northern hall that connected to the room, and Eden nodded in response, turning from the demons. Yuki then approached the head scientist.

"Are there any prisoners here still? Demons, humans"—she crouched in front of the demon, her expression darkening as she hovered eerily close to him—"children?"

Expression solemn, the scientist raised his head and shook it. He then glanced at the northern hall.

Yuki stood, returning to Eden's side without another word.

"Captain," Valeria began, holding her wrist up with the holographic interface from her hunter gauntlet showing, "the elevator in that hall should lead to the prisoner holding. You and Schaefer should check it out."

Eden's gaze flickered, and he looked at Yuki, seeing her gaze firmly fixed to the ground with her hand tightly squeezing the hilt of her saber.

"Agreed." Eden touched Yuki's shoulder, pulling her out of her thoughts.

"Right ..." she muttered, and Eden glanced at the others.

"The rest of you keep an eye on the demons. Our connection may break for a bit once we descend. Flare your signatures if you need to get our attention."

Once the squad gave their confirmation of his order, Eden took to the northern hallway, and Yuki followed behind him.

With a heavy sigh, Kendra folded her arms. The ensuing silence jarred her. It wasn't an alarming quiet, but the kind that begged answers to a looming mystery waiting to be uncovered. The odd shadows cast from the floating blobs of flesh in the vats were the most apparent subject of her curiosity.

She had studied chimeras in the compendium, never having encountered one personally. They were rare, created artificially, and the technology that produced them had been relatively primitive—less than a century old from the first reported sighting. The splicing of DNA, while perhaps a mimicry of the mutation she had undergone, was much more complicated than she'd deign to guess. Then there was the confusing ordeal of consciousness within them.

Despite the Hunters' efforts to research them, no specimens they had acquired proved anything useful beyond learning the genetic profiles of the chimera. Whether they could truly perceive and feel as a living creature did was indeterminate, nothing beyond what wraiths were capable of, according to their inconclusive studies. Wraiths were corrupted omens that amalgamated into spirit-like forms, waiting to be exorcised, and chimeras the Hunters encountered behaved just as they did. To see one in its infancy, pulsing within the amber-hued vat, evoked a dull ache within her chest.

For several minutes, Kendra hesitantly patrolled the room, idly scanning the different fleshy amalgamations with a divorced curiosity. Though they writhed and pulsed, there were no further hints of life. She circled one of the vats, peering at what appeared to be the most developed of the subjects. Writhing energetically, there was a similar undulation of its flesh to whenever her wounds regenerated. She focused on it further, and a twinkle of heat grazed her as its energy signature thumped against her own. Like tiny tendrils latching onto the essence of her soul, she could detect whispers of life from within it, however minuscule and alien it was.

She gasped, backing up as the flesh expanded and squirmed. Then, an orifice opened, revealing an eye. It was glassy and lacked detail, but it was an eye if she ever saw one.

The more she scrutinized it, the more Kendra's chest tightened. The thing that she watched appeared to squirm in a way she could only describe as panicked. The eye's features developed in front of her, becoming a brown iris fixed atop a black void. Up until then, the liquid in the vat had been still, but a single bubble ascended from the corner of the eye as it stared. The longer their gazes connected, its likeness caused her breath to quicken. While unrecognizable in appearance alone, the pervasive sentiment within it—the fear—was eerily familiar.

Something human.

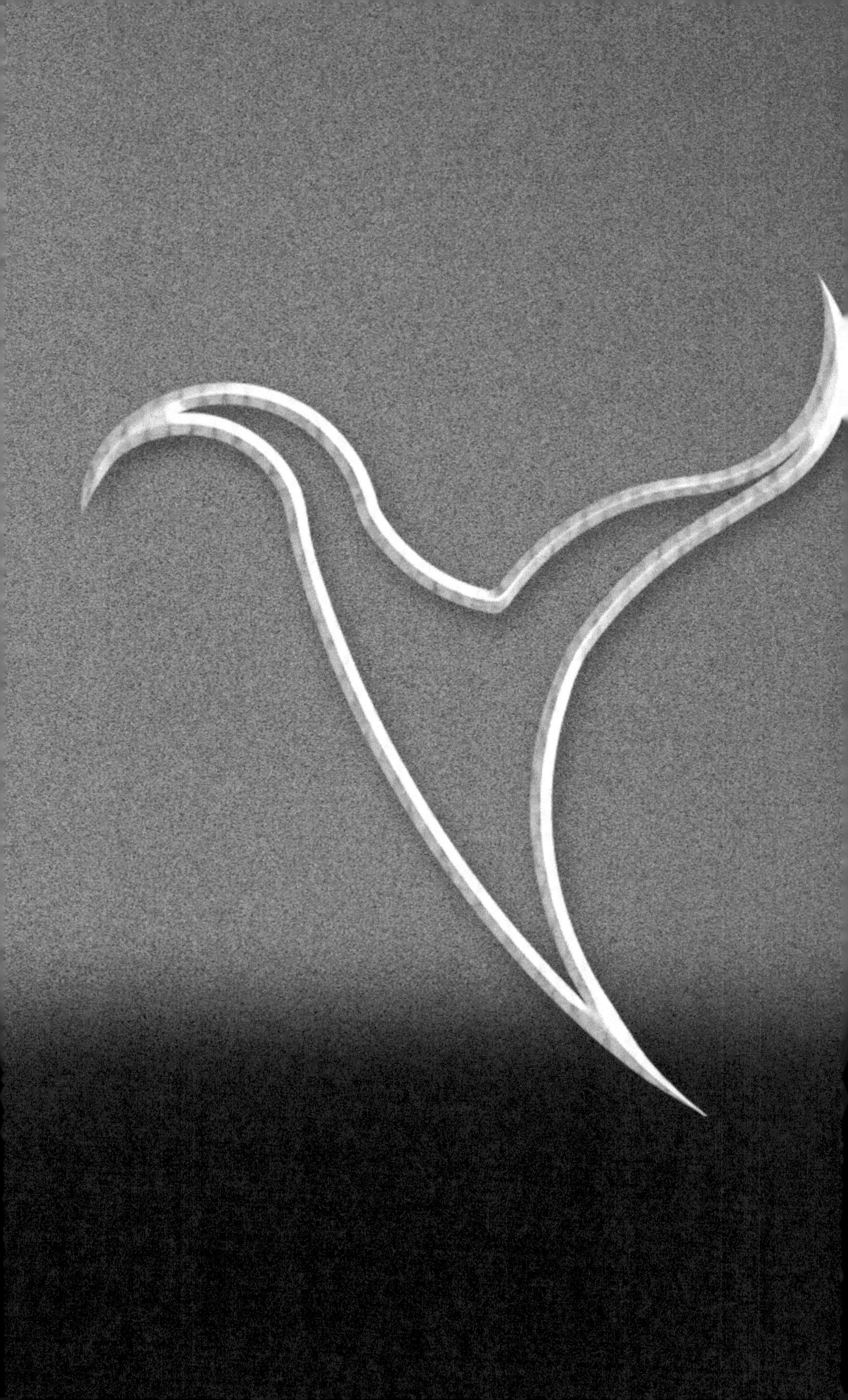

Two

Embittered Reticence

THE EYE BEFORE KENDRA stared with eerie sentience within its depths. She knew such a polarizing look, even if no expression could accompany it.

Darkness.

When Kendra had first lost her humanity several years ago, a similar grief had invaded her own eyes—like looking through a cloudy lens at a world that once felt safe, now confined within an inescapable cage. She had seen it. She had felt it. But while she had found peace with what she was, she suspected it could never. She wasn't entirely sure it fathomed the severity of its state. Even so, its pitiful, grieving gaze begged for freedom—to awaken from the nightmare.

The elevator opened within the adjacent hall, snatching the hunters' attention. Marching from it, Eden rapidly approached the restrained scientists, ire festering within his red eyes. And despite Kendra's initial questioning of the urgency behind his approach, he ignored her in his adamancy. Lunging at the lead scientist, Eden snatched him by his throat and held him up, only tightening his grasp as the man choked and gasped.

"You sick fucks are going to tell me *everything* that you know!" Eden growled.

Kendra's attention snapped to Yuki as she followed behind him, lacking the same urgency as Eden, but her face was inscribed with a similar contempt. That look marring her delicate complexion was a visceral omen of what Kendra anticipated learning.

"You made them suffer until the very end, and like you worms always do, you took everything from them!" Eden hissed, his grip tightening with an audible crackling from the power building in his hand. It was tight and painful, yet deliberately nonlethal in how he applied the pressure.

"No! The doctor wasn't the one who proposed that idea … it was me!" one scientist proclaimed from the group who helplessly watched Eden strangle the lead scientist.

Eden slowly turned his gaze to the man who spoke. Young, lighter in complexion than the others, he appeared to be of similar age to Andrew. However, youthful appearances of a demon weren't as indicative of age as they were for humans. However young he was, Eden lacked a whisper of sympathy.

He dropped the lead scientist, who gasped for air but quickly squirmed to sit up, sweating profusely as Eden approached the youthful scientist.

"No, boy! Don't—"

Eden's leg snapped back and kicked the lead scientist in the face. He tumbled across the floor, splatters of blood painting the white tiles. Eden then marched over to the young scientist and snatched him by the collar before pointing to the closest vat.

"The hunters you captured … you're making them into chimeras, aren't you?" Eden hissed.

The squad was silent for several moments, their eyes snapping to the vats with manic bewilderment and disgust alike. Finally, the scientist Eden questioned nodded.

"Tell me. The vulcans we fought in the surrounding forest—were they chimeras?"

"Y-yes, but not in the technical terms. We augmented their brains with the ones from the prisoners the OCN delivered to us," the demon scientist spoke, cowering from Eden's glare.

The Oxium Corporum Nexus was a syndicate headed by ferali and umbra demons that had declared independence from the noble houses and the authority of Avernus, formerly headed by an umbra demon called

Salem. The ferali were especially formidable—powerful, resilient enigmas comprised only of females. When they were under the rule of their matriarch, Cecilia, they had stolen souls from the living and denied them an audience with Sere, the Primordial of Death. For this, their existence was especially damned by humans and demons alike.

The Hunters actively worked to destroy them. However, they hadn't been prioritized for various reasons—their comrades' abductions a crucial one. Eden was concerned upon hearing of their continued operation, but he sought to confirm it.

"The Nexus? How long ago was this?" Eden demanded, and the scientist nodded promptly.

"Several weeks ago. I can tell you where Salem is, just ... please don't hurt my colleagues. We were just following Onaga's orders." Upon hearing this, Eden glared skeptically.

"Don't waste your breath. I killed him over a year ago, and you'll be next if you don't tell me where Onaga is!" Eden pulled the scientist closer, causing him to flinch as he dangled.

"We don't—" Eden tossed the scientist into a nearby wall, and a loud crack was heard as he fell to the floor, dazed and groaning in pain.

"Eden! What are you doing?" Kendra called out, rushing over to Eden, but Yuki snatched her by the shoulder, shaking her head.

"Don't, Mallory ... he won't compromise the mission," Yuki spoke, eyeing the scientist as he struggled to sit up.

Eden, with laser focus, lunged at him and pinned his head beneath his boot, causing the scientist to let out a cry of pain.

"I don't know!" he repeatedly cried out, stirring the lead scientist from his stupor as he squirmed on the ground.

"We were being truthful earlier, Blackwell!" the lead scientist spoke, and Eden eased his boot from his subordinate's head. In that moment, the air grew heavy as Eden's fingers curled into tight fists, and he turned to face the lead scientist.

"You know of me, so you'd also know why I need to find him," Eden growled.

"Y-yes, of course. I ... we just don't know. Otherwise, I can assure you we would have told you. He moves often and seemingly appears without a trace."

Eden paused, scrutinizing the scientist's face to glean his sincerity, but he returned his attention to the youthful scientist at his feet.

"What is this research for? There's a reason, so what is it?" he demanded snappily.

The young scientist peered up at Eden, blood spilling from his lips as his skin sizzled, slowly regenerating from the damage Eden caused him.

"Biological fusion and magic synthesis. Artificial vessels and instilling the essence of life into them ..." spoke the scientist, and he glanced at his senior with fear in his eyes.

The red omens in the air surged around Eden, and the expression on his face darkened as he stared down at the demon. The answer, whatever meaning Eden ascribed to it, had set off something observably malicious within him. Kendra's eyes widened, and she acted within that instant, rushing at Eden. She slid and caught his boot before he could bring it down on the demon's head. A crackle of red electricity erupted around Eden's form as his attention landed on her, and when she raised her head, she hardly recognized who was staring back.

"Eden, what the hell are you doing?" Kendra grunted out, shoving his leg back before she stood. For several moments, he stared at her, the darkness within his eyes slowly fading. He then closed his eyes, turning his back to her.

"Blair," Eden called.

"Sir?" Bonnie answered, perking up from the stasis that she and the rest of the squad had been in.

"Have Andrew put you through to Command. They need to send an intelligence unit to scrape this place clean."

Bonnie lifted her wrist, interfacing with the projection while nodding in confirmation.

"Consider it done, Captain."

Kendra eyed Eden warily, watching as he walked back to the elevator on the opposite end of the room, where they had initially emerged.

"I don't advise it, but if you've got the nerve and stomach for it, go observe the prisoner holding. These ... *experiments* are a grim reminder of why we took our oaths," Eden spoke, propping himself up near the elevator. He took deep breaths and reached into his coat, removing pills that he promptly swallowed before falling silent.

Kendra glanced at Valeria. They had both heard what the scientists said, but even then, it was difficult to understand what had angered Eden so much. Chimeras weren't new, but human integration was. An affront to ethics was too lenient a descriptor for such evil.

"I'm going to take a look ..." Kendra hesitantly decided. She preferred not to, but the idea of purposefully avoiding it seemed more disrespectful to the memories of her fallen comrades.

Before Kendra could reach the elevator, the sound of rapid steps followed her, and she glanced over her shoulder to see Valeria, who pursed her lips as their eyes met.

"I'm going too. We said we'd stick together when we graduated, so I can't let you be the only one who bears this ..." she said.

Kendra gave a reluctant smile, nodding before they moved through the hall. Together, they entered the elevator and descended into the bowels of the facility. Anticipation brewed, even with the gruesome scenes they had seen throughout their short careers. Whatever they would uncover suggested itself to be far more grave. Demons rarely left behind favorable circumstances, and she hoped it could grant justice to Eden's rash anger.

The moment the elevator doors opened, both of them flinched in disgust at the scent that smacked them. Sulfur was the least offensive of the discernible sources in the stagnant air. The acidity could be tasted, and the revolting, pervasive rot was even more intense for Kendra. The cramped halls, lit with a dim red hue, felt as if they would swallow them whole, condemning them to the several prison cells within their stretches.

"This is ..." Valeria retched, clenching her stomach. However, with a shake of her head, she swallowed hard.

Kendra's lips pursed tightly as she pinched her nose and entered the halls. The hazardous layout begged many questions beyond ethics, and she imagined it had been purposefully designed as such—far more inhospitable than the warehouse basement she had been stuffed into years ago. The cells were filled with the prisoners' decomposing corpses, and insects gnawed away at them, their limbs still bound in the shackles bolted to the floor. As inhumane as their subjugation was, it had been the more lenient of the fates the remaining prisoners suffered.

The sounds of chains rattling from farther down one of the halls caught the pair of hunters' attention, prompting Kendra to slow. Valeria carefully raised her SMG, a rifle being too big to maneuver within the halls. The energy signature they detected was indescribable—abominable, even—and the gurgling grew louder the closer they got to the cage. Most disturbing of all, there was something familiar within the malformed signature.

They came to a stop in front of a larger cell, where they saw *it* bound by several chains—one for each of its six malformed limb. Taut, leathery gray skin hugged the bony curvature of the creature that writhed within the cell, and within its chest was a throbbing amber sack that audibly thumped. Each time it did, a low gurgle left the thing's animalistic maw. Its teeth were too big for it, even with its size, and its eyes, like a spider's, bulged uncomfortably from its ill-suited face. Disoriented, the eyes danced around, searching for several moments until they landed on the hunters outside its cell.

Kendra peered into those knowing eyes, and the sack within its chest throbbed sporadically. It moaned softly through its jagged teeth as it reached out with one clawed hand.

"Ken ... Val ..." it hissed in a garbled voice, struggling to maneuver its body effectively.

Kendra's gaze narrowed, and for a moment, embers left her palms as she debated slashing the cage open. Eyes gaping, they stared at the thing's form. Fixed to its neck was an object they knew well from their time as cadets. The bastion of their cadet squad, Draugr Six, had always carried around a necklace containing a silver mark coin passed down through his family. It had been caked in blood and rusted over, but its engraving was still legible. He had shown promising talent that Jessica personally commended. They had taken the final exams together—graduated together. In that moment, they became nauseous, but Valeria lost face.

"*Steiner* ..." she cried before collapsing to her hands and knees, beginning to vomit.

The longer she held its eyes, the more she could decipher the sheer despair buried within them—even with the monstrous appearance. And the thing, trembling with what Kendra could only assume were distorted sobs, spoke.

"Kill—me ..." it began but suddenly squealed as the sack in its chest convulsed painfully.

As the shackles echoed, so too did the memory of the chimera's eye inside the vat. Far beyond a mere loss of humanity, they were stripped of everything they were—left a malformed husk birthed by sinful curiosity.

The true extent of Onaga, the fallen angel Eden sought, had dawned. The original demons who fell were few and far between, most swallowed within the sands of time. Onaga, however, remained, and so long as he did, the depths of his darkness would strip all before it of Ichor's grace. Human or demon, all would become subjects—consumed by insatiable greed.

"I knew him ..." Kendra said. "Steiner was a good man, very talented. Nobody deserves to have suffered like that. I was never religious ... but it feels like something beyond blasphemous," Kendra spoke to Yuki, her legs crossed atop her bed. No number or length of showers made her feel clean. What she had seen was on par with the insidious machinations Intico had made her witness. Being a dithered suddenly seemed tame in comparison to her comrade's fate.

She hadn't delivered the killing blow to what remained of Steiner—she couldn't bring herself to. His quirky exuberance roiled in her memories fervently, and she froze when she thought to. Unlike Valeria, she was able to at least stand steady on the way back out. The fate of the chimera was left to the intelligence unit sent in after her squad, she had been told. She just hoped it would be quick.

Kendra and Yuki shared a barracks room, both dressed in their night-time casual wear as they settled in for the evening. Kendra, gray joggers and a black tank top. Yuki, black and white shorts and a white crop top. The tropical scent of the incense box on Yuki's nightstand filled the room. Unlike other artificial scents, this one hadn't bugged Kendra—she actually found it pleasant.

Yuki was brushing her long white hair, holding it with a tight fist as her eyes held Kendra's gaze from the dresser mirror she stood in front of. She was mulling over Kendra's statement, but after a moment, she sighed.

"Agreed," Yuki said. "Alicia used to talk about him, said his aptitude was quite high for a human. And only half a year into his career, like you"—Yuki shuddered—"It's beyond awful. Knowing that they suffered … I can't blame Eden for snapping the way he did." Yuki sighed, glancing back at Kendra before setting her brush down, spinning around to face her.

Yuki always had a toned form that Kendra admired, but whenever Yuki was in casual attire, Kendra caught glimpses of the stretch marks on her stomach—the only ones on her body. She had always hesitated to pry. Shaking the stray thoughts from her head, she pursed her lips and spoke,

"I … never saw him like that. Not even when he fought Intico. The look in his eyes was beyond loathsome. I don't even know the word to describe it," Kendra said, muttering the last part to herself as she reclined back on her bed and pressed her head into the pillow. "You guys are always talking, so you'd know more about that."

As the Harbinger of Greed, Onaga was the demon who ushered the deadly sin into the hearts of many angels when he fell. Since then, many of his schemes had unfurled over humankind. Of all the notable demons Kendra had read about, he was the most prolific and ancient of threats to humankind. Since the inception of the first hunters, he had been relent-lessly pursued for the evils his experiments and thirst for knowledge had wrought across the world. Much of the history of his deeds had been erased when most of humanity was disconnected from Ichor, but its echoes rippled in ways unseen.

There were many reasons to hate Onaga. His ambitions served as an affront to all extents of decency and morality. However, Kendra thought the animosity Eden had shown was entirely different from just his conviction to hunt demons.

Kendra's gaze suddenly landed on the empty glass and empty syn-blood packet on her nightstand. Scrunching her face, she reflexively sat up and sighed.

"Hey, Yuki? Feel free to say no, but Eden has really been adamant about these Fracti Alas missions we've been going on. Onaga is a genuinely evil guy and all, but is there something that happened between them?" Kendra asked.

Yuki's light eyes shifted away from Kendra, and she approached her nightstand with silent steps, opening the drawer and pulling out a pink rectangular handheld gaming console.

"I won't speak on his behalf, but ... I'll say the way he reacted is more tame than it could have been, believe it or not. He was rash, yeah, but I understand why," Yuki spoke, turning to face Kendra and offering a wry smile. "What we discovered was just a bit too much for him mentally. I wasn't exactly thrilled to give mercy, either, but they're more useful alive. We just have to hope the intelligence team and interrogations can yield something good from it all."

Yuki's eyes betrayed her saccharine tone, and the more their gazes met, the more Kendra could see the topic was sore for her. She had enough sense to not delve further, and she offered her own smile in return.

"We all have our breaks here and there. I shouldn't judge him too harshly," Kendra remarked. She unclasped the straps attached to the temples of her glasses and removed them from her head, set them on her nightstand, and rolled herself into her blanket. "I think I'ma catch some Z's. Early day tomorrow and all."

Yuki sat on her bed, uncurling an old pair of earphones—the kind with a jack cable—that she plugged into the game console. She curled into a ball, flipped the dual-screened console open, and switched it on.

"My sleep schedule is pretty bad at the moment, so I'll be winding down."

"Oh, I've been meaning to ask about that thing. I haven't seen that console before. Pretty ancient, right?"

"Older than me by two decades, but I like retro gaming more than you like being a Ken-burrito," Yuki said. She then smirked to herself and turned her lamp off. "Sleep tight," Yuki said and placed her earbuds in.

Kendra nodded, turning her lamp off before turning to face the wall, yawning as she relaxed into her bed.

"Night, Yuki," Kendra murmured, shutting her eyes.

While Kendra wasn't really into gaming, she couldn't help but imagine that Kendall and Yuki would have gotten along well. They were both sweet and friendly, and she would have wagered Kendall would have even developed a crush on Yuki like she did on Natalie. As much as the memory of her late younger sister left a bitter taste, she took solace in how jealous she would be to know Kendra was a demon hunter. As Kendra drifted into sleep, she could practically hear Kendall complaining.

Not everybody has cool hell powers to fight demons!

The westerly winds brushed through the frigid valley, carrying with it the floral scent of sassafras. It was dry in December, and as fall transitioned to winter, so too did the leaves descend from the canyon just north of it. The surrounding forests, typically a mix of lush greens and vibrant reds, had become a faded gradient. Light clouds obscured the sun, bathing the land in the afternoon light.

Subtly, a light blue shimmer rippled in the sky. The barrier encompassing the Rosemary Fortress was boundless, and it was sometimes easy to forget it was there. Capable of staving off all encroaching threats, be they demonic or human, its massive presence promised peace to the hunters, but Eden doubted such a promise.

He overlooked the valley below, observing several cadets marching through its routes, and for a moment, he remembered watching Kendra when she was still a cadet. She had been an athlete prior to her initiation, so the drills weren't particularly difficult for her, but mastering the techniques hunters used had been the daunting obstacle for her. While imprecise, she was gifted with flinging flames and using her claws. However, she had struggled to become proficient with the other uses of Ichor. Augmentation, barrier conjuration, tethering, and other techniques had been a challenge for her, but he and Zane had helped her overcome the learning curve.

The flap of his jacket swayed in the wind, and the breeze tossed the structured strands of his black hair. He had run through several drills and exercises with Seraph Seven that morning. Structuring their team coordination was his prerogative as captain. He still wasn't entirely accustomed to it. However, both Yuki and Bonnie, who were in several squads before Seraph Seven had formed, suggested he did well as captain. Confidence in his own combat capabilities was one thing—faith in the abilities of others was different.

Yuki approached, taking to his side before the cliff. After a quiet moment between them, she spoke.

"You seem tired."

Eden continued staring down at the valley with a blank expression.

"Is it obvious?" Eden asked, prompting Yuki to nod.

"Having trouble sleeping again?" Eden was silent for several moments before sighing.

"The medication isn't working anymore," Eden spoke, his hands tensing as he gripped the cloth of his coat. "Every time I close my eyes ... I'm there again."

"Some nights, it's like we never left," Yuki said, pursing her lips as she reached out and took his hand. Briefly, her thumb circled along the back of his wrist until his tension eased.

"Alicia and I have plans soon. You gonna be okay?" Yuki asked, smiling softly at him before releasing his hand and taking a step back. She glanced over her shoulder, seeing Alicia smiling at her from the tree she leaned against.

"I'll be fine—just watch over Alicia," Eden said, his eyes still glued to the valley below.

"Such a protective cousin. You can count on me, though. Be safe." Yuki patted his back and turned, jogging off toward Alicia before they rejoined the squad.

The rest of the squad assisted Andrew in packing up the mobile communication center they had utilized during their exercises. At the bottom of the hill, they loaded the equipment into a utility cart. The barren center, consisting of dry terrain, was surrounded by the lush greenery that marched all the way to the cliff where Eden was.

Joseph placed a cylinder, the retracted communication tower, in the cart and turned to Kendra, who huffed at him.

"Show-off—making that seem easy," she spoke sarcastically.

"You should see the shit Dad made me lift," Joseph said, dusting his hands before placing them on his hips. "Doubt anything you did for him would have compared."

"Was it even heavier than his attitude?" Kendra suggested with a smirk, hoisting a large case from the ground.

"Ha. Guess you got me there, but I took that too," he said, rolling his eyes. "Tell the old man I said hey when you head home tomorrow. Already used my vacation for Thanksgiving," he said, slapping her arm as he walked past her.

"I'll consider it."

The case was the last piece of equipment left, and she hoisted it onto the cart. She let out a relieved sigh as Andrew eyed her with a pout, rubbing his left arm as sweat dripped down his brow. Meeting his dejected gaze, Kendra chuckled, flashing him a reassuring smile.

"You have to remember I've got hellhound DNA and years of athleticism on you. Can't beat yourself up for not being able to lift what you said, in your own words, is a collapsible server."

"I should be able to lift my own equipment without throwing my back out. I've been practicing my form and trying not to rely on augmentation for everything," Andrew huffed. He slapped the oval gem embedded into the handle on the cart, and in a flash of light, it and the equipment inside of it transformed into a slim metal brick. He then slid it into a pouch on his thigh.

It still astounded Kendra the kinds of things pocket dimensions could do for transporting and displacing stuff. The limitations and specifics still escaped her, and while Alicia had tried explaining it once, it went over her head. She'd imagine that her father would have an aneurysm trying to chart it out in scientific terms, based on how he reacted to Kendall's explanations of Wicca.

"Well, next time, just tell Bonnie not to take it off the cart," Valeria spoke with a chuckle. She slapped Andrew on the back, causing him to stumble forward.

Letting out a yelp, metal devices attached to Andrew's calves engaged, shooting metal anchors into the ground to keep him from falling.

"Careful! I'm only a hundred pounds and a laptop!" Andrew let out, pouting as the anchors retracted from the ground, clicking back into place.

"Made some gains? Good job!" Kendra said and ruffled his hair.

"I need to put on more muscle, so Dad's been keeping me on a strict diet and weight-lifting routine outside of this. Really sucks sometimes," Andrew said.

Valeria snorted and applauded Andrew.

"I'll need to ask Major Carter to make me a regimen. You're looking stronger day by day," Valeria said, causing Andrew to blush and look away.

"Speaking of which ... time to eat. Need thirty more grams of protein for my daily macros. You guys wanna join me for lunch?" Andrew asked.

"Could go for some nugs right now," Valeria commented, and Andrew perked up.

"Oh! I have some dino nuggies in the barracks' fridge," Andrew said.

"Dino nuggies? You're fucking adorable, Andrew," Kendra chuckled out, but Valeria elbowed her rib with an indignant smirk.

"Fuck yeah, dude! Those are the only kind I'd accept," Valeria said, holding her hand up for Andrew.

Snickering, Andrew gave her a high five and glanced at Kendra.

"Val's in. What about you?"

Kendra rolled her eyes and cracked her neck, glancing over her shoulder to see Eden still standing at the cliff. After a moment, Kendra flicked her wrist at the two.

"Go on ahead. Gonna see if I can convince Eden to join."

With a quizzical look, Valeria glanced at Eden before cocking her eyebrow at Kendra.

"He always says no, though," Valeria said. She tugged her beanie down to cover her ears, her breath visible in the cold air.

"I should at least try. He always skips breakfast, so he's gotta be hungry after today's drills," Kendra said, her eyes spelling concern the longer she looked in Eden's direction.

"Mm, okay then. Hope to see you soon," Valeria sighed, walking backward while waiting for Andrew.

The glimmer in Andrew's blue eyes shone as he nodded eagerly at Kendra. She flashed a smile in return.

"All you now," Kendra said. She winked as Andrew mouthed his thanks and walked after Valeria. The two proceeded to grab their backpacks and disappeared from sight when they descended the slopes connected to the training ground.

Kendra turned to face Eden. She silently watched him for a moment, wondering what kinds of things he was thinking about. He was broodier than usual recently, and while she hadn't overly concerned herself with it, the distant behavior was disconcerting even for him. She assumed it had to do with the history between him and Fracti Alas.

Killing her hesitation, Kendra made her approach. Her footsteps were dampened by the grass as she ascended the hill, and she stopped right behind him. She adjusted her glasses, waiting to see if he'd acknowledge her, but he kept staring down the cliff. The drifting clouds eased the harshness of the sun, diffusing the light for Kendra to see the still shadow Eden cast. His perceptiveness was high, as she had come to learn. She knew he was aware of her presence.

"You okay?" Kendra asked. As if the wind had feared her words, it, too, became still, and all was quiet once more.

"Just ... thinking," Eden spoke, unflinching.

"You're always thinking. Might get worried if you keep doing it while staring down a cliff," Kendra teased, taking a few steps forward and looking up at him. The moment she saw his eyes, she tensed, seeing a glimmer of the intense condemnation she saw when he was interrogating the demon scientists. However, with only the two of them present atop the cliff overlooking the valley, she wondered why he thought about it then. It didn't sit well with her.

"Didn't mean to worry you," Eden said, finally turning to face her.

Staring down at her royal-blue eyes, Eden could see her skepticism—though that was nothing new. She was always wary of what he claimed, given how brief he had always been.

"Need something?" he asked.

Kendra, with a stark gaze that challenged him, could see his head was still elsewhere, and she could already hear him declining the offer with such a distant mind. Very few things actively distracted Eden, or so it appeared. For years she had known him but still knew so little. But one thing she did know—he appeared most alive and engaged when he was fighting.

"Now that the others are gone—spar?"

Eden cocked a brow, shifting his feet as he turned to her directly.

"Why wait until the others were gone for that?"

"You know how I get when I'm pushing myself. I don't have the full extent of my abilities under control yet, and I don't want to put the others in harm's way."

Eden glanced down at her hands. Seeing they were already in tense fists, he remembered seeing her hands aflame as she struggled to contain the sweltering power throughout her training. With mishaps aplenty, he had helped her hone her focus and control as best he could. Admittedly, Zane was better suited to that task and had given the advice that mattered, but Zane couldn't delegate as much time to Kendra.

"Fine, but we blunt our attacks. And avoid using your chaos flames. Don't want any accidents," Eden said, and Kendra snickered in response.

"Doubt I'd hurt you even if I didn't," Kendra suggested.

She suspected she'd lose. Eden often blitzed the entire squad in the sparring exercises—even when it was all of them against him. As an elite squad, he insisted it was important they could work together to deal with powerful enemies as a team. Ethan, who was chiefly charged with training blades, did the same when he was a captain. Incredulously, Yuki had also mentioned Ethan was less gentle than Eden was. She didn't believe her, despite Ethan previously being declared the strongest blade of the Hunt.

The two marched down to the dirt lot carved into the mountain, and they took their places several yards apart from one another. As the wind rustled their hair, the sun slowly peeked through the clouds, illuminating the sharpened gazes that met. Upon Eden's countdown, they began.

Kendra dashed at Eden, reeling her hand back as her claws manifested with bright flames flickering atop them. With a swipe, the ground was ignited with rows of flames that shot after Eden. He leaped to the side, and Kendra gave chase. Though she tried to attack him, he deflected them all, and he soon sent her tumbling back with a boot to her abdomen.

The wind had nearly been knocked out of her, but she recovered quickly, holding her side as Eden dashed at her. There was a spark in his eye, and his hand lowered to Avenger's hilt. One swipe could end their session prematurely, and she made the split decision to channel her demonic power entirely.

With a growl, her flames swarmed around her form, furious and hot, prompting Eden to abort and leap back. Her human visage was eclipsed as the abyss swallowed her eyes, and from the center, her scarlet irises carved through as her sharp teeth bared. With an exhale, flames licked the air around her form and spilled from her lips, and she lowered herself close to the ground. With her sharpened focus, her barrier shimmered faintly around her arms and hands in a selective concentration of energy—just as he had taught her. So far as she maintained that concentration on her limbs, she could block his attacks.

Eden drew Avenger, slanting the black odachi defensively. In the following moments, Kendra aggressively closed in. She deflected Avenger from its defensive front and jabbed at Eden with a fiery arm. But he caught it, causing the wind to scream. They continued to clash several times, causing embers to scatter as hot air surged between them.

Eden's skin rippled, his crimson aura undulated as an intense pressure brewed. With crackles of red electricity, he kicked her, and she slid back. With adamance in her form, she remained upright and firm despite the dull ache surging in her chest.

She scarcely had a moment to breathe before he closed in on her, and the intensity of their collisions caused the ground to crack beneath their respective might. For the next several seconds, they danced in a flurry of clangs and bangs as they aimed to subdue the other, but Eden kept a solid front. Flames, claws, and kicks were swatted away.

The moment came when Kendra retreated with a leap, spinning as she took to all fours with a familiar pressure built in her chest.

Inhale.

The air surged around her, embers creating a brilliant display as her fiery visage danced in the sweltering heat building inside of her. But even as Eden watched this, he stood straight with challenging eyes. He wouldn't dodge.

Release!

Kendra's mouth opened wide as a wave of fire shredded the ground in front of her, advancing on Eden with a fiery hiss. The world around them was consumed by the hellish light. As if everything paused, a flash of red tore through her vision, then the flames suddenly reversed course. She had barely seen him move when they shot back toward her and dissipated into blinding light. Though she was stubborn to keep him in sight, he had leaped out of view when she flinched. When the world before her dimmed, the ground splintered from the impact of Eden landing from above, and she froze when cold metal touched the back of her neck.

Avenger hovered ominously atop her neck, the black blade's tip firmly planted in the ground. It hovered in the corner of her eye, informing her that their spar was over. Conceding, she dropped her head. A shaky breath left her trembling lips as she relinquished her focus, and her demonic features receded.

"You may be able to heal, but you'd be hard-pressed to find a demon capable of regenerating their head. Make sure you guard it more than anything else," Eden spoke. He lifted Avenger and sheathed it before holding his hand out to Kendra.

Kendra sighed, grasping his hand before standing.

"How did you do that? I was barely holding back my hell flash," Kendra huffed.

"Hell flash?" Eden cocked an eyebrow.

Kendra rolled her eyes. "Thought I'd name the attack—it being my trump card and all," she said, and Eden shrugged.

"Just don't go calling it out when you use it," he muttered, shaking his head. "What I performed was a sort of parry, a technique my grandfather came up with. I think I showed it to you back when you were a cadet; recall how I didn't shout the name when I performed it."

"Oh yeah, that thing. Didn't think it could deflect attacks of that scale," she said.

"But don't be mistaken. I could have easily dodged it with the same result, just like Intico did when you used that move on it." Eden crossed his arms and glanced back at the ground, which had been scorched black from the flames. "On that note, you can't always rely on that technique of yours. Uses a lot of energy, so if your opponent dodges it, you're probably screwed."

"Not like I can speak while doing it, anyway," she grumbled. "What do you suggest I do from now on, Captain Blackwell?" Kendra asked sarcastically, brushing her thighs off as she examined the waistcloth on her right thigh, noticing it had gotten a bit shorter from repairing the frays of her suit.

"What's the fun of me telling you?" Eden said, finally breaking his serious demeanor and offering a small smirk.

"Oh, now you have a sense of humor?" Kendra huffed but failed to contain her snicker as she adjusted her glasses. "I'll work on it." She watched him for a moment as he held out his gloved fist to her.

"Good match," Eden said.

Kendra nodded, tapping her knuckles against his.

"Good match," she agreed.

As the sun settled into its throne in the sky, no longer obscured by the drifting clouds, Kendra held her stomach as she recalled her original intentions.

"I'm hungry enough to eat a cow. Wanna join me for a late lunch?"

Eden quizzed her for a moment, then shook his head with a sigh.

"Not hungry. I won't hold you up, though."

"Not hungry? I know you don't eat breakfast, so how is that even possible? It's almost three in the afternoon. Do you even enjoy food?" she asked, and he shrugged. "There has to be something you'd want. At least a snack, like chips or fruit?"

Eden was pensive for a moment, shifting as he averted his gaze.

"Apple ..." he spoke quietly, prompting Kendra to give a knowing look. The irony was not lost on her.

"Wow, didn't know you were such a pretentious techie," Kendra teased, and Eden rolled his eyes.

"That's my least favorite kind of apple," Eden muttered.

Kendra folded her arms, smirking as she nodded.

"Well, you can snack on an apple while I eat. Deal?" Kendra asked, and Eden slumped his shoulders in defeat.

"We'll be here a while if I say no."

"Correct," she affirmed, and Eden sighed. He cracked his neck as he walked over to a tree and grabbed his backpack.

"Let's go then."

Kendra grabbed her backpack, fished her utility bottle from it, and took a long drink. Once done, Kendra slung her bag over her shoulder before walking after him.

They descended the hill, finding the path that would lead them back to the training field. Given how long of a hike it was, it would take half an hour to reach the tram that would take them from the valley to the training field. Kendra much preferred the buses in Chicago, which were cozier, but she assumed that comfort wasn't at the forefront of the tram's design. Also, heights still scared her.

As she held onto the bar in her seat next to Eden, she glanced out the window overlooking the valley as they descended the mountain. She wondered what kind of hike she'd go on with Natalie that weekend when she'd take her vacation. It had been over a year since she last saw her, and she wasn't able to use her smart band's network throughout most of the Rosemary Fortress. That further crippled the contact she had with her on her neglected social media profile.

"Have you taken your vacation this year?" Kendra asked.

Eden shifted in his seat beside her, glancing to the side.

"No, but General Blackwell will probably make me take it." Eden sighed as if he dreaded the idea.

"Then you don't have any plans?" Kendra inquired, and Eden shook his head. "You should totally join me back in Chicago then. Dad and I are doing dinner this Saturday, and there's a bunch of stuff I've lined up leading into the new year."

Eden gave a wary look, pursing his lips as he considered it for several moments.

"Sure. I was just going to be home, anyway. We only live a few miles apart."

Kendra smiled brightly, nudging him playfully.

"If only you were always this easy to convince."

Snow fell from the sky, softly caking Chicago. The cold in the air nipped at Eden and Kendra, but its bite appeared to bother Eden more, given

Kendra's body was far more resistant. Even with the thick layers of his long wool coat and fleece underneath, Eden's hands retreated to his pockets. He kept closer to Kendra than he usually would, her warm body temperature serving as a ward.

"I hate winter," Eden huffed out, shivering.

"I used to," Kendra bragged, smirking as she brushed snow off the nylon of her coat. Their boots sank into the thin layer of snow with each crunchy step, and Kendra squinted to see better. With the way the light reflected off the snowflakes, even with the sun having set, they blended into a beautiful spectacle with the omens. Light blue and white, they twinkled in a way reminiscent of a glitter-filled snow globe.

"It's a bit lighter than the last time I was here. Earlier this year, the omens were still pretty gloomy," Kendra mentioned, holding her hand out to touch one of the sprites, which drifted away from her when she did.

"They're typically more purple this time of year, seasonal depression and all. Something must be lifting spirits."

"I somehow doubt it's Santa," Kendra joked, prompting Eden to crack a smile.

The street beside them had been cleared of snow throughout the week, but Kendra could smell the salt that was used to mitigate ice formations. Even with it, she doubted it was much fun driving on the roads. She recalled when her mother drove her and Kendall to school one winter, and the car lost traction. They hadn't been in an accident, thankfully, but Kendra had been turned off from learning to drive after that.

"Hey, you drive a motorcycle, right?"

"Hardly when it's like this outside. I walked to school when it snowed or rained," Eden informed her then buried his face in his black and gray scarf.

"Obviously, but it's kind of funny that you took up riding one pretty early on in life. You look the type, I mean, but you could have just as easily taken to driving a car instead," Kendra said.

Eden was quiet for several moments before he shook his head.

"I'm claustrophobic. I don't like driving one."

Kendra cocked an eyebrow, walking ahead of him slightly before turning to face him.

"You? Claustrophobic? That's surprising."

"Is it?" Eden asked, shyly averting his eyes.

"You just come across as a person who's fearless in general," Kendra said, clearing her throat. "I mean, we've nothing to fear but fear itself, yet ... you looked at Intico and said, *try me*." Kendra lowered her voice when mimicking Eden.

"I never said that," Eden huffed.

"You were totally thinking it though," Kendra teased. "If you're struggling with my humor, you won't survive a dinner with my dad." Kendra turned back around and continued walking, ducking beneath the branch they approached—the same one she and Vicente used to walk beneath years ago. She had visited his gravestone a few times since and sent his family gifts on the holidays. His wife was a lovely woman. That sudden surge of guilt provoked a sigh as she shoved her hands in her pockets.

"You're someone I admire, Eden. I'm glad we're friends."

"I'm not someone you should admire," Eden spoke flatly, pursing his lips as he looked down.

"Well, to each their own," Kendra dismissed, speeding up her pace when she saw her house. "We're here, so no more mopey talk. Just clench your cheeks and get ready to endure good food and cringe dad-humor." She flashed him a smirk, and Eden snorted, hiding his lower face in his scarf.

"Roger," Eden said.

The two-story home, same as Kendra always knew, was glazed in snow. The lawn was completely covered, and the driveway had a narrow path between two piles of snow—just enough for Kendra's father to get his car in and out. He was mostly lazy outside of work, so she imagined that was all he could bring himself to do.

Racing to the porch, Eden in tow, Kendra knocked on the front door before she fished her keys from her pocket. However, before she could insert the key, the door swung open, and on the other side was her father.

Aaron looked the same as when Kendra had last seen him, perhaps less kept with the crows-feet beneath his eyes and his less tidy brown locks.

Those same hazel eyes beneath thick glasses showed an amiable warmth that welcomed both Eden and Kendra.

"Ken! I missed you more than I miss summer," Aaron said, holding his arms out. Without pause, Kendra leaned forward, hugging him with a chuckle.

"No promises that I missed you that much," Kendra said, breaking the hug before gesturing to Eden.

"This is my former classmate, Eden. I'm pretty sure you saw him at graduation," Kendra said, and Eden gave a simple nod.

Aaron cocked his eyebrow, a smirk forming on his lips as he held his hand out.

"Eden, huh? If I'd known your name, I'd have made garden salad instead of Caesar."

Kendra groaned aloud. However, Eden gave a quizzical look before taking Aaron's hand, shaking it.

"Caesar's fine," Eden said.

Aaron gave a tepid nod, releasing Eden's hand and beckoning them.

"Well, come on in. Cold isn't gonna feed you guys, after all."

Eden and Kendra entered, taking their boots off in the foyer before hanging their coats up. Beneath, Kendra wore a black sweater. Eden also removed his fleece, revealing a black long-sleeved collared shirt and a red gem hanging from his neck. Kendra knew he kept his gear within the necklace—a feature she still wanted for her suit, but Alicia hadn't gotten around to it yet, and Jessica was busy. The degree of magical proficiency it took to make the enchantment was higher than she could comprehend.

"I thought I had another half hour before you guys came, so I didn't have a chance to pick up a pie from Auntie Angie's. I'll go pick one up once we're done eating instead," Aaron began, then cleared his throat. "On the menu tonight, we have applewood-smoked ham, gravy, mac and cheese, cranberry sauce, yams, green bean casserole, the aforementioned Caesar salad, and a bottle of some fancy merlot from France," Aaron said, leading them through the hallway and into the kitchen.

The circular table came into view when they turned the corner. Several pans and dishes were neatly arranged, completed by a festive squash-shaped vase with an assortment of warm-hued flowers and the bottle of wine in the center. Above, a warm light emitted from a decorative casing.

"Wow, really outdid yourself, Dad," Kendra complimented. "There's no rosemary in this, like I asked, right?"

"I didn't forget. No rosemary. Don't need you having a reaction like last time," Aaron said.

"Yeah ... kind of slipped my mind to mention the allergy before when your spaghetti gave me a fever." Kendra cringed. While it wasn't deadly to demons in low doses, it was more than uncomfortable. Aaron still didn't know about her change, and she intended to keep it that way if she could help it. His connection to Ichor was like most humans', rendering him ignorant of it all.

Aaron sighed, walking over to the chair and pulling three out for them.

"Bit of a pain to make things from scratch, but I had to learn anyway. Eating out all the time sucks."

Kendra took her seat, then her father, and Eden sat beside her. There were four plates and three wine glasses on the table. Kendra stared pensively at the plate, silently pondering for a moment before grabbing a fork and using it to place a single slice of jellied cranberry sauce on the plate beside Eden's—Kendall's.

Eden glanced at Kendra, who gave him a forlorn smile as she shook her head.

"She liked cranberry sauce," Kendra explained, and Eden nodded. Neither spoke for a few moments.

"Well, go ahead and help yourselves," Aaron said, using the utensils on the trays to make his plate.

Kendra and Eden crafted theirs after—Kendra's own with a lot more ham than any other item. She had acquired quite the appetite for meat after her change, which was no surprise to Eden. Contrary to his large frame, Eden crafted a modest plate with a bit of each item, earning an amused chuckle from Aaron.

Aaron implored Eden to take more, but Kendra was quick to chastise him over it. She was just happy he ate at all. While he tried a bit of everything, she indulged in the ham with verve. Eventually, Aaron broke the stretching silence.

"Military been good to you both, then? I honestly never expected you'd join. Navy SEALs, right?" Aaron asked, trying to spur conversation again.

"Even more secret than that. We can't even talk about it," Kendra mentioned, shoveling a large slice of ham into her mouth.

"We'd have to kill you if we did," Eden said in a deadpan voice, earning a shocked stare from Kendra, who suddenly choked while trying to swallow her food. Eden glanced at her, hiding the smirk forming on his face with a chunk of yam on his fork. "Just a joke," Eden said, then nodded at Aaron. "The food's good."

Aaron burst out laughing, reaching out and patting Kendra on the shoulder before leaning closer to her.

"You make great friends, Ken. Kat would have loved that one," he said, letting her go.

Kendra gave a wry smile, glancing down at her plate and jabbing at the macaroni. They bounced around subjects: her father's projects, her workout routine, Eden's favorite dishes—he didn't have one. Soon, the topic landed on her mother.

"I miss talking with her," Kendra said, prompting her father to rub her back.

"You and me both. I visit her every free moment I can. Just ... hope she can hear what I'm saying. I tell her everything still, that she's beautiful. Like it's the same as it's always been."

Kendra's time as a dithered surfaced again. However far it had seemed, she had heard Eden's voice in the forsaken place she was imprisoned in.

"She hears you. I'm sure ... it keeps her going deep inside," Kendra spoke vaguely, lowering her head and smiling. A moment later, she leaned over and hugged her father.

Eden carefully scooted his empty plate away, pensively eyeing the glass of wine centered on the table. Something about it was familiar to him, but the thought escaped when he felt Kendra shift next to him. Having noticed him retreating into thought, she thought to steer the mood elsewhere.

"Hey, I was thinking that Eden and I could just walk to the bakery and pick up the pie. Should bring back an appetite to enjoy it with the wine," Kendra said, offering her father a sweet smile before turning to Eden.

Eden stood, sighing as he nodded.

"Sounds fine to me," Eden said, although he was secretly dreading heading back out into the cold.

"It's awful out there; you sure? It's only a ten-minute drive."

"We'll be fine. Our training involved trekking through all kinds of treacherous weather," Kendra said.

"Wait ..." Aaron cocked his brow skeptically. "Don't tell me. Eden may kill me."

This caused Eden to chuckle, and Kendra snickered, seeing him finally crack.

"He finally got you." Kendra feigned disappointment, shrugging before walking through the hallway, beckoning Eden to follow her.

Eden nodded at Aaron before turning on his heel and following Kendra. He took care not to linger on the family portraits on the wall, spending brief moments examining them before joining Kendra in the foyer. The two then layered themselves again before leaving the house.

Though they stayed close, the distance in Eden's gaze increased, soon disguised within the snow. Kendra searched for what to say—something to pull him back. He had seemed normal minutes ago, but it always went like that. Normalcy. Reclusion. She was damned to witness it, but she had invited him on the vacation to ease him out of his head.

She racked her head, thinking of what was said over dinner. They had discussed a few things. There was melancholy, but there was also levity. Then she recalled the last subject that had cropped up—her mother.

A swarm of white clouded their vision, and the omens drifted before Kendra, greeting her. She once noticed that the sentiments they carried often corresponded to her own thoughts when she was alone, but while the blue and purple danced, she caught glimpses of red. In the corner of her eye, Eden treaded with his eyes downcast, and without thought, she reached for him.

Heat brushed her knuckles, and she stumbled as a gasp escaped her lips. Before she could fall, Eden's fingers curled around her wrist, keeping her upright. His crimson eyes, faintly glowing, were masked by the red omens, but their light faded as Eden released her, his face rising from the safety of his scarf.

"What happened?" Eden asked, his eyes now grounded to reality again.

It wasn't the icebreaker Kendra was looking for, but she accepted her unintentional success, chagrin aside.

"Just slipped. Or maybe I wanted to see if you were paying attention," she said, sheepishly smiling as she tugged her collar down. He stared skeptically but shrugged.

"Satisfied?"

"Plenty," Kendra said, nudging him playfully.

Soon, they reached the plaza where the bakery was. Kendra pointed at the snow-covered sign featuring a rustic wooden carving of the shop name, outlined by warm light shining from the grooves. The L-shaped building consisting of several businesses was made of brick, denoting how old it was compared to the more recent structures built throughout the city.

"Forgot to ask, but have you been here before?" Kendra asked, and Eden pondered for several moments before replying.

"I believe so. Years ago, when I first moved to Chicago," Eden replied.

"They're good, and Auntie Angie is such a sweetheart," she said, and Eden tucked his face into his scarf, giving a tepid nod before Kendra snatched his arm. "Alright, let's get inside."

Kendra led them toward the twin glass doors. Frost crept in from the corners, and in the middle was a poinsettia caked in snowflakes. Kendra pushed the door open, causing the bell hanging from the door to jingle before the warm, sweet aroma flooded her and Eden's noses.

Kendra let out an audible moan, feeling her hunger resurge at the smell and sight of the baked goods lining the display case beneath the counter ahead. Even Eden indulged in the scent, and he removed his hands from his coat, rubbing them together. There weren't many patrons dining inside the bakery's lobby, predictably, but shortly after they entered, a woman emerged from the room behind the counter.

"Ken! Oh my God, it's been so long! You look good, dear," the large older woman, Angela, said from behind the counter. Her black skin and large, warm brown eyes shone within the sepia lighting cast over the room. She raced to the double doors leading to the front of the restaurant and held her arms out.

"Hey, Auntie. It's so good to see you again. Been busy with life after graduation and being in the military and all," Kendra said, approaching the woman, who then pulled her into a firm hug.

Once they separated, Angela looked at Eden, cocking her head for a moment before smiling.

"I've seen you before. I've got a bad memory sometimes, but I always remember people who have pretty eyes," she said, causing Eden to blush.

"Thank you ..." Eden muttered shyly.

"You liked apple pie, and you ate every bite, mhm."

"That's ... a really good memory," Eden said, a smile tugging at his lips.

"Remind me your name again, sugar-puddin'?"

"Eden," he replied, and Angela nodded in approval.

"Mm, you got a good name. Beautiful and biblical," she said, prompting Eden to look away timidly.

Kendra placed her hands behind her back, snickering to herself at Eden's bashfulness.

"Dad was supposed to drop by earlier, but he's bad with time management, so here we are, coming for the holiday reaping of your famous blueberry pie," Kendra said.

Angela nodded enthusiastically before she shimmied back through the door and rushed to the register.

"Oh, I'm sure you are. Aaron comes every other day. Usually gets sandwiches and the occasional pie," Angela said.

"He's been busier lately, and he's still not entirely used to managing the house by himself."

Though Angela thought to comment on Katherine, she realized that it wasn't a good idea to spoil the mood—even to encourage her. Instead, she hurriedly booted the register back up.

"Well, I could talk your ear off, but I'm sure y'all are in a hurry. You in town for a while?" Angela asked.

"Next two weeks, yeah. I'll stop by again for an extended chat sometime next week."

"I'll be waiting too," Angela warned playfully, grinning brightly as she cackled. She tapped the screen on the register, and the terminal in front of Kendra popped up the order. "Do you want anything, Eden? Some apple pie again?"

Eden shook his head, citing a half-true dietary limit he imposed on himself. Angela was more than understanding, commenting on her own desire to do the same as her fingers danced on the register's tablet.

"I'll get the order ready. Be about ... fifteen minutes, so hang tight, sugars," Angela said and turned, heading into the back again.

Kendra and Eden walked over to an empty booth adjacent to the counter, sitting across from one another.

For a few minutes, they didn't speak, and Eden stared out the frosty window, mind adrift like the swarming snow that fell from the sky.

"Apple pie, huh? I'm beginning to notice a pattern here," Kendra said, shooting him an amused look.

"Not surprising, I suppose," Eden spoke flatly, and Kendra poked his arm, drawing his attention from the glass to her.

"Auntie makes the best apple pies, right? You should have asked for one to take home."

Eden shrugged, leaning forward on the table before glancing at the various decorative cakes and pastries on display.

"General Blackwell used to make apple pie for me over a decade ago. She was never much of a cook, but when I was young, she discovered I loved it and must have made a thousand of them throughout the years. She got really good at it," Eden said. Although the memory rang of a sweet reminiscence, his face suggested something akin to dejection.

"Hard to imagine your mom baking, considering she could wipe the smirk off a demon lord's face with her stare alone," Kendra said before she glanced out the window. Her mother wasn't an amazing cook either, but she stuck to recipes she could make. The thought of the times they spent cooking as a family made her wonder what it was like for Eden and his mother growing up.

"Say ... I noticed something," Kendra began. "You never call General Blackwell *Mom*. Why?"

Eden perked up, his gaze meeting hers with hesitation brewing behind the reticent depths. His fingers brushed the table, curling into a fist as he began to tap the table lightly—a distracted habit he defaulted to when he wasn't comfortable.

"It's complicated."

Kendra cocked her head, her brown strands spilling from her scarf. It had always been jarring; she yearned deeply to speak to her mother again, and Eden had all but scorned his.

"And I'm smart," Kendra insisted.

Eden sat up, glancing down at the table before returning his gaze to the window, seeing his reflection. The warm light obscured the glare of his red hues, and as he focused, those eyes became indiscernible from his mother's. Staring back at him, he saw his reflection, uncannily similar to hers, transform into her visage. Vaguely, the mix of his reflection and the snow outside made it seem like tears were falling from her eyes, and the memories, colder than the snow, replayed.

He heard her knock against his door at night and their soft weeping that swept through their barren home. Her muffled pleas sounded so far away each time he tried to remember what she'd said. Now, there was only the indignation in her tone each time she'd scolded him for defying her orders or being *reckless*. Unlike him, Kendra could speak of her mother with fondness and sorrow. As his mother's visage melted away in a swarm of red omens, Eden shut his eyes and spoke.

"You wouldn't understand."

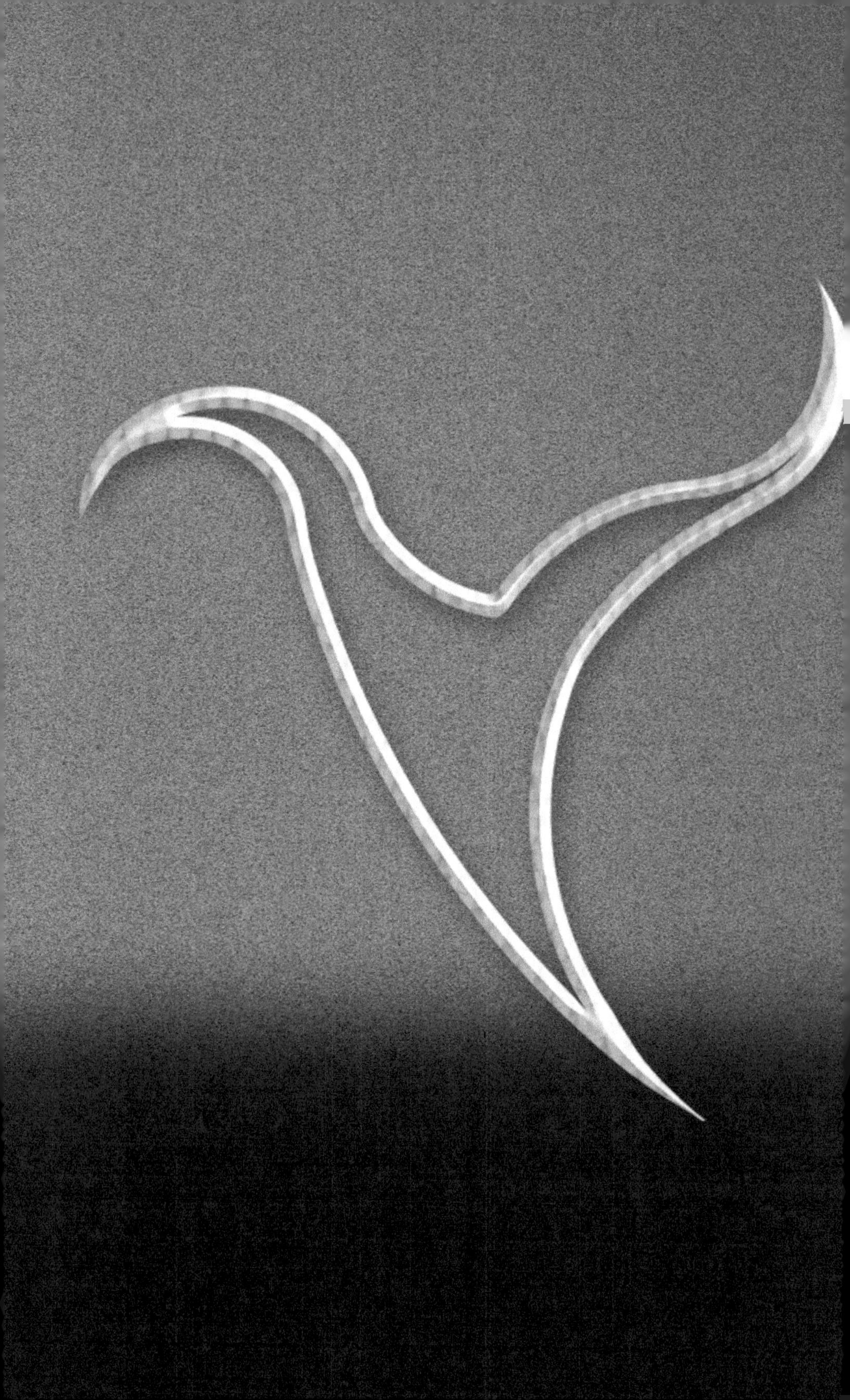

Three

Vacant Vows

"A TRAITOR IS AMONG US ..." Ethan spoke quietly, his hazel eyes scanning the several documents before him. On his left, the American branch of the Sieghart family, and on the right, a list of the Hunters' own personnel.

"And you are sure of this?" Jessica asked as she approached the desk, removing her hat and tucking it against her lap.

"Not in the strictest sense," Ethan admitted, flipping open the file pertaining to Allen Sieghart. His expression became bitter, and he curled his hand as his index finger glided down the information he had compiled. "There is an incongruity of accounts, and while I initially expected that the Siegharts had just been prepared with contingency plans, that wasn't the case—at least according to what I gathered from subsequent interrogations."

The warm lights above subtly flickered as Ethan scanned the documents. Soon, he landed on a string of information pertaining to Allen Sieghart's social media presence, and he used the projection from his desktop to navigate to one such profile. The last post had been made back in September 2042, a short time following the Hunters' establishment in Chicago for their investigation of the Covenant of Augury. Jessica circled the desk, standing behind him as she peered down at the projection.

"Allen Sieghart is a curious case I feel should not have slipped past us. The moment Kendra was attacked—around the same time we suspected the Siegharts—we should have run a report and investigation into him. Things that we should have caught on a lazy afternoon, let alone the full-sail investigation we launched. Is that not the least bit suspicious?"

Jessica's eyes narrowed, and she gave a soft sigh. She placed her hat over the personnel files and leaned down, pressing her palms into the desk.

"The boy erased his presence using that eye of Jugo, yes? Orchestrated assaults on behalf of his father with those strays of the Alastairs. Given the circumstances of sleep deprivation, would it be a far stretch to suggest carelessness? Occam's razor."

"Unlikely," Ethan suggested, sitting up straight as he scrolled the social media page idly. "A certain amount of incompetence is indistinguishable from maliciousness. We're left with a question of espionage, and I intend to get to the bottom of it." Ethan then tapped the last video posted.

On the projection, there was a field where a soccer game had been taking place. A player with the number seven on her back, Kendra, drove the ball with a ferocious kick into the enemy's goal. A whistle rang, and the crowd erupted, Allen's own cheers filling the video. Kendall's face came into view as the camera panned, and she stood from her spot in the stands, rushing to the sidelines to meet Kendra. The two cheered and danced together until the voice of Coach Springfield called out.

"Kenny! Game's beginning again!" Natalie's voice called out, and both girls looked toward the camera before the video ended.

He examined the profile—friends, content, and comments. Hacking it for an investigation of his correspondence could be beneficial, if possible. He had heard that Allen was less than cooperative in custody, bordering on catatonic. Kendra had been more than cooperative, but she didn't have social media to begin with. Then he saw Kendall's profile on his friends list, but delving into her profile was beyond problematic. If public comments had been anything to go by, he figured it was an appropriate compromise.

Ethan clicked on her profile and was greeted by a Wicca-themed page with videos posted from her vlog series. He assumed there were several hours of video, of which he'd dread combing through. With a labored sigh, his shoulders dropped before he glanced up at Jessica, who shot him a concerned look.

"Maybe a rest is in order," Jessica suggested, standing straight.

"I'll be fine," Ethan insisted. "My vigilance is required here now. And if my estimations are correct, things have yet to reach the apex of what is really going on."

"I'm sure that is true, but you are only human in the end."

"I need to be … *less* than that. Demons will show no mercy to a human, nor to other demons for that matter. To protect our hunters, I have to be something worse than a demon—or at least pretend to be," Ethan said, and Jessica huffed as she shifted her hand to her hip, eyeing him warily.

"Careful. You might just become the next thing we hunt if you succeed. Perhaps … don't abandon that bookworm I've known since I was a girl," Jessica mused, glancing at the documents peeking from beneath her hat. "You are certain the Siegharts knew nothing further than the covenant schemes we uncovered?"

"They are due for more questioning, to whatever their memories can offer years after the fact," Ethan said. He shook his head as he leaned back, staring up at her from behind the glare of light in his glasses.

"Demons have remarkable memories. They need them to hold their vendettas," Jessica insisted, smirking to herself as she snatched her hat and circled the desk. "I trust you will find some conclusive answers in time, but be sure to save your energy for the more important endeavors," Jessica claimed. She then waltzed to the door, dragging Ethan's gaze with her.

"I promise to try," Ethan said, propping his head up with his face hidden behind his joined hands.

Zane's auburn gaze flicked around the foyer leading into the living room. A chubby, blond-haired woman, Eva Kohen, led him through the hall while humming to herself. Her hands were joined behind her back, resting just above the white ribbon that fixed the white silk dress to her frame.

A sharp contrast to the typical décor of noble demon homes, the halls were wide, with burgundy walls and dark brown molding framing them—the type of chic vibe Zane was subconsciously fond of. He was far too acquainted with flashy displays to care for them anymore. Whether it was pretentious or seemingly ripped from a generated image of a gaudy mansion, they burrowed into his nerves in a way he despised. Simple and functional impressed him far more.

"Like what you've done with the place, Eva," Zane said, earning a snort from her, and she shrugged.

"Gotta pull my weight around here somehow," she said, coming to a stop in the living room. She gestured over to a man whose sandy-blond head peeked above the back of the couch. "Well, Asher's right there. I'll be back in a few," Eva said before turning on her heel and walking through a doorway leading elsewhere in the house.

Zane cracked his neck and sighed lightly as he approached the brown leather couch. On the TV, he saw a cooking show playing, wherein several contestants of a challenge were being yelled at by a comically angry man for their mistakes.

The Kohen family was pleasant compared to other branches of the noble families he had met. Most of the Hunters' diplomats thought so when the family had brokered the peace treaty between the noble demon families and humanity. They had always been amenable to humanity and other demon families—save for the Siegharts. After the events in Chicago, Zane understood their hatred of one another more intimately. Asher had even indicated that he'd give up cooking if it meant not having to see Oliver again.

"Zane the flame!" the man, Asher Kohen, called and paused the show. Standing, he circled the couch and drew his arm back, palm outstretched, and they dapped one another with a boisterous handshake and half hug. Once separated, Zane inspected the baggy white suit jacket Asher wore. As was typical of him, he hadn't even bothered wearing the matching pants, instead sporting jeans and brown dress shoes. Zane chalked it up to the fact they were cool with one another.

"Sup, Ash? Been a while, man," Zane greeted, flashing a grin. "Wouldn't have happened to make something good for our meeting? I still have dreams about those cinnamon roll baklavas you made."

Asher shook his head and spoke.

"I didn't even have time to throw on my Sunday best, let alone go buy the ingredients for baklava, but I got some leftover butterscotch cookies, if that's your speed. But damn, dude. Must be pretty damn important for you to be here if the Mistress of the Hunt requested for me to meet you." His lips curled into a sheepish grin. "For a badass witch known for slaying demon lords, she's pretty lax. Chatted me up for advice on baking pies before asking me to meet with you. Talk about buttering me up before tossing the oven at me."

Asher gestured to the couch, and the two circled before sitting next to one another.

"Oven? I'm more like a blast furnace, except that furnace is fueled by an abundance of caffeine and carbs," Zane said, snorting.

Asher reached for the short, hexagonal glass of dark whiskey sitting on the coaster. Inside of it, diamond-shaped ice was half melted. While subtle from where Zane sat, the smoky scent beckoned his attention.

"I've seen you eat. You're definitely underselling that, dude," Asher replied, beckoning Zane to give a shameless smirk.

"Best thing about this meeting, compared to the usual ones, is the fact I don't have to wear my typical suit. Wool and hellhound fur blend feels much nicer than the other types they have us wear," Zane spoke, sighing happily as he tugged the sleeve of his suit. "Helps that I'm seeing an old friend too."

"Hell yeah, dude. Pretty stoked to see you again. What yah been up to?"

Zane propped his leg up on his knee, leaning back into the couch as he sighed.

"Oh, you know … lollygagging, disturbing the peace. The usual." He glanced down at the glass Asher held. "We'll have to catch up soon in a more casual setting, but for now … been looking into something you could maybe help with."

Asher shrugged, slapping his free palm on his lap before taking a sip of whiskey.

"Of course. What's up?"

While Zane would have loved nothing more than to share stories from the past three years, he focused his thoughts on what he had been sent to look into.

"You're familiar with the Fracti Alas labs, I presume?"

Asher frowned, pursing his lips before setting his glass down.

"Of course. Although … far from a fan, to put it politely. If the Kohen have dealings with them, it'd have to be through a proxy of some kind. We would never deliberately play ball with them—even avoid dealing with the Xiao for that very reason."

The noble demon family of greed, the Xiao, were the descendants of Mammon, the Cardinal Sin Ordinance of Greed. The family had once openly allied with Onaga—a respect to his heralding of the sin that defined them. While many of the family's leaders openly professed their disassociation from the harbinger, in accordance with the Kohen Treaty, many alleged it to be insincere. Zane thought that assumption to be correct.

"I figured that much, so I wanted to go over any potential anomalies in the usual patterns you might have noticed recently."

"I'm not the head of the family, so I'm not entrusted with many insider details, but the cursory ledgers of our shipments have a couple of things that stand out," Asher spoke. He leaned back and rested his arms on the back of the couch, gaze fixed on Zane. "You're a smart man, Zane. I trust you aren't gonna go picking a fight you can't win."

"Correct," Zane quipped, snorting as he tapped his knee repeatedly. "Whatcha got for me?"

"Rubidium fluoride compounds, lots of it. It's for our demon-affiliated clients for obvious reasons, namely for environmental transformation. Avernus gets most of it usually, but I've noticed an uptick in the amount

we've been sending to some enterprises affiliated with the OCN recently. Kinda sus, in my opinion. They've been cozying up to the Xiao, if
my sources are correct ..."

Zane pondered the thought, knowing the OCN had been far more
interested in shadow brokering in their ventures; they had a monopoly
on rare Inferos materials and a notoriously complicated trafficking
network. Providing subjects to Onaga was the obvious guess, but he
doubted they were starving for rubidium with how fractured they had
become in the year prior. Once he had considered the ramifications, he
nodded before he snapped his fingers.

"Outside of simulating Inferos's flora conditions, there's only one
other notable use they would have for rubidium." Zane's eyes narrowed. "Demon alchemy," he spoke aloud, and Asher chuckled, looking up at the ceiling.

"Yeah, go figure. Can't imagine a reason the Nexus would want
to grow Inferos vegetation. Given that my family has a stranglehold
on both that and the human stuff, we charge the Alastairs extra just
because of how much they demand. I can easily see an *unassuming*
reason for the Xiao to use the OCN as a proxy."

"Still, kind of odd to hear about their involvement. Cecilia and
Salem are dead, and the rest of the ferali are scattered thanks to one
of my comrades. Gotta wonder who's at the helm of that shtick now."
Zane scratched his chin. "On another note, the noble demon family of
greed working with the Harbinger of Greed's nefarious research efforts
is beyond expected."

Zane thought back to his scarce interactions with the Xiao. They
were hardly the friendly sort in any meaningful way—very detached
and focused on materialistic acquisition. There was a bare minimum
effort from the family's head to cooperate with the Hunters in following the Kohen Treaty.

"Why would they need this for demon alchemy?" Asher asked,
reaching down and lifting his glass again before downing the rest of
the whiskey in it. With a flex of his brows, he shook his head and sighed
heavily before setting the glass down on the table again.

"Well, there's two primary uses, among others. You can use it medically to restore rubidium levels in the blood—like a shot of demon adrenaline. I use it for my blaze serum to maintain my demon form longer," Zane began, his eyes shutting as he sighed heavily and leaned forward. "The only other use I can see being the case ... is chimera research. Demonic cellular synthesis dialed up to eleven. Real nasty stuff when you get into the weeds of it, and I know you'd especially hate to lose your lunch and dinner hearing about it."

Asher squinted as he raked his thighs, his fists balling with the fabric of his jeans.

"Chimeras are gross, yeah. Had the displeasure of seeing one of the monstrosities used by the Siegharts before. Thing would vomit everything it was given, so it starved to death before they could use it." Asher shook his head and groaned. "As a demon of gluttony, I'm real sensitive to seeing things starve and being helpless about it, but that thing was hardly what I would consider alive. Whatever they used to simulate it ... I don't wanna imagine."

Zane nodded, slapping his knees before standing.

"I've got theories on it, but I don't practice that kind of demon alchemy. I thought of it once ... but I went with my gut when it told me not to dabble."

"Good gut, man. Demons can be pretty volatile, but there are some boundaries you just don't cross, y'know?"

"Definitely not. Although ... can't say that Arionne felt the same. He tried pushing me to study it, but I think that my little stunt of making a pile of flesh explode on him turned him off from the idea." Zane snorted.

"Did it on purpose?" Asher pried, and Zane nodded in response, a smirk tugging at his lips.

"Fuck that guy and the shit he tried to make us do. He was probably more twisted than Zaldionne. Hard to believe, I know." Zane shook his head. "Think you can send me a copy of that ledger with the shipment information?"

"Depends ..." Asher began. "No Hunter meeting ever happened, right?"

"If the feds ask, I was meeting an old chum for a drink and a chat."

"Damn right," Asher said before lifting his sleeve and navigating through the projection from his black smart band to the document Zane requested.

The brightness and clarity from the projection differed from the smart band models civilians carried. Zane had always assumed it was the kind of thing available only to those of higher status, usually with an abundance of secret documents.

"It'll come through a double encryption through the usual tunnel we'd use. I'll give you the password after that drink, k? Oh, wait ... can you actually drink right now? Job regulations and all?" Asher inquired.

"Not officially on duty, so it won't be a problem, but I do still have to go check something out after this. That said ... just one for me."

Asher snickered, offering a jagged grin.

"Got this excellent duskberry wine from Syberia, and boy, does it slap!"

"Ooh, maybe another time on the wine. Was really curious about that whiskey you just had. Smelled kind of sweet."

Asher's gaze shifted to his empty glass, although his amusement remained despite Zane's rejection of the wine.

"Oh right, you do fancy yourself some whiskey, huh? Was made with smoked cinnamon. Aged in Torr wood barrels for at least a century. The trees only grow on the border of Torreo and the Gloom Woods, so it's pretty damn hard to get here. I'll let you try some."

Zane's brows raised, his nostrils flaring as he stifled a laugh.

"Jeez, guess I'm a better friend than I thought. A single liter has gotta be worth my year's salary at least," Zane said, prompting Asher to roll his eyes and shoo Zane with his hand.

"Come on, man. This is me we're talkin' 'bout," Asher said. "Eva, can you bring the whiskey and another glass?" Asher called out.

"Yeah!" Eva called back, and shortly after, she came with an empty glass and an intricately decorated bottle. Eva set the glass on the table, uncorked the bottle, and proceeded to pour whiskey for both of them. Once she finished, Asher lifted the glasses, handing the fresh one to Zane.

"This'll be a nice way to usher in the shit-show that's awaiting you, eh?"

Zane laughed sardonically before taking the glass and clinking it against Asher's.

"Couldn't have said it better myself."

The forest in the evening was far from what one would consider hospitable, between the swarming insects and the humid air clogging Zane's pores. He had done away with his jacket in favor of his combat vest. It housed his ammunition and serum, not that he expected to use either in what he considered a simple recon mission. With an intelligence team present within the confines of the hidden laboratory, he expected to play lookout and simply monitor their communications in secret. Andrew, thankfully, had also provided him with the encryption key for the channel they occupied.

He fiddled with the earpiece as he mumbled under his breath about how gross the humidity was. Given that Seraph Seven had ensured that no threats remained in the forest, and the lack of rifts from Inferos from which feral demons could invade, he hadn't expected any demonic threats. Regardless, he remained vigilant, as any former assassin would.

Perched on the cliffside above the laboratory, he listened in on their conversations. However, it had mostly just been procedural jargon, and he yawned as the minutes droned on. Monotony in the night ambience was hardly on his itinerary, but such was the tedium of all great discoveries. Alysium had hammered that into him.

"All clear here ... but the floor smells like cheap coffee and whiskey. Place's quality really was shit, but guess that's what you'd expect from one of these minor labs," a male voice spoke over the radio.

"They were working with really niche chimera research, yeah?" a female voice replied.

"Says nothing about their crappy security protocols. Great minds don't make great guards, they say."

"True enough."

Zane cocked an eyebrow, hanging on to the oddly casual tone of the intelligence team; he was usually bored beyond description reading their reports. Perhaps they were friends, but there was a tonal inconsistency the further they spoke on the findings—something divorced of human sympathy to the horrors Andrew had informed him of.

The team was to collect samples for the biology reports and recover the corpses of their fallen comrades. Even in their desecration, they were due a proper burial for their families and friends. A creeping paranoia clawed into Zane, but despite his aversion to *superstitious* thinking, he wasn't one to ignore his gut.

With a sigh, he mustered his energy to prepare for a stealthy intrusion.

"Insenseilin." A subtle blue aura enveloped him before becoming a shadow that cast over his being. His body was submerged in the shade, and with the incantation active, his presence became as the silent night. Now, both his form and sounds were made minuscule within the magic he had so often employed during his allegiance to the Alastairs.

Zane leaped from atop the cliff, effortlessly landing at the entrance to the laboratory without a sound. The door Kendra had breached made entry easy, allowing him to walk in without using his own flashy methods. He quickly discovered the team was sequestered deep within the depths of the lab, and as he ventured after them, they continued speaking their vague observations aloud. Upon reaching the main lobby, Zane glanced down at the sticky puddle of whiskey and the stale half-eaten donut next to it. The subtle scent of dried alcohol stung his nose, making him cringe as he continued through the lobby.

"Here I thought *my* bouts of the munchies were diabolical ..." he muttered. Following the floor plan Andrew gave him, he continued through the western corridor to the elevator and rode it down to the research center.

While the incantation didn't make him literally invisible, he could remain discreet as long as he wasn't in plain sight. If he remained by the elevator, he'd be no more conspicuous than a cobweb. The end of the hallway leading into the research center was already open. He rubbed his chin and mused quietly, determining how he'd go about snooping. Once decided, he raised his wrist and positioned his hunter bracer. The surveillance microphone engaged, aimed toward the room, and he listened through his earpiece.

"Kind of eerie how far along these things are. DNA splicing or some crap like that, right, doc?" one of the hunters spoke.

"DNA splicing and grafting existing tissues as we infuse an antibiotic bonding suspension ensure rejection doesn't occur. Taken to the extreme ... the human brains are still intact and aren't being rejected in most of the samples—assuming their connection to Ichor is exceptional. Optimal conditions appear to be between thirty-seven and forty-two degrees Celsius. Onaga's little runt had a good guess, it seems," an unfamiliar voice spoke.

"Must be one hell of a teacher for a kid to guess that."

"I would have determined this a lot sooner if that accursed daughter of his wasn't actively destroying our research centers."

Zane's brow furrowed. The laboratories were difficult to find, but of the handful the Hunters had managed to locate, a few of them had been completely incinerated prior to their discovery. The archives and structures alike were reduced to nothing, leaving no discernible information.

Zane thought it was poetic that Onaga's own daughter was sabotaging his research. As the daughter of two harbingers of sin, she was considered demon royalty—the youngest to date. Princess Lucifina, daughter of Onaga, the Harbinger of Greed, and Lilith, the Harbinger of Lust and queen of the succubi and incubi. Her nature as a princess of sin was speculated upon by many, but Zane cared little for the rumors.

"You'd think he'd hunt and catch her then. Couldn't be that hard to track her down, right?" another hunter mused.

"They tried several times. Even diverted some of the Venatum to go after her, but she's killed every single one. I hear that succubitch has chaos flames, so tough deal messing with her."

Venatums. Zane perked up at the mention of the term, recalling his own encounter with them a long time ago. Originally, they were angelic disciples of Onaga, who then fell and became his personal guards and warriors—ancient and formidable. That Onaga's daughter had killed any number of them made the hairs on the back of his neck stand on end.

"Well, we'll just have to hope we don't meet her now, won't we? If you vulgar lot are done gossiping, you can begin destroying the subjects and data. Thankfully, the group of hunters that were here didn't find anything crucial," the unfamiliar voice spoke.

"Damn, not even gonna try to save some of these poor things?" a hunter asked. "I couldn't care less about the hunters that went into them, but they're good bioweapons."

"Unnecessary. The current chimeras are far superior for now. The data is all we needed."

With their intentions made clear, Zane sighed as he looked down at his vest. He inspected his equipment momentarily before checking his breath and tidying his hair. Satisfied, he marched toward the research center. He formed a terra-diablo with his hands and built power in his palms as he drew closer to the opening. Upon reaching it, he slammed his palms into the ground, causing the tiles to crack and ripple. The concrete beneath then reformed around the bodies and limbs of the hunters and the doctor.

"Pardon the intrusion, folks, but I've got a few questions for you colorful bunch," Zane said, eyeing the several beings struggling in his makeshift restraints. His attention then shifted to the source of the unfamiliar voice. A doctor with a demonic appearance. The grooves of his curved horns jutting from his forehead and the subtle maroon tint in his grayish skin differed from a standard umbra demon. Based upon the particularly chaotic energy signature he gave off, Zane deduced he was a primonium—*pure* demons typically born within Inferos.

"How did he sneak in without being detected?" the doctor demanded as he glared at the others.

"Zane? Well, aren't we just fucked," one hunter hissed as he struggled within the tightening confines snaking around his wrists and neck.

Zane stood, nostrils flaring as he shook his head.

"I regret to inform that there will be no fucking. Just questions and witty remarks," Zane mused aloud, dusting his hands before walking into the room, eyeing the several vats filled with the embryo-like creations suspended within them. "So, I am guessing the security of this lab intentionally sucked so as not to stick out as much to Lucifina? Could have at least installed one of these crappy AI systems that can't even play the song you asked for."

"You're not supposed to be here," a hunter growled, and in response, Zane formed the terra-diablo sign again and stomped his foot, causing the concrete to form around the hunter's mouth.

"Mic's mine right now, pal," Zane said before scanning the group again, squinting his eyes with a skeptical expression forming. "Now … how many of you are actually human? It smells like glamour." He clapped, and a rush of flames washed over the group. Although they screamed, the flames were superficial. Once they dispersed, the *hunters* he had caught were exposed. Their visages had faded from their human likeness to their true demon forms. "Called it." Zane clicked his tongue, his gaze showing a hint of malice within it as he crossed his arms.

"We're not telling you dick," a female demon spat, glaring with glimmering orange irises.

"Oh? Good, 'cause I'm not a big fan of hearing about any other than my own." He flashed a saccharin smile at the demon whose mouth he had covered. "But … I'm not afraid to cut one off if I need to," Zane warned. "Since you interrupted me earlier, I'll take that as you volunteering."

Zane approached the man, who began to shake his head the closer he drew.

"Relax, drama queen. I won't actually do any dismembering. I'm more of a shake-and-bake kind of interrogator. Speaking of which, Lucifina was the one burning these labs down, right? She no longer affiliated with ole pops?"

The man glared for a moment, muffling his response into the concrete, prompting Zane to perk up and chuckle.

"Oh, sorry. Hold up." Zane flicked the concrete over his mouth, causing it to recede down to his neck.

"Fuck, man. If I tell you anything, I'm as good as dead."

Zane rolled his eyes and sighed as he raised his arm and then slapped his outer thighs.

"Hate this cliché so much. Who's this nefarious gentleman commanding you? Or is it a lady?" Zane stared deep into the demon's eyes as if he were transparent before him. After a few moments of pensive silence and the expression of the demon remaining unflinching, he smirked. "They-dy?" The demon's eyes twitched, and Zane laughed. "Okay, so they're well dressed and probably have some obnoxiously philosophical reason for their evil. This is gonna be fun," Zane said, circling the man before leaning against his back to prop himself up. "Alright, who's the boss of this scheme you guys are cooking?" Zane spoke, his tone dropping as he waited.

"I can't say," the man muttered.

Shaking his head, Zane stood straight and stretched before he walked toward the next demon that was bound. As he did so, his gaze became paradoxically cold, and he raised his hand before snapping. As the pop echoed through the room, a spark ignited before the previous demon burst into a screaming effigy of flames.

"No!" the demon yelled out as Zane approached him, beginning to hyperventilate the closer Zane drew. He just stood there with an ominous gaze, unspeaking. When the other demon was sufficiently burned, the flames subsided, leaving him squealing in pain as he regenerated. The demon before Zane freaked out as he tried to cobble together an answer.

"Yes, Lucifina has been attacking the different labs! She's been on a warpath for years now, so we've had to hide the labs and make the security less obvious!" he sobbed out as Zane nodded along. Once finished, Zane reached out and placed a finger on his forehead.

"Ah, the bird is squawking now. What else you got for me?" Zane spoke, his smile returning, albeit shallow and still threatening.

"I ... uh ... know that this research used hunters captured throughout the past few months."

"And how have you been going about capturing them? Since you guys were parading as hunters and were here on official orders with official equipment, somebody sent you bunch here specifically, yeah? Are the commanders in on this? How did you infiltrate the org?"

"They ... don't, I think. We're a layer removed from who we take our orders from," the demon spoke, shivering as he glanced at the doctor, who glared at him.

"They get their orders through a proxy, Hunter!" the doctor spat, and Zane shot him a glare. Given Onaga was the progeniture of demon alchemy, Zane was wary of the doctor's capabilities. If he was an ancient ally of Onaga's, as he suspected, lowering his guard was dangerous.

"Distractions won't get you very far ... but fine, I'll bite. This is the part where I ask you what you know, and trust me, there's a *lot* that you do know. Sing for me." Zane turned from the demon he was interrogating, giving him a playful slap before marching over to the doctor. "You're one of Onaga's trusted colleagues, yeah? I made sure to bind your fingers in a way that if I feel any energy surges from you, they will be crushed, so don't get any funny ideas."

"I'm anything but a comedian, Hunter," the doctor hissed, grunting as he looked to one of the vats. "There are many hunters we have captured throughout the centuries. These are no different from routine captures we make among many who aren't within your faction." Zane rolled his eyes and shook his head.

"Bullshit. Hunters have been going missing at a high rate, nor does the little narrative you spun resolve the problems that follow the infiltration thing I just spoke about. I'm going out on a limb and guessing that the Covenant of Augury's schemes were also tied to this? Fracti Alas doesn't seem the type to pull those kinds of high-profile stunts ... no. There's someone else at the helm of this. The impostor among us hunters." Zane glared hard. "Who is it?"

"I am being honest when I tell you that—"

Zane snapped his fingers, and a flash of flames rushed through the pillar like a torrent, searing the doctor. Cursing and yelling, the doctor breathed hard when the flames stopped, his skin smoking as his regeneration engaged.

"Try again," Zane said in a bored tone.

Staring with his bubbling eyes, the doctor slowly composed his erratic breathing before shaking his head.

"You've exaggerated the extent—" the doctor began, and Zane prepared to snap his fingers again. "Inferos, no!" the doctor begged. "Yes! It is as you expect, but I don't know who!" he swore, and Zane searched his eyes deeply for a moment, sighing in annoyance.

"I assume somebody here should know. Who is it?" Zane asked, waiting for a moment before the doctor nodded his head toward the woman from before. Seeing her comrade sell her out, she hissed and glared at the doctor.

"And you primonium act so high and mighty compared to us novas. You spineless vanity-humpers have no balls!" she hissed, causing Zane to stifle his laughter.

Novas were the colloquial reference to the demons more acclimated to Earth, often capable of disguising their demon forms to preserve their energy—much like himself. While they were respected when hailing from the noble umbra families, those of unnoteworthy origin were often denigrated.

"In fairness, I'd probably be a bit pissed if I were you too," Zane said. He stopped in front of her, eyeing her for a moment before touching the concrete below her hips. In the next moment, the concrete receded to reveal the pouches strapped to her thighs. "Anything gonna poke or stick me?" Zane asked before rummaging through her pockets.

The woman rolled her eyes and sighed in disgust.

"My dick."

"Geez, you're really obsessed with those, huh? You chose the wrong line of work, ma'am," Zane mocked. After a few seconds, he removed a data chip, and he held it up for her to see. "Contraband, eh?" Zane clicked his tongue and slipped the chip into his vest before the woman spat on him.

He didn't flinch, however. His stare went cold again, and flames danced on his cheek, burning away her saliva.

The tense moments dragged on, their gazes clashing with frigid disposition, but soon, the woman's expression finally cracked. Her frustration bubbled to the surface as she thrashed as best she could, but it was to no avail.

"I can't say their name, damn it!"

"You're not shy," Zane said. With a glimpse of the human eye staring at him from the vat, he scowled. They would sooner be fried alive, yet, he wasn't keen on submitting to the devilish desire to burn them all to a crisp like he had the other demon. He'd only kill if necessary.

"I ... can't," she spoke in a shaky voice. With a high-pitched breath, her head dropped as she began to sob lightly.

"Funny ... I wonder if you were this remorseful and worried when you took my comrades and tore their entire beings apart. Seeing you sob ... it's clear you're gutless," Zane spat, shaking his head. "Alright, I'm done with the philosophical grandstanding. You have three seconds to give me the name before you all end up being crispy creme."

As if time itself announced the countdown, the woman raised her head, her cheeks going pale as she stared with despondent eyes at her comrades. The group began voicing their opposition to her giving the name, begging her to refrain.

As if giving herself to resignation, she met Zane's gaze, her despondency melting as if his flames had thawed it, but the air quickly grew stagnant as her lips parted.

"Their name is ... Or—" The words caught in her throat, and she choked. A white glow flickered from the rune etched onto her tongue as she convulsed. The air in the room went cold, and a static white engulfed it as a loud explosion erupted from the woman's body.

In that blaring moment, the explosion obliterated everything within a short radius, and all else had been scathed by the insidious energy. When the dust cleared, the once pristine white floors were entirely shredded down to the earth beneath, and every other discernible life in the room perished—except for one.

Concrete shifted as a hole within the ground opened up, and from within it, Zane climbed to the surface, his hair disheveled and soot covering his form as he exhaled heavily.

"What the fuck…" Zane breathed out, searching as he tried to detect the others. It quickly became apparent to him that they had all died, along with the creatures that had been growing within the vats. He sucked in a sharp breath before cracking his neck and glancing up. His nerves slowly settled, and he considered himself lucky that the entire building hadn't collapsed.

There was only one possibility to explain what had happened: a hex triggered by attempting to speak a name. Despite the grisly nature, it was unlikely to be the consequence of a pact, which typically yielded more insidious results. Those details rendered a troublesome conclusion.

"Void magic," Zane spoke through gritted teeth. He then understood that whoever their mole was, they were either one of a few notable demon lords, or they weren't a demon at all.

In his spiraling thoughts, the fear he had aroused within the demons became clear. They had effectively been coerced into suicide. He pursed his lips and sat on the ground, crossing his legs as he contemplated the mistake. *Old habits die* hard, he thought. Old and bitter. The way he once conducted himself had since been renounced. He knew he needed the senseless deaths to count for something.

Having meditated on these sentiments, Zane stood and glanced around the laboratory, thinking of what he should do. Several malformed chimeras were still imprisoned below, likely slated for euthanasia. Despite all the research that had been destroyed in the blast, he assumed that their mole would still eventually come to investigate. He finally determined that the Hunters couldn't know he had been there.

He arranged to burn the laboratory, like Onaga's daughter had allegedly done to several others. That fact still baffled him, but he knew that the stories of demon families—especially those of great prominence—were embroiled in a hidden turmoil. That had been the case with Darrel Carver, and it could be the case for Onaga's daughter as well.

Chaos flames were beyond Zane's ability to conjure, but he knew how they moved and raged. His flames were a part of him, and he could feel everything they tore through. Mimicking chaos flames was easy enough, and the way normal fire affected structures was hardly different if he made them burn hot enough. Making his way to the elevator that would take him to the prison, he reached into his vest and grabbed one of the vials of his demon serum.

"This is going to take a lot more calories than I have on hand," he muttered, thinking to himself before nodding. "I was having tacos in Los Angeles, and they can think Lucifina burned down another lab with the intelligence unit inside of it. That'll work."

The Rosemary Fortress was still in its tranquil might. While the maliciousness of night brought with it the threat of rifts opening, the base was safer than any other hold on Earth. The last of the sunlight was wrung from the skyline. The only noise filling the night was the ambience of the patrolling vehicles on the roads stretched throughout the base. Blending in with the dark, only their lights could be seen from the windows of the men's barracks.

Andrew's blue eyes shimmered as he stared at the monitor on his desk, a vibrant scene of shouting animated characters clashing with an intense orchestral arrangement. His left hand idly gripped the tail of a dinosaur nugget that he dipped in ketchup atop the plate. Immersed in the scene, he was completely startled when he went to take a bite and was interrupted. The hunter gauntlet on the opposite side of the desk buzzed abruptly. Dropping the nugget onto the plate, he groaned as he wiped his fingers clean on a napkin and snatched the module from the gauntlet's socket. There was a message from Zane, but he didn't bother to view the content.

Instead, he peered at his second monitor to see that the sensor in front of his door gave a positive reading.

"Hold on ..." Andrew sighed out in annoyance, standing from his desk and pausing the video on his screen before tearing his headphones off. He marched to the door and opened it to be met with a wide grin and a large hand ruffling his head.

"Lil bro," Zane spoke with hushed exuberance, immediately tucking himself into Andrew's room before closing the door behind him.

"What are you doing here so late? Did anybody see you? I'm not supposed to be up this late as it is," Andrew said and swatted Zane's hand away.

"I know. That's why I waited to come and speak with you. Had to be sure that nobody knows we met."

"I'm not a fan of breaking the rules like you, you know," Andrew said, sighing before he walked back over to his desk. "That stunt we pulled could get me in serious trouble."

"It's all with a good purpose ... which is why I begrudgingly ask for one more teensy little favor for your good ole big bro."

"Anything else to add before I do?" Andrew asked, and Zane shifted over to the bed, adjusting his black hoodie before taking a seat.

"Am I that predictable? Promise you'll keep it extra-double secret, k?"

"You've been skimming some of my nuggies, Zane. I keep count." Andrew frowned as he gave Zane a harsh stare, earning a nervous chuckle from the shameless man.

"Oh, uh, guess that is worth mentioning too. I'll buy you some more when I go into town next week. But, uh ... it's pretty serious. Do I have your word?"

Andrew sat in his computer chair and spun around, facing the monitor before he held a finger up. He double-checked one of the windows featuring several lines of code atop a black background, nodding after a moment.

"You have my word ... we're all alone at the moment. Go ahead."

"Good call on your part," Zane said, giving a wry smile before shifting his gaze to the window. "We have a mole in the Hunters, one who's been sending our comrades to their deaths and sabotaging our operations. They were probably involved with the Covenant of Augury as well, but I don't have any evidence to directly suggest that yet. In retrospect ... there were a lot of things off about the response from HQ, and I assume that could have been the mole's doing."

"Woah, hold on," Andrew said, his voice hitching an octave higher as he spun to face Zane. The once nonchalant expression Zane wore was replaced by one of solemnness and concern, a troubling indication of the gravity of his words. "A lot of people died, and ... our communications were legitimately down that night, yeah?"

"They were," Zane agreed. "The problem lies in the contingency planning and operations. The moment our communications stopped for any duration of time, it would have been clear something went wrong, and HQ would have investigated it promptly. If I know General Blackwell and Commander Ardon, there's not a snowball's chance in my jacket that they wouldn't have sent the cavalry immediately. But it took our message getting through to Command several hours later. If Harvest was any bit as serious as the Athens incident, they would have taken an hour tops to mobilize our forces." Zane leaned back. "Know what I'm saying?"

Andrew was quiet, exhaling shakily before nodding, and Zane continued.

"Then you know why I'm looking into this more seriously now that I've got some leads. These disappearances have been fishy, oddly reminiscent of the way the police officers' were. But demons aren't just chancing upon careless hunters. I coerced one of the intelligence unit members you and Seven called to that laboratory into telling me the truth." Zane took a deep breath and stood up, walking over to Andrew as he reached into the pouch on his cargo pants.

"They weren't really our comrades—just pretending with glamour. There are demons in our ranks. Couldn't tell you how many ... but it's enough to know we can't trust just anybody."

"What?" Andrew gasped, his fingers tensing as he gripped the bottom of his hoodie.

"Unfortunately, I couldn't find out who is behind it all, given they kind of blew up when they were going to tell me," Zane said. He removed the data chip from the pouch and held it out. "I did snag this, however."

As Andrew laid his eyes on the chip, he bit his bottom lip and tensed up.

"If they find out that I'm helping you uncover this ..."

"I'll make sure that you stay safe. Always do." Zane grinned. "Don't I, lil bro?"

"Well ... we're not on the same squad, but I guess I made it through Harvest with only a few nightmares since then," Andrew said, taking the data chip as Zane laughed. Even with the dire insinuations of his continued assistance, he couldn't help but crack a smile as Zane stood over him, granting his reassurance.

"Think you can crack it? May be encrypted."

Andrew rummaged through his desk for a small cartridge that he plugged the chip into, and after a moment, he connected a cable to the cartridge before plugging it into the computer.

"If it was encrypted, there wouldn't be a single thing I could do about that, unfortunately. But ... I'll wager it probably isn't. The security system there was so *bad*," Andrew said as he returned his attention to his monitor.

"Let's see," Zane said.

As Andrew navigated to the file system of the computer, he tapped the screen to click on the chip as it loaded into the registry. The folders then slowly appeared.

"There we go. Told ya," Andrew said, snickering before flashing his signature grin.

"Hell yeah," Zane said, smirking as he leaned closer. "Mind if I peruse?"

"Nuh-uh," Andrew said, shaking his head before tapping the cartridge with the chip inside of it. "It loaded, but it isn't necessarily verified to be safe yet. I'm going to run a scan and duplicate the files to ensure there aren't any trojans or tripwires. But ... seeing how this thing is several terabytes large ... that'll take a day at least. You'll have to come back tomorrow night."

Zane hung his head, sighing dramatically before shoving his hands into his hoodie's pockets.

"You'd think that technology in the year of our lords 2045 would be faster."

"This kind of scrubbing would have taken a week a decade ago. This is about as fast as we can hope without submerging a data center in ice to handle the kind of processing going on. My humble rig will run the program at its own pace, thank you very much," Andrew claimed, reaching down and grabbing the nugget he'd been interrupted from eating. "Jeez ... I was going to finish this series tonight, but now I'm assisting with uncovering another conspiracy. Hope you're happy."

Zane nodded and yawned.

"I just love saving humanity from certain peril when I could be stuffing my face and napping. Well, guess I'll go get some well-deserved sleep and worry more about this tomorrow," Zane spoke, slogging through his words as exhaustion finally caught up to him. His soul still shivered as if it were in a freezer after burning down the lab earlier, and even the small feast he had after wasn't a replacement for a long date with his bed.

"Before coming back tomorrow, go into town and get more dino nuggies to replace the ones you took."

"But you have plenty in the freezer still. Can't that wait until next week?" Zane complained.

"It could if it were just me, but Val is joining me for a movie tomorrow."

"Oh?" Zane cocked a brow. "Consider it done then, Casanova." Zane saluted Andrew and spun on his heel, walking toward the door. When he reached for the knob, something hit his shoulder, a pen tumbling to the floor. When he looked over his shoulder, he saw Andrew glaring at him with a venom in his eyes he rarely ever saw.

"Make sure they're gluten-free. Don't need a stomachache to go along with the headache."

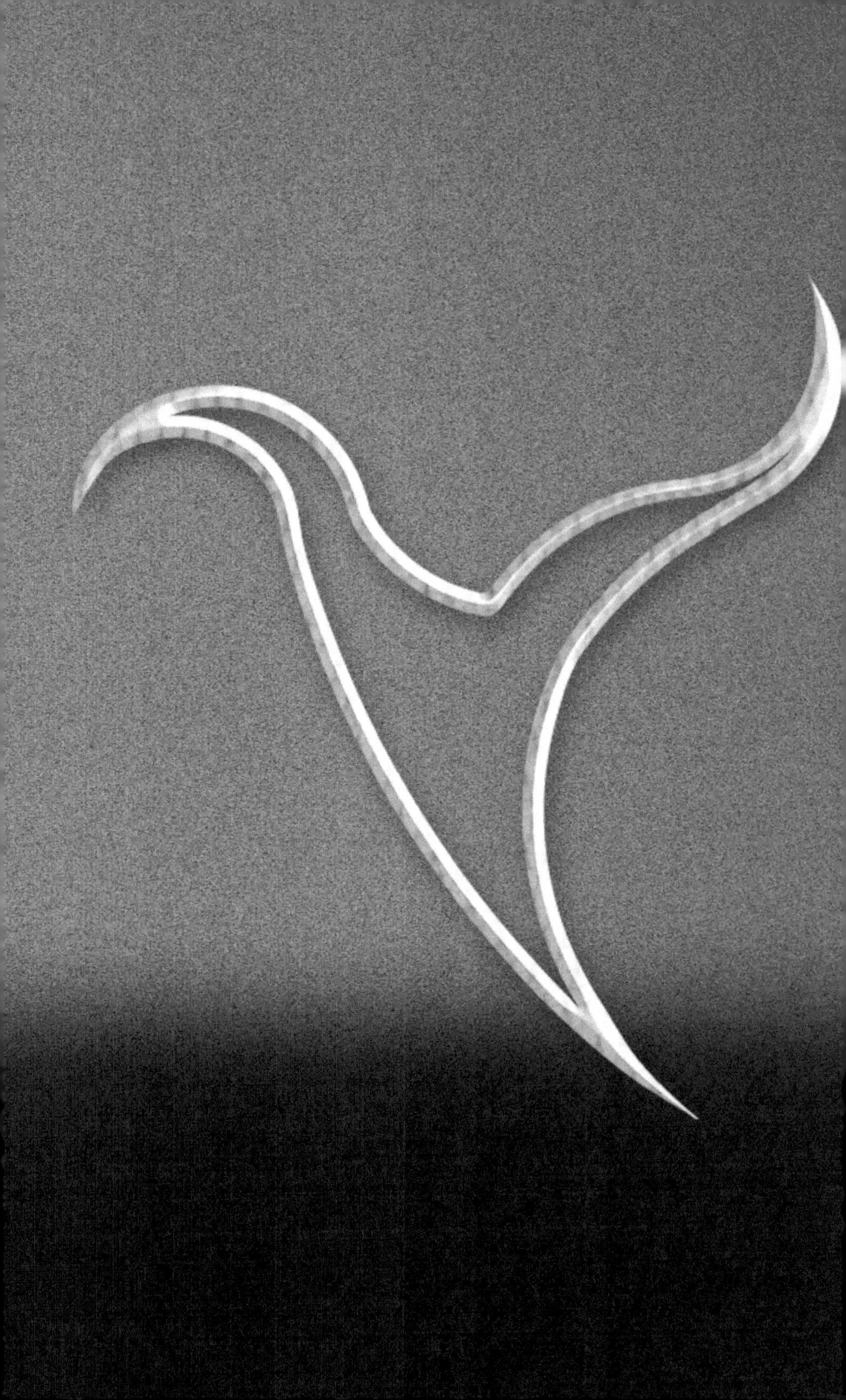

FOUR

Elations in the Cold

O HM'S CADENCE was hardly different in the aftermath of Harvest. The entire business district had various damage scarring it, but most of it had been repaired years later. For Ohm's Cadence, however, the scored exterior glass had never been replaced. The thick pane hosted four jagged marks on its surface, stopping shy of the door handle. Most of it was covered by a crudely placed poster featuring robotic limbs and the store logo of the Ohm's Law triangle, featuring a metronome in the middle. Kendra had always laughed reading it when it had been in the lobby.

Need a kick? Full service of prosthetic limbs offered at prices that should be illegal!

The afternoon bustled with cars zipping through the streets, angry honks of horns, harsh accelerations, and screeching tires at the intersections. The impatience of the average Chicago resident baffled both Eden and Kendra.

"This is the Chicago I adore," Kendra said sarcastically as she removed her arms from around Eden before dismounting his motorcycle. She removed her helmet, which had admittedly been a bit spacious for her liking. As she fixed her hair, Eden dismounted the bike and grunted with begrudging agreement at her statement.

"I abhor it," Eden said, and Kendra nudged him playfully.

"Hey, that rhymed," she teased, waltzing to the door and tucking the helmet Eden lent her under her arm. She noticed there were holes in the pavement where the bike rack had once been bolted. It was adjacent to the damaged glass, so she assumed it, too, had been damaged and was never replaced.

She went inside, peering around at the familiar lobby that had been a staple in her routine. The robotic pod that was Chelsea floated from its perch, blue eyes opening on the glossy black screen to greet them.

"Welcome, Kendra. Welcome, Mr. Blackwell," Chelsea chirped in its robotic, female voice.

"You remember!" Kendra squeaked, racing toward the counter and setting her helmet down.

"Mr. Blackwell ..." Eden muttered, earning a wink from Kendra as he took to her side.

"Of course. Mr. Ardent has never wiped my memory banks of your personnel file despite your resignation." Chelsea blinked, hovering to the counter as it looked between them. "How can I help you both today?"

"Just stopping in to see James," she said.

"I'll page him for you. Stand by, please," Chelsea said, its eyes closing as a ring circled on the black screen.

Eden set his helmet atop Kendra's and crossed his arms, looking around.

"Haven't been here in a minute. Used to be more convenient to bring my stuff here than to base," he said.

"Didn't they decommission the Chicago base just before I deployed for training?" she asked, and Eden nodded.

"Only really was established for us to deal with the covenant. No sense in wasting resources to continue operating it."

"No other demonic activity here?" Kendra inquired, and Eden shrugged.

"Last I heard, Detective Stroth became our eyes and ears here—even made some allies with other demon citizens. At least that's what Zane said," he sighed, shaking his head. "Don't really keep up with the guy."

"He and my mom worked together, so it'd be nice to say hi some-time—see how surprised he'd be to know I'm a hunter now as well," Kendra said.

The door opened behind them, and they both turned, Kendra smiling upon seeing a familiar face.

"Well, well, well," Jones said as he entered the shop, a grease-stained brown bag in hand.

"Jones!" Kendra called out, holding her arms out as he approached. He gave her a half hug, holding the bag away from her.

"Got some parmesan breadsticks. I don't wanna get grease on ya," Jones said. "Want any?"

"Is it from Franko's?" she asked, squinting at the bag as she broke away. "I'll pass this time. Had a ton of bread yesterday," she lied, recalling Franko's Italian Kitchen used a lot of rosemary in their seasoning.

"More for me, unless you want some, kid?" Jones asked, holding the bag up to Eden, who shook his head.

"I'm good," he said, giving an insincere smile as he paced to Kendra's side.

"Kind of glad you both said no. I just wanted to be polite," he admitted sheepishly, chortling as he opened the door to the back of the store. "Come on. James is probably locked in on that executive's prosthetic he's upgrading."

They followed him, and Kendra glanced at the shelves and workbenches. Messier than usual, she couldn't help but wonder how things had been since she'd left. Arman's desk was the same as usual, but Sal's desk looked barren, caked in a light layer of dust.

"Where's Arman? Did Sal move benches? He's too much of a neat freak for his bench to look like that," Kendra commented, cocking her head.

Jones was quiet for a moment, pursing his lips before he shook his head.

"Really has been a while, huh? Arman's off today, but Sal's still in the hospital since that Exsomnis attack. No progress yet, and J-man's been sinking his own bread into funding this experimental treatment they've been floating. Really miss that grouch ..." Jones mused, clearing his throat as he tossed the bag onto his bench. Nobody spoke at the mention of

Exsomnis for several seconds, then Jones broke the silence. "I wanna know what you've been up to, though, to change the subject."

Eden watched Kendra mull over the thought. Abruptly, she slapped her cheeks and released her breath. She knew much damage had been left in the wake of the somnium's conquest, but she wanted to keep the vacation positive—especially for Eden's sake.

"I'm in the military now. Part of a special operations force that I'd have to kill you if I talked about it," Kendra said. Hearing this, Eden gave a playful scoff as he walked past them, shaking his head.

"Oh? Hunting down Exsomnis, maybe?" Jones whispered, leaning forward against his workbench.

Kendra held her index finger to her lips, winking as she walked past him.

"I'll get back to you in a minute. Need to talk with J-man real quick!" Kendra claimed, waving as she joined Eden at James's workbench, where he was carefully installing wiring into the frame of a gold-plated prosthetic leg.

Hovering in front of him, Eden folded his arms as James grumbled beneath his breath, attention fixed on the leg with his goggle lenses zooming in and out.

"What is this gaudy abomination?" Eden asked, cringing at the sight of the leg.

"My retirement fund," James grumbled as he connected a wire and then snapped the compartment shut, where a connector port was fixed for charging the device. "If it was one of our own, they'd get the model without the power port and something more functional than gold plating, but hey, it's his money."

"What did you even do to it? Don't recognize this model," Kendra mumbled as she eyed it with less disgust than Eden.

"Newer one. Came out a week ago, and the guy already wants it outfitted with the tech of next year and some additional capacitors for the fancy add-ons some lousy quack upsold him." James sighed, standing up with a crack of his back as he groaned. "I could afford a new spine if I get another job like this one."

Eden rolled his eyes and said,

"Could get those things way cheaper without installing it into his leg."

"Go hunt him down and tell him that," James grumbled as he rubbed his eyes and blinked several times.

"Is he a demon?" Eden asked.

"Worse. Hedge fund manager," James said and tore the goggles from his head.

"Ew," Kendra said, her face twisting in disgust. "I guess you can put the money to a good cause—balance out all that negative karma."

"Already am," James sighed as he folded his arms. "You two on winter vacation or something? Surprised ole' Captain Lord Slayer here is payin' me a visit."

"Actually, I'm here to pick up my last paycheck," Kendra sardonically joked, and James rolled his eyes.

"I definitely gave it to your pa for you years ago," he said and tossed the goggles in the black bin beside his bench.

"Under the table," Kendra teased, shaking her head. "Also, Eden and I *both* took Intico down, thank you very much," Kendra said, folding her arms with an expectant look.

"We did," Eden affirmed, flashing her a knowing look as he shoved his hands in his leather jacket.

"My bad. Captain and Private Lord Slayer," James said, huffing as he circled from his desk and grabbed a towel from the rack above him. Once he wiped his face clean, he looked at them. "As long as y'all are keeping Joe safe."

"He's doing fine. Lot more skilled than you'd give him credit for."

"I've seen him work. I know," James said and gathered his silver locks and redid the tail it was tied into. "I'm sure he's pulling his weight. Just wish he had become an engineer instead—give me someone to pass this place down to when I kick the bucket. It'll probably go to Jones at this point."

"He doesn't care about tech beyond weapons," Eden affirmed, shrugging.

"Just his special interest, I guess. Like Eden and his motorcycle. Just boy things," Kendra said sarcastically.

"Hey, I reckon you'd be into some cycles if you had the right one. Maybe the 2030s line of Kite N Key choppers. Lot better than the Wattz Eden swears by," James explained.

"Kites are too loud," Eden argued, frowning. "Those decibel levels are egregious. Might as well have gas motors with their artificially bolstered noises."

"What, and kill the joy of riding a bike to begin with?"

"It's about the speed, not the roar."

The two bickered for a while longer before Kendra slapped the bench, clearing her throat performatively.

"I prefer the bus and a pedal bike. If I want to ride so bad, I have a perfectly good demon hunter right here to take me," Kendra proclaimed, flashing Eden a smirk.

"Killjoy," James huffed, walking past them to the back. "Hate to let y'all go early but gotta have this thing done by tomorrow. What you two got planned after this?"

"Just hanging out at Eden's place. He's got some art to show me too." She smiled fondly. "Just a chill kind of day before I go watch the show at midnight," Kendra said with a soft smile.

"Yeah, mhm, sure," James said, grinning to himself as he entered the storage room. "Just be sure to use protection."

Both Kendra and Eden perked up, expressions flustered. Eden was quiet, but Kendra glared and huffed loudly.

"We're *friends*."

Kendra sighed in relief as the motorcycle finally came to a stop inside Eden's garage. She felt somewhat claustrophobic from having to breathe through the oversized helmet. At some point, some of her hair came untucked during the ride, and she was too occupied with holding on to Eden to readjust. She unlatched the strap that tightened it to her head, and when she yanked it off, she took a loud breath.

"That would have been much more fun if my hair and your helmet agreed," Kendra commented, setting the helmet down on the backseat of the bike. Eden snorted, lacking the same urgency as he engaged the kickstand.

"Apologies for not having a smaller one," he said, removing his helmet and clicking it tightly to the bike handle. He then grabbed the one he lent her and placed it on one of the garage shelves next to an old box of tools before turning to face her again.

"Definitely not. You'll have to pay the Ken-tax for that one," she demanded insincerely, pointing at him.

"Ken-tax?"

"I made it up. Think of something you have to do for me," she joked, brushing her black jeans off before removing the matching faux leather jacket she styled with it.

"I'll keep it in mind." Eden sighed, walking toward the door that led into the house. He then clicked the button that closed the garage behind them. He fished his keys from his jacket before unlocking the door and ushering her inside, and instinctively, he checked the walls like he used to.

Upon seeing the runes decorating the home, Kendra cocked an eyebrow. She had recalled seeing Alicia drawing them on a kind of paper a few times, knowing they were used for some enchantments.

"What are these for?" she asked.

"Protection. Ensures that things won't detect our energy signatures while we're within a certain perimeter from them."

"Why would they come after you?" Kendra probed, pointing at Eden. "You're like a boogeyman to demons, if what I gathered is accurate."

"That's exaggerated," Eden alleged, shaking his head before tapping the center of the blood symbol on the wall. "It's not like I'm doing much boogey-manning when I sleep. Best to be on the safe side."

Eden removed his jacket and hung it by the door before gesturing to the empty hook next to it, and Kendra set her own jacket on it. He directed her to follow him to his room while she inspected the environment. She hadn't quite imagined Eden would live in such an ordinary home, runes aside. It was the kind of middle-class suburban home she was used to.

The interior styling was bare, and even the kitchen they passed by lacked a spice rack or even a knife block. She couldn't imagine him or Jessica cooking, but he had mentioned she used to make pies. It wasn't the kind of home that seemed broken in at all, but Eden had mentioned that he and his mother had only moved to Chicago halfway through his junior year.

"Why Chicago?" Kendra abruptly asked, and Eden paused at the base of the staircase.

"Huh?" he responded.

"What made you and your mother move here?"

Eden sighed, placing a hand on the pillar of the banister, and his fingers drummed on the orb-shaped head.

"James," Eden replied. "Meant that General Blackwell could keep a better eye on me. She's protective, as you've seen."

"Oh, yeah. I feel dumb for not putting two and two together. I mean, we just left his shop after all," Kendra said. "I was ... distracted back when we were in school. The supernatural stuff was still pretty strange," she said with a wry smile, and Eden nodded sympathetically.

"Not so strange anymore," he suggested, eyes drifting before he turned and made his way up the staircase. Kendra followed, smirking at his demeanor. He showed sympathy in odd ways, but he had always been considerate and protective. Years prior, he had refused to kill her even as Intico controlled her body, or when she initially mutated. Back then, she had found him scary, his presence unnerving. Now, those crimson eyes were a beacon of comfort.

The pictures lining the pale walls caught her attention, and for the first time, she caught a glimpse of a time unknown to her. In his infancy, Eden was on Jessica's lap while he ate an apple half the size of his face. Behind them, there was a younger, clean-shaven Ethan, greatly contrasting with the uptight formality she knew him for. Fondness glittered in his eyes as he looked down at Eden and Jessica, and she couldn't help but notice his hands were placed atop Jessica's shoulder and Eden's head.

Perplexingly, she barely noticed that Eden's eyes in the picture were green. It hadn't crossed her mind before whether she could see their true color in pictures, but it was one of many mysteries surrounding him.

"You and Ethan go that far back, huh?" she asked, prompting Eden to glance at the photo.

"Since I was born," he confirmed. "He and General Blackwell shared a squad once." Eden's gaze softened, and he continued down the hallway that led to his room. "He's like a father."

"Oh ..." Kendra muttered, offering a sheepish smile before rubbing her head. If she had known that much, she wouldn't have complained to him about how much he had put her off initially. Eden hadn't commented much on it when she had. Somehow, Ethan was harder to read than Eden, but even so, she hadn't thought him to be terrible.

Eden opened the door leading into his room, and light spilled through the blinds. A queen-size bed filled one corner. Adjacent to it was a large desk covered in notebooks and old, rolled-up blueprints. The only other furnishing was a simple dresser opposite the bed, and Eden's suitcase sat atop it, among other common belongings.

"This is different from what I was expecting," Kendra murmured, her eyes landing on the desk to see a case of art supplies.

"Not very exciting, I take it?" he asked, and Kendra chuckled.

"Not what I said. Just kind of expected something more ... mystical and dark. The kind of room you'd see belonging to a demon hunter. This just looks like ... a room."

"Didn't see a point in decorating. I tried not to be home a lot." Eden paced to his desk, taking a seat on the chair before directing Kendra to his bed. Walking over to it, Kendra took a seat, pressing her palms into the mattress. It was firmer than the one she owned, perfect for someone like Eden.

"First time having a girl over?" Kendra joked.

"How'd you guess?" Eden asked, playing along while he grabbed one of his mechanical pencils. He then twirled it in his fingers, glancing at her.

"Little birdy down the way says I was your only friend from school." Eden cocked an eyebrow.

"Birdy?" Eden chuckled. "I like birds, so … compliment accepted."

"It wasn't meant to be," she huffed, smirking. "I could come up with a much better compliment. Like … your eyes are really cool." Kendra snapped her fingers, sitting straight before pointing at him. "By the way, why don't your red eyes show up in those family photos?"

Eden snorted, leaning back in his chair as he looked past her, out the window.

"Remember what you learned about the supernatural and surveillance?"

Kendra pondered for several moments, hunching forward before standing.

"Yeah, but that only applies to demons, right? They're the only ones that don't show up on camera as they are," she said, but Eden shook his head.

"Because of the veil, supernatural things are obscured and changed in recorded mediums. My eyes are the same, so normal cameras don't pick them up. That's why you couldn't see them until you became connected—which is also why I had assumed you became connected that night at James's store."

"Oh, right. You slayed the hound that night, huh?" she asked, and Eden nodded.

"Luckily, I was there that day for maintenance on my gear," Eden began, tapping his pencil. "He made the maneuver device I use. Even invented the quantum motors you see in a lot of our equipment," Eden said while Kendra nodded along.

"He'd talk over my head a lot, but I'm sure he and Andrew could monologue on tech stuff for hours." As Eden chuckled at her assertion,

Kendra stroked her chin, thinking for a moment. "Wait … I think my dad was on that quantum motor project. Said it was the crown of his career. Pretty sure that's how he met James too."

"Makes sense. Not everything we use is manufactured by other hunters," Eden said and turned in his chair before flipping open a sketchbook. He scribbled something on the page, mulling over the thought more. "Most of our weaponry is just modified versions of existing military models and designs."

Kendra crept over to him, peering over his shoulder to look at what he was drawing, but there was only a vaguely feminine form on the page.

"You like tech things too, yeah?"

"Some things …" Eden said, tapping the tip of the pencil above the head of the figure, as if pondering what to do next.

"Your bike comes to mind," she said, thinking of his bickering with James.

"I always wanted one as a kid, so I put my salary into buying one to work on over time. Made it quieter rather than louder, unlike what *some* like to do. Helps that Wattz bikes are already pretty quiet to begin with." Hearing this made Kendra laugh, and she kneeled next to him while eyeing the sketch.

"Oh yeah, I forgot to ask when you picked me up." She glanced out the window. "Are you doing anything tonight? I was gonna watch the holographic fireworks show with a bottle of wine. You're welcome to join me if you're free."

Eden stared solemnly at the page, his expression deviating along with his train of thought. His eyes never diverted from the page, however.

"Sorry. I am, actually. I'm going somewhere special to me."

Kendra frowned. Being so close to him, Kendra couldn't help but notice the dark circles beneath his eyes. The idea flashed through her mind that perhaps a somnium had been present and haunting him, but she knew that wasn't the case. Eden had always appeared tired—then more than usual. The fact that he was sleep-deprived so often worried her just a bit, but she never thought to mention it. He would always deflect and refrain from divulging his brooding topics.

"Is she special?" Kendra teased, attempting to wrench his mind from the darkness she saw him retreating to. But rather than showing mutual humor or levity in his mood, Eden sighed with a subtle tremble in his voice.

"I'll be back," he said, standing, and Kendra moved to give him room.

"I'll be here," Kendra said, forcing a smile as he walked out of the room. *Nice one, Ken,* she thought with a sigh.

When he closed the door, Kendra returned her attention to the sketchbook, examining the half-drawn figure and the vague familiarity that it evoked. Her fingers had subconsciously drifted down to the desk. They glided down the edge of the page, curiosity consuming her as she thought to see more of his work. She had only caught glimpses of it in the past. Eden's talent with art was something that intrigued her the more she considered how little of it he had shown.

Page by page, Kendra flipped through the book, examining all the unique sketches and ideas he had jotted down: gear, hunting attire, and several other practical things. There were a few pages of anatomy practice she had seen, but nothing that really embodied a specific person. Then she came across the one drawing that stood out the most, buried within the pages in such a way she had almost missed it. A girl.

Large eyes with a serene depth stared with a bright smile that Kendra swore would have glowed in reality. Her long, wavy hair fell wildly along with the curly bangs that dared not obscure her round face. She wore a white dress that hugged her small form, but what stood out most were her large white angel wings. They enshrouded her body, feathers flying around her like cherry blossom petals.

The sketch, unlike the others in the book, was far more detailed and showed a great deal of care. The lead on the page had since weathered, the lines slightly smeared. Why Eden had placed such a thoughtful sketch within the book baffled her, but she assumed there was some elusive reason. Whoever the girl was, she wasn't daft enough to believe that she wasn't of some importance to Eden.

The sound of a door opening down the hall stirred her from her stray thoughts, and she realized she had been snooping too long. She hurriedly flipped the sketchbook back to the original page and walked over to the dresser before leaning against it. Inconspicuously, she then fixed her attention on the ceiling.

When Eden returned to the room, she offered him a smile but saw he had been avoiding her eyes as he returned to his seat.

"Everything ... alrighty?" she prompted.

"Yeah," Eden said with feigned assurance. "Something I remembered I needed to do."

"Well ... if you say so," Kendra said, returning to his side. Seeing the vaguely feminine figure again, Kendra leaned against the desk, and an idea came to mind—a distraction of sorts. "Would you draw some combat attire for me to graduate into one day?" she suggested, earning a quizzical look from Eden.

"We'd still have to get the material necessary for making it fireproof; otherwise, it'll be just as prone to burning as the standard stuff, let alone the approval process."

Kendra pouted, recalling the troubles she had faced in getting her power under control when she was a cadet. Jessica personally had to enchant her uniform along with adding a waistcloth that it could siphon material from for automatic repairs.

"Well, isn't there something we can get? I mean, Zane has stuff like that, right?" she inquired, and Eden nodded.

"He does, but grants aside, he spends most of his salary on buying those ultra-rare materials—and gorging himself like a pig. I swear I try to forget when he ate an entire rotisserie chicken in under a minute," Eden spoke, muttering the last part, and Kendra rolled her eyes.

"I'm sure it was at least a minute and ten seconds," Kendra joked. "I'll talk to him about it sometime. So, how about we just get a design down?"

Eden shrugged before grabbing his pencil, tapping it against the sketch before looking to Kendra for a moment. She looked at the page, then to him, her gaze expectant. He glanced between her and the page repeatedly, then he sighed upon realizing. Promptly, he corrected the figure he had drawn to widen the hips, earning a laugh from Kendra.

"There you go," she mused, nodding in approval.

"Do you have an idea of what you'd want?" As he looked at her, she gave a sheepish smile and took a step back.

"Okay, so, I suggested it ... but I hadn't really put *that* much thought into it."

Eden sighed and set the pencil on the page before shooting her a look.

"I'm not fashionable like you, but I could maybe come up with some ideas based on how you typically fight."

"How I fight?" Kendra questioned, inspecting herself in the mirror. A mischievous smirk found her after a moment.

"Just don't undress me on the page with something that has my boobs practically popping out," Kendra snapped insincerely, arms folded atop her chest with a feigned poker face. Eden gave no reaction, eyes fixed on the page.

"The opposite, actually. Something that would prevent that ... *one* incident when you were a cadet."

Kendra squeaked, blushing furiously as she recalled the embarrassing memory of when she had flared up and burned her shirt off when she first took the blade exam. He had been quick to cover her up with his jacket then, but the chagrin burned all the same. Without hesitation, she slapped Eden's back and huffed.

"Of course you'd remember that!"

Golden light caressed the cityscape as the encroaching night marched over the horizon. Its emptiness invited the spectacle that Kendra so awaited. New Year's Eve and what it heralded suggested something new that await-ed—something better, or so she hoped. The large black bottle in her grip was as much a representation of her uncertainty as it was an agent to numb her doubts. She disliked most alcohol, as she had liberally learned with the several cocktails she tried after her graduation from being a cadet. Wine, however, was palatable. It was almost ironic how she found most things a deep shade of red to be delectable—something that once dismayed her.

"Blackberry wine ..." Kendra spoke listlessly. The depressing idea of drinking the bottle alone as she watched the fireworks brought her back to Kendall. The desire to see her again bubbled from the grave she'd dug for it. It never remained dead for long, if it had died at all.

The life that could have been—taken by demons. She became a hunter to deny such a thesis for others. That shared sentiment with Eden allowed them to become closer, in spite of the distance he imposed.

Wonder where he is, Kendra thought, her face twisting into a scowl. She turned her head when she heard a little girl's voice, and she tucked the bottle in her jacket, offering a kind smile to the child. Ignoring Kendra, she passed, returning to the waiting arms of her mother.

Chicago didn't feel as large as it once had, and the more she traveled through its crowds, the more it offered a brief antidote to her rumination. As if she were pretending to be normal once more, she cherished the moments. Finally, she relaxed while venturing toward the place she and Kendall used to occupy for firework shows—a building that stood half the height of Willis Tower but still offered a miraculous place to spectate from. She doubted she'd have to sneak in anymore either.

Next to it was a hospital whose rooftop was rarely occupied beyond the occasional patient who would sneak atop it to smoke. Even before her change, Kendra hated the scent of tobacco that the wind carried across. With the photos she had seen of a smoker's lungs in biology class, she'd never deigned to try it either.

Shaking the stray thought, Kendra untucked the bottle from her jacket before she awkwardly wedged it within her pocket. She eyed the building, mentally mapping out how she'd scale it. It was still too light out upon her arrival—too many onlookers. She dreaded waiting longer than she needed to.

After a moment's consideration, she slapped her forehead at her mind's absence. With a deep breath, she ducked into a smelly alleyway.

"Insenseilis," she whispered, and her form shimmered light blue as the incantation took effect. The sensation was subtle and barely discernible in the physical sense, but the heat of her aura had dampened significantly, along with the omens circling her. Now practically invisible to humans, she took her first leap, landing atop an old balcony ledge, and she kept jumping to similar protrusions until she reached the top. Ironically, it had been easier than when she would hack the back door's lock and climb several flights of the cramped stairwell.

The top of the building was mundane, primarily consisting of ducts that peeked from the building. The ledge was where she, Kendall, Natalie, and Allen would gather to watch the fireworks. On the last Independence Day they had spent together, the three girls had been the only ones to show. She ventured a guess as to why Allen couldn't make it, but she was glad that memory was untainted. Now, Natalie was back home celebrating with her family in the countryside, and she hadn't thought to contact anybody else.

"Kind of sad when I think about it ... all alone with a bottle of wine on New Year's," Kendra muttered, pulling the bottle from her pocket. Peerless and empty, the dark sky reflected on the surface. Suddenly, light twinkled on the glass. For a moment, she thought it was illegal fireworks being set off from one of the adjacent suburbs, but there was no sound.

Kendra turned to see the hospital rooftop that was a story lower than the tower she stood on. There she saw the source of the twinkling lights—*omens*. Dazzling, they carried a familiarity that erected the memory of a man she had since forgotten, and the pale, princely visage flashed in her mind. And as if manifesting from those recesses, she spotted him.

Shimmering, with his silver hair flicking in the wind, he stood at the edge of the rooftop, palm held out as energy coalesced around him. The omens that danced, as if commanded by his presence, spread, dispersing the winter's chill that had been mild that evening. With it, snow gently cascaded through the air to cake the city in its frigid embrace. Captivated like last time, she found herself nearing the edge to take a closer look.

When they had met before, Kendra had lacked a strong grasp of the supernatural. Now attuned to the forces that once eluded her understanding, she could unequivocally determine he wasn't a threat. Instead, he invited calm. Swallowing hard, she acted without thinking and took a leap, plunging several feet. She landed a bit more oafishly than she had intended, stumbling to catch the bottle when it slipped from her grasp.

A heavy sigh of relief escaped her, and she turned her gaze upward to meet those icy blue hues she remembered so vividly. As she met those incandescent, icy depths, she couldn't help but wonder what his true form looked like. There was little information pertaining to the rime within the demon compendium, but it was said they had blue skin.

"Azazel," she spoke softly, digging his name from the recesses of her memory. And in response, he smiled.

"Son of Azazel," they spoke in unison, but she suspected he plucked those words from her mind to know she would speak it.

"How auspicious that we met in this city again. I should have expected this, however. This is your home, I assume," Azazel spoke, his calm voice carrying with it the delicacy of a snowflake, yet all the warmth of a hearth.

"You have a lot of correct assumptions. It's almost creepy," she said, huffing as she realized how unnaturally cold it was now that she was close.

"I assure you that I am only making guesses, Miss—" He lowered his gaze, touching his chin as he searched his mind. "You never gave me your name," Azazel concluded.

"Kendra Mallory, daughter of Katherine and Aaron," Kendra said, snorting as he gave her a knowing look. In the next moment, the omens had gone quiet and disappeared.

"It is a pleasure to see you again, Kendra. Would it be another creepy assumption if I said you've become a hunter?"

"Only if you're not honest with what gives it away," she said, setting her bottle of wine down before crossing her arms beneath her chest with an expectant stare. His expression remained unflinching. His eyes roamed, inspecting her in a way she would have been unnerved by if not for his calm aura.

"You appear significantly more capable than when we last met," he spoke, offering a sly smile as she shot him a skeptical look. "Ah, and that technique they employ encompasses your body," he spoke, chuckling. "Or perhaps you have stumbled upon an ancient archive and taught yourself the requisite tongue to rehearse its knowledge?" he suggested jokingly.

"There we go," Kendra said, daring to approach him now. "And your intentions here? I don't imagine it's your curiosity to see the bean, nor do I think there's another conspiracy your king has you investigating."

Azazel cocked his brow.

"The bean?"

"Big, shiny art piece that looks like a bean—kind of a tourist attraction here. Looks clean, but I wouldn't recommend touching it." Kendra's face scrunched at the thought.

Azazel snorted, letting out a sigh as he focused on her other question.

"Odd reason for a visitation, but my purpose here tonight is connected to my presence here last time," Azazel began, eyes flitting away from hers. "There is much insight I've to glean on these somnium and the phenomenon they have inspired. I feel compelled of my own volition," Azazel spoke, a frown marring his pale features.

"You're not here on official business then? Just research?" she asked, tilting her head.

"Research contains a purpose. The more insight I discern, the sooner we could understand the machinations still plaguing your kind. It, perhaps, may provide us the means of remedy."

"You mean like"—Kendra trembled, daring to entertain the idea of seeing her mother again—"returning them to normal?"

Azazel raised his head, giving a tepid nod. "If it is possible. But I've yet to determine so," he spoke, his tone dropping. "Adamance is a virtue I shall maintain, nonetheless."

Kendra pursed her lips, the brief flitter of hope fleeing once again, but she forced a smile.

"Well, then I suppose I won't have to try to be an official hunter tonight and report our encounter. I somehow doubt anything good would come of that, anyway." With her words, Azazel's expression thawed.

"Wisdom is very becoming of you. With the formalities of our respective vocations suspended, perhaps there is much we would discuss?" he suggested.

Kendra took to his side, nodding in agreement before holding the wine bottle up.

"I was going to drink it by myself originally, but now I feel we'll be talking for a while and ... well, you've seen the movies. Drinking while exchanging our tragic stories seems fitting."

"Movies?" he asked, cocking his head. "Those motion pictures you humans immerse yourselves in?"

"Dude, how old are you?" Kendra interrogated, making Azazel chuckle.

"Demons like myself age differently, and with the time dilation between Mortale and Inferos, it's hard to answer that question honestly. A few centuries is a safe guess, perhaps."

"You say that so casually!" Kendra huffed as she tried to contain her exasperation. "Is that why your hair is silver?"

Azazel glanced up, blowing a cold breath to shift a strand from in front of his eye.

"Most rimes have silver hair, actually. In demon years ... I suspect I'd be just past my teenage years, but it's hard to say. I suspect the royal librarian in Avernus could better determine it," Azazel spoke, offering a coy smile. Pouting, Kendra shook her head and turned, walking over to the wine bottle and snatching it.

"Do you like wine?" she questioned as Azazel tugged the hem of his coat.

"Depends ..."

The two eventually approached the edge of the rooftop, taking seats as Kendra used the tool on her keychain to uncork the bottle. She then realized she hadn't brought cups. Azazel smirked and held his hand out to her, and a twinkling white light encircled his palm as shards of ice formed into a crystal-like goblet. With an amused expression, Kendra reached out, tapping the side of the glass.

"It isn't cold. Will it melt if I hold it? I'm pretty hot," she said, and Azazel shook his head.

"While I agree with your proclamation, this isn't typical ice—it's permafrost. Only cold to those I seek to harm."

Kendra's eyes darted down to the goblet again, and she examined it carefully.

"Guess I'm not—wait." Kendra raised a brow. "Was that flirting?"

"Perhaps." Azazel shrugged, offering a bewitching grin devoid of shame.

Kendra huffed, shaking her head before she poured herself a glass. Once it was filled, she turned her gaze back to him to see him holding an identical goblet out, still sporting that expression. She filled his cup before setting the bottle down beside her.

"This is the part where we toast, yes?"

"You know about that, then? Guess your knowledge of human stuff is sporadic."

"I am possibly as old as that specific custom," Azazel sarcastically spoke.

"Fair," Kendra said, failing to contain her smirk.

Once they clicked their goblets together, they enjoyed the wine in silence for a few seconds. With the edge removed and the night descending upon them, they exchanged stories. She began first, explaining her human life, how it ended, the Covenant of Augury, and becoming a hunter.

"Now, I'm on vacation, and here we are. Still alive, emotionally scarred, needing more therapy ... but alive."

Azazel, pensive with a daunting gaze that showed his attentiveness, slowly raised his goblet to his lips before finishing what remained in his cup.

"Like wisdom, perseverance is also a becoming feature for you. I suspected you were strong already, but your story is vindicating."

"I guess you could say that. Can't say I feel very strong." She sighed, setting her goblet down beside the bottle.

"Nobody feels strong," Azazel spoke, pursing his lips as he peered into the night. The last glimmer of the sun disappeared behind the horizon, and he focused on the sparse stars above. "It's persisting in our perceived weakness that determines strength."

"That's courage," Kendra challenged.

"Almost. Courage denotes a near certainty in our demise, or at least a recognition of it. Strength is something more perpetual and pervasive within our being. Courage and fear are ephemeral feelings that can be challenged or conquered by strength. It's not mutually exclusive either. We can be strong yet fearful, or weak yet courageous."

Kendra stared quietly, mulling over his words in silence as the wind rustled around them. As much as she felt compelled to disagree or refute him, she found herself in total agreement, much to a phantom chagrin.

"If I understood what you just said, then I'd rather feel weak again. It was a nicer feeling."

Azazel reached across her and snatched the bottle with nimble fingers before setting it beside him instead.

"*That* wouldn't be very becoming of you," he spoke, smirking as he glanced down at his goblet. "I'll share some details about myself with you now, if you would lend your ear."

Kendra snorted, shrugging before she pretended to grab and toss her ear at him.

"All yours, Plato."

Azazel chuckled lightly, his eyes twinkling with amusement.

"I do know of him, at least." He tapped the rim of his goblet, a light chime humming from it before it dissipated into nothing.

"I was born in Inferos, son of King Azazel of the rime. Now, I am all that remains of my clan—the only remaining ice demon as far as I am aware, and believe me, I have searched." Azazel's tone dropped but remained as calm as his aura, clashing with the grim nature of his story.

"What happened?" Kendra asked, holding on to every word.

"Paimon," Azazel answered, a wisp of venom in his tone as his eyes narrowed. The city reflecting in his icy depths mirrored the cold he harbored toward that name. "The demon of agony, inheritor of wrath. While he once liberated demonkind from near extinction so long ago when the Primordials sought our eradication, he surrendered his sanity. Eventually, he deemed the rime as insubordinate in his ambition and eliminated us." Azazel took a deep breath, the cold air marshaling before him. "I survived and fled to Mortale, where Paimon could not reach me, and here I persist as their ghost, seeking to exist as my father had—benevolent to the world and all that would live within it." As his words died, Kendra considered how to respond, but as she examined him, her gaze went soft.

"A forlorn prince ..." Kendra spoke quietly, a sorrowful expression washing over her. His face nearly shined in the shadow of night, incandescent as to almost blend with his silver hair. To escape the weight of the stretching silence, Kendra continued in the only way she knew how. "Just so we're clear, I won't go calling you *Your Majesty* or anything like it. But it's definitely fitting."

"Fitting how?" Azazel inquired, eyes still fixed below.

Kendra pursed her lips, giving a sheepish smile.

"Guess it could be considered kind of a girl thing, but like ... I feel safe. Not just interpersonally, but there's a vibe that you'd be the noble type who'd lay down their life if needed." Kendra sighed and shook her head before averting her gaze to the building she had leaped from. "Kind of dumb since I hardly know you, but it's just a feeling. I could be entirely wrong."

Azazel's lips curled into a smirk, suspending the bitterness he had momentarily adopted. Finally, the frigid breath he had imprisoned released, and he turned to her with renewed confidence.

"I pray not."

In the ensuing night, he continued to speak of the kingdom of Avernus, how it resided outside of human comprehension with old magics very few could bypass. This included the Hunters. With many comrades and subordinates, he had become the captain of the vanguard—a force of elite demons reporting directly to King Asmodeus, serving as the frontline against all threats to demonkind, among other duties.

Avernus had many cultures within, demons of all walks and considerations that coexisted within the towering walls. The food, vegetation, and sentiments of demons combined within a capital that invited demons to prosper. The summary of it all inspired many questions for Kendra, but midnight approached.

"It's almost time," Kendra said, interrupting Azazel's explanations of demonic cuisine. She raised her wrist, a projection showing they had less than three minutes.

"Ah, so it seems," Azazel said. Prematurely, the sounds of fireworks thundered in the distance. "I suppose patience isn't reliable in determining this outside of the newer clock devices humans have."

"Yeah, lots of people kind of suck like that." Kendra chuckled. "If demons in Avernus celebrate it, what was your favorite thing to do leading up to it?"

Azazel snorted, giving Kendra a curious look.

"I could hardly condense it with the time we have left before midnight."

As Kendra had noticed, Azazel was artfully aware of how to avoid giving certain details, much like she had neglected mentioning Allen, among other things. It was ironic how disjointed her curiosity was from that fact. She cursed her propensity for meeting elusive, supernatural beings. The thought manifested as a pout that she did her best to hide but found herself reaching for the bottle that wasn't there anymore.

Turning back to Azazel, she found him holding the bottle out to her, hovering right above her lap as he gazed over the city. As if it mirrored fondness, she glimpsed the longing in his eyes, a kind smile in tow. *Reminiscence.*

"Never mind," Kendra said and shot him a similar smile, but as the seconds ticked, her thoughts slipped more and more.

Three. Two. One.

A cacophony of thunderous pops and crackles erupted throughout Chicago, and the sky shined to life with a display of eagles soaring throughout the fireworks. She had never investigated how they did it exactly. It was a marvel of human ingenuity that compelled both Kendra and Azazel to give it their full attention.

Kendra's memories flooded, finally reaching a break. With starry eyes and quivering lips, tears fled her eyes, clashing with that smile she wrestled to maintain. Catching herself in the following moments, she exhaled shakily and shifted her glasses to wipe her eyes. She had hoped that Azazel hadn't seen. Even with the safety she felt, she thought it inappropriate to break down in front of him.

"I never knew my mother," Azazel spoke, cutting through the applause of noise that settled into ambience. "She died shortly following my birth, according to my father."

Kendra hurriedly composed herself, turning to face Azazel, where she met his daunting gaze.

"Yeah?"

"If your mother is like you, I imagine she, too, possesses incredible strength capable of triumphing over darkness."

Kendra bit her bottom lip, air jetting between her teeth as she cast her head down.

"I want to believe that, but she's like the others who were merged with."

"You were merged with as well, yes? What would you think differs?"

Kendra's thoughts retreated to those final moments in that void Intico had placed her in—those haunting crescent eyes that undulated within the dark until Kendall's soul found her.

It's never too late to change your story.

Perhaps those words alone reminded her of the strength she so neglected to find, that she felt she had lost since. The questions thrummed in her mind—the darkness within, fear, and the death arcana Kendall had drawn for her.

"I embraced it. That I could change the fate awaiting me. I was afraid of how I had changed, and what more would change, but ... I knew that if I gave in, we would have been doomed to something even worse. It's like a paradox. Embrace fear to beat it." Her lips pursed. "Sounds stupid as hell, but if it works, it works." Kendra laughed softly, standing as she shook her head. "I really just didn't want us to die. It's not as deep as it seems."

Azazel leaned back, his eyes looking at the moonless sky with renewed curiosity.

"I wonder about that. As I said before, wisdom is very becoming of you," Azazel stated, letting out a long sigh and swung himself upright, turning to face her. "Daughter of Katherine and Aaron, you should show more pride."

Kendra cocked an eyebrow, snorting as she waved her hand.

"A demon telling me to be sinful was the first thing on my bingo card for 2046."

Azazel shook his head, standing with his hands sliding into his coat pockets.

"Sin and virtue are in perpetual balance. Too much pride becomes arrogance. Too little becomes vanity. Both denote a center on the self, yet it is within that we become of use."

Kendra stared quietly, her expression warming the more she considered what he said, no matter how cliché she thought it to be.

"I like you, Zel," Kendra said, turning away from him. "I would love to talk more, but I should head home now." She brushed her jeans off and straightened her jacket, only turning when she heard him begin to laugh loftily. She frowned, seeing him holding his stomach with a glee she had thought demons incapable of, but it was a laughter that was endearing. "I say something funny?"

"Royalty, former or current, is usually regarded with such a degree of respect, hesitant and restrained. Then a mortal woman so cavalierly addresses me as *Zel*."

"Oh … uh, sorry. I should have asked if I could call you that. Just kind of assumed you'd be okay with it." Her expression lightened when he smiled at her.

"I like it."

Hearing this, Kendra's eyes brightened, and a burst of fireworks erupted behind Azazel. The lights colored the sky, snatching her attention, and as her eyes shimmered, a flash of white flickered over them in a subtle but chaotic spectacle that beckoned Azazel's attention. His gaze hardened, eyes peering deep into her own. When she noticed his scrutiny, her heart froze for a moment.

"Something on my face?" she asked disconcertedly.

Azazel's gaze softened after several moments, and in his chagrin, a bashful smile formed.

"Apologies. My imagination was playing a trick on me. Alas, it was but an illusion of the wine." As they stared, Kendra huffed as she looked away.

"You're so hard to read, Zel. No refunds on the nickname, by the way." She smirked before gesturing to herself with her thumb. "Call me Ken from now on—if you like."

Azazel raised his hand to his chin, blinking in confusion before lowering his gaze.

"It's my understanding that names of endearment in Latin-inspired languages prefer feminine inflections. Is there a reason you don't prefer Kenny?"

Kendra paused, a forlorn look flashing through her eyes, but she banished the thought quickly.

"I've always been a bit of a tomboy growing up, or at least that's what my grandma called it. And when my mom called me Kenny, Kendall threw a fit. I preferred Ken anyway, so I made a point of making people call me that. Wouldn't have it any other way, either." Kendra feigned a confident smile.

"Would it be fine if I continued calling you Kendra? It's a lovely name I would be remiss not to utter fully."

"Only because you asked nicely," Kendra said, failing to hide her smile.

"Kendra," Azazel began, peering into her eyes. "I sincerely have enjoyed your company tonight as we have entered this new year. Perhaps, next we meet, I will share more of my customs."

"Oh, right!" Kendra said, shaking her head and raising her smart band. "Can I have your contact details? Or a number? I don't imagine we'll keep running into each other in the city, after all."

Azazel shot a puzzled look as he eyed the holographic screen that shot from her smart band, as if he peered at something entirely alien.

"I do not use such devices as humans do," he said, crouching down and grabbing the nearly empty wine bottle before approaching her.

"Oh ... yeah, guess that makes sense, since you're so old and stuff," Kendra teased sheepishly, reaching out as he handed her the bottle.

"But ... I can teach you another means of reaching me, if you are so fond," he spoke, making Kendra cock a brow.

"Like what? Sacrificing a lamb or something?"

Azazel snorted, scrunching his face.

"That would summon a random prodigium without the proper rite and ritual."

"Prodi-what?"

"Feral demonic beasts, like the ones you spoke of. Not very capable of speech or higher thought, typically," Azazel explained, and she nodded.

"Right. Well, what's the correct way of doing this?"

"Instead, you would merely need to speak my title and name, then you would recite a specific incantation into any surface or object made of ice. I may or may not answer, depending on when you contact me." Azazel cleared his throat. "Channel your attention and energy onto the surface, and speak, *Ku Azazel, Gotelu neo.*"

Kendra bit her lip to keep from chortling but quietly committed the term to memory. During her training, she became vaguely familiar with the demon tongue, Indiox—a language, too, derived from Latin, given the demons were originally fallen angels. Latin, allegedly, had been made to communicate with humans long ago. She was privy to it, as it harbored similarities to French.

"Forever here, Lord Azazel," she recited, humor dripping from her tongue. "Speaking ancient tongues into an ice cube sounds a lot funnier than it should be," she said.

"That would be truly humorous, yes, but there is a more practical remedy." Azazel held his hand out, light swarming his palm as shards crystallized into what appeared to be a hand mirror—except it was composed of permafrost. "You won't even need to toss it in one of those cooling containers your kind makes. It will never melt as long as you don't purposefully try to destroy it. When it shimmers and chimes, it means I am contacting you."

"Huh, this is pretty neat," Kendra commented, carefully taking the ice mirror and examining her blue-tinted reflection that rippled on the surface. "This is even better than the hand mirror I keep in my drawer," she said, earning a wry smile from Azazel, whose face soured with the comparison.

"Do refrain from using it for facilitating cosmetic rituals," Azazel pleaded.

Kendra spun the ice mirror in her hand, sliding it into the inner pocket of her jacket. Returning her attention to him, she flashed a mischievous grin before she turned and walked away.

"No promises, Zel."

Groggy mornings were the norm for Kendra lately. With an unholy amalgamation of a poor sleep schedule and a busy mind, she found herself struggling to stay asleep. Instead, she stole small intervals throughout the night. Muttering obscenities, she grabbed the syn-blood tablet and dropped it into the glass of red liquid by her bed. She found that adding a berry-flavored water enhancer made the drink tolerable, albeit still unpleasant.

Kendra ran through her morning routine before tossing on a pair of leggings and a Decker T-shirt, then made her way downstairs. The scent of toast her father was making greeted her before she made it down, and she began craving a croissant. Regrettably, she had neglected to pick any up when she and Eden visited Angie's. The jar of hazelnut spread on the counter practically mocked her, making her wish she had.

"Morning," Kendra spoke in a raspy tone as she shambled over to the counter, checking the notifications on her smart band.

"Hey there. You look"—the toaster went off, beeping as the toast popped up. This snatched Aaron's attention. He played hot potato with the slices as steam rose from them, tossing them onto two plates.

"Like what?" Kendra asked while cleaning her glasses with her shirt.

"A billionaire," Aaron alleged.

"Creatures that shouldn't exist," Kendra muttered. "I'll take a coffee fit for a serf, thank you very much," she said, and Aaron gestured to the coffeepot.

"You sure? It's decaf. Been tryin' to wean off the caffeine lately."

"Ew." Kendra scrunched her face and circled to one of the plates of toast. "I'll just order from Angie's for my fix," she said while pulling up a delivery app on her smart band.

"Angie's, huh? Could have sworn you preferred Cosmic Cash's frappés," Aaron said, pouring a cup into a heat-activated mug that displayed the Milky Way. He added an abundance of creamer and sugar before daring to take a sip.

"I'd prefer to take *your* hard-earned tax dollars and support something small and local instead. Something-something America and all that jazz," she said, yawning loudly as she snatched the bottle of hazelnut spread. She applied liberal dabs of the sugary confection to her toast, then flipped it into a sandwich that could earn Zane's approval. Nodding in satisfaction, she took the plate to the table and resumed ordering her drink.

"Yeehaw," Aaron said sarcastically, soon joining Kendra, having made his toast into an identical sandwich, which he proceeded to consume between sips of coffee.

"Battle Bots finale is next month. Finalists are Ebon Jaw and Starscreech. Interesting matchup." Aaron smirked, reaching out as he pulled up a video on his smart band. He scooted closer and practically shoved it in her face before jumping into his speculation.

"Maul uses an electromagnetic shield that it can open, close, and bash with. Anything touches them, they get locked and pushed into the arena traps. Meanwhile, Screech is fast as hell, can jump with pistons, and stab the top of other bots with these harpoons that it can aim. Very hard to pull off, but the guy who operates it is good at using it."

Kendra listened passively, still building her perfect latte—one that had enough espresso shots to put down a demon lord. As absent as her gaze suggested she was, she nodded along and absorbed everything he said. He regularly emailed her updates whenever the show was in season, and she felt obligated to remember everything since he used to watch it with her mother.

"My money is on Jaw, honestly. Real tricky to penetrate its defenses, fast or not. Very low chance Screech outmaneuvers it," Kendra pontificated, sticking her tongue out at her father when his smile widened.

"I'd put my hard-earned tax dollars on that too."

"Then the congress of Mallorys arrives at an agreement," Kendra announced.

Aaron raised his mug to take another sip, but a buzz shot through his wrist as his smart band played his ringtone, prompting him to set the mug down. When he looked at the notification, he pursed his lips and answered.

His expression showed equal parts surprise and concern, but Kendra didn't bother to question it, instead returning to add the finishing touches to her coffee order. However, her attention shot back to her father when his tone suggested urgency and jubilation. Their gazes met—glistening eyes, unsteady and marred by tears.

"On the way!" he huffed out, hanging up before he turned on his heel. "Go get ready!" he began, his lips trembling as he blinked the joyful tears from his eyes.

Kendra knew that starstruck look that seeped to the surface. From seeing her father her whole life—that look only arose when he was with her mother. She thought it too good to be true as she stood up, her breath barricaded behind shut lips. But as if the nightmare of over three years had ended, he spoke her wish into reality.

"She's awake."

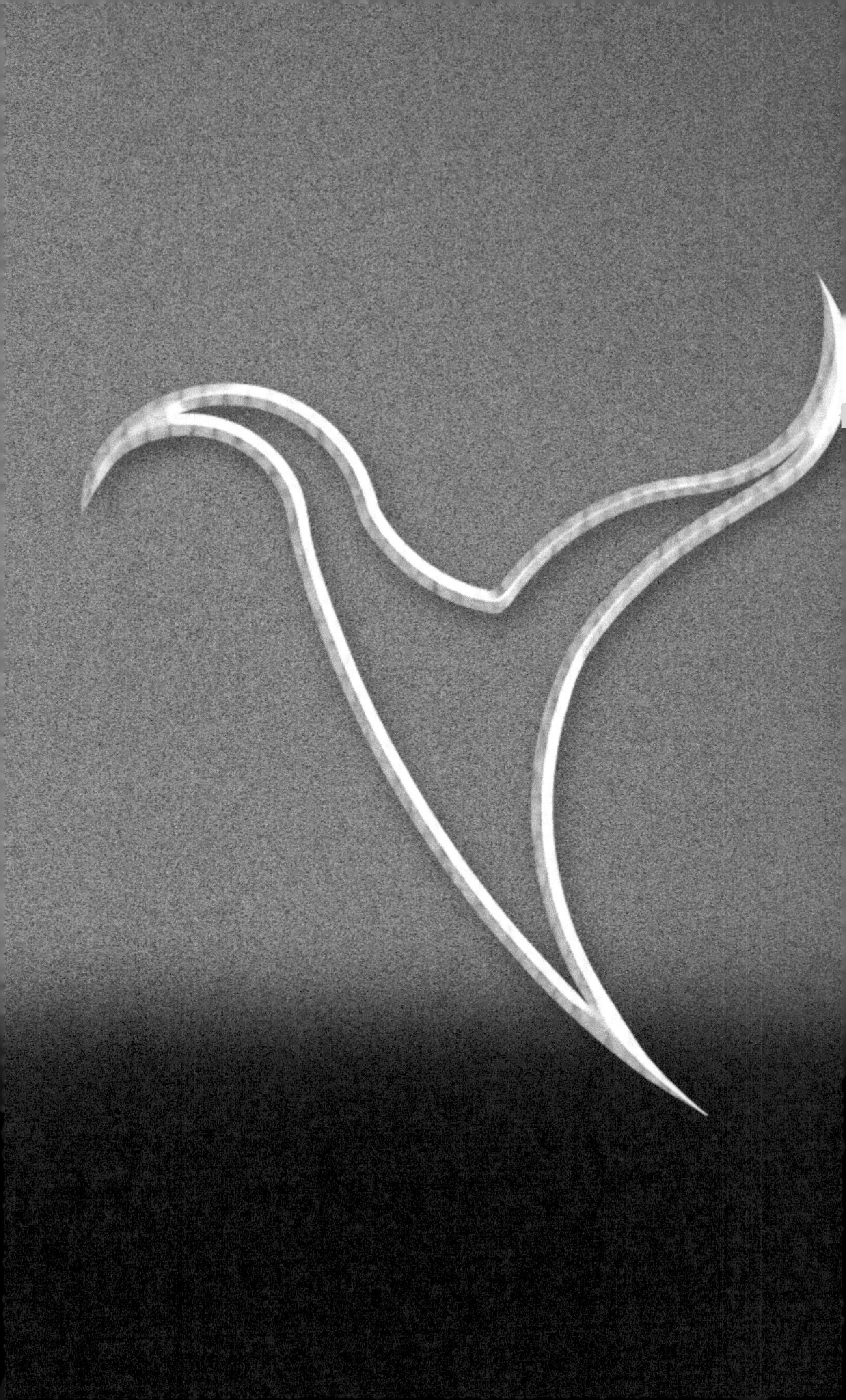

FIVE

LAMENT OUR SHADOWS

"IT WAS LIKE A DREAM,"** Katherine spoke in a raspy hush. She inhaled shakily as her royal-blue eyes found Kendra and Aaron. "Glimpses of things I can't remember now, but I know they were awful and terrifying. I was just ... suspended in it all," Katherine said, her eyes drifting as she reached out with trembling, emaciated hands to grab a paper cup on the bedside table. As her fingers wrapped around it, she whimpered lightly, struggling to lift it.

Aaron quickly reached, assisting the cup to her lips as she took a long drink. No matter how difficult a sight it had been, the paradoxical smiles that stretched on the tear-stained canvases of their faces spoke of their joy.

"You're safe now," Aaron said as he returned the cup to the table.

Kendra reached out, brushing the messy brown hair from her mother's face. It had grown long and tangled compared to the shorter style she had once sported, but through the once-lustrous tufts was a visage she adored—a comfort she had long sought, like the day Kendra had returned to her after the mutation.

"There's so much I want to tell you, Mom, but I don't want to be selfish." She swallowed the building tension in her throat. "I ... I've missed you so much," Kendra said, leaning closer to her.

"We're too alike," Katherine said, offering a wry smile before glancing at Aaron, her hazy gaze becoming pensive as she mulled over what to say. "Dear, I want to speak with Kendra alone for a moment," she said, her face scrunching as she sucked a breath in through her nose as she composed herself. "Before I lose the thought." Her pained expression wasn't lost on Aaron, and he rubbed her hand before standing.

"I'll be waiting," he said, hesitantly slipping away from her before leaving the room.

Now alone, Katherine's eyes bore into Kendra, her lips trembling as she focused.

"I know ..." Katherine said with a pained smile before sobbing lightly.

Kendra wished she had been confused. Within those lamenting depths, she saw the grief that had been slumbering with her mother—that she knew the harrowing truth.

"You're connected," Kendra whispered, leaning closer as she touched her mother's cheek. Though reticent, her mother's eyes reflected a familiar fear—one wrought by the likes of the somnium.

"Those ... *things* tormented our family, took my little girls—hurt them. They left me and many others like this. I know. I saw it among the things I can still remember. It wasn't all a dream, was it?" she asked, coughing dryly into her hand as she forced herself upright. With tenacity in her struggles, she placed her back against the wall and breathed out heavily.

Kendra knew better than to try to help her in that moment, knowing how stubborn they both were. The recovery would be tumultuous, unforgiving of her weakness. Both of them abhorred such sentiments in their respective plights.

Combing for what to say, Kendra's hands retreated to her sides, and she met her mother's gaze with all the conviction she could cobble together.

"One had merged with me for a short period, and it showed me that night over and over again, reminded me how powerless I was. It was their leader who took the souls from people to enact what they called Harvest. Then, when I really needed her, Kenny came to me, spoke to me, helped me realize I wasn't powerless." Kendra's gaze lowered, thinking back to the final conversation she had with Kendall. She always remembered it when she felt low.

"Is she at peace?" Katherine asked with a pensive stare, and Kendra nodded.

"Yeah. It would be difficult to explain it all now, but she's with the Primordial Goddess of Life. And ... she wanted me to tell you that she loves you and Dad a million," Kendra said, shaking her head as she stifled a chuckle. Katherine's expression shifted, her lips curling into a smile.

"That's her ..." Katherine murmured as she cocked her head to the side and closed her eyes. "I have so many questions."

"And I have answers. Shoot, detective," Kendra said.

"*Organization X* ... who were they really?"

Kendra shoved her hands into the pockets of her coat, walked to the adjacent wall, then leaned against it.

"Demon hunters. Hidden faction in the government," Kendra began. Her lips twisted into an assuring smile as she turned her head to look down at her mother. "And I'm one of them now."

Katherine's eyes widened as she examined her daughter, and Kendra's reveal prompted her to examine her more closely. If Katherine's memory had immortalized anything, it was her family. Somehow, she knew her daughter now differed, and she slowly reached up, fingers uncurling to take Kendra's hand.

"You've changed so much," Katherine said, and Kendra reached out, gently giving her hand a squeeze. "But no matter how you change and grow, you'll always be my little girl."

Kendra could practically taste the sweetness from the once-catatonic gaze, and the hollow pit she had fretted over just the night before had all but disappeared. As if winter had subsided, she felt a great warmth blossom within her, giving birth to a smile.

"Always," Kendra agreed.

Katherine rolled her shoulders, coughing lightly before she grabbed the cup of water. With renewed strength, she hoisted it and took a drink.

Kendra gave light applause. The elation that bloomed in her chest crept further up, and she did everything in her power to contain the torrent of things she wanted to say. The mystery of how her mother had returned to sentience peaked above the others.

"How did you wake up? Or what do you remember?"

Katherine's face tensed, and her eyes shut as she breathed out with a light sigh.

"Let's see ..." she began. After a few moments, she rolled her head and her eyes opened. "There was a voice. Captivating and light. Like snow. It ... reminded me of what I should cherish, how my fear didn't define my failures. I remembered the urgency I had to protect both you and Kendall ... and I rose from the bed I was stuck in. Then that tall demon appeared and taunted me. So ... I strangled it."

The explanation caressed her nerves. The familiar recollection told her what had happened, and she reached up, her hand settling beneath her throat.

Azazel.

Her own explanation of pushing Intico out of her body—overcoming fear—came to mind. She knew he had some degree of magical influence over the mind, and in consideration of his efforts to treat those who had been left ill-fated by Harvest, it had to be him. If he had been there in that moment, she dared to think he'd be in danger with how hard she'd hug him, and she laughed softly.

"I'm so happy to have you back, Mom. There's so much more I want to talk about, but I don't want to hog you from Dad."

Katherine smirked and set the now-empty cup down before gesturing to the door.

"Is this something you'd report to those demon hunters?"

"Oh shit, you're right!" Kendra said, propelling off the wall as she turned her attention to the door. "I'm going to go and handle that, and ... you can catch up with Dad, k?" she proposed hurriedly, making Katherine laugh softly. She stopped herself after a moment, coughing a bit before holding her sides.

"I won't be going anywhere. Promise."

Kendra was torn between two imperatives: Longing and urgency. She recalled many nights when her mother skipped family time to attend to her duties. Due to her mother's lived experience, Kendra assumed she would understand it better than she did. Pushing through her confliction, she opened the door, where she saw her father leaning against the wall beside it. He immediately perked up, and his brown eyes met Kendra's.

"All yours, Dad. I have to go attend to something for a bit, but I'll be back." Kendra smiled and playfully smacked his shoulder. "Try not to swoon too much."

Aaron stood straight, peering into the room briefly to see Katherine wave. With his smile returning, he huffed lightly.

"Too late," he said before entering.

Kendra made her way through the hall and down the stairs. When she reached the bottom of the stairwell and exited into the lobby, she thought to determine whether her mother was the first to wake.

She idly brought up the browser on her smart band and typed several prompts to find something relevant. Most of the prompts included Ex-somnis, and she homed in on local outlet reports. After a few attempts, she found an article from Chicago Daily that included a live broadcast. She tapped it, and there was a high-end hospital that the cameras panned over, complete with footage of several families lined up to see the waking patients. In that moment, she was glad that her mother had been moved to a local, more obscure facility.

Kendra carefully shuffled past some of the staff and placed herself in one of the chairs. She reached into her coat, removing an earbud case and placing one in her ear to listen to the broadcast.

"Here at Northwestern Memorial Hospital, several victims of Exsomnis are also awake. While they have been monitored for several years by the country's top experts, there are still no answers as to why they are waking now."

The camera cut to a doctor who sat in a red chair across from a reporter who held a microphone up to him.

"If I had an explanation, I'd happily tell you. That's the dilemma with matters of the mind. We hope we'll understand more as we probe into patients and really try to understand their recollection of things."

The feed cut to a middle-aged woman who sat in a bed, her frail hands being held by another woman who sat beside her as she smiled into the camera.

"It was a nightmare, but there was a man speaking so sweetly and gently. He said everything would be okay and to hold on to what is precious. I thought of my daughter, and I just knew I shouldn't be afraid anymore."

The camera then cut to an older man beside a young boy who lay in bed.

"It's one of Jesus's miracles. Not a doubt in my mind. Jesus set him free from the devil."

The broadcast went on in much the same way, with many who were interviewed mentioning a male voice—most attributing it to Jesus. With an odd relief having taken root in her chest, she displayed a humored smile and giggled to herself. She shook her head and lowered her wrist to dismiss the hologram before migrating outside of the hospital.

After a brief conversation with Eden, he indicated he would be there soon, and she waited for several minutes. Soon, a news crew arrived in a van just out front. At breakneck speed, they began unpacking the van, presumably to interview and report on the patients in the facility her mother was in. Within five minutes, the reporter was rehearsing quietly in preparation.

Both their speed and choice of reporting location were astonishing. It was impressive even, and she thought Andrew would have gotten jealous of how they handled the heavy broadcast equipment. Still, she wanted nothing to do with it and promptly relocated to avoid being interrogated.

"Nothing should surprise me anymore," Kendra muttered aloud. In response, a light, flowery voice from behind her giggled.

"Would you make a bet on that?"

Impossible.

Time became ensnared in the webs of disbelief—like a bullet had sounded in her head and pierced her heart. A sacred burial was unearthed, and her blood turned to ice in her veins.

"Told yah," Kendall spoke, circling to stand in front of her. Just as the day Kendra had held her in her arms when Harvest had ended, she was there before her. A saccharine smile colored her image, and as she walked backward, her eyes flicked to the crowd forming around the news team.

"I don't have a lot of time to explain. Come on," she said before running away.

Although her entire body had seemed petrified, Kendra's legs moved instinctively, even though everything else was trapped in the memories that told her it wasn't true. Even so, she ran after the *ghost*.

Soon, they were in a secluded alleyway, where Kendall retreated further from the entry. The solitude was irrelevant to Kendra. Her eyes, wide with dismay and confusion, refused to focus on her dead sister. The smile she knew so well, the familiar twinkle within her hazel eyes, and her sweet mannerisms—all resurrected from memories she had once laid to rest.

"I'm not really back, or at least not yet ... it depends on you."

"*You're dead*," Kendra whispered, her voice straining through her chattering teeth as she hesitantly approached.

"I am," Kendall confirmed, her smile fading as she lowered her gaze to the ground. "It's hard to really explain ... but there is a magic that was used to bring me here temporarily—not that I really understand it, honestly. I was with Mother one moment, and then I was called back. I was told it could be for real."

There was a parade of questions enshrouded by intense emotion, and any semblance of what Kendra could have asked or said was lost upon her faint breath. She thought it to be a trick—glamour by a demon seeking to deceive her—but as she focused, she couldn't detect the precursors of glamour. No subtle sulfuric scent. It was exactly as she remembered her.

"I missed you so much. You, Mom, and Dad. I want to hold you all again and go back to how things used to be," she said, frowning lightly. "Death isn't what it seems, right? That's what I told you after our tarot reading." As Kendall stared at her, Kendra struggled to compose her breath. Though labored, Kendra resurrected the words.

"It's ... the end of one thing—"

"And the genesis of another," Kendall finished, giving a forlorn smile as she raised her head, tears streaming down her face.

"I'd have given anything to have you here again ..." Kendra sobbed, barely holding herself up.

"I know," Kendall said. "It isn't going to be easy, though. It means that ... someone else would die."

"Why?" Kendra asked. She lowered her head as she trembled, and Kendall slowly approached.

"The Gates of Oblivion bypass both life and death. I've temporarily been brought back through it, but I'll be called back to Mother's veins again soon. Without a soul to maintain balance—a means of taking my place—I can't remain."

Kendra slowly lifted her head when Kendall approached her.

"Gates of Oblivion?" she questioned. "Who—why?"

"Does it matter? We could be together again." She exhaled unsteadily, as if on the verge of tears. "I barely understand any of this, but you can bring me back. There has to be someone—anyone—who can take my place."

Kendra shook her head and stepped back, breath hitching in her throat. The brewing turmoil roused her claws to emerge and pierce her palms, causing blood to gather on her fingers.

"You'd pick them over me, then?" Kendall asked, tilting her head as she bit her bottom lip. "I ... want to live."

"And they would too," Kendra said, shaking her head before clenching her chest. "There's already been so much suffering."

Kendall reached out to Kendra, carefully pulling her into a tight hug. As if eternity had stretched its arms around her, Kendra hesitantly reached out, embracing Kendall as if she would disappear or fall lifelessly into her arms like she had before.

"You saved so many already, though. And you can save even more."

"I could never forgive myself. I can't," Kendra whispered breathlessly, sobbing lightly into Kendall's shoulder. With her rigid fingers, she ran the blood-covered digits through Kendall's hair. "I would sooner die," she continued, prompting Kendall to whimper.

"Since when have you been so doom and gloom, Kenny?"

Kendall's words siphoned all trepidation from Kendra's body, and the cold fled from the festering heat of her thundering heart. She shoved Kendall away, eyes wide as her claws extended defensively.

"*Who are you?*" she hissed, her eyes narrowing as her irises flickered with infernal light. The wounds on her palms sealed shut, and the tears that had stained her cheeks dissipated into steam as embers leaped from the hairs of her body.

Kendall's eyes widened, and she took a hesitant step back. Her breath quickened as she clenched her chest.

"What?" Kendall questioned, her voice barely above a whisper. She gestured to herself in a way that suggested disbelief.

"Cut the shit!" Kendra hissed. "You're not my sister. She would never ask me to do this, let alone forget her own nickname!"

The ambience of the city filled the silence of their tense stares. The crackle of flames spilling from Kendra's form was drowned out by the rustling wind and blaring traffic from the street behind her. Quickly, their threat only magnified as Kendall's once warm eyes became cold voids.

She directed her palm out, but Kendra closed the distance quickly. Visage demonic, flames gathered atop her claws. With a swipe, she cut through Kendall, painting the alleyway in blood.

Kendall crumpled to the ground, whimpering as she writhed in the puddle of blood forming beneath her.

"It hurts! It hurts ..." Kendall's voice cried, slowly fading. Her skin rippled as the pigmentation became void black. The form, robbed of its integrity, became a lustrous ooze that contorted on the ground soundlessly. "*That you'd see me die again,*" an indistinct, hollow voice spoke.

She spun as the black ooze stretched behind her and formed into a humanoid figure that defined itself before her. Tall. Imposing. *dreaded.*

Allen stood dressed in the plain, unassuming clothing that once distinguished him from his wretched family. Uncertainty surged in her muscles as she backed away, realizing that the entity sought to cut off her direct route of escape. Her fingers, caked in the blood she had spilled, sizzled, turning to the same ooze the being was composed of.

Kendra knew she had struck them, but they had effortlessly reformed. It was unlike the regenerative displays of the several demons she had encountered—it was far too quick. Regeneration was rarely ever so rapid, even for her. A display unlike anything she had studied from the demon compendium.

"Who—"

"Anyone," the entity spoke, slowly drawing toward her, expressionless. Their unfathomably cold eyes scorned any evil she had ever known, but their malice was just as palpable.

"What do you want from me?" Kendra demanded, the air weighing down on her suddenly. Conjured distortion now isolated them from the rest of the world, sourced from the entity before her.

"You'll know soon, Kendra." The entity approached her slowly, and in response, Kendra hurled a wave of fire, engulfing them. Yet they continued walking, even as the flames melted their flesh. The black ooze merely resurfaced, and it formed anew.

Standing in front of her now was a face she wouldn't forget—Vicente's.

"Maybe you enjoyed watching me die."

Kendra's body glowed, and the flames enveloping her arms became fierce and scarlet red. In the next moment, she yelled as she hurled several lashes of chaos flames at the entity, repeatedly bathing it in them. Even as they screamed using Vicente's voice, she gritted her teeth. When she finally stopped, the pavement where they had been standing was smoldering, and ashes polluted the alley.

Even with the veil, she could imagine that the spectacle would have garnered attention from the nearby humans. What they had perceived was beyond her, but she knew the veil had its limitations. For the briefest moment, in her waning focus, her barrier had relented. Her coat had mostly burned away, brittle and falling from her body. Hesitantly, she tore the remainder from her form.

Chaos flames were taxing on her energy reserves. She only ever conjured them if needed, and even with her brief display, she panted. From within the smoke and ash, a silhouette emerged, tantalizingly slow in its approach as the bleeding, blistering visage of Kendall emerged, and those hollow eyes found her once more.

"Told you," the being spoke in Kendall's voice, followed by a distorted giggle.

Kendra's chest pulsed, tightening as she prayed to wake from the torment before her. Even if it wasn't really the ones she knew, the sight and sound of them were indistinguishable. Chaos flames had proven useless, and she then knew that the being before her was not a demon.

"That's a good look on you," the being spoke, twisting Kendall's face with a remorseless smile. They held their hand up once again, dark energy undulating in their palm as it neared her face. Kendra's lips agape, she gripped her chest and growled in an unholy mix of despair and anger.

Before the impostor could attack, their head flew from their shoulders as blood splattered. The black bevel of Avenger dripped as Eden appeared from behind the smokescreen.

The impostor turned into black ooze again, appearing once more as Kendall, their focus now fixed on Eden.

"There you are. How convenient."

The quiet tension brewing between the impostor and Eden was beyond palpable—two forces of malice colliding with cold disregard. Eden held Avenger's hilt firmly, fist clenching tight as he eyed the threat. It was unlike Eden to show visible reactions to his foes. That moment was no exception.

"They can't die …" Kendra said, her gaze never leaving the impostor for an instant.

"They're a voidling," Eden said, but the impostor refrained from answering, instead offering a sickening smile.

"That your guess?" they mocked.

"Ephemeral energy signature—lacks any conclusive pattern. You're mimicking others." Eden shifted, turning Avenger's razor edge toward the impostor and placing his other hand at the bottom of the hilt. "No matter how many bodies you've collected, I'll just continue to kill you until your reserves are depleted."

Eden's energy control and detection were in a class of their own among the hunters. Of the few who were capable of such a determination, he was one. While not talented with magic himself, he was versed in the machinations of all forms of Ichor's utilities—a byproduct of being the son of a homuntium witch who had been trained by ancient covens. Among such knowledge was void magic, rare and unintuitive even for the most proficient of magic users. While he was confident in contending against the being, the underlying dread of their trail of death remained—how many bodies they had subjugated.

Voidlings were usually known as peaceful, detached beings who harmlessly spectated life. They were born from the fragments of the unnamed Primordial deity that encompassed the unknown, referred to by others as *Void*. However, for reasons unknown, some voidlings were expelled from their protective umbrage. Some called them doppelgängers for their ability to assume the appearance of others—distinct and more intimate than glamour—but what entailed their exile wasn't apparent.

Their detached eyes reflected within his own crimson gaze. Akin to evil—arguably worse. Forces of nature weren't capable of feeling, and much the same, voidlings were considered something below even that. Purposeless and beyond the measure of beings of Ichor.

"Eden Blackwell," the voidling began, still donning a manufactured smile. "I never considered humans to be smart, but it's baffling that you'd waltz right up to me, even when understanding how fragile your *freedom* is. Do you miss your chains?"

With a flash of red, the voidling was sliced in half, and Eden kicked the torso. Its body bashed against the side of the trash bin, causing it to slide back with a screech from the rusted wheels. The result was the same, however, and the ooze became a humanoid shape once more, but it refrained from borrowing a form yet.

"I love playing with your nerves, demigod. Your anguish—"

Eden hurled Avenger, the blade piercing it through and spearing it into the wall of the trash bin with a loud impact ringing through the alleyway.

"I can see why Intico desired your body."

The voidling formed into a puddle that shifted from where Avenger was, forming next to it as a tall, feminine figure—gray, flawless skin, long scarlet hair and eyes, and a stunning allure brimming with feminine appeal.

They stepped forward, the pure red demonic eyes somewhat obscuring the malice that had been present within them before.

"In retrospect, it would have been much easier dealing with you personally. Such potential is squandered with human sentiments," the voidling spoke. "It's been how long since we've seen each other? A decade? I wonder if you're stupid enough to still have feelings for me."

Eden held his hand out, and Avenger tore free and flew back into his grasp. With a shaky breath brimming with unfettered rage, red electricity rippled around his form. With crackles that blared through the alleyway, he dashed at the voidling and pierced them through into the wall. He then proceeded to pummel their face into the bricks until his knuckles dripped with gore.

Kendra flinched, distancing herself slowly as she braced against the power he emitted. His palpable anger brimmed, spurred by the voidling's cynically weaponized adoption of familiar forms. Such torment whispered through his energy, somehow rivaling his outburst in the laboratory.

The voidling continuously reformed after every fatal blow inflicted. The ooze of their being leaped onto the wall and bounced behind Kendra, reemerging at the end of the alleyway before it slowly took on another figure.

"You said you'd keep killing me, but here's the real question ..."

Unrelenting, Eden dashed past Kendra to attack once more. He closed in as the voidling took on a new visage—one only known by Eden. The moment he reached them, preparing to remove their head with Avenger, he froze, as if halted by an immovable wall.

"How many times would you watch me die?"

The fury of burning red energy around Eden ceased, as if a blizzard had siphoned both his power and his anger. Eden's expression was one she had never thought him capable of showing. It betrayed his indomitable stoicism and evoked dread, but hers must have paled compared to his. Though she feared the sight of what had arrested Eden, she compelled herself to turn and face the voidling.

Now wearing a form like fresh clothes, the voidling became a short woman. Peering at them were incandescent lilac eyes, framed by shimmering white curls that spilled down her shoulders. Unlike the demonic woman before, Kendra had seen her visage—the drawing in Eden's sketchbook. Although her glimmering wings were absent, both the tattered white gown and the serenity her angelic appearance inspired were indisputable from what Eden had captured on paper.

"Now *that's* a good look on you," the voidling whispered in a sweet voice, its undertones vicious. "What's wrong, Eden? You were going to kill me, right? Go ahead. You've seen it once already." A saccharine smile painted the angelic face, daring Eden to forgo his petrification.

His eyes were distant, locked behind an abyss. Those eyes he so adored in memories long since passed rendered him into stone. And the more the voidling spoke with her voice, the deeper he receded.

"Cassie ..." Eden whispered, his tone forlorn and stripped of his prior malice.

"You left me there all alone," they chastised, their expression dropping.

"I ..." His voice strained as he barricaded the sorrow that boiled within him. The roiling turmoil squirmed through his mind, stretching its tendrils down his limbs to become shackles. *She was dead.* However, this truth didn't register in that moment.

"You left me, and I've been waiting." Slowly, the voidling reached out, dark energy gathering on their delicate fingertips.

"Eden!" Kendra called out, jumping forward and snatching him by the shoulder. She yanked him out of the impostor's reach, tucking him close to her.

"I've been begging to be free, yet here you are. *Pretending.*" They glared. "But that'll change soon. You'll come back for me, won't you?" the voidling spoke in a dejected tone—a cruel performance only Kendra saw through.

"Who are you?" Kendra demanded again, shuffling in front of Eden to guard him in his paralysis.

Without speaking, the voidling's eyes landed on Eden, remaining fixed for several moments before they shook their head.

"Many call me Orphan," they began, their face darkening. "Nothing else matters."

Sirens wailed in the distance as the smoke behind Kendra and Eden cleared, and the pressure in the area alleviated. The distortion dissipated, and the omens ceased crying as the world resumed once more. Shadows latched onto Orphan's feet, stretching along their porcelain limbs and engulfing them in darkness.

"Eden?" Orphan called, and those serene depths became impossibly devoid of anything resembling the celestial solace that haunted Eden. Everything but her image disappeared before him, now hijacked by the voidling as they declared the *truth* he could never escape.

"*You'll never be free.*"

Before Kendra could rekindle the distortion, the voidling was already gone, leaving Kendra and Eden alone in the alleyway. She cursed herself for allowing them to escape. With their immediate threat absent, she released her demonic aspect and surrendered the tension from her muscles.

"Eden, you okay?" Kendra asked, turning to face him. His perturbed expression pulled her from her despondency over the encounter. As if thrust into a pit of despair, his attention was absent, and agony was etched within the grooves of his face. Her expression softened, and she reached up, grabbing his shoulders. "Eden, we have to go."

Eden's gaze slowly focused on her, expressionless as he nodded silently. The two obscured themselves before retreating, finding another silent haven on the rooftops. They leaped from building to building, far away from the alleyway they had been in. Kendra suddenly took Eden's hand, halting them in their tracks as she turned to face him.

"We both knew it wasn't really them. This ... isn't like you," Kendra began, releasing a breath heavy with grief. "What happened?"

Eden shook his head, summoning the familiar, stubborn disregard he usually portrayed.

"It's noth—"

"Fucking stop!" Kendra snapped. "Eden, gods, please stop trying to hide away. We're friends, and this idea that you can continue keeping these things from me is just stupid." Kendra clenched his hand tightly and looked up at him, her eyes mixed with both scorn and concern. "*What happened?*"

Eden averted his gaze as if hers would sunder him if he didn't. And as he clenched his chest, his shoulders dropped, and he shut his eyes in resignation.

"I don't like thinking about it, let alone talking about it. But fine."

Kendra slowly released Eden's hand, waiting for him to look at her, but he instead reached up to the ruby necklace he wore, cupping the gem delicately in his palm.

"There's a place. We'll talk there."

A narrow stretch of trampled vegetation lined the path to the retreat Eden led them to. Moss clung to the jagged walls, shrouded in curtains of vines along its stretch. The mid-evening sun blared through the matted branches of the trees. The frigid breeze made them sway above the journeying pair, leaves shaken loose, jerking shadows above them like falling feathers.

It was an odd tangle Kendra couldn't imagine discovering organically. As they ventured closer to the entrance, an odd presence lingered inside, something resembling the energy that permeated Chicago when the souls had been freed from Intico.

Eden ducked through the screen of moss that obscured a small crevice leading into the connected mountain face. As they fled from the light spilling through the entrance, a glimmering cyan light soon took its place the moment darkness nearly swallowed them. The dim hue welcomed them into an open expanse of stone, petrified roots, and a glowing pond. Completing the alluring beauty of the cavern, an ensemble of omens danced to a subtle symphony of chimes above the pond.

"Clusters of sentiments within the omens have been known to meet the seams from when reality had been stitched together. When left un-polluted, they create these pockets," Eden spoke. His eyes narrowed as he conjured those words—an explanation once recounted to him. "I call it the Grotto of Serenity."

"This is ... beautiful. Even more calming than you suggested," Kendra murmured as she stopped behind Eden, who froze in place.

He glanced at her over his shoulder before pointing to the root that hovered at the shore of the pond. As they shambled over to it, reluctance whispered in his every step; Kendra almost thought a ghost would appear to affirm his hesitation.

They sat on the root, feet dangling before the pond as Eden breathed in the respite that the silence brought.

"You already know a little—about me being sought by demons because of my divinity," he said, and Kendra nodded.

"Intico made that much clear. But it presented nothing new to me. It was one of many who had tried before. The worst, however, almost nobody knows the extent of—not even Alicia." He swallowed hard. "Yuki does. I asked her not to speak about it." Eden's crimson gaze clashed with the blue tone to create a glimmering violet color within his eyes, reflecting a bitter memory in its hue. "The same goes for you now."

"Of course," Kendra spoke, reaching out and picking his wrist up. She curled her pinky around his, giving it a slight shake before returning his hand, and she gave a sympathetic smile.

Eden lowered his head, his eyes shutting while he gathered his thoughts.

"The red-haired woman you saw—that was Onaga's daughter, Lucy," Eden began, taking a moment to mull over her memory after speaking her name. "I was always moving around as a kid. It was dangerous to stay in one place, but I liked exploring. One day, I found this place. She was here, and against Ethan's prior warning about trusting demons, we became friends." Eden shook his head. "I didn't care about her being a demon—I really should have."

"What did she do?" Kendra hesitantly asked, her fingers digging into the hard surface of the root they occupied.

"Nothing for the first few years. But then, one day, she came to me in the middle of the night. Wanted to show me something. It was an ambush by Onaga's servants, and they took me away to one of those laboratories." Eden's lips quivered, and his eyes opened, meeting his rippling reflection in the water below.

"I was imprisoned to be studied. You know why." Eden paused, his eyes peering hard into the pond. And within the subtle ripples on its surface, he thought of *her*. "I wasn't alone at first. That woman you saw—her name was Cassie, a celestial who was also being studied. They thought it was fitting to have her prison cell be across from mine." His face contorted as his fingers became rigid. "She was beyond kind. She would cheer me up, heal me—even when they hurt her as well." Eden's body trembled, and the omens that danced took on a red hue in response to the malice that swelled from within him. "They took everything."

Kendra reached out but faltered as she saw tears welling in his eyes. Turmoil defined him as the omens' scarlet light painted them both with their terrifying sentiment, but he still conjured the truth for her.

"They took our blood. Experimented on us. Violated us in every conceivable way. And when Onaga had found a need for it, he wanted our lives too." Eden took a shaky breath, hiccupping as he gritted his teeth. "I begged and cried and pleaded. Still, he killed her right in front of me, and I was helpless to save her." Tears finally journeyed down his face, eventually falling from his chin and making the pond ripple.

"I hate demons," Eden hissed, the venom in his words growing more pronounced. "They take, and take, and take ... until nothing's left."

Kendra tugged Eden by his arm, capturing his head in her palm before resting it in the crook of her neck. Quietly, she shushed him as she held him close, holding back the tears in her eyes. The unbreakable wall she had always thought him to be seemed frail. Such vulnerability was a grim reminder of the humanity she had neglected to see within him. The mask he wore, while not disguising his pain, had done well to hide its depth. And now, the gravity was all too prevalent—too real. The selfish demand she had made seemed daft in the revelation of what he had been through.

Soon, the omens became blue again, and the warmth surrounding them had quelled for the moment as Eden wrangled his breath.

"I'm sorry I made you speak about it," she whispered, biting her lip as she held him tightly. Seeing his mind shackled and distressed reminded her of the oath she took to protect humanity. Somehow, she never considered Eden to be one of those who needed her protection. He was the personification of what it meant to be a hunter, but she found herself remembering the humanity she had been robbed of years ago.

The true nature of strength was elusive. She'd thought Eden was strong, and she still did. But her understanding of what it meant waned. Even so, her ignorance would never keep her from defending what was precious to her. Wrought in her burning blood, she resurrected that oath she took when she was sworn in as a hunter, when her hand was placed upon his blade.

Solemnly, as a purveyor of humanity's continued existence, I would give my life to defend it, she had said.

Her gaze sharpened as she felt Eden's heartbeat, his anguish thrumming through her fingertips.

I would give my life to defend you, she amended to that vow.

Eden wouldn't have doubted it. He wanted to tell her, as his friend, that she deserved to know what haunted him. However, no words came forth from his strained throat. Even in the peace the respite offered, the tragedy continuously tore through him.

Cassiel's words still compelled him to persist against his shadow. He had spent midnight mourning her death in the grotto he now shared with Kendra. Tears blurred his vision, and though the blue light shimmered within the safe embrace, his mind only saw darkness as he stared into the pond, and *greed* stared from within it.

Much like everything he had proclaimed to have been taken, feathers that had been stripped from their wings sunk into a pool of blood. Eventually, they drowned and turned to ash, robbing what remained.

Light that no longer existed.

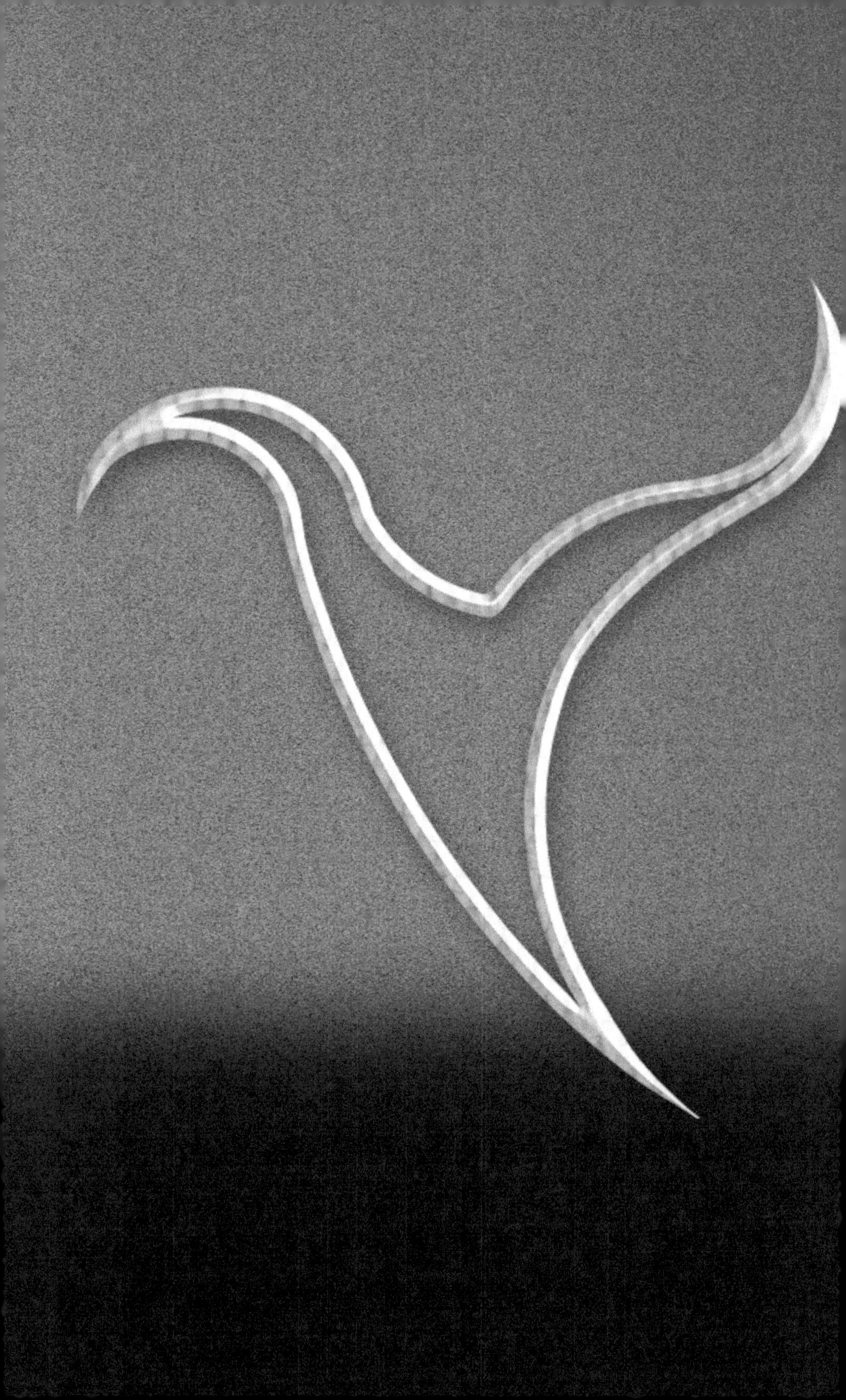

SIX

ALL THAT IS TAKEN

“**W**HAT IS YOUR NAME?”

Eden slowly lifted his head, heavy shackles biting his wrists. Cold and merciless, the tight vises that bound his arms restricted his movements and bolted him to the ground. The runes etched into the metal pulsed with a dark energy that rendered his powers mute, as if he were disconnected from Ichor. The sickening fatigue accompanying it was even more alien, incomparable to any ailment he'd known before.

Here, he had only been twelve years old—a young, growing boy who had been led into a trap by the girl he had considered to be his best friend—the girl he had come to love. He had struggled for over an hour since his untimely capture, and the wounds of Lucy's betrayal still tore at his heart, further pilfering his focus.

The voice that spoke to him came from the cell across from his own. Still dizzy from his struggle, his eyes adjusted until he had gleaned her incandescent features through the thick bars of the cell.

Pearl-white locks of hair that, although unkempt, shimmered brightly, along with her lilac eyes resembling the heavens that peeked through thunderclouds. Even with her dirtied complexion, she was as radiant as her other features, all confined to a white, tattered dress that hung loosely on her small form.

“Me?” Eden asked in a strained voice.

The girl nodded, and her pink lips curled into a soft smile.

"I suppose I should start then. I'm Cassiel."

Eden was quiet, slowly shifting to move the chains from his thighs. When he peered into her curious depths, he glimpsed no sense of malice, but seeing as he thought little of his own judgment now, he was hesitant for several moments.

"Eden ..." he answered. As if peering into his soul itself, she greeted his dejected eyes with an unusual innocence in her own. She mulled over his name, her smile widening.

"That's a nice name," she said, slowly shifting onto her knees before sitting on her ankles. "I'm glad to have someone here with me, even if the circumstances are dismaying. It seems selfish, but I don't feel like it is."

Eden's gaze dropped again, and he curled up to refrain from leaning against the jagged wall behind him. Even as he retreated, Cassiel's impervious smile never wavered.

"You hail from divinity, right?" Cassiel inquired.

Eden didn't respond, and as he found some sense of solace with his face buried between his legs, he wept softly. The image of his mother and Ethan pervaded the dark forest of his mind, and Ethan's warning boomed again.

Demons lie and betray to take that which is closest, and it is in their subjugation of what we call love that they will teach you despair.

He had been a fool, led on and cheated by the woman he had felt closest to—a demon. What he had felt was real, but so cruelly, Ethan had been proven correct. Both his mother and Ethan had warned him, but he had dismissed them, convinced they knew little of what infernal beings could offer.

They had much taken from them, lost innumerable comrades. His mother had lost her father. For Ethan, his younger sister and family. Now, he continued the cycle, another memory to be lamented.

Eden and Cassiel sat in silence, disallowed from speaking in the advent of Eden's cries. The colorless halls soon filled with numerous footsteps, and Eden instinctively tightened his self-embrace. Several scientists wearing long black lab coats came to a stop in front of his cell, all possessing ashen skin and unique sets of horns that protruded from their heads.

"Alright, demigod. Up," one of the demons spoke, his cold red pupils landing on Eden with venom swirling within.

Eden deigned to look up, but upon seeing such eyes, he ducked back down and bit his lip to stifle his whimpers.

"Not asking," the demon said, using a key on the cell door before throwing it open. As he approached, the rest waited listlessly, and he reached to grab Eden. "Now."

Eden shot up and took hold of the demon's arm, yanking him down and quickly using his chains to choke the demon. In the struggle, the demon gagged and grabbed at the chains, but Eden tightened his grip on them until the coarse metal tore through his skin. Although he was young and not acclimated to any real combat yet, he was still abnormally strong for his age.

Witnessing Eden's retaliation, the demon's colleagues showed disinterest in subduing his efforts. Instead, the demon he was choking grabbed his arm and bit down with sharp teeth. As they gouged his forearm, Eden yelled out and released the demon.

"You accursed child!" the demon spat, the formal indignity in his tone replaced with seething hatred. He stood and grabbed Eden by his head, hoisting him from the ground with sharp nails digging into his scalp. "What a stupid little stunt."

Effortlessly, the demon pushed Eden into the wall, holding him firmly while his other hand opened the clasps of Eden's shackles, freeing him.

"If you think of pulling something like that again, you will sorely regret it, boy," the demon whispered harshly into Eden's ear, his breath jagged knives against his neck. The demon tossed Eden into the waiting grips of his colleagues, causing him to stumble before they subdued his wrists and locked cuffs on them. Even as his arm throbbed and bled, they hoisted him along, dragging him through the halls with no further difficulty from his resistance.

"The boy got you pretty good, Modeo," a colleague spoke. This earned a scoff from Modeo, whose neck sizzled as it healed. He refrained from speaking, instead scorning Eden with his gaze every chance he got.

The scenery before Eden was hardly notable, but it burned into his mind. Every room, every path, and every grisly glimpse of the laboratory rooms. The experiments hidden behind each door evoked dread, every detail gleaned etching itself into him. However, one peek he had caught of a tank with a bleeding, fleshy substrate inside was enough to persuade his preference for ignorance. Frantic red eyes darted around, searching for a means of escape. Eventually, one of the demons took notice and yanked his hair, causing him to yelp.

"Quit that," the demon grumbled to him, holding his head straight for the rest of their journey through the oppressive corridors.

Eventually, they came to a stale white room. A large table was in the center, several stations ripe with tools surrounding it. North of it, a long shelf was lined with innumerable vials filled with clear liquid.

Without warning, the demons yanked Eden's clothes from his form, restraining him as he struggled. Left in only his underwear, the scientists hoisted him onto the table, and within moments, he was restrained to it by several metal clasps anchoring his limbs.

"No, let me go!" Eden yelled out, tugging his wrists to no avail. Restraints had always felt like suffocation—even something as innocuous as a blanket draped over his face. If the chains in his cell were hell, this was something worse.

"Shut the fuck up already," Modeo spat. "The doctor will be in shortly."

Eden's eyes flicked to the door as he listened for footsteps, but no sound ever came. Anticipation gnawed at him, his heart drumming as he sensed something dark but couldn't pinpoint the source. The black feather that fell from the ceiling evaded both his sight and hearing, and silently, the fallen angel manifested from it. How, no one understood—not even his closest confidants.

Eden turned his head, peering up at the towering fallen angel, who wore a similar black outfit to the scientists. His ashen skin, not dissimilar to other demons, bore a stonelike quality with his unflinching facial features—chiseled and inhuman, possessing long pointed ears. Boring into Eden's eyes, remorseless, abyssal purple eyes stared as if he were beneath a living creature, something invaluable. No emotion existed behind those eyes—not even malice. There was no intent to harm, but that didn't assuage him. Neither his life nor sensibilities meant anything to the fallen angel; that much was clear. It was just as Lucy had described of her father—*Onaga*.

"Interesting ..." Onaga's deep, transcendent voice rang with an unfamiliar accent. "Divinity sequesters within your soul itself, brimming through its windows for all to discern."

Eden's breathing stopped, as if he were drowning in a sea of darkness that flashed over him. In the next moment, he returned to reality. What stared into him was far more than he could have fathomed—something ancient and yearning. Fear wrapped around him—feather by feather. His finite flesh was all he could offer, but he feared it would not be enough for the insatiable greed before him. Silent before the curious leer, he shivered at the terrible darkness that he carried.

"I wonder ... the extent of your heritage. Does it reach your flesh, blood, bones? Or is it merely this incorporeal essence that you exude? Are these questions you have ever pondered?" he asked Eden, but he couldn't answer.

For several moments, they remained staring at one another, and Eden reached deep to find his voice, afraid of keeping an answer from the fallen angel for too long.

"No," Eden whispered. As if his answer had been insincere, Onaga's invasive gaze of the fallen angel caressed his very bones.

"You truly have no idea ... but fret not. We will discover this," Onaga spoke flatly, turning his attention to the other scientists. "Prepare to take the tissue samples to the biology center. I estimate no more than seventy-two hours for tangible results for your teams to render ostensibly useful data. They will be ready in under three minutes."

One of the scientists eyed Eden, blinking in confusion. "Only three? Extracting distinct, viable samples surely—"

"Three minutes," Onaga repeated. His black wings suddenly unfurled, shooting out to their full expanse and causing his long black hair to sway in the encroaching draft. As the wings loomed, their shadow stretched over

Eden. It was eerily silent at first; only the glimmer of twinkling purple from Onaga's eyes remained as he became a silhouette. Then Eden fell unconscious.

It was unthinkable, spared only in the visceral display due to the nature of its precision. Black feathers became arrows that curved across and through Eden. Both large and small, they rapidly excised flesh from his body, leaving not even a trace of blood. In their incisions, they sewed him closed after each extraction.

In under three minutes, as Onaga had promised, the vials surrounding the table were neatly sorted with small samples from Eden—organs, muscle, flesh, and bone marrow. A precise procedure, guided by an ancient, angelic technique. The wounds had healed into scars already when the feathers darted back to Onaga's wings, unsullied and clean as before.

Although they were visibly exalted, the scientists carefully collected the vials and made their way to the door, only pausing to listen when Onaga spoke.

"I expect the results within the timeframe I have given. I will be in my study."

As suddenly as Onaga had arrived, he disappeared without a trace.

Crimson eyes drifted open in the dark. The permeating light was only challenged by the shimmering of a faint light flickering from several cells away. Only a semblance of light shone for Eden's eyes to see. Frigid stone beneath his feet informed him he was on the ground. It had been hard to tell in the remorseless grasp of the dark.

Groggy was too insufficient a descriptor of his state; his head swam as the air in his chest weighed heavily. His blood was ice, as if he had been stored in a freezer. In his recollection, Onaga's wings had unfurled, and as if a tsunami had swept him away, he had succumbed to the overwhelming fatigue that clawed him into the abyss. Only discomfort lingered, and he failed to determine why in the darkness cloaking his body.

"H-hello?" His hoarse voice echoed in the hall, and the grating sounds of rattling chains roused his attention, making him flinch. Metallic links clashed against the floor as a muffled moan cut through the following silence.

"Eden?" Cassiel's light voice called out. Her lilac eyes caught the light, appearing faintly red when her gaze found his. "I can see your eyes," she informed, her tone suggesting awe.

Eden was aware his eyes tended to glow in the dark if he didn't consciously suppress energy, not that he needed to in that instance. Why they glowed while his power was bound was beyond him.

"Cassie?" Eden called out, unable to see her face.

"Yeah, it's me," she spoke quietly with a smile. "You were asleep for hours. Do you feel okay?"

"I don't know," Eden said, coughing as he searched the dark. *Thirsty,* he thought. Finding a cup of water was unlikely, but his dry throat compelled him to search. It proved fruitless, and he quickly gave up, unable to make out his surroundings.

"I want to go home," Eden spoke, curling up again as the chilly air assailed his form, which was barely covered in a white gown. The lack of cushioning or a bed hardly helped either.

"Me too," Cassiel spoke, her voice soft and forlorn. "Were you abducted from your parents?"

Eden was silent, thinking briefly as he moistened his lips. "My mom and dad."

"You know both? It's very unusual for deities to remain present."

"How did you know what I am?" he asked, and Cassiel giggled.

"How couldn't I? Your energy is similar to a celestial's, yet much richer in depth. I know what their energy feels like, and yours is ... more than that," she spoke, smiling brightly.

Eden swore he could see her form shimmer briefly, but he assumed his eyes were tricking him. Her words, while having initially invoked his anxiety, calmed him. It was the kind of comfort one found in being understood in a way most others didn't.

"My real father isn't around," he said. "My mother's boyfriend is also my mentor—so I call him dad. Mom said he likes that."

"That's sweet ..."

"They don't know I was captured, I think, but they'll find me soon—I know it."

"You think so?"

"They're hunters and strong. Lucy's father wouldn't stand a chance," Eden asserted, certain in his claim.

Cassiel didn't speak after that for several minutes, and Eden retreated into thought. Lucifina's condemnation when her father's Venatums ambushed them echoed repeatedly. The prospect of being sought by her father had never crossed his mind. He had kept his friendship with her a secret. Realizing this, dread crept into his soul, and he wondered if they would have any idea of where or how to find him. They would search, but he became unsure if they would find him.

They had spoken of demons' treachery, but Lucy had shown only kindness, warmth, and a philosophical curiosity he adored. Such an intelligent girl, yet she had shown an interest in what he thought. She had always begged to see his drawings, regardless of the fine art she spoke of in her home. He had been completely enthralled during their time together.

Eden was shaken from his thoughts when he heard footfalls and scraping along the hall's floor, and heavy breathing filled the air. The scent of sulfur permeated the air and stung his nose, and with it, the light of embers pulsed along the walls. He instinctively shrank into the corner of his cell, seeing it draw nearer.

The eyes of the creature banished the darkness. Before him and Cassiel, a hellhound's glare burned ferociously. Embers ascended from its bristles, and its nose twitched as it glared into Eden's very soul. In the next breath, its teeth snapped at the cell's bars, and growls thundered from it as it tenaciously attacked the barrier separating it from Eden—the would-be prey.

Eden let out a cry. His heart pounded with such force he thought it might break through his chest. His breath was trapped by his clamped lips. The cell that imprisoned him, ironically, became his only respite from the fiend before him, and he prayed it held.

"Warden!" Cassiel's voice called, and the creature drew back, its sharp teeth still bared while turning its attention to Cassiel. "Here, boy … come here. Treat!" she called, and the hound turned around eagerly, licking its maw before trotting across to her cell. A chunk of old meat tumbled outside of the cell, and the hound hungrily consumed it, licking its muzzle clean afterward before it took a seat in front of Cassiel's cell.

"Good boy, Warden …" Cassiel spoke, hushed, her chains tumbling as she relaxed in her cell again. "They never feed him enough, so he's always excited when they bring a new prisoner here. I try to calm him down by saving some of my own food for him. He prefers meat, but that's not surprising for a dog."

Eden breathed out hoarsely, composing his breath.

"That isn't a dog," he said, making Cassiel giggle.

"He's close enough. Hardly seems different from the one I had growing up, minus the hunger-induced aggression and fiery fury."

"It's a demon," Eden spat. "It would kill us if it could." He kept far from the bars. Because of the chains, he couldn't reach it if he wanted to.

"He lives just as we do, and though his nature seems problematic, he has desires just as you and I do. Be they infernal or not, all beings of Ichor deserve love."

Eden went quiet as he eyed the hound. It sat by Cassiel's cage, as if waiting for her to toss more food to it. Cassiel appeared underweight, and he wagered that feeding the hound some of her food contributed to that. The portions given to them were already meager at best.

"There is no being that is inherently evil, I believe. Nor inherently good. We mold ourselves and look to the world to discover the principles which define us," Cassiel challenged.

"Does the difference matter? We all have sin, but they're ruled by it—born in it."

Cassiel's lips curled into a soft smile. Her eyes softly rested on Warden, whose drowsy gaze simmered with a similar fondness.

"Suppose that is true ... would that prevalence solely define who they are?" she began. "We look within to discover the world that surrounds, and as often as we miss the forest for the trees, we miss ourselves for our minds." Cassiel shifted, seeing that Warden had fallen asleep by her cell door. "Should you allow yourself to be defined by what you think yourself to be, you'll never discover who you are—who you can be."

As her words washed over him, he exhaled unevenly, shaking his head in refusal of what she said. Once, he had been more amenable to such thinking, but recalling how such an idea was now what he believed led to his capture, he admonished it greatly.

"I wish I could believe that ..."

Much to Eden's relief, the hound remained asleep for the rest of the night, and Cassiel resorted to humming a melody until she drifted off herself. Eden, much to his detriment, refrained from sleeping, afraid of prying his eyes from the hellhound in fear it might wake and try to breach the cell.

Though his eyes were heavy, he endured the fatigue. Eventually, the lights turned on, and Warden dashed through the hall, disappearing from sight. Eden closed his eyes and leaned his head against the wall, finally seeming to relax as the tension fled his body. Though the lights from outside of the cell burned through his eyelids, he preferred that discomfort to the menacing presence of the hound.

The rest was all too brief, and some odd hours later, the banging of a rod against his cell woke him up. Several demon scientists were lined up outside his cell, opening the door with such force that the impact reverberated in the hall. Eden's eyes opened, his chest tightening as if he had just been punched.

"What are you doing to him?" Cassiel called, her voice firm despite its soft tone. They ignored her, however, wheeling in a machine that was used for drawing blood. Eden was hoisted up to his feet by Modeo, who he recognized from the day prior. Judging from his intensifying glare, Eden knew a grudge had formed.

"Cooperate, or you may get hurt, boy. We're taking blood," Modeo spoke.

Eden inhaled sharply, shaking his head in refusal as he tried to yank himself free. However, the Modeo's grip was too strong, and he tightened it on his wrist as a warning.

"You're stubborn, but if you don't quit it, this will be painful, and we'll miss your vein," Modeo said, gesturing for his colleague to approach.

When Eden tugged his wrist again, the demon squeezed it harder. He let out a cry as the demon extended his arm, and another demon stabilized it as they inserted the needle. Eden began hyperventilating, and he was reminded of his hatred of needles while watching his blood siphon through the tube.

Cassiel persisted in yelling at the scientists, but they paid her no mind. One of the bags attached to the cart filled with blood, and when it was filled, the scientist withdrew the needle. The abusive man holding Eden's wrist pressed a thumb to the wound, energy surging in his finger. The wound sealed, and the demon let Eden fall to the ground before they wheeled the cart from the cell.

"Was that so hard?" Modeo said, crouching down. "You're giving me so much trouble, and that needs to stop. I'm the one in charge of dealing with you, outside of Onaga, that is." He glared hard. "Make me an enemy, then I'll be an enemy."

Eden raised his head, clenching his arm with a challenging glare directed at Modeo.

"Fuck. You," Eden said.

Modeo's colleagues watched him hesitantly, but he waved them off. Dismissing their hesitations, they nodded and wheeled the machine and the blood away.

"I can't kill or harm you in any way that is detrimental to our continued research into you ... but rest assured, I can show you agony even with that restriction," Modeo said with a sardonic smirk.

"No! Leave him alone, Modeo!" Cassiel shouted, yanking on her chains as she tried to move toward her cell door.

"Shut the hell up, stupid dove!" Modeo hissed, his head whipping around to face her. Eden took his opportunity and jumped at the demon, but the demon caught him by the neck and pinned him to the ground. Modeo glanced between the two prisoners, unperturbed by Eden's relentless struggle.

"Celestials and deities all think the same. That they're *above* demons. That I'm evil just because I was born one. No, I choose to be the demon they think me to be because they pretend to be righteous. I hate pretenders. I'm sure truly benevolent beings would never murder parents in front of their child they sacrificed themselves to protect, but they did. At least I'm not pretending my path isn't paved in blood," Modeo hissed, glaring at Eden.

"If that's all it takes to make you do this, then maybe they were right. They should have finished you," Eden hissed in a muffled voice, his cheek mashed into the floor. And as he met Modeo's glare, it darkened.

"I think you need to be taught a lesson, boy ..."

Modeo snatched Eden's arm that he had drawn blood from, his grasp clenching hard enough that Eden's bone ached. In one motion, his jaws snapped onto Eden's arm, piercing his flesh with his jagged teeth.

Eden yelled in pain, howling as the demon increased the pressure, sucking the blood that dribbled out. Despite his efforts to break away, both the pain and his grip were impossible to overcome. In desperation, he professed his regret, apologizing and begging for him to stop. The pain burned into him as if he were being burned and siphoned all at once. But Modeo ignored both him and Cassiel, indulging in Eden's pain and blood alike for several seconds before releasing him.

Blood dribbled from Modeo's lip, his tongue quickly lapping it. His infernal eyes bored into Eden sharper than his teeth had.

"You're more delicious than putrid angels," he claimed, glancing at Cassiel briefly. "I could get addicted if I'm not careful," he warned, chuckling darkly as he pressed his palm to the bite wound on Eden's arm. Energy ran through the wound before he tossed Eden into the wall, but the wound on his arm remained. "I stopped the bleeding, but you can sit with that pain for a few hours and think about your insolence."

Eden grabbed his arm, staring at the wound with wide eyes as he choked. He began weeping, his arm throbbing as he looked away with humiliation inscribed on his face. Although no blood seeped from the wound, the stinging assailed him incessantly.

"Eden, please don't cry ..." Cassiel's voice called, her eyes fixed on him, glossy with tears as she shared in his pain. Her voice barely reached him, and his tears streaked down his face as he sobbed from the pain.

A pain all too familiar.

Cassiel raised her hands, the shackles on her wrists heavy as her dainty fingers outstretched toward him. She focused intently on his energy, diminutive and inscrutable beneath the hex that confined it. As if searching for a wisp in the dark, she found it there and took hold. She whispered in Latin beneath her breath, and a light breeze fanned over Eden, who opened his eyes to a shimmering light shining where Cassiel stood. It was soft, permitting him a glimpse of her soul—her light.

Serenity greeted him. His wound cooled, liberated from the fiery pain that plagued him. When he looked down, the twinkling feather that sat atop his bite marks sealed his wound shut.

"You've but to call for me, and I will grant you my light ... so please dry your tears, Eden," Cassiel begged with a troubled smile and glistening eyes. Behind her, he saw her white wings spread, ethereal in stark contrast to the dark expanses of Onaga's.

"You're ... an angel?" he asked, reaching up and taking hold of the feather that rested on his arm, absorbing its silkiness with fond fingers.

"Nephilim, to be exact," she admitted, her wings slowly retreating into her back as she panted heavily, the hex eating at her energy once more. It took everything in her to heal Eden, and now, nausea washed over her as the runes on her shackles glowed.

"Then you're like me. A halfling," he spoke. He stood, his muscles relaxed in the afterglow of Cassiel's healing. "Are you alright?"

Cassiel nodded, sitting down as she caught her breath.

"I will be," she promised. "I couldn't stand to see you cry. Something in me weeps when you do, and I wouldn't be able to live with myself if I didn't try to help."

Eden's eyes drifted down. Suddenly, the scorn he showed toward the love she permitted the hound earlier felt both daft and cruel. The sentiments she had shown him, her healing and her light, all culminated into a blossoming admiration toward her. *Beauty,* he thought.

"I wish I had wings like yours …" Eden said, his hands retreating to his side.

"Oh?" Cassiel's brow furrowed.

"They're beautiful, and your feathers are soft. I liked flying with …"

Cassiel lowered her head, lips pursing.

"Lucifina?" Eden met her curious gaze.

"You know her?"

"Somewhat. I mostly heard of her through Onaga since he talked fondly of her. I only met her once or twice."

Eden sat down again, sorrow washing over him now that she had entered his mind again. Cassiel watched him, studying him curiously. With a small smile forming, she giggled.

"It's settled then. When we're free, I'll have to take you flying."

Eden laughed uncontrollably as he tugged at his chains. Meanwhile, Cassiel giggled.

"I won't stop until you admit you're not a bad artist," Cassiel warned. Her feather lashed out at Eden's abdomen, evading his attempt to catch and swat it away.

"Okay! Okay! I guess I'm not that bad!" Eden sputtered, holding his sides as Cassiel's feather returned to her wings. Afterward, they receded into her back as she stuck her tongue out at him playfully.

"Good enough," she claimed, her gaze returning to the image of her face he had carved into the stone wall behind him using the links of his shackles. "It's so good, especially considering you did it without an actual tool."

"I moved around a lot, and holographic sketching is just weird and non-tactile, so I avoided it. Scraping stone isn't that different from sketching with a pencil," he claimed, relaxing as he rubbed his sides. Still sensitive from Cassiel's tickling, he guarded them as if she would change her mind about the mercy she granted him.

"I'm a fan of paper and crayons myself. Call me childish, but there's ... less pressure to be good with those," she said, rubbing her head while showing a sheepish smile.

Cassiel returned to the small mattress tucked into the edge of her cell, and Eden did the same. He was glad that they had given him a mattress the week following his imprisonment, but it was still less comfortable than the ones in the hotels or the dorms he'd stayed in.

"They're not super precise or versatile, but they're nice and easy, and plenty of diners have them. My mom isn't a very good cook, so I used those a lot," he said, hiding his smile, longing to be home. It had been months already, but despite the abuse, he enjoyed Cassiel's company. The nights were harrowing; between the cold, the dark, and the sparse uproars from Warden *disposing* of inessential prisoners, it was hard to relax. Whenever the dark took hold, Cassiel's wings unfurled and shimmered—a comforting nightlight. Without it, he couldn't sleep.

As Cassiel thoughtfully peered into Eden's gaze, her smile became a welcoming hearth.

"Momma always cooked well. Comfort foods, mainly. It was better than what my foster mom made ... if she served at all. Claimed she didn't want me fat and made me skip meals," Cassiel said, her smile fading as she spoke, and she tucked her legs into her chest.

"That's awful ... she sounds like the kind of person who should be here instead of you," Eden asserted, but Cassiel snorted, shaking her head.

"She wasn't great ... but nobody deserves this."

"You especially don't ..."

Eden retreated into thought, but for once, he was thinking more about her. She had told him about the time she had spent with Onaga before she was locked away in the cell. He initially assumed it was for experimentation and research, like him, but he suspected there was more to it. Modeo was the only one who bothered her, which didn't resemble any kind of research endeavor.

"Your mom ... what happened?" Eden asked, peering through the bars at her. Cassiel pursed her lips, sighing lightly.

"She got sick when I was younger. Something to do with an adverse aging effect of time dilation."

"Time dilation?" Eden inquired, and Cassiel gestured to herself.

"When Mother met Father, she was not in Mortale. She never mentioned which realm, but I suspect Caelum, since my mother was human. When she had me, she was with my father, but she grew ill—unable to maintain herself within that realm. He sent her back." Cassiel frowned. "Though ... apparently, we were suspended within the path between to avoid being detected by the sages, who would surely have killed us. When we made it here to Mortale, she deteriorated no matter how much of my light I shared with her."

Eden had learned of the sages once before—beings of limited sapience who existed as guardians of the realm bridges. Time dilation, however, was a concept beyond his understanding. Still, he couldn't help but wonder how old Cassiel was. She didn't seem much older than he was, but he thought it too rude to ask. It was too late, however. Having noticed his stare and his lips ajar, she giggled lightly and shook her head.

"Before you ask, I don't really know how old I am. Legally speaking, Sweden thinks me to be nineteen, but I'm a lot older, I suspect."

"I wasn't going to ask ..." Eden protested, but Cassiel scrunched her face, clearly doubting him.

"Subject change, do you know which Primordial is your father?" she asked. Eden shook his head and looked away.

"Mom doesn't talk about him." He pouted. "There are only twelve though, right? Which ones are male?"

"Technically speaking—they aren't strictly bound by sex and can appear however they want, but Void doesn't involve itself in mortal sentiments. Of the other eleven, I learned of their afflictions during my time here—before I was caged, that is." Her expression soured, but it quickly resolved. "Do you know of the deities and their roles?" she asked, but Eden shook his head.

"I know about Ichor, the Mother of Life, and Sere, the Father of Death. That's about it." Cassiel gave him a bright smile, her gaze softening further than he thought possible.

"Maybe we can find out together? I know a little about how the others are described."

Eden was all too eager to hear her speak about the other deities, whose former pantheon had long since been erased from human record. He knew its remnants remained throughout other mythologies and cultural regards of the divine, however. Cassiel began explaining the Primordials to him, the domains of reality they embodied.

Those regarded as feminine were explained first: Irene, the Primordial of Peace; Nyx, the Primordial of Darkness and Sin; Helena, the Primordial of Light and Virtue; and Eris, the Primordial of Order.

Two Primordials were often regarded as being ephemeral in how they were perceived: Verse, the Primordial of Space and Time, and Aegis, the Primordial of Order.

Finally, there were the Primordials regarded as masculine: Romanus, the Primordial of Conflict; Izanagi, the Primordial of Creation; and Draqul, the Primordial of Destruction.

Cassiel and Eden speculated to no avail. Eden's only point of reference was that Jessica liked Ethan. He was a stoic man—well-spoken and sharp, prompting Eden initially to believe his father was Izanagi or Aegis. Cassiel regarded them as best fitting those qualities in the texts of old.

Soon, she fixed her gaze on his red eyes, her lilac hues twinkling as she peered deep into them. Eden couldn't help but blush, but as she began speaking, her face dropped as her limbs became taut against her body.

Upon hearing a door open, their attention was torn to the western end of the hallway, only one set of leisurely steps parading from it once it snapped shut. The tapping of heels and an infamously familiar and slow tune being whistled filled the halls. Both of them retreated into the corners of their cells, tucking any exposed skin into their gowns.

Their gazes remained low as Modeo approached. Their joyful expressions and breathing evanesced, amalgamating into silent fear. The tapping stopped, and a low hum vibrated in such a way that the hairs on their necks stood on end like knives. Eden's jaws clenched tightly, becoming a shield he knew was necessary.

"You two are more meek than usual. Something the matter?" Modeo spoke, but neither of them replied. He inspected them in their cells, his eyes briefly glancing to the depiction of Cassiel that Eden had scraped onto the wall, a dark grin forming. "Wow, staying busy? Good for you. Really. Maybe I should bring you some paper and ink, then you could use one of Cassie's feathers as a quill."

"Don't call me that ..." Cassie grumbled with indignation, eyes still glued to her mattress.

"Call you what, little dove?"

"You know my name."

Modeo frowned and moved toward her cell with leisurely steps, understanding the slow approach was torturous for her.

"Eden calls you Cassie, so why not me?" he asked sarcastically, shaking his head. "Angels. All the same. Why hide your wings? Afraid I'll pour ink on them instead?" he asked, musing on the thought while squinting at her. A devilish smile formed, and he snickered before pulling a key from his belt and unlocking her cell door. "They'd look better black, anyway."

"And you'd look better red and blue," Eden growled, raising his eyes to glare at Modeo.

"Oh, I'm sure you'd love to see that, but I don't have much of an appetite to make you eat those words. The caged bird here looks more tantalizing right now."

Modeo's eyes cast down onto Cassiel, who shut her eyes. It was as if her whimpers were music to him, each step of his approach evoking a crescendo.

"You're quiet now, *Cassie*. Say something ... or would you rather I open your mouth for you? I have something you'll enjoy," he spoke, his words dripping with lecherous venom.

Cassiel finally raised her head, her lilac eyes devoid of their radiance and kindness as she stared at him, expressionless.

"I don't enjoy the taste of lesser evils."

A crack filled the hall as Cassiel's head was slammed into the wall, her pearly hair pulled taut and spilling through Modeo's fingers. His thumb pried her bottom jaw open before he fumbled with his belt, tears spilling from Cassiel's eyes as the sounds echoed in her cell.

"No! Leave her alone, Modeo! I'll do whatever you want, just don't touch her!" Eden begged, his voice swelling with panic with each repeated iteration.

"We always go through this song and dance, demigod. You'll try to resist and bite. You always make me beat you into submission," he spoke flatly, divorced from any moral disdain of his own statement.

"I won't—I promise. I'll do whatever you say! I'll do what you say from now on ..." he spoke. When Modeo ignored him, he hung his head and sobbed audibly. "Please don't hurt her anymore ..."

The loathsome demon stared down at Cassiel with a hint of hesitation, his fingers loosening on her hair as he laughed darkly.

"Oh wow, you really do like her a lot, don't you? It's sweet, really. You wouldn't catch me dead crying for anybody," he said, shoving Cassiel's head away as he turned on his heel.

"Eden ... no, please. Don't do this for me," she breathed out, her voice strained and distressed as she cried. Even as her head throbbed and her vision danced, she unclenched her teeth to breathe her pleas. "Modeo, plea—"

"*Rikara!*" Modeo hissed, a dark energy pulsing across Cassiel's lips, muffling her voice despite her continued attempt to speak. "You're spoiling the moment," he said, finding a twisted pride in his effect on Eden. Shutting Cassiel's cell, he locked it before turning to face Eden again. "You promise, boy? I will use her instead if you dare to break it."

Eden looked up, glassy-eyed as his tears stained his cheeks. He stifled his hiccups and sobs, giving a tepid nod.

"I promise," Eden whispered in a broken voice.

Modeo gave a salacious grin, moving closer to Eden's cell as he held the key up.

"Good," Modeo purred. "I like you better anyway."

Day by day, Eden grew weaker within the confines of his cell. Atrophy and dwindling determination took hold, and soon, the solace offered by Cassiel struggled to breach the creeping darkness within him. Be it his broken will or physical weakness, the shackles on his wrists were too heavy to lift. He struggled with basic movements, but Cassiel continued offering a smile and encouraging him, despite the agony the sight brought her. Her shimmering feathers, while no substitute for proper nutrition and freedom, eased his pain.

It had been several months beyond a year—he lost count. His seclusion was magnified by his degrading health, but he always called for Cassiel when he began slipping too deep—thoughts that disturbed him far more than the demons did.

He heard the voice again that afternoon. While it boomed, he stood with buckling legs, shaking his head in denial as his long, matted hair swung. Cassiel peered at him from her own cell, her eyes glossy with dried tears staining her cheeks. She sought to give all she could, but it was never enough to bring him back for long.

The turmoil continuously fermented within his soul, refusing to die. Divinity tarnished, or so she feared. He had grown physically during his captivity but shrunk in every other way. This, too, Cassiel could not explain. A great sadness thrummed in her heart the more her scattered thoughts reflected on his own ramblings. The mumbling in his sleep, the random outbursts of refusal toward someone who wasn't there—he was suffering despite her efforts. She gave all she could give.

It was never enough.

Modeo hadn't visited in over two months, as if he had vanished as a specter that they collectively imagined, but that was wishful thinking. They knew all too well that neither of them could conjure such vileness prior to their torment. There was no reason or explanation given. Eden had been tested regularly and given treatment for his ailments, but still, he deteriorated. It boggled the scientists, but it was all too clear to Cassiel what gnawed at her dear friend. An immutable sentiment incompatible with his divinity—with the Eden she cherished.

In the dark of night, she caught glimpses of it when he'd stir from his sleep. A gravity erected from him that squeezed the bars of their cells and scorched the air. Suffocating and terrifying, she saw such sentiments within those glaring red eyes. Like she had asked, he called her name, and she knew to shed her light upon him when he did.

"Go away ..." Eden whispered between heavy breaths as he dropped to his knees, nausea washing over him. Something tugged his heart toward his throat, its cadence erratic, but he wrenched his breath back from the phantom that grasped it.

"You don't belong here ... you can't," Cassiel spoke, her voice barely above a whisper as she shakily released the breath she had been holding. Her eyes widened as her feathers danced around Eden, shining her light upon him until he became conscious. "Eden?" she called.

"I'm here ..." Eden said, his voice wavering as light returned to his gaze, meeting Cassiel's glistening eyes that watched him, perturbed.

"Thank Ichor. You were gone for so long." She gasped deeply. "I was worried."

Eden's eyes widened, his head cocking as confusion carved his visage.

"How long?" It had been a brief darkness that had absconded with his vision. The flickers of blazing red within it had commanded his attention for but seconds as the voice spoke to him again. Once again, it sought to compel him, but Cassiel's voice pulled him out again.

"Too long ..." she said, her wings slowly receding as her feathers returned—all but the one that rested in his palm. "It's taking longer."

"I called your name," Eden swore. Cassiel was silent for several moments, shaking her head as her eyes narrowed.

"I never heard you," she breathed out, her face etched with adopted guilt.

Eden finally composed himself and crawled back to his mattress. The wall, while still cold and rugged, had the odd effect of grounding his thoughts. Should his mind go asunder once more, he feared Cassiel would never hear him again.

They sat in silence for several hours, but Eden kept studying her lilac eyes. It was haunting to see their luster disappear night after night. As if her gaze was tethered to the floor, she hadn't looked at him since they last spoke. He feared whatever could make her ruminate—she never shared what.

By evening's arrival, she glanced at the western end of the hall again. She vigilantly watched and waited but soon surrendered her attention when nothing showed.

"I haven't seen Warden in over a week ... I hope he's okay," Cassiel spoke, her voice devoid of the brimming optimism she had always channeled.

While Eden cared little for the hellhound, he knew what the infernal creature meant to Cassiel. She had been alone with Warden prior to his arrival. The hound had shown something akin to affection for her, playing with her and chasing her feathers without a hint of malice. Eden could only see the gluttony within its burning eyes, a facade that it disguised itself with. It was friendly, but not a friend.

"It's only us now. Maybe that's why they don't need him patrolling the halls." Eden offered, forcing a smile, but she didn't flinch. She shrank into herself and tucked her head between her knees. Shortly after, he did so as well.

This moment didn't last long, however.

"Something's wrong," she whimpered, her eyes going wide with terror.

Immense pressure washed through the entire facility, bringing a wave of nausea that slammed into both of them. Pain and sorrow alike, scorching hot, burrowed into their hearts as the suffocating air became heavier.

All other things were drowned out—no sounds or cold. Even their eyes barely perceived the swarm of black feathers that flashed over their vision as two demons appeared before them. Onaga and one other.

The unknown demon's dark dreadlocks undulated within his aura, sporadically flickering scarlet-red. A tamed inferno that flared in stark contrast to his ebony skin washed over them; that deathly energy was diminutive compared to what they sensed within him: a tsunami of despair that could drown an ocean.

Agony.

The sentiment erected itself as they gazed in fear, yet tearing their gazes away was impossible. Intangible, eating away at the world they once understood. And then his gaze fixed on Eden. With what those blasphemous eyes heralded, Eden lurched forward, falling to his hands as he vomited. Before its inferno, the voice he so feared within himself was but a spark.

"*You* are what will liberate demonkind?" the man's deep voice growled. Contrary to his tone, the question was both a demand and a prayer.

Unflinching, those eyes immolated Eden's visage. He was nothing within them, not even kindling, but he would still burn. It was unending—just like Onaga's gaze, but their sentiments were far from alike. They were reminded of that when the fallen angel answered on Eden's behalf.

"Kuzaku Paimon, I have uncovered the depths of his being. Together, they are what will untether us from obliviousness and subjugation alike," Onaga spoke.

His dark voice made Cassiel flinch. Rather than torture herself with the sight of him, she tore her gaze away and tightly shut her eyes. Vitriol bloomed in her soul, and she dared not grant Onaga further thought—she couldn't contain herself if she did.

"With their union, we may forge a new reality, and your exile will cease," Onaga continued, causing Paimon to give a grave grin as he gazed through Eden.

"It is only fair ..." Paimon began. "For so long, divinity has erased us. Robbed us. It is only fair you offer yourselves to rectify their injustices." His gaze narrowed, a darkness expanding within them that turned his burning irises into supernovas that obliterated their voids.

Blossoming wrath.

"You're a demonium," Cassiel's voice squeaked, a chime that broke the rumbling fear that consumed Eden and herself.

Paimon stirred from his declaration, as if robbed of his respite. He turned slowly, his gaze finding Cassiel's and declaring war. As if magma had met ice, two paradoxes collided. Serenity and Pain, peering through one another in a moment that stretched beyond their understanding, but Cassiel was the first to declare her glimpses.

"You're suffering ..." she alleged, whimpering as if she did as well. "You don't belong here either ... do you?" When she asked, Paimon's eyes softened, and the inferno that raged became a silent storm.

"Your eyes are just like his ..." Paimon whispered, but his words were not meant for ears. They were a rebuttal of what he had desired to believe, and a hint of sorrow glared back at him.

Onaga's wings jittered, and his gaze shifted to Paimon as his aura was consumed by black, and shadows latched at his form while he gazed upon Cassiel.

"You are out of time," Onaga spoke.

Paimon raised his head, closing his eyes as he breathed in deeply, basking in the air he despaired to depart from.

"Do not disappoint my father again, harbinger," Paimon said. Several shadowy arms clutched his form and cascaded around him until he was no more than a silhouette. In the next breath, he was torn from Mortale and returned to Inferos.

Although the pressure was alleviated from the air, the cold of Onaga's presence granted Cassiel and Eden no ease of mind. Eden remembered to breathe, and when he looked up, he met those fathomless purple eyes. Much to the harbinger's title, their greed pilfered his mind once more.

Onaga turned on his heel, facing Cassiel without a ghost of an expression to color him. Cassiel hadn't needed to see it to know that. It was beyond typical. *Despicable*, she thought.

"Long ago," Onaga began. "Mortale was created by Izanagi, whose infinite hands crafted every atom. I orchestrated much of this process as their seraphim. But it was Ichor's heart that breathed life into it. Accompanying it was an intimate power that could not only be wielded but manipulated to find all that she would touch. Her heart, stolen by Lucifer, was used to craft Inferos, but it was expended. Such is the case of love and betrayal ...”

As he spoke, Cassiel's gaze deigned to meet his. Accursed and deserving of her scorn, she loathed the memory of his meaningless monologues, lectures disjointed and devoid of a deeper meaning he was slow to reveal. It was something she had once found endearing, but the once sweet fondness only allowed her to taste bitterness as she listened.

“Why do you pretend to care whether we know or not? You're here to kill us,” Cassiel alleged, venom beneath her monotone voice.

“You know well by now that I abhor ignorance, be it within the living or the dead,” Onaga spoke, his eyes softening.

“And you know I don't care for your lectures, so enlighten us already,” she snapped, prompting Onaga to shut his eyes.

“I seek to combine the realms so we may discover a singular truth, a knowledge untethered by wanton borders that establish creed from arbitrary sentiments unknown to us. All the concepts that exist outside of omens and sentiments thereof—we will know.”

“And then?” Cassiel asked, her eyes wavering as tears gathered in their corners. Onaga fell silent, and tears spilled down her face, maiming her once impregnable serenity.

As if Cassiel had shared these brewing emotions with Eden, he desperately adopted her pain. Borne through the bond he had formed with her—a pure altruism, and despite knowing it was a vain effort, he subconsciously tugged his chains.

“You ... don't know, and you never will. It will never be enough. There will always be something more to know and discover. More to desecrate. More to strip of dignity. More ... to take, and take, and take!” Cassiel shouted as she gritted her teeth, shivering as she held back a fit of sobs. “What more would you know then?” she shrieked, her face twisting with sorrow.

“I cannot fathom such a concept, and that is why I must achieve omniscience. There is no greater liberation to be had. To put an end to the tyranny of ignorance.”

"There is no liberation!" she snapped. "Your yearning will become your demise. I tried ... I tried to pull you from it, to allow your endless curiosity to serve love for once!" Cassiel's head dropped again, sobbing loudly as her tears drummed the floor. And in the chorus of her lament, Onaga was quiet with that same emotionless stare. Neither he nor Eden dared to interrupt.

Eden couldn't contain the tears from spilling down his cheeks, sharing in her overflowing sorrow. He hadn't understood how much Cassiel had loved Onaga before, but he knew such vitriol could not be born without a betrayal so deep. *He knew it all too well.* As she wept before the fallen angel, he discerned no such reflecting sorrow from Onaga—a silent, unrequited condemnation of her feelings. Cassiel knew before he did, and she sought to damn it again.

"You know nothing of love—you refuse to learn. As much as you wish to know, your curiosity ends when you are met with the uncertainties that can only be remedied in our hearts and souls. Truths that rely on more than just you to be understood. *Solipsistic Gnosticism*, you called it, and yet, here you are. Our lives as the catalyst to set you free. It's ironic in the sickest of ways," she spat, her voice hoarse and strained with grief.

"You couldn't accept that we were incompatible in producing life, and you coldly ripped our forsaken child from my arms. Yet, you still expected me to feed your desire for knowledge. In that *one* way, we were incompatible, but you couldn't accept it." She heaved as she growled in distress. "You tried to drown my light and make me fall as you raped me ..." she whispered in disbelief, her eyes wide with an unheeded plea.

Remorselessness. That was all she could remember when she had held the soulless child in her arms. Ichor refused to recognize her and Onaga's union—their child's life. Ichor would never breathe life into the spawn of demons and angels—something Cassiel had learned through tears and unanswered prayers. Onaga cared not, and she resented him endlessly through her broken heart. It wasn't that he had hurt her, but that he had sought to strip her of the virtue she held—to make her fall as he had.

She refused.

"My feelings meant nothing, be it to love or hate, and what am I now? Just a means to your dreams of omniscience? I have given you all I can!" She gasped as her breath fled. "You will always know nothing—you could know every secret and machination and still never understand ..." She fell quiet, her voice disappearing as she ran out of breath.

Onaga's black feather fluttered before Cassiel, and he appeared inside of her cell, kneeling before her with his eyes fixed adamantly on her. Unflinching. Unchanging. Unfeeling. He observed her with something suggesting fondness, an intimate fixation.

"You vex me so, and I would unravel your mind and virtues more and more, dear Cassiel. Your subjugation was suboptimal, for when I found you, it was with the intention of uncovering the light you brim with. Nephilim are exceedingly rare, as the angels are expected to remain detached, among many other virtues expected of them."

His eyes were briefly shrouded, slit purple irises daring to peer from beneath his physical form.

"While I only speculate, I believe you to be the Cardinal Virtue of Charity. A selfless soul embodying its desire—to give without an expectation of return." He shook his head. "Regardless, I would see you flourish with no mysteries to impede you if it were possible. You would never be tethered by uncertainty or doubt," he whispered softly, reaching for her chin, but he faltered when a tear fell atop his fingertip.

Onaga's wing extended, the edge slashing open the lock of her cell with ease. He turned, opening the cell door and stepping from within it. He turned to face Eden, and while only giving the boy a glimpse, something tumultuous painted his face for a fleeting moment.

"With your soul, and his body, we will forge a new heart of divinity. The light of virtue and the love it offers, amalgamating with the power of divinity to serve as an artifact akin to Ichor's heart. It will be briefly painful, but soon, perhaps when your soul converges with my own ... I may truly understand you and the love you speak of. Or perhaps your hatred. Whichever you feel I deserve, I will defer to your understand-ing."

Eden's eyes widened as Cassiel fell silent. A familiar pitter-patter greeted their ears. With it, dread reemerged. Eden thrashed hard, more than aware of what Onaga intended next.

"No, you can't ... please don't do this to her!" Eden said, his voice pitching higher than usual. The shackles cut into his wrists and put pressure on his bones as he tugged against them. He tried to dash but fell to the ground as the chains' resistance remained firm.

Cassiel stared past Onaga, seeing Eden beneath the framing of his dark wings, as if casting a shadow over him. Even through her broken heart, she saw his crimson eyes that were plagued by worry and panic, and she gave a forlorn smile. It was unbecoming to welcome any further sadness—to let what remained be taken by the voracious greed she once dared to love.

If she were indeed the Cardinal Virtue of Charity as Onaga had proclaimed, it mattered little. Cassiel would offer all she had left.

Hope.

"It's okay, Eden. You'll be okay," she hushed, her strangled voice waging a war to be heard by him.

Eden's vision blurred with tears as he recognized her resignation. That damned smile she gave lied, suggesting her life was not about to be stolen. And though she had done nothing but give, she still offered it as a paradoxical retreat.

Cassiel's wings shot from her back, shimmering brightly. A single feather, brimming with a glaring radiance that erased even Onaga's shadow, floated toward him, and as she had predicted, Onaga let it reach him.

"Whenever you enter that dark place, just know you're not alone. I'll be right there with you if you call my name. I promise," she said, her voice as light as her feather. And much like it, both found Eden.

There, in his open palm, the feather's warmth chastised the cold months they had both endured. Even as he felt the biting pain disappear, the ache in his raging heart remained alongside her smile. The feather's caress quickly became a dagger that plunged into his chest.

Coming into view, Warden was now an emaciated, starved creature that displayed a wild hunger in its flickering eyes—the hunger Eden had so feared from it. Slow and unsteady in its jagged movements, it stumbled toward Cassiel, throat glowing with a desire to consume. Yet, even in its starved state, it recognized her. Its teeth chattered in confliction as drool dripped from its maw.

Before its terrifying visage, Cassiel gave Warden that same serene smile, her expression divorced of fear and hatred, for she had none to give. She had given all of her remaining sentiment to Eden in her feather, and what remained was immutable peace.

"Eden … just make me one promise. I never ask for anything ever, so can you make me just this one promise?"

Warden lunged.

"*Live.*"

Eden's screams and rebellion were ceaseless as she was consumed until nothing remained. Soon, his voice gave way, erratic and sputtering despite his attempts to wail. His eyes never fled, refusing to cower in her final moments. As if he could manifest a sentiment—power—he sought to change the verdict. But soon, she was gone.

Gore dripped from the whimpering hound's maw, eyes twinkling as her soul filled it with power. Onaga lifted the hound by the back of its neck, his energy sedating it, and his remorseless eyes continued gouging into Eden. His screams had since stopped, but he still thrashed and tried to summon his voice, which was no longer there. His eyes, wide with a malformed marriage of hatred and sorrow, never left where Cassiel had been. They refused to surrender his one remaining desire.

Onaga averted his gaze, having garnered all he could in his scrutiny.

"I will come for you in due time. The catalyst for your union must be prepared first," Onaga stated in a monotone voice, and in a flash of dancing black feathers, he disappeared with the hound and Cassiel's soul.

For an indeterminate stretch of time, Eden stared with eyes devoid of the determination and rebellion he had expended. He had no more to give.

The blood that painted the floor became a blasphemous image in his mind. His failure. His weakness. There was nothing he could do, but what he feared most was his inability to fulfill the promise she asked of him.

Eden's head fell, no strength left in his body. He waited with his chaotic vision cemented to the frayed feather. The once glowing white was now dull and saturated with his tears, crushed in his struggle. If he had seen it anywhere else, he would never have imagined it came from Cassiel.

And just as the light fled the halls, darkness crept in around his vision like inky tendrils. Soon, he was in that place once again. He didn't call to Cassiel, for no such delusion ruled him in those despairing moments. While nothing he possessed remained, there was something else yet known.

He had almost forgotten about it. The festering sentiment that plagued him so within the dark place. It spoke of vengeance, of a damnation yet delivered unto those who take. Cassiel couldn't pull him from it as she had before. No choice—no hope—remained.

He surrendered to the voice, possessing no more resistance.

But *it* did.

Would you allow them to continue to take?

"*No*," he replied.

The chains snapped from the floor, and his memory absconded, no longer his own. Images flashed from within the darkness he surrendered to, glimpses of reigning violence.

Terrible and heavy, his clenched fists were warmed for moments gone too soon. Blood dripped from the walls and pained shrieks ascended. It was like he was drowning, but the wrath that once suffocated him became the air he breathed.

Suffer, the voice demanded of those distant and muffled cries. They had to, just as he was made to. Retribution or justice, whichever it was, his demand was paved in death. Eventually, the torturous halls he could never escape became a distant memory—banished to his nightmares.

When Eden opened his eyes again, he was beneath the sun. Bright but unfamiliar, he reached with blood-caked fingers and inhaled. His body was numb, but he yearned to fly into the sky, to touch it. It didn't feel real, and he expected to wake in the cell as he had many times before. A part of him wished he did. With such a terrible desire, there was the hope he'd see Cassiel again, calling him from the dark once more.

Stinging warmth spread through his fingertips, and the luster in his eyes faded along with his strength. His arm fell as the sun above shone on him, and the sentiment that liberated him slumbered again. Resting in his open palm was Cassiel's blood-soaked feather.

The only thing that remained.

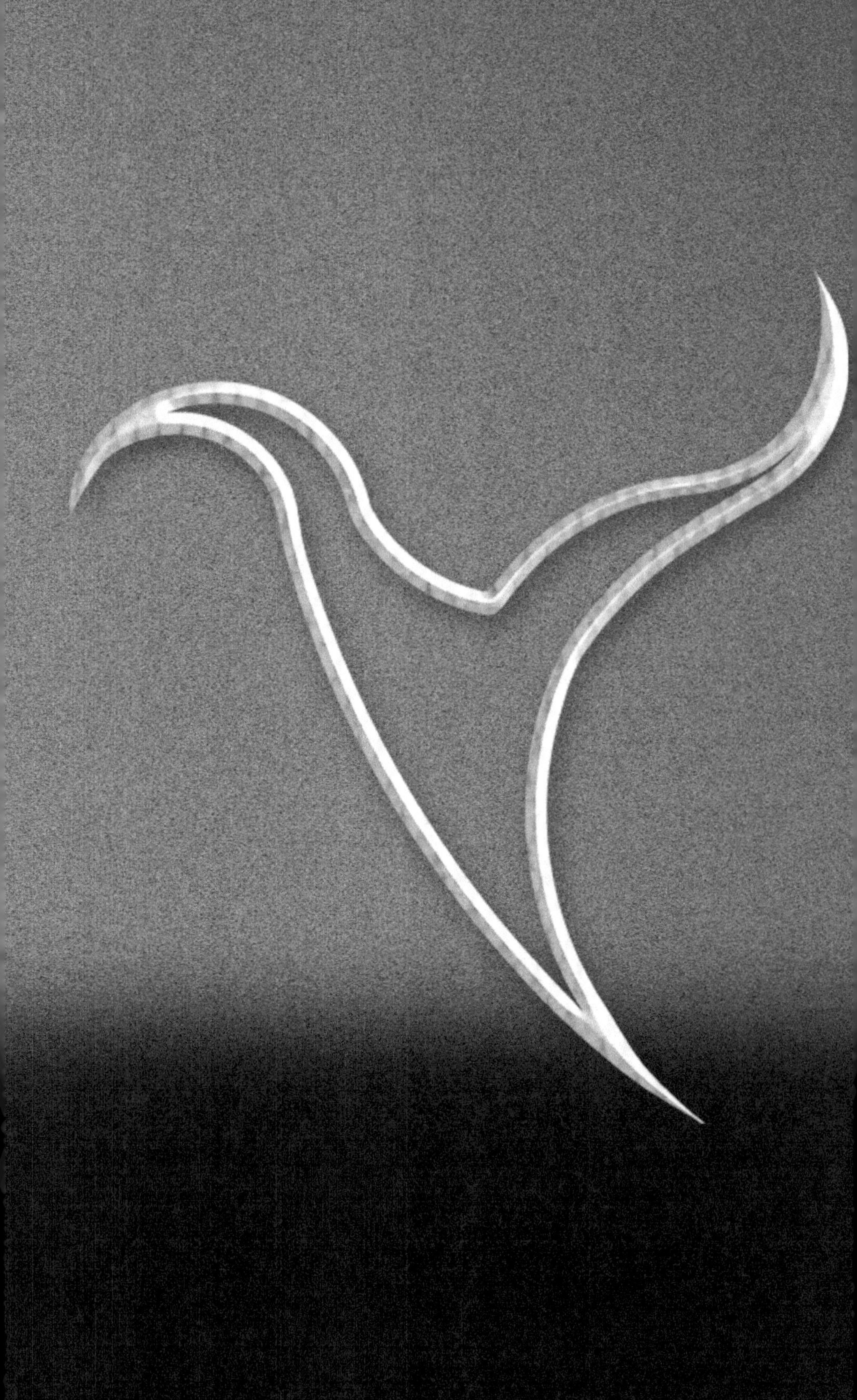

SEVEN

TORMENTED VAGRANT

ETHAN'S SHARP EYES danced across the pages in front of him—a knife that finely minced whatever it touched, and no minute fact escaped him. The personnel files he had religiously inspected were piled to the side. In that moment, his scrutiny was directed at Andrew's background sheet. There was a silent question that bubbled in his mind; no matter how revolting and bitter it was, he dared not let it fade.

He was pulled from his thoughts only by Zane entering the room, and the two guards outside closed the door behind him.

"Wanted to speak with me, Commander?" he asked. Ethan shifted, sitting straight as he stacked the papers and pushed them across his desk.

"I'll try not to take up too much of your time, Captain Larson."

Zane sat at the desk and clasped his hands in front of him.

"Considering I was napping, I'd say it's already too much," he spoke, dispensing the tension slightly and earning a snort from Ethan.

"I made an effort." Ethan's gaze flicked back to the desk, and he reached for another paper, spinning it to face Zane.

"In light of the recent incidents, we have begun borrowing from squads to supplement the afflicted teams. Right now, I am constructing a provisional squad, Angel Forty-Seven, for a mission, and I will be borrowing hunters from Seraph Nine and Seven to render it sufficient for operations."

Zane perked up, silently watching Ethan before nodding. The situation was eerily familiar. All hunters knew of the tragedy of the Sage Fortress in Berlin being wiped out. Such a similarity warranted greater attention from him.

"Alright ... who do you need from Nine?" Zane asked.

Ethan grabbed the stack of profiles, three of which were stapled. He then set them in front of Zane, spreading them out for him.

"Sergeants Anderson and Hopkins from your squad. I've pulled Private Carter from Seven."

"Andrew, huh?" Zane questioned, leaning forward and resting his chin on his knuckles.

"His results with Seraph Seven have been fruitful. He should prove auspicious for the mission."

"Really vamped up my gunblade recently. Kid's a genius. You should consider expediting the grants he's been seeking to upgrade the equipment we carry," Zane said, sitting up straight as he slid the papers back over to Ethan. "I'll make sure my people watch over him."

Ethan nodded, assured of Zane's declaration.

"It's the first thing on my agenda once the budget audit is done," he claimed, his gaze casting suspension and becoming steel. "I assume you understand the other matter I called you in for."

"Was waiting for you to prompt me. I have many thoughts on it," he said with an unpresuming stare.

Ethan stood and turned away from Zane. The tense silence built, and he took a deep breath.

"Does the name *Orphan* mean anything to you?"

"Unless we're discussing a masked vigilante billionaire, I can't say it does." Ethan turned, furrowing his brow.

"You know what a voidling is, I presume?" Zane's expression contorted, his eyes thawing from their cool disposition.

"Vaguely," Zane answered. His focus retreated to memories long since fractured, obscured by a deep sorrow. He refused to unearth it again and buried it once more. "Voidlings can pretend to be anyone, and we'd be none the wiser. I'm guessing that this Orphan individual has been playing the long game, but you suspected that already," Zane alleged, prompting Ethan to affirm his claim.

"My vigilance is unwavering, much to my detriment at times. From back when I sent you to Chicago to investigate the Covenant of Augury, I had my suspicions."

"Right under our noses, near and far. That's the only kind of fire I hate playing with." Zane clenched his hand, cracking his fingers as he let out a loud sigh. "Something specific happen recently to bring this to your attention? Can't imagine you pulled that name from nowhere."

"Yes. Private Mallory and Captain Blackwell of Seraph Seven encountered this voidling during their vacation in Chicago. Reviewing their report hasn't given me any clues, thus why I called you in. I considered bringing in the detective you recruited nearly three years ago, but he has been delegated to other matters already."

"Detective Stroth, huh? Considering how close he came to solving that matter as just a human, he'd probably be a better fit for this than me. I don't have any concrete suspicions," Zane claimed. He smirked, thinking back to when he last spoke to Julian. "But … if I were a betting man, I'd say it was someone pretty high up—someone facilitating operations."

"You'd be correct, I surmise. Though—it may not be *that* easy." Ethan turned again, his eyes drifting to the framed photo propped on his desk, his eyes faltering for a moment. "What is my body temperature, Captain Larson?" he asked, making Zane pause with a bewildered stare.

"Approximately 96.4 degrees Fahrenheit. A minuscule amount lower than usual, but I could chalk that up to the winter weather. Your heart rate is likely in the range of forty-eight BPM."

"And are you being charitable or coy when you suggest that?"

"The Ethan I know wouldn't be so trusting, is all," Zane said, staring blankly at him for several moments.

Ethan raised his sleeve, revealing his hunter bracer beneath it. With a few taps, a holographic projection shimmered, a small display showing his vitals appearing.

96.3°F

45 BPM

"Your answer did calm my nerves slightly, I admit. Only you could have guessed that with such a high degree of accuracy. Most would assume a variance within the average human temperature, but only you would know about my bradycardia without accessing classified files." Ethan lowered his sleeve, a smirk plastered on his face.

"You already knew that I wasn't Orphan, though. They could be the most talented voidling and still not replicate the flame of my soul," Zane said, expression puzzled before he began to chuckle. "Oh ..." Zane cooed.

"You really did just wake up," Ethan needled.

"Assuming that this Orphan fellow isn't a top-tier hacker with unsupervised access to our servers, I guess you're disqualified."

"As much as I should show indiscriminate skepticism, having people you can trust is that human thing I can't bring myself to relinquish," Ethan said, giving him a sheepish smile.

"If patterns held, I'd be inclined to agree." Zane sighed and relaxed in his seat. "Who're the suspects?"

Ethan placed his hands behind his back, recollecting details for a moment. The suspense in the room had resurrected, practically rumbling within the walls as the two men's gazes met

"While I have no hard evidence, I suspect someone a part of or adjacent to those who oversaw and managed communications in Chicago. This places several engineers, operators from Command, and even Commander Evans in the spotlight. I have already temporarily reassigned several operators while I investigate their logs further, but preliminary findings indicated some inconsistencies from that time period—forgeries, likely."

"Then during the raid on the Sieghart mansion, I assume our communications with Command and base were being jammed?" Zane asked, and Ethan shook his head.

"Not so overtly. It appears that the reports and information were received, but only partially, and with inconsistencies from the reports I received from you and others on the raid team. Given that Sergeant Jackson perished that night, I can safely assume his involvement was either minimal or nonexistent. No malfeasance indicating brainwashing was sifted from the husk of his spirit, and the audio logs pulled from his hunter gauntlet suggested nothing pertinent to the concern. This leaves Private Carter as the only engineer from the raid team, but for obvious reasons, I highly doubt he sabotaged communications prior to or during Harvest."

Zane listened, his chest tightening the more he had learned. In his own snooping, he never found anything unusual, but he recalled Eden telling him about the cowardly behavior of Commander Evans. He had seen the man refrain from flinching when a wraith exploded in his face, an indomitable certainty placed within the strength of his barrier and his lieutenant's aim. While he wouldn't claim Commander Evans was dauntless, it was suspicious that he froze before Intico. Still, he didn't think that to be overtly conclusive—just as Ethan insinuated.

Andrew, on the other hand, was an impossible option. The once-frail boy who was resigned to death behind the lenses of curiosity that had saved so many. If not for such a curiosity persisting, Zane doubted they'd have uncovered the scheme that sought to rob him and several other sick children of their lives.

"Andrew is a good kid. The best of us, even," Zane claimed, sincerity shining through his stark eyes. He had recruited Andrew personally, after all.

"I prefer believing that ..." Ethan spoke, bittersweetness lingering in his following silence. Regardless of what they believed, it was understood that those sentiments were the exact thing that could be used against them.

"There is no optimal way to look at this, and there likely is no simple explanation. I further suspect, with Seraph Seven's recent mission, that Orphan is actively working with Fracti Alas and seeking Captain Blackwell's recapture. To that end, I am keeping an especially close eye on him," Ethan continued, and Zane's expression twisted with a hint of annoyance.

"As you should. He's tough as hell, but rash when pushed. Orphan would exploit that," Zane said. The time Eden had briefly spent as his lieutenant had taught him that much.

"I'm sure the conference table we've yet to replace would corroborate your assessment," Ethan said, flashing a knowing smile, and Zane flexed his brow in amusement.

"Remember when you arrested me after the Athens incident? When you recruited me all those years ago?" Zane asked.

"Of course," Ethan replied. He took a seat and swept his silver hair over his shoulders. "You were quite determined to not wear the uniform," Ethan said, and Zane gave an unapologetic shrug.

"Still not a fan of them, in case you were wondering."

"I'm aware." Ethan rolled his neck and glanced down. "What about our initial meeting has you sentimental?"

"I was cracking sardonic jokes and feigning detachment. You didn't buy it one bit," Zane said, his eyes sharpening. "You decked me good and told me to stop playing pretend. Saw right through me." Ethan's unflinching steel gaze pierced through him once more, and he gave a sardonic smile. "Guess that was the cold water I needed to start working through my issues. You knew that wasn't me, or at least not who I wanted to be, truly. You reignited the embers that had faded when my mom died. I respect the hell out of you for that, and I'd lay down my life for our people ... uniform aside."

Ethan refrained from responding, merely meeting Zane's gaze with the stoicism he was known for. Zane stood and turned, approaching the door of the office. With his fingers firmly gripping the handle, he paused for several moments.

"If I discover who has betrayed us ... I won't hesitate to end their life."

"I know." Ethan stood, turning away from Zane. He peered at the image of his departed family that hung on the wall. "That's why I recruited you. You would do what I failed to so long ago."

Zane left the office, the guards outside the door taking to his side as they led him back to the elevator. He didn't speak with anybody else as he left the HQ building. The black SUV waited for him at the curb across from the front entrance, and he slowed down as he approached it. Insistent on unburying what was dead, his thoughts strayed with a spade again.

Voidlings.

He loathed knowing of them. One had killed his mother. He never divulged that to anyone else—not even Alysium, nor could he address it without losing face. No flame could overcome the coldness it brought.

Bitterness stung his tongue, a fermenting question. He found it difficult to mull over the idea, but the thought of Orphan and the unknown voidling from long ago prevailed against his efforts to suppress it. The indispensable bond with his mother, starved of embers, invited his scrutiny once more. Severed but bound to his soul, it kindled a bravery he had lacked. Even as a cold-blooded assassin.

It was a warmth he longed for more than any other, dreaming of the days her flames of dawn caressed him. Due to their golden hue, she was known as Irenaya, a name that meant *golden sky* in the blaze dialect of Indiox. He still rehearsed it sparsely in her memory, perhaps the sweetest of words he knew in the language. She had always tried to teach him, but he was slow on the uptake between already learning Serbian and English. It didn't help that he struggled with Latin languages.

Zane squeezed himself into the backseat of the SUV, his eyes finding Donovan, who furrowed his brow upon glimpsing Zane's expression in the rearview mirror.

"That ain't the kind of look you give, kid," he prompted bluntly. His black eyes scanned Zane with concern, and he huffed as he slapped his steering wheel. "Whatcha need?"

"Need to disappear for a few hours." Zane curled his fingers into quaking fists atop his lap. Donovan snorted, pulling onto the winding path that led out of the towering walls around the Rosemary Fortress's HQ building.

"I'll take you to your spot. Don't worry about the travel log—I dropped you off at the cafeteria as far as anyone will know."

Zane adjusted his tan parka, the fur collar snug against his neck as he fumbled with loose threads in the pockets. As finely crafted as something could be, it eventually weathered and frayed—many a time in places unseen. While red was his favorite color, he had always adored his mother's golden hair. He used to run his fingers through the silky tresses like he was petting fire itself. The fond warmth that once clung to his fingers towered above any he could ever hope to mimic with the thickest of fleeces.

When Alysium had asked why he wore the coat, he had refrained from being completely honest. No matter how warm he was physically, he was always cold. An eternal winter swarmed in his heart each time he dared remember his mother's voice calling him by the name she had given him.

Zaikio.

The wisps of her voice still wrapped around his ear, and he dared to reminisce again. The grassy field, wild and overgrown, stretched alongside the dilapidated street. It wound around several towering weeping willows, forming a garrison with swaying leaves that created a mask to hide away their secrets—*his home.*

Blaze magic pervaded the willow branches. Perception syncopation was an enchantment that steered eyes from scrutiny, only dispelled by familiar blaze flames. Near and far, it was roughly a hundred miles from the Hunters' base. Yet, for eighteen years, he had never visited.

The last he had seen, much of the home was charred by his flames. Anticipation filled him, although he was unsure of what he was searching for. He had long since abandoned the idea of closure. In his mother's absence, he doubted he'd ever know such maternal warmth again. Such vulnerability was beyond debilitating.

With a flick of his wrist, fire washed over the willow branches and arrested the spell. The modest house, made of thick slabs of stone and other non-wood materials, would have once been considered welcoming. Stretching around it were several pots and plant boxes where his mother had fostered her garden. Discolored and caked in soot, the soil was dry with thick, tangled weeds. His mother loved growing exotic flowers, but not one of them remained in the absence of her tender hands, and they were now strangled by the weeds.

Zane pushed through the dead grass, treading on the compressed foliage opposite the small black footprints that etched the ground. When he stepped inside, the brittle, rusted door crinkled beneath his boots, and he paused.

The living room blended with the same terrain that crept in from outside. Not so much as a picture remained. For a moment, Zane wished he still had the cellphone from long ago—a device that had never been connected, but he took many pictures on it. He wondered if it was still where he had left it in his room. Pushing through the ruins of the living room, he navigated to the east end of the home.

Zaikio, you are my sun. When Earth's rises in the sky, its light will touch you first, and when it departs at night, I will still feel its rays through you.

Her voice paraded, reminding him of the meaning of his name. *Wild Flame or Zaney.* Such rebelliousness was apt—perhaps self-fulfilling, the more he thought about it—but he pushed the impertinent thought down as he breached his old bedroom.

Across from the bed frame, a small piano remained, tucked into the corner. The taps of his footsteps dampened against the dirty tile, and he came to a stop before the piano. Trembling fingers extended, and he hit one of the keys. A detuned note chimed from the soundboard. The fact that it still worked was astounding, and in the absence of the stool that had burned away, he crouched to be level with it.

After pondering for several moments, he formed his hands into the ventus-diablo sign, making a weak gust of wind that cleared the keys of loose dust and ashes. His hands lowered, taking position before playing a simple song. As expected, it was horribly out of tune, but that added to the odd charm he found in its resilience. Deft fingers glided across the ivory keys, collecting the remaining soot that coated them. When he sought to finish the song, one key for the final note never played, lacking tension as it sank down into the slot.

Zane stood, cursing as the feeling returned to his legs. He peeked inside at the soundboard to see that one of the strings had snapped. There were spare strings tucked somewhere in his mom's closet. The shelf had been too tall for him when he was ten—just a year shy of his big growth spurt.

He still wasn't as tall as she was, nor any other pure-blooded blaze, but he could still imagine being called her *izirra*—titan flame.

Hesitantly, he ventured through the cobweb-covered halls. A hot aura licked the air in front of him, burning the webs away to give him a clear path. In what remained of her room, the furniture was either disintegrated or melted into deformity. Her closet was shut, albeit the door was compromised like the others. He carefully pried it from its hinges, setting it gently on the adjacent wall. Inside, her clothing remained intact, as he'd expected. Many of her dresses were from Inferos, made of threads capable of withstanding even the most intense flames—unlike the home.

The shelf had managed to not melt away like the other metallic furnishings in the home, and atop it, coils of golden wire were stacked neatly, albeit covered in dust. His palms never left his sides, clenching his jeans as his head dropped.

What would she say? Would she hate the kind of man I was? Would she forgive me for what I've done?

His shoulders bounced, and the fortress around his heart became ice once more. Ascending his throat, a million needles pricked his head as tears gathered in his eyes.

"Eighteen years and I'm still so cold without you," he spoke, his voice quiet and cracking. A dying fire inside of a chimney, his sobs were but the remaining smolders. Begging for kindling, they mixed with the frigid air as he turned, shaking his head. "No. Hold it together," he chastised himself, sniffling as he wiped his face with his sleeve.

He had allowed himself to reminisce too vividly. Abandoning his quest for the piano strings, he turned to leave the room. Down the hall, his father's study loomed, a room he had hardly entered—the room where he and his mother had died. The accursed day was something he'd never forget.

He had picked the last remaining scarlet celosia from his mother's garden as the sun set, and a man he hadn't recognized approached their home. Zane rushed inside to let his mother know, and she tucked him away in the cellar within his father's office, insisting he stay quiet inside of it. She had welcomed the man inside, knowing him to be a colleague of her husband's. While his mother was always kind and cordial to most, her tone that he had heard from beneath the floor was uncharacteristically cautious.

The noise that had ensued confused him, but he felt her flames lashing out and attacking to no avail, and gunfire roused his worry. Rather than staying put, however, he had foolishly raised the cellar door, peeking out to see the man holding his mother by the throat. When he lunged, the man easily knocked him away and pointed his pistol. There was a bang, then everything went dark. He had submerged into the shadows, their cool embrace inviting him into the infinite darkness to be erased and born anew. To the current day, it was the scariest thing he'd experienced, making him afraid to be in pitch-dark spaces ever again.

A bright golden light—his mother's flame—pulled him from the dark, and as if he had slumbered peacefully, he opened his eyes to see what remained. Only the husk of her being, both her soul and flame alike, absent. In his grief, his flames raged and razed the home. When he'd exhausted his power and fury, he fled, leaving the place behind.

There was a silhouetted figure on the floor now. There, the remnants of her body had faded, crumbling into dust. Unlike a human's body, blaze corpses never remained, instead disintegrating into cinders. The walls were stone like the rest of the house, but they were eroding. Unexpectedly, there was one piece of decoration that juxtaposed itself, having survived the hottest of his flames. A drawing.

In red ink, a weathered sheet of paper with the periodic table remained fixed to the wall. Zane had drawn it for his father the year before he and his mother had moved from Serbia. The thought of him stirred turmoil in the pits of his heart. He had resented his father's absence leading up to his mother's death, blaming him for not being there for them in the final years. It was childish, but that resentment boiled over. With a growl, he hurled a fireball at the drawing before collapsing to his knees and pounding the floor.

For years, even with the resources granted to him by the Alastairs, he had scraped every database and turned every stone in search of his father. Unfortunately, it was as if he had vanished from the earth. He once idolized the man so much that he sought to surpass his expertise—now, it was out of spite. A renowned human scientist in biochemistry, his contributions to the field were considered invaluable. He had worked with the Hunters long before Zane had even known of them. Many stories had not been shared about it all, for he was too young for his mother to have considered it—he resented that especially. It was why he had forgone the second half of his childhood.

His waking hours had been spent studying chemistry and demon alchemy, going so far as to neglect everything except his duties as an assassin. As formidable as he had become, he still preferred to preserve his energy for studying.

Zane was close to finishing his doctorate degree. Ethan had encouraged him to focus on it, even having sponsored his collegiate efforts with his influence. However, with everything that threatened the Hunters then, delaying his studies was a self-imposed obligation. He would never allow himself to remain idle while the lives of those he cared about were threatened.

Having calmed down at last, he peered up. There, facing him, the drawing remained—no different from when he rashly decided to burn it. Weathered as it was, its integrity and legibility were resilient to fire—his flames especially. As if having activated it somehow, his flames traveled along the ink and sequestered to a handful of the elements. He stood, approaching it curiously.

Of everything in the office, it was the only thing not only incombustible but actively resonating with Zane's flames. Some materials existed within Inferos that were immune to blaze fire, some even compatible with it in uncanny fashions. The sheet used for the drawing was torn from a sketchbook given to him by his father. He suspected that it was made of such material—likely to have kept from being burned in one of his tantrums. The ink simmered into a low gold, suggesting itself as more peculiar than his glance had suggested. *A message.*

Zane pried it from the wall and carefully inspected it. Upon flipping the page, his eyes widened when he saw a familiar amber resin fixed on the back. Cinros, a fireproof resin compound used in blaze architecture. The size of a thumbprint, he carefully peeled it from the paper. In his palm, he could see through it, noticing a proprietary data chip—the kind specifically for hunter technology. He pinched the resin between his fingers, determining there were two layers. Without hesitation, he pried it apart to release the chip.

It was intended to be found by a blaze, he determined. However, he knew of no other blaze residing in Mortale, let alone being affiliated with the Hunters. He suspected his father wouldn't have magically anticipated him becoming one either.

He shook his head, setting the drawing on the ground as he raised his sleeve, revealing his hunter bracer. He interfaced with it, scrolling through the options that projected before him. Once he opened access to one of the ports, he inserted it, waiting for the device to read it before it flashed a request for an eight-digit encryption key.

"Shit ... he had to have left the code somewhere," Zane muttered. There were tens of millions of possible combinations. He sighed and lowered his wrist. A brief search ensued, but he quickly gave up. He returned his attention to the drawing again, suddenly reminded that only a few of the elements had been glowing earlier. With the fire having faded, he scooped it up. With precision, flames coursed through his hand once more, and the elements illuminated again.

Vanadium, oxygen, iodine, and darmstadtium.

The arrangement was odd, but his eyes flicked across the atomic numbers and weights, scrutinizing it carefully. Of the elements, he could extract eight of the atomic numbers, but in what order to arrange them, he was initially confused. Moments stretched, and his eyes widened, the memory of the voidling roiling in his head. Why the being had sought his mother wasn't known, but he had heard their muffled voices speak of her golden flames. They were exceptionally unique, and on the page, their golden shimmer was present.

The idea manifested within the gnawing memory and golden glow on the paper. If blaze fire was intended to highlight the elements, it was intended to obscure the data from someone it wasn't intended for—someone like the treacherous voidling. That much, he had determined upon arranging the elements from the table.

V-O-I-Ds.

Zane saw it clear as day, albeit spelled differently due to the constraints of the elements' letters, but it was close enough.

2-3-8-5-3-1-1-0.

Zane keyed the numbers on his hunter bracer, watching as the menu of files expanded before his eyes.

"What the hell, Dad?" he huffed in amusement.

It wasn't the cleanest directory—the kind of thing he imagined would give the hyper-organized Andrew an aneurysm if he saw it. Odd formatting aside, the niche terms pertained to collegiate-level chemistry, something he could mostly understand. He was bewildered, doubting it was only research notes.

He arduously sifted through each file, refusing to neglect a single detail. An oddly placed folder titled *Dearest Irenaya* stuck out, juxtaposed beside the technically titled documents. Dated November nineteenth, 2024—a time prior to when he and his mother abruptly moved to West Virginia. Killing his hesitation, he melted the ice in his veins, tapped the file, and read its contents.

The research conducted by his father, Kalinik Lazar, meticulously detailed the machinations of his mother's unique flame and how it defied all that they knew of demons. Whereas infernal power typically harmed and subjugated Ichor, her own had coordinated with it in a way that was unprecedented. Her flame sought not to harm or malform, but to heal and remedy that with which it was originally ordained.

The golden flame was what allowed Irenaya safe residence within Mortale, whereas other blaze, as primonium demons, would struggle to maintain their being substantially. This was due to the energy demands of blaze's sweltering bodies. That problem alone was too great to overcome. Novas, the demons who evolved within Mortale, had no such issue. Unlike Inferos, Mortale was not so easy for demons to refine their power within, effectively capping their potential. Even Zane, a demonium, could only maintain his demon form for a few minutes due to the tremendous calorie demand. Refining Ichor to channel his infernal soul was just an additional hurdle to that issue. Irenaya differed, as Kalinik detailed.

Within the paradoxical nature of her power, it was something that he had studied. The report spoke of its secrecy between him and the blaze who permitted Irenaya's journey to Mortale. In a grave turn, Kalinik had come to suspect her golden flames were no longer a secret.

There had been an encounter with someone who had pretended to be his colleague—a voidling child banished from the mysterious paternal nature of Void—an *orphan* of it. Kalinik had seen that the golden flames stripped voidlings of their physical forms for reasons unknown. With his escape, he had penned the report for Irenaya as an explanation for why they had to leave: to protect herself and Zane.

The peculiar details of the voidling suggested their disguise was beyond mimicry. They had channeled near-indistinguishable characteristics of who they pretended to be. If not for the voidling accidentally brushing against the flame, he would not have known of its ruse. Without further evidence to conclude for certain, Kalinik suggested that the voidling could steal deeper knowledge somehow and cautioned Irenaya to use her flames against anyone she was uncertain of.

Zane lowered his wrist, suspending the projection temporarily as he gathered his thoughts about everything he had read. The timeline compiled, and something tugged at his heart as if trying to pry it from his chest. *He had been wrong.* His father had disappeared to protect them. But as hopeful as he could pretend to be, he knew the truth: his father was dead.

When they had moved, his mother changed his name to Zane. Contrasting greatly with her warm nature, she was near-militant in ensuring he memorized his new identity. She taught him how to get to and from home, disguise his energy signature, and everything necessary to remain obscured from prying eyes. He didn't know that at the time, however. The espionage of the voidling mirrored what Ethan had told him, and he reached a stark conclusion.

The voidling who killed his parents was Orphan.

Zane took a deep breath, stumbling back toward the wall as he processed this realization. The grisly implications imprinted themselves as a fresh doubt within his mind and an understanding that the mimicry that Orphan employed was far more troublesome than he'd initially assumed.

There were only a handful of people he knew he could trust, and he needed to confer with them in private.

He propelled himself from the wall. With dried tears staining his cheeks, he wiped them away using his sleeve and left his home. Emerging from the front door, he glanced to the left when a noise startled him. A raccoon pushed from beneath a collapsed tarp, dragging it a few feet before escaping into the wilderness. With the moment having passed, he laughed at himself as his eyes locked onto a single familiar red hue peeking from within the dead, overgrown grass. A single scarlet forest-fire celosia brimmed with radiance. He thought that the last of them had died long ago without his mother's care, but one survived somehow. Zane approached it and crouched, his fingers extending as he touched its petals. As if reacting to him, it became more vibrant against his fingers. Now close to it, he gleaned a golden hue nestled within its core—a beautiful flaw he had never seen in them.

Blue omens buzzed around him as he peered into the scarlet petals. The soft flower made his fingertips tingle, as if trying to convince his heart to thaw. A neglected warmth soon bloomed, if only for a moment, and for once since his mother's death, the cold retreated.

Zane had made his way back to the base, functioning under a generic guise of seeking out more palatable food from within a city. Something had bugged him when he had spoken with Ethan—namely, Andrew being pulled into a provisional squad. He always worried about him.

Andrew had come a long way from being a frail, bed-bound child brimming with enthusiasm for tech. Something about his optimism softened any fraying of his nerves. It had certainly served to keep him centered when they trekked through Chicago and jetted to the top of Willis Tower, not that Andrew knew of such a truth. He'd wager Andrew considered it the other way around on that trying night.

Seraph Seven, much like Zane's squad, was considered elite and highly capable. As much as he found Eden disagreeable, he considered his former lieutenant more than capable of taking care of his subordinates. With Andrew being pulled away from his umbrage, Zane's doubts mixed with the dwindling warmth from his discovery back home. However selfish it was, he wanted reassurance leading up to the heavy conversation approaching him.

Zane typically avoided driving to the Engineering Center, given its unpaved roads dirtied his car that he actively cleaned after every use. Instead, he walked from his squad's garage to seek him out. As he arrived at the stout stone building, he heard three voices from behind the garage, quickly spotting Alicia's SUV to deduce one of them. He had deliberately tracked Andrew's energy signature, so he was left with the mystery of who the third voice belonged to. He circled the garage to see him standing with Valeria and Alicia on a concrete patio, preparing to test one of his experimental devices. Rather than announcing himself, he smirked and watched in secret for the time being, intrigued to see what Andrew had been preparing.

Andrew clenched his fists, taking a wide stance with his dominant leg behind him as he braced himself. After a brief countdown from Valeria, metallic anchors shot from beneath the mechanism attached to his calves and bolted into the concrete beneath his feet. Shortly after, the exoskeleton of his suit locked into place, and he released his breath.

"It worked! That's much better than before!" Andrew said, his eyes wide as he laughed. Valeria let out a bright cheer as Alicia folded her arms, inspecting him as she gave a nod.

"It bolted you in about four inches, so it should be stable enough. We can't test out the cannons here due to the noise ordinance. Instead, I'll hit you with a sustained energy wave to simulate the forces you'd be subjected to when using them," she said and circled to stand across from him. "I'll catch you if those things disengage, of course."

"Roger," Andrew said, forgetting to lower his goggles under the assumption he wouldn't need them. He then braced himself with his arms extended out as if he were engaging the aforementioned cannons attached to the base of his gauntlets.

After a brief countdown, she recited a spell, and energy shot from her palms, causing a continuous force that tossed Andrew's hair. He stayed upright for several seconds until the energy died down.

Alicia clapped, giving him a nod as Andrew pumped his fists.

"Nice job, Drew. I'm pretty sure that'll serve you well for keeping the flying things away from your nests," she claimed, walking over and slapping his back.

"It's meant to be a way of dealing with both those and hordes of ferals that may bum-rush—like that one time in Cleveland." His face soured in thought. "Ohio was scary," he said. Valeria nodded in agreement, but Alicia shrugged.

"Eh, you should see Indiana. Gary is no joke with the concentration of rifts I looked into there," Alicia said. Shortly after, she pointed at Andrew's head. "By the way, your goggles flew off."

He reflexively grabbed at his forehead, stumbling for a moment as he prematurely disengaged his anchors as his suit's exoskeleton unlocked.

"Oh crap. Did you see where they flew?" he asked, his head whipping around as they searched for it. In a nearby tree, they spotted it dangling from a branch that would have been too tall for them to reach. Alicia had prepared to use magic to knock it down, but Zane whistled to grab their attention.

"I got 'em," Zane called out as he jogged to the tree, snatching them with ease before walking over to him. "Here you go, lil bro!" he said with a grin.

"Thanks, Zane. What are you doing over here?" Andrew asked as he took the goggles.

"Just thought I'd drop by and see what you guys are buzzing about today, given my squad is all wrapped up for the evening." They stared for a moment, but Andrew shrugged, reattaching his goggles to his head before folding his arms.

"Just finished testing out the new and improved anchors for use with my sonic cannons." Zane cocked an eyebrow in confusion, and Andrew continued. "New thing I'm hoping to unveil soon," he informed.

"Oh, *those* things," Zane nodded. "You've been talking about those things forever, huh?"

"I finally got enough money to go through with it and got approval from my dad and the Board of Engineering," Andrew said.

"Major Carter signed off on it? Congrats!" he said and glanced at Alicia and Valeria. "I'd take you out to celebrate if I had time, but maybe next month when things have calmed down a bit. New year, new headaches to deal with and all." He ran a hand through his shaggy hair.

"We'll have to see, I guess," Andrew said, meeting Zane's gaze and frowning. He looked away momentarily, turning his attention to Alicia and Valeria. "I'll meet you guys inside to head out in a few. I totally forgot I have to discuss the gunblade maintenance plan with Zane. I shouldn't be long," he said, earning a nod from the others.

"Alrighty. Let me know if you need me for another test before we head out," Alicia said as she turned and walked to the front of the garage. Valeria gave Andrew a kind nod, patting his shoulder.

"See you in a bit," she said and joined Alicia, leaving Andrew alone with Zane.

Before the two spoke, Andrew activated the jammer on his hunter gauntlet, and he sighed gently.

"You've always got the weirdest timing, but I also wanted to talk about what I was reading in those files you brought me a few weeks ago."

"You're getting better at reading between the lines—but actually, I was here about something else. It can wait, though," he said, giving a wry smile as he beckoned Andrew to follow.

The two made their way to the tree Andrew's goggles had landed in, and Zane grabbed a sturdy branch above his head as he leaned against the trunk.

"What's up?" he asked. Andrew crossed his arms and leaned beside him, eyes glued to the ground.

"There were a lot of people included on the list of hunter subjects Fracti Alas got ahold of. There wasn't too glaring a pattern from what I saw, but I did dig into the personnel files more to confirm one of my suspicions," Andrew explained. His gaze then lifted to meet Zane's.

"What suspicion is that?" Zane asked.

"It's targeted toward the hunters with high node counts. If you recall, I was doing a lot of the node mapping before I graduated into a squad. There were lots of people in the files that I personally took scans of, including Steiner." Andrew frowned. "That's what made me suspicious originally. Most of the subjects in the files I could recognize had a node count of eight hundred or higher—very rare, so I doubt it's a coincidence."

"Shit, really? That's probably 5 percent of our people, tops. Definitely has to be for their chimera research." Zane sighed, shaking his head. "What happened with the node maps you scanned during that time?"

"They were stored locally, as opposed to on a big server. The only ones who had access were the high-ranking hunters and a few other engineers." Zane was quiet for a few moments before replying.

"That's a big pool to suspect foul play from, but I'll keep it in mind. That all you got for me?"

"Yeah. Not much else I could decipher from it all." Andrew shrugged, standing straight before turning to face him. "So, what are you actually here for?"

Zane snickered lightly, his eyes softening as he glanced away.

"You won't believe me, probably, but I was just feeling sentimental about my lil bro." Zane sighed. "Lot on my mind right now, and I was just remembering when we first met at that children's hospital. I'm ... just glad I went with my gut and took you seriously after you hacked our comms."

"What has you thinking about that now? It's been six years." Andrew cocked his eyebrow.

"Just ... decided to let the emotions run a bit, and I started thinking back to my days with the Alastairs. I saw many people your age who I paid half a mind to. I can't help but feel like ... that one arbitrary decision I made to believe you is what gave me one of the best friends I could ask for. Has me thinking of all those damned *what-ifs*, you know?" Zane mused, memories of the demon children the Alastairs oversaw playing in his head, comrades and enemies alike he had seen perish—some by his own hand.

"I don't know why you paid much mind to a dying kid back then, when I think about it, but you really saved my life by vouching to have me become a hunter. Without the experimental treatment they gave me for the cancer, I'd have been a goner." He smiled wryly. "Even with you and Yuki breaking protocol to bust those OCN goons who wanted to feed my soul to the ferali." Andrew chewed on the inside of his cheek, his gaze flicking between Zane and his gloved hands. In response, Zane chuckled softly, shaking his head as he shrugged.

"I had a feeling about you—that you were the kind of guy I ought to break the rules to help. Maybe it's that you reminded me of myself when I was young—minus your bright smile, crazy intelligence, and every physical quality." Andrew cracked up, holding his sides as he shook his head.

"What are you even getting at?"

"I mean the fact you kept your head up and persevered despite your death prognosis. Said you would be lucky to make it to sixteen, and now look at you!" Zane gestured at him. "You're almost twenty and a badass demon hunter. Not bad at all, huh?"

"Still not strong or tall like you. Nor being someone every girl talks about like they do you or Eden," Andrew muttered with a pout.

"Oh, trust me, none of that is all it's cracked up to be," he said with a snicker, snatching Andrew into a half hug. "I'm sure Eden would sooner make out with his blade than give a girl a chance." Zane crinkled his nose. "Also, among the blaze, I'm considered tiny. My mom was nearly seven feet tall, and many are even taller. It's all about how you carry yourself more than the height or looks, I'd say." Zane leaned closer with a smirk. "Besides, what you've got cooking with Val is worth more than all the relationships I've had combined."

"I could still bear to be sturdier," Andrew claimed, nudging Zane and pulling away. "I never had a family until I became a hunter, and now I've got a whole lot of people to live for and protect. To use the second chance I was given the way you would." He pursed his lips. "That's part of why

I'm risking my neck hacking and snooping for you. If I don't pull my own weight, what kind of friend am I?"

"The kind I'd die to protect," Zane said without hesitation. "I became a hunter as a way of atoning for my past, but saving you, without a doubt, was a decision I felt genuinely good about." Zane held his fist out. "Weak or not, just know your big bro will always have your back."

Andrew stared in disbelief for a moment. Soon, his doubts numbed, and he flashed a bright grin as he fist-bumped Zane.

"Ditto."

Jessica's unyielding gaze trailed down the paper in front of her as her nails idly raked the lacquered wood of her desk. Hesitation plagued her mind the more she scanned the contents—several names of importance before her. The soft hum of a crystal suspended within a decorative glass case filled the silence. In its gentle ambience, she carefully reached for the mug beside it and lifted it from the coaster. The earthy scent of the tea was accented by rich citrus, and she took a long sip. She abhorred coffee, but it wasn't as if she enjoyed many teas either. It was almost ironic for a witch, but it was better than resorting to the half-empty bottle of gin tucked away in her cabinet.

Something truly tumultuous flared in her soul each time she saw her son's name on a page. She reasonably knew that he would handle himself as he did most times, but there was always the possibility he wouldn't. The guilt of what had happened with Harvest plagued her, and her absence from assisting Eden and her hunters alike roiled in her blood. Her oath as the Mistress of the Hunt and her obligation as a mother were both challenged again and again. She refused to yield to the evils before her, lest she prove herself correct once more.

Failure.

The Witch of Death, she was called. The reputation meant little before that festering opinion of herself. The suffering that many endured before her was all she could think of. Her father had died saving her and her sister over two decades prior. Her son had been subjected to unspeakable horrors, and even now, she failed to reach out to him.

Signing off on the assignments he'd endeavor were but reminders of how she had failed to protect him. Becoming a hunter meant he'd adopted that same desire to protect—to sacrifice. She desperately scrutinized the altruism her son declared.

His eyes were much like her own. In the rare chance she could peer into them, it was uncanny how they mirrored hers—submerged in darkness and drowning within its sentiments. Again and again, she learned she was powerless to save him from its toll. Vengeance, she knew. The toll she paid had been her father's life, and the toll it demanded of Eden she feared more than anything else.

She would have rejected any assignment his name was attached to, but she knew that denying him the duty he tenaciously adhered to was a fool's errand. She'd be remiss to see him adopt despair in place of courage once more. The image of his emaciated younger self was something she would never allow to come to fruition again—even if the compromise still tore her apart on the inside.

A single sharp knock roused her attention, and she inhaled lightly before setting the mug down. Her posture straightened, and she placed her hat atop her disheveled black hair before shoving the papers back into their folder. She turned on the small jammer hidden beneath her desk before conjuring a spectral hand that opened the door for Zane.

"Hello, General Blackwell," Zane spoke cordially, entering the office. The door slid closed behind him, and he approached her desk.

"You seem more agreeable than expected." Jessica's gaze sharpened. "Have you uncovered something pertaining to Fracti Alas since we last spoke?"

"A lot, and more to come, maybe," he admitted, giving a wry smile.

"You have been good to us, Zane—more than we deserve, I fear," she spoke, her eyes searching his own, and she relaxed a moment later.

"I wish I could believe that, madam," Zane sighed. "I discovered some things when I ... visited home."

Jessica's lips parted, her eyes widening a bit. She felt the semblance of grief on his breath.

"That must have been hard, dear. What provoked you after all this time?" she asked. Zane approached the desk and sat across from her. The menu of his hunter bracer flashed, and he navigated it before ejecting the data chip.

"I was speaking with Ethan about the voidling Eden and Kendra encountered. Infiltration aside, it reminded me of my own encounter with one long ago—the voidling who killed my mother. Nearly killed me too." Zane breathed shakily, his face scrunching. "Still unsure about how I'm here after that." Zane took the data chip and placed it in Jessica's palm, followed by a slip of paper with the key written on it. "I believe they're the same voidling we are dealing with now, as my father details in a letter he left for my mother. He hid this data chip in such a way that it could only be found and deciphered by her."

Jessica gripped the data chip firmly, her gaze drifting down to her hunter gauntlet.

"This is an old model—about two decades old. The data on this should be illegible by now," she suggested.

"It was stored in cinros," he explained.

Jessica stared in amusement, but she opened the data chip slot of her device and inserted it. Upon entering the encryption key, her eyes widened as the documents appeared. After scrolling for several seconds, she returned her focus to Zane.

"Kalinik Lazar is your father?"

Zane cocked a brow.

"You a fan of his work? I could have sworn I mentioned my dad was a biochemist."

"Your lineage was muddied in several veneers of paperwork, if I recall correctly. As if you began a brand-new life as a child. We thought it impertinent, given how you helped during the Athens incident. But this changes everything." Jessica navigated to the letter that Zane pointed out, tapping it.

"Dr. Lazar was a renowned scientist by human standards, but his insights were invaluable in studies of demon biology. He and several of his colleagues were contracted for a period under my father, Desmond, when he was the Master of the Hunt." Jessica scrolled lower on the directory, her brow furrowing. "His research revolutionized the Hunt. While he wasn't exclusively with us, it taught us to treat demon afflictions, allowing a second chance as homuntiums. His research quite literally saved me and my sister's lives."

"I imagine that wouldn't have been a good bedtime story for a kid," Zane spoke sardonically, chuckling darkly as he buried his face in his hands. He had hated the man for so long, spurred by his naivety and ignorance of the truth.

Silence followed while Jessica reviewed the letter further, her expression souring the more she read.

"Orphan ..." Jessica whispered as her eyes found the passage that had inspired Zane's suspicions. "They could be almost anyone, and those who would be involved likely also have that obedience hex you spoke of."

"Yeah," Zane spoke, his eyes shutting. "When I checked out that laboratory following Seraph Seven's breach, it turned out that the intel team were demons parading as us. Don't know what report you got back from that, but there was a hex placed on their tongues—obliterated the immediate area when one tried speaking that name. At least I presume she was going to. My memory was foggy trying not to get blown to smithereens."

"The intel team we sent were impostors then? That bodes poorly," she muttered, frowning. "I will have to see if a report or investigation was opened pertaining to them. I can hardly catch everything that pops up in a week, let alone a day."

"I did manage to get a different data chip out of it, though. Cracked it open with a little ... help. It's pretty dire, but some of our hunters have been abducted for research purposes. They're incorporating them into the chimera," Zane said, his teeth grinding at the thought. "Allegedly, the more pronounced connection to Ichor that the hunters have is relevant—yielding *promising* results in their experiments to synthesize them into those abominations. And we haven't even touched on how Orphan infiltrated us."

Jessica scowled as Zane explained the experiments, her fingers raking her desk. Zane then reached into his jacket and removed the data chip he had taken from the demons before handing it to her. She took it in her fingers, watching him with sharp eyes.

"I had it checked before bothering to open it, and it's all green. Just in case you need it." She shakily exhaled, relaxing her fingers as she tucked the chip away in her uniform, but her expression remained expectant.

"Do you have any suspicions of who Orphan is?" she asked.

"As cunning as they are, I highly doubt they can conjure the memories of who they parade as. It's like glamour on steroids, in a word. The rest has to be research and theater. Think a Hollywood try-hard." His fingertips rubbed along the grain of the desk rhythmically, thinking back to his conversation with Ethan.

"I can detect thermodynamic contrasts within the environment, like how Ethan is colder than most with an abnormally low heart rate. Small details that very few would know could be used as a trap—a way to find our mole." His eyes narrowed. "But ... thinking back to the fact they've been taking hunters with a greater connection to Ichor, including some of the cadets, gives me some ideas. Whoever is working with them must have greater details of their performance—their node maps and aptitude for squad placement. Many of them have been bastions, those with a higher aptitude from the get-go. Bears giving thought to the ones who oversee training."

Jessica didn't react to what he had said, her gaze fixed on the desk in deep contemplation.

"I've much to review then ..."

Zane pried himself from his seat, standing as he clenched his fists.

"Likewise. Would it be fine if you returned my father's chip to me when you're finished with it? I know protocol would demand procured evidence remain secure with a requisite authority, but—"

"I understand. More than you may suspect," Jessica spoke softly, lowering her wrist as she tilted her hat down. "I will keep it safe. If you discover anything further I should know about, don't hesitate to tell me." She pursed her lips and swallowed. "You may leave."

Zane gave a forlorn smile, the tension in his hands easing as he turned and approached the office door. As the bastion of all hunters, he knew his trust was best placed with her. There was no barrier he could imagine manifesting before Jessica that she would not be capable of overcoming. His trust was solid, but he imagined her trust in him was stronger.

Zane glanced over his shoulder, glimpsing the fear fermenting within her. It mirrored his own—impending loss. Orphan couldn't hide from her. It was a decision he'd hesitate to make if it was as he suspected.

"No matter how harrowing it may be ... I know that you'll do what's required."

After Zane left her office, Jessica released the breath that had become poison in her chest. The desk below her face became saturated with tears. Despite the absence of the vengefulness she had long forgone, another toll presented itself.

Without a doubt, she then knew she had proven herself correct again.

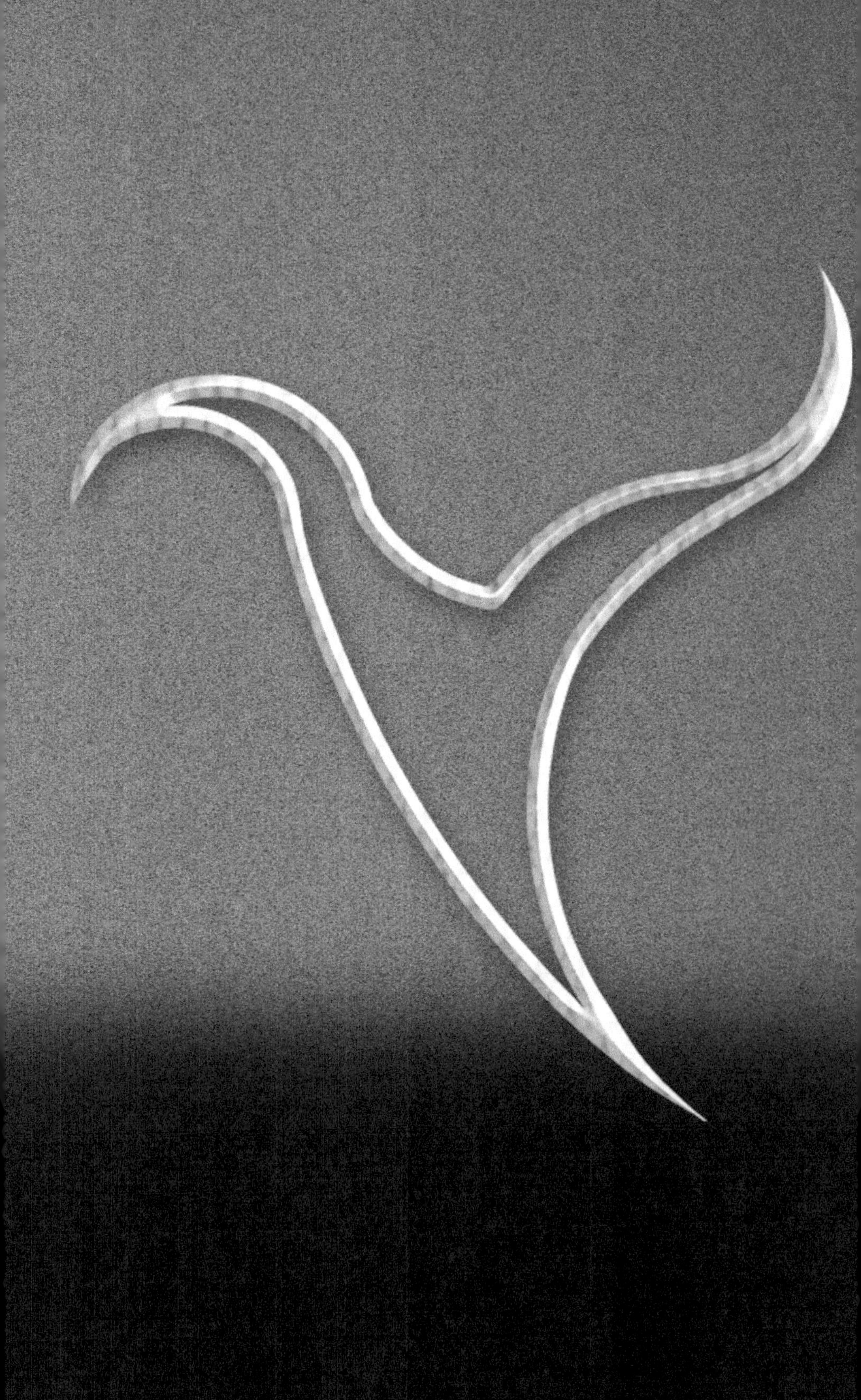

EIGHT

Indispensable Bonds

"ARCANAS AREN'T CUT AND DRY, and many times they're contextual," Kendall spoke in the video Kendra was watching. She had maintained the website hosting Kendall's vlogs, keeping it as a memorial. She rarely went through it, but she had felt reminiscent that afternoon and decided to watch the final one she had made.

"Your mindset and sentiments majorly influence what is drawn and what it means. Depending on the order and position you draw it in, its meaning differs. Tonight, I drew the death arcana for my sister. In the context of the two I drew before it, death represented the end of one thing and the genesis of another. It still freaked my sister out, but hey, change is scary!" Kendall reached toward the camera. "This has been Tarot with Kendall. I'll see you all tomorrow with another video. Bye-bye!"

The video then ended, and Kendra dismissed the hologram. She removed her smart band before tossing it into her nightstand drawer and standing from her bed.

The tarot cards she had taken from Kendall's deck were in her dresser drawer, and she made her way over to inspect them again. After moving her clothes out of the way, she spotted them next to the gleaming ice mirror Azazel had given her. The thought had been lost after Orphan's arrival, but upon seeing the mirror again, she remembered she had intended to speak with him afterward. She silently condemned herself for not expressing her gratitude sooner.

Kendra snatched it from the drawer. After reciting the incantation, which she had thankfully written down, the mirror pulsed with light as if ringing. Moments later, it shimmered with Azazel's visage manifesting on the surface.

"Hello there," Azazel greeted, flashing a cheeky smile.

"First of all, you could have told me what you were planning. I missed my coffee that morning because of you," Kendra huffed, her faux irritation drawing a laugh from Azazel. She paced around her barracks room.

"I assumed that her lucidity would be more effective than that concoction," he alleged. "In truth, I hadn't been positive that my theory would work, but the insight I garnered from you was more than applicable. I'm but one rime, so it may take a while to cover the some odd thousands afflicted."

Kendra leaned back on her bed, hoisting the mirror up as she stared into it.

"Regardless, you have my gratitude. Thank you, Zel. Really..." she spoke, shyly averting her eyes. "I'm guessing that healing my mom first was payment for the insight?" she asked coyly to shift the subject, and Azazel tilted his head.

"It was nontransactional. Consider it a courtesy from and for a friend," Azazel said. His frank tone spoke to the sincerity he commanded, and Kendra couldn't contain the sheepish smile forming.

"Friendship is an important commodity, some say."

"But what do *you* say?" he quizzed as his environment shifted. However, due to the lack of visual clarity, it was indistinct beyond his face.

"I think the commodification of human connection is dumb." Kendra squinted, looking away as she mused on the thought. "Actually ... I guess connections between anybody, seeing as I don't think that *human* part applies to either of us exactly. My point stands," she huffed out, making Azazel laugh lightly.

"It is interesting, the dichotomy of colloquial expressions. Demons are often hyperspecific when speaking Indiox, primarily due to how literal we must be. You would almost never find such a broadly optimistic saying—especially with interspecies camaraderie," Azazel mused, flinching when Kendra flicked the mirror.

"And what do *you* say?" she interrogated in return.

"I'm unconventional, but I imagine you suspected that."

Kendra fell quiet for a moment, jumping from the bed and adjusting the waistcloth of her hunter uniform.

"That makes two of us," she murmured. Azazel frowned, his visage getting closer within the ice mirror.

"Unconventional or not, I can tell something is troubling you. Pray tell?"

"Dealing with a lot right after my vacation. Actually ... the problem began the other day, so I cut the vacation short to deal with it." Kendra perked up and gathered her thoughts. "What do you know about voidlings?"

Azazel's expression suggested graveness, but it mellowed quickly.

"They are particularly mischievous on the best of days, quite playful and innocent should you be lucky to see one," Azazel began, his eyes darkening. "However, that innocence obscures the threat they can pose. They are unfettered by the boundaries of Ichor and the realms, and as such, they are capable of much that we are not. Should one be unfortunate enough to be ejected from the void, their one limitation is effectively neutralized."

As Azazel spoke, Kendra paced nervously, her fingers dragging along the dresser as she trained her eyes on the floor. Back and forth. Innocent and naïve were far from the adjectives she'd have used to describe Orphan during her encounter with them, but Orphan was perhaps atypical even among their kind.

"They pretend to be people?" she asked, her voice low.

"They can," Azazel answered. "Not typically with cause for concern, given energy signatures differ from being to being. Even if they are talented in that ability, it is mostly relegated to appearance. I would deign to call their true essence something akin to a soul, but its energy signature is distinct if you understand how it operates."

"Is there a but?"

"There have been times when they were exceptionally talented in their deception, so take what I said with a grain of salt. I am no expert." The helpless nature suggested by Azazel gnawed at her, creating her next question.

"How do you kill one?" Eden had indicated that he just needed to keep *killing* Orphan's forms, insinuating a limitation. That wasn't something she dared to bet on, however, especially given that drawn-out attrition was disadvantageous for her.

Azazel pensively held her gaze, but he let out a long sigh after a moment.

"If you could call it killing, there are two methods to dispose of them. You may attack until they deplete their corporeal essence, from which they mold their appearance, or you may bind their being to a form and dispose of their essence directly. Unfortunately, the second method is inaccessible to most without extensive arcane knowledge." Azazel frowned, tapping his chin as he considered the infernal nature of the voidlings.

"Void magic is dangerous to contend against, especially if you are blindsided by it. It does not abide by the laws of our reality, and its nature is volatile," Azazel said. Suddenly, a muffled female voice spoke to him, prompting him to look away from Kendra. "Yes, Koyaku," Azazel spoke cordially, releasing a sigh. "I must take my leave. Do exercise caution in your coming plights."

"Thanks, Zel. Until next time," she said, giving a small wave before hanging up and making her way back to her dresser. Her gaze lingered a moment too long on the three tarot cards. Orphan's despicable parading as her dead sister spurred another flash of rage to course through her. Once she cooled her head, she set the ice mirror inside next to them before snapping the drawer shut.

The Engineering Center was a complex of several garages, some including warehouses for the larger machinery. It was south of the training fields, directly across from the primary armory. ATVs were recommended due to the terrain not being paved—a purposeful decision by the original architects of the base, according to Bonnie. Not many cared, however. Many standard vehicles belonging to hunters were present by the garages.

That afternoon, Seraph Seven was scheduled for equipment maintenance, and Eden suggested they have the first squad meeting of the new year take place in tandem. Kendra suspected that he got there early on account of his sleeping troubles. Their encounter with Orphan wouldn't have helped either.

She sat in the back seat of the hoodless ATV, the wind whistling and flicking her braid as they crossed the dusty terrain leading to the garage assigned to her squad. The buildings were imposed beside each other, occupied by squads who assembled for gear maintenance, utility drills, or simply to sit atop coolers while speaking.

A familiar face presented itself in the group of hunters from Seraph Nine in front of garage F-17—Cassius Moreno. He was a young man with cocoa-colored skin, short black braids, and sunglasses that covered his golden-hazel eyes. He wore the standard hunter uniform but superimposed a long black coat with a bulky collar that framed his sharp chin. Upon spotting Kendra riding by, he smirked and flipped her off.

Responding in kind, Kendra stuck her own middle finger up, its claw extending to one-up him. It successfully drew a laugh from his squad members beside him. Kendra relaxed back into her seat, smirking with satisfaction as her driver, Sergeant Devon Charles, chortled.

"Best of friends?" he asked, glancing back at her as he slowed down, approaching the garage assigned to Seraph Seven, F-19.

"Yup. That was our way of communicating birthday plans," Kendra said. With the not-so-healthy rivalry they had during their training to be hunters, she made it a point to insult or show him up whenever she got the chance. It wasn't out of malice in the strictest sense, considering he still insisted on calling her *Kendra Malarkey*. She had no reservations responding in kind. The hours of vulgar language and jabs she endured working for James left her uniquely equipped for that. Ethan was mildly amused when he had witnessed them argue, but the humor was lost when he made them both clean the toilets with toothbrushes—on a Tuesday night. Her sensitive nose could never forget.

They approached the building, and she eyed the closed garage door as they came to a stop in front of it. Beside it on the right side was a normal door. Eden had sent out a memo about the garage door undergoing repairs; otherwise, she was used to entering through it. The civilian door was a mild inconvenience she could live with.

"Feel free to pop in for a cold drink before you head out."

Devon shook his head, patting the hydro flask next to him.

"Nah, already had my Claymore this morning. Don't need to kill my heart *and* liver before I'm thirty."

Kendra flinched, grasping her heart performatively. She remembered the particular energy drink brand as being way too strong.

"Isn't that stuff 450 milligrams a can? For shame, sir." Kendra clicked her tongue and patted his shoulder before hopping out of the ATV. She waltzed to the building door, glancing back and raising her hand. "Later, Charmander," she chirped, remembering how he collected the cards from that series.

"Says the woman who breathes fire," Devon said with a sigh before pulling off.

Kendra scanned into the building, walking through the hall that led to an open lounge area with several workstations, shelves, and machines bordering the room. Kendra eyed the node scanner in the northeast corner of the room. It consisted of a large circular pad with several scanners attached to arches looming above it. Nodes were the access points through which Ichor flowed from and into each person. Given node networks differed, the machine revealed where the nodes were for the hunter suits to be adjusted accordingly.

For those who refused to wear the standard uniform, such as Eden and Zane, the machine wasn't particularly useful beyond gleaning insight or enchanting other gear. For Kendra, she had learned that the clusters around her hands and throat were the most prominent. That didn't surprise her. Manifesting flames in her palms and breathing fire were particularly easy.

Her attention shifted to the others of Seraph Seven. They were mostly gathered near the workbench Bonnie occupied, where she was busy using a screwdriver. Upon Kendra's approach, she saw one of Eden's maneuver bracers, freshly reassembled. Bonnie slammed the screwdriver down with a satisfying smack and inspected the bracer carefully for several seconds before nodding.

"All done with the second, Cap'n," Bonnie said and tossed the bracer to Eden, who caught it.

"That was quick," Eden said, appearing amused.

"Would have been quicker, but calibrating the motors takes a bit of time. The new power cells should notch up the torque about 15 percent or so, and I added a second trigger for the variable gear ratio system I installed. For the new trigger, send quick pulses through the nodes on your wrists to prioritize speed once you've got some momentum going. The standard you'd still use from lower stationary or lower vantage points. Should be more efficient on the energy demand that way," Bonnie explained. She wiped her brow with a rag as she spun around to face the squad.

"And if I want to yank a demon from the air, which is preferable?" Eden asked, making Bonnie scrunch her face.

"Don't recommend it since physics is a thing, but since I know you're going to do it anyway ... standard trigger is still the best. More torque," Bonnie said, rolling her eyes.

Eden nodded silently, setting the bracer down on an unoccupied workbench before he unclasped his jacket and removed it. He wore a black vest beneath, exposing his arms as he placed the maneuver bracers on.

Kendra's gaze was fixed on the light scarring that lined them—jagged teeth and claw marks, most prominently—but her attention diverged in discomfort quickly. Kendra cleared her head and glanced over to a distracted Valeria, who was staring up from her tablet at Eden. The two girls' gazes met, and Kendra acknowledged her with a knowing wink. Valeria huffed and made a face at Kendra before ducking behind her tablet to hide her blush.

The rest of the squad was locked in conversation. Alicia, Damion, Emily, and Joseph bantered, and Yuki took to striking up a conversation with Eden, which was almost too quiet for her to hear over the others talking—a discussion about his sleep, she had gathered.

Upon realizing it was of a more private nature, she tuned them out and looked around for familiar blue eyes she hadn't yet seen. Andrew had been absent, and she frowned, wondering why. She approached Bonnie, her fingers gripping her waistcloth as she searched the room.

"Andrew okay?" Kendra began, and Bonnie gave a nod.

"Yeah. He got pulled this morning to work with a provisional squad for a mission."

"Oh, and here I was hoping he'd have that info I asked him to look into," Kendra said, secretly dejected she didn't get to see that signature grin of his.

"Oh, about adjusting your suit to mesh with your most recent map? He left notes on that, so I've been looking into it already. I can adjust your suit right now. Should only take a few minutes," she said, patting her bench to invite her over. Kendra nodded and approached, leaning against the bench as Bonnie prepared her desktop to interface with her suit.

Kendra glanced at Alicia while Bonnie did her work, and she remembered she was going to speak with Alicia about the incantation that Azazel spoke of.

"Yo, Alicia. Got a minute?" she asked, rousing Alicia to peel her attention from the others, and she held a finger up. Excusing herself, Alicia walked over, arms folded across her chest.

"What's shakin', Ken?" she asked.

The similar appearance between her and Eden still bewildered her when she saw them up close. Those jade-green eyes were a prominent feature she had known Eden for prior to her connection. It wasn't lost on her how that small detail had likely saved her.

"Apparently, Val when she saw Eden just now," she said teasingly, making sure Valeria could hear her, which prompted the girl to roll her eyes.

"What can I say? Ladies can't resist us," Alicia said, glancing at Yuki.

"Getting to the point ..." Kendra continued. "I wanted to probe you about some magic stuff, since you're General Blackwell's apprentice and all."

Alicia cocked her eyebrow before blowing a strand of hair from her face.

"I'll see what I can tell you."

"Hypothetically, if I was fighting a demon like a legion, and I didn't want it splitting into potentially hundreds of forms, is there a way to prevent that?" She knew the question lacked credulity, given the demon's rarity. Legions were human once, only becoming demons once a possessed person had been infested by several wraiths. They were tricky to deal with, even under the best of conditions.

"A legion? Very rare you'd ever fight one, but it'd be easier to exorcise it," Alicia said, her gaze skeptical.

"I like to be prepared for anything. Like, what if I got hit with a silencing hex? Or just accidentally bit my tongue really hard?" This made Alicia snort.

"That'd be very unfortunate, but alright. There's another method, but saying it's difficult would be underselling it." Kendra nodded.

"Hit me," she prompted, and Alicia held a finger up.

"A soul binder is the way to go, and yeah, it'd be even easier if you had one, but getting one is the problem. You'd need to know eighth-circle magic, and I'm barely learning seventh." Alicia shifted her hand to her hips, glancing away. "Two, you'd have to manufacture a conduit capable of anchoring a soul, which is difficult for a variety of reasons. Either you need an intact reaper gem from a ferali, or a duscillium crystal. Good luck getting either." Her brow furrowed. "The crystals only form in Inferos, and the only source on Earth is through the Nexus, which isn't an option for obvious reasons."

Kendra sighed lightly, rubbing her head as she shifted against the bench. While Kendra never encountered a ferali, she knew they were usually angel-classed or higher. Neither were they common to encounter, from what she knew. She doubted one would willingly give away her reaper gem—something tantamount to suicide.

Her attention returned to Bonnie when the woman patted her thigh.

"Brace yourself. The synchronization of the new profile is commencing," Bonnie warned.

A jolt of warmth flashed across her body, and her wrists and collar vibrated, causing her to tense. After a few seconds, her suit returned to normal, and she sighed in relief.

Bonnie clasped her hands together and disconnected her terminal from Kendra's suit before closing the projection.

"Done. Should be calibrated to mitigate synthesization overload around your wrists and neck. Your flames shouldn't run as wild with the bottleneck I installed too. But don't slack on upping your skill—ain't no substitute for that."

"I'm working on it," Kendra groaned, clenching her hands repeatedly. She couldn't feel a difference, but she didn't doubt her comrade. "Thanks, Bon-Bon."

Kendra looked back at Alicia, giving a wry smile before holding her fist up to her.

"Appreciate the insight. Let me know if you ever come up with a better enchantment to keep me from burning my suit off."

Alicia bumped the back of her fist to Kendra's, smirking deviously.

"And ruin the fun?" she teased, and Kendra stuck her tongue out.

A sharp clap rang through the room, and a gruff voice called out. "Attention!"

As if activated, the squad stood straight, turning to face the voice as their hands snapped behind their backs.

"Commander Evans, sir!" they spoke in unison.

Commander Evans eyed them sternly, nodding approvingly after a moment before he gestured his hand forward. Behind him, Jessica strode forward and came to a stop, peeking from beneath her hat.

"Hold your salutes. You may ease your stances," Jessica said, a ghost of annoyance in her tone. Her eyes flicked over to Eden, who was the first to drop his hand, stepping forward. She eyed the scars along his arms and neck for a moment, lifting her head as she pursed her lips.

"I hope the elite hunters of Seraph Seven are doing well today, especially the young bloods. Please step forward, Privates Mallory and Alma."

Kendra and Valeria approached, stopping in front of Jessica as she scrutinized them briefly. Jessica circled around them to place her back to the rest of Seraph Seven while she spoke with the two, who then turned to face her properly again.

"I trust you have both acclimated to the challenges that have been imposed on Seraph Seven. It has been about half a year, after all," Jessica prompted. Kendra was first to answer.

"Yes, ma'am. I have worked closely with—uh, Captain Blackwell and Lieutenant Schaeffer to ensure I properly execute what is expected of me as a blade," Kendra spoke. She bit the inside of her cheek, cursing her slip of almost calling Eden by his first name. While Jessica's expression suggested she didn't care, Commander Evans winced.

Valeria perked up when their attention turned to her, and she prepared a response.

"I have also worked closely with both Captain Blackwell and Sergeant Rigs to execute the duties expected of me as a cannon," Valeria spoke stiffly, her face taut.

Jessica gave a nod, spinning on her heels to face the other members of the squad.

"And your summaries of their performances?" she asked, and Eden began first.

"Privates Mallory and Alma have both shown exceptional courage in the face of demonic threats in the course of our operations. Neither has shown any significant mistakes unbecoming of privates. Any erroneous behavior I have witnessed has been coached against, and advice was administered accordingly. While not required, I have kept track of their combat effectiveness," Eden stated, earning a confused expression from Kendra and Valeria when they glanced over their shoulders.

"Private Alma has exactly sixteen kills, three of which are unconfirmed. Private Mallory, on the other hand, has fifty-five kills, fifty-six if you count Intico prior to her enlistment. Of those kills, twelve are confirmed."

Commander Evans's face contorted in bewilderment, and he glanced at Kendra before raising a brow at Eden.

"Why so many unconfirmed?" he asked.

Eden's eyes narrowed, and he bit the inside of his lip for a moment as he composed himself.

"Tallying efforts are challenging given Private Mallory's tendency to run hot."

Seraph Seven chortled at the explanation, as did Jessica.

"Well in line for a squad of this caliber."

"If we're counting from before I became a hunter, then fifty-seven is a more correct number. I killed that one somnium at the police station too," Kendra added, and Eden nodded.

"Fifty-seven total kills, thirteen confirmed," Eden stated.

Jessica waved her hand, turning her attention to Yuki while Commander Evans stood silently.

"Do you have any comments, Lieutenant Schaefer?"

Yuki stepped forward, flicking her white braid over her shoulder.

"Private Mallory has adapted well to close-quarter encounters and exhibits a keen awareness of her surroundings. Both that and her reflexes show her capable of executing her missions and roles within the commands given by Eden and myself," Yuki explained.

Jessica turned her attention to Damion, her eyes expectant, and he folded his arms, staring at Valeria pensively.

"She's a steady shot, quick to react and adapt as necessary. Can't say I have any complaints. She knows more about weaponry than anybody else in the squad, Lieutenant Blair included. It's nice having a walking encyclopedia on the squad, so I give my praise," he spoke. While the two superior hunters weren't looking, Valeria nodded in approval.

Jessica and Commander Evans listened intently, exchanging glances as the squad members went on. They privately deliberated once they were finished, and while Kendra had thought to listen in on them, her high-strung nerves made that impossible.

With scrunched faces, Kendra and Valeria glanced at one another. Calling Eden by his first name would have been a ticket to being *smoked* by Commander Evans, something nobody wanted. It hardly helped that Commander Evans insisted on calling her *Kenny No-shirt* when he'd chew her out—something she chalked up to chauvinistic disdain for her least prideful training moment.

Jessica and Commander Evans turned their attention back to the squad, finding Eden and Bonnie. With a tense confrontation of gazes, Eden opted to shift his position and grab his armored coat to disguise the suspicion in his eyes before Jessica began speaking.

"While Private Carter isn't here, I am obliged to also inquire about his performance," Jessica said, and Eden slung his jacket over his shoulder.

"Private Carter, while not physically noteworthy, has been an important asset to Seraph Seven. He has seamlessly integrated into his role and provides several valuable insights throughout our missions and operations." Eden then turned his gaze to Bonnie, who appeared less skeptical than he did.

"Like Captain Blackwell said, he's got some physical work to do, but his expertise really shines. Audio frequency tuning, positioning, and elimination of disadvantageous obstacles to continued communication and hacking procedures. He's got it all on lock."

Commander Evans's eyes hardened, darting between Eden and Kendra.

"No breaches of procedure or unauthorized equipment?" he asked, his firm gaze boring through Bonnie as she shook her head.

"No, sir. Everything he uses is approved beforehand. He's got a million ideas for us, but he complies with the ordinances we have in place with the engineering directors."

Eden's eyes narrowed further before he looked away. With a soft sigh, he placed his coat back on and snapped the front shut, finding Jessica as she relented in her questioning.

"Excellent. My hopes have been rather high for the boy. I am certain Major Carter will be proud to hear such damning praise of his son," Jessica spoke, feigning a smile as she waved her hand. "I won't keep you all, but I would have a word with you, Captain Blackwell and Private Mallory." Jessica directed her gaze to Bonnie next. "Lieutenant Blair, stand by. You are needed for a separate matter." She turned and relocated to an unoccupied corner of the room, and Commander Evans repositioned to the primary doorway.

Seraph Seven went back to speaking with each other, and Eden exchanged glances with Kendra. The two carefully approached Jessica, their gazes infirm upon stopping in front of her. Eden decided to dispense with his feigned ignorance, folding his arms as he broached the topic.

"That was unusual," Eden muttered.

"There is a reason you're a captain," Jessica reminded, folding her arms above her chest as she tilted her head down, hiding her face with the brim of her hat. "I won't discuss anything here, but there are matters arising quickly, and Commander Ardon would speak with both of you personally. In two hours, you will be contacted through and will be transported to a private entry of HQ."

Kendra furrowed her brow, bewildered by the highly unusual circumstances being proposed, but before she could speak, Eden nudged her.

"Understood. We'll go prepare," he replied without hesitation. Jessica's gaze narrowed when she peeked up at Eden, eyeing the darkening marks beneath his eyes.

"Perhaps rest as well," she whispered. With no further words, she walked past them to stand at the door, waiting for Bonnie.

Bonnie had finished gathering her things, then gave her farewell to the squad before she left the room with Jessica and Commander Evans.

"What's going on?" Kendra asked Eden in a whispered voice, both pensively eyeing the door. He shook his head dismissively, gesturing to the rest of the squad. Anticipation ate away at her, rousing an unsteadiness in her anew. When he returned to the others, she dragged herself behind him, stopping once she was beside Valeria.

Eden snapped his fingers loudly, garnering the squad's attention.

"There is nothing further I have prepared for today. With that, I disband Seraph Seven's very first meeting of 2046. You may commence with the rest of your day as you see fit, but as always, I highly encourage training," Eden said. He then placed his hands in his coat pockets before walking toward the door.

The squad seemed confused for a moment, but they quickly took to making lunch plans, except for Valeria, who tried to speak with Kendra. However, Kendra held a hand up, shaking her head.

"Sorry, have to attend to something too. Catch up later," she whispered, and Valeria gave a tepid nod before slumping back onto the couch. Kendra then took off after Eden, following close behind as he emerged outside.

"Hey, hold up, Eden," Kendra called, taking a deep breath as she conjured her barrier. With it, the wind and dust deflected away from her face. She stopped when he stood still, and Eden glanced over his shoulder at her.

"I was gonna go catch a nap back at the barracks."

"Oh, uh ... got it. Not that important anyhow," Kendra sighed, hoping she'd have gotten to pick his brain more. She had skipped eating when she got up that noon, and her negligence became apparent when her stomach rumbled. The regret in not joining the squad for lunch was strong, but she imagined she could still catch them.

"Eyo!" a familiar voice called out to Eden and Kendra, and both looked to see Zane approaching.

Kendra thought her gut instinct to be accursed, the rumbling a herald of Zane's arrival rather than hunger. It was one aspect of the humor she found, as she could practically hear Eden's groan from his expression.

"Sup, Seven?" Zane continued, stopping in front of them and holding his hand up, presenting a gleeful smile as he eyed the two.

"Nitwick," Eden spoke flatly. Zane grimaced at the nickname, and Eden crossed his arms to avoid high-fiving him. Instead, he showed skepticism in his gaze. Kendra was less hostile, but feigned aloofness as she reached up and tapped his hand.

"Sup, Zane?" she asked.

"Just lollygagging, thinking of catching a bit to eat," Zane began.

"Andrew's freezer is off limits. He told me to make that clear to you if I saw you," Eden interrupted, and Zane clicked his tongue.

"I figured with you hanging around Mallory, you'd be less cold," Zane alleged. "No worries about that. He cleared it recently, anyway. Besides,

Schaefer had invited me to join them for lunch, so I came to talk with them about it."

Eden cocked his eyebrow, and Kendra shrugged, thinking little of it.

"You're paying your own way if you're tagging along. You'd empty the meal stipend for our entire squad by yourself," Kendra said, indicting Zane's eating proclivities.

"It's cool. I get extra," Zane said with a sardonic smirk. "Speaking of eating, I've been meaning to have you come and try out the new syn-blood formula I've been working on for you. We've been talking about it for a while," Zane said, flicking his ear and twisting his wrist to flash his hunter bracer.

Kendra glanced at Eden's deadpan expression. She hadn't talked with Zane about a new syn-blood formula for several months, and his accompanying gestures definitely caught her attention. Cocking her brow, she knew something was amiss.

"Sure," Kendra said, her tone unassuming. "Captain Blackwell comes with me, though. Just in case your janky formula makes me want to rip a throat out," she suggested, and Eden folded his arms, staring at Zane with a mix of exhaustion and concern.

"If you must insist ..." Zane sighed insincerely, giving an appreciative thumbs-up before gesturing in the direction of his squad's garage. "I'll take you in my bird. It's easier." Zane walked off, leading them to the garage, Kendra and Eden slogging behind in silence.

When they reached the open garage center, several vehicles, both personal and armored, were parked within. Zane clicked the key fob in his pocket, and one of the vehicles, a satin black Akicita Thunderbird, revved to life. The low purr of the electric engine made Kendra wince. Instinctively, she reached into the pouch attached to her belt and removed two noise-canceling earplugs Andrew had made her, placing them in her ears.

Zane chuckled lightly, folding his arms as he clicked another button on the fob, causing the muscle car-styled coup to back out and stop between them.

"EVs bug your hearing?" he inquired.

"Just the American-made ones," Kendra mumbled, and Eden smirked at her remark. Zane rolled his eyes dismissively. The two doors slid open, and the front passenger seat slid forward to let them inside.

It was a short ride back to the barracks. Once parked, they promptly made their way to Zane's room, being across from Eden's in what both of them considered a cruel joke by their superiors. Zane marched over to his bed, reaching beneath the frame and hitting the jammer switch before he sighed in relief.

"Good thing you guys caught on," he said.

"You never use last names off the wave," Eden replied, marching through the room and leaning against the dresser. He locked his attention on the blinds, where diffused light bled into the plainly decorated room.

Zane relocated to his desk, which was akin to the ones in chemistry labs. He tugged the cabinet door open and rummaged through it for several moments before he tossed a Ziploc baggie of small tablets at Kendra. She caught it and shot him a confused look.

Unlike her usual syn-blood tablets, they were a redder coloration with a dubious crystalline sheen to their surface. Seeing Kendra's face twist, Zane snickered and waved his hand.

"I wasn't joking about the syn-blood formula. Spruced up your standard dose to be a lot more amenable to your energy demands. It's a reapplication of my serum formula distilled into a tablet. Should give you some extra kick for those tough days out on the field."

"Doubt they're FDA-approved," Kendra said, a scowl forming. "Why is it red and shiny?" Kendra demanded, squinting at it before clenching the bag.

"I infused it with the power of Inferos and human misery," Zane dramatically claimed, snorting as he shook his head. "It's a rubidium compound, sugar, and some shit you couldn't pronounce. Berry flavored, like you suggested," he explained.

Kendra bit back her laughter and shook her head. Demons possessed rubidium in their blood—a necessary element in their biology. In ways she failed to understand, it was instrumental in refining Ichor into a state their bodies could use. It also happened to be that several variances of demon, primarily those maladapted to Mortale, relied on human blood to replenish their rubidium levels.

"Why are we really here, Zane?" she asked, circling the desk to stand beside him.

Zane pursed his lips, plopping into his desk chair and relaxing into it.

"I heard you guys had a run-in with a certain voidling. That means you guys are being targeted."

Eden turned his attention back to Zane, a glint of anger in his eyes as he thought back to the loathsome interaction.

"I know that much," Eden claimed, but Zane shook his head.

"Not in the usual way—at least overtly. I meant that you're being targeted by someone in the Hunters. Someone pulling the strings to sabotage us." Zane sighed and looked down. "I visited that laboratory you guys infiltrated, scoped out the intelligence team that was sent. They were all demons parading as hunters. However, when I interrogated them, a hex on their tongues utilizing void magic detonated. My guess? Orphan didn't want them squealing."

Kendra's face contorted in confusion.

"Who sent you? What made you go snooping?"

"Me, myself, and I. And that dastardly trio has lots of suspicions," Zane began and looked to Eden. "Remember when we were recruiting Julian after Harvest? He mentioned something that I've been investigating since, and only Jessica, Ethan, and I are aware of Orphan, as far as I know. Can't trust others, as far as I'm concerned."

Eden's eyes darkened.

"Then we've been infiltrated for the longest time. Could mean that Orphan was behind our failsafe not being triggered during Harvest. I'm venturing a guess that General Blackwell has you looking into it—she likes using you for these things, I noticed."

"Precisely that," Zane said with a snort. "The moment the raid team stopped sending updates, Command would have investigated and sent the cavalry, but apparently, communications had been forged during Harvest. The only ones overseeing that at the time were Bryce and Andrew. With Bryce dead ..."

"Andrew's possibly being framed," Eden concluded, not deigning to suggest Orphan was parading as Andrew, or that he was a traitor. Kendra was of the same mind.

"Not a chance," she concluded, and Zane shrugged.

"I'm with ya, but you have to look at the circumstances the big guys see. Andrew's hacking allowed us to find Kendra was held captive by the Siegharts. This triggers a raid, then Harvest begins while we're most vulnerable. Communications get fabricated—phantom signals and reports being sent from the Chicago base. It's almost too convenient how indicting that is."

Kendra growled, her fists curled and audibly cracked as her fangs grew in her mouth.

"Bullshit!" she hissed, shaking her head. "Why Andrew?"

"Collateral damage or a vendetta? Hardly matters. All I know is that he's innocent, and we need to find who the actual mole is. Either of you have any ideas?"

Eden clenched his fists, mulling over the question. Seconds later, he gave a nod.

"Evans is a good guess. Was in charge of Chicago, oversaw communications between Command and the convoy, and not to mention the coward showed little urgency in mobilizing our units when I reached the Chicago base."

"That's too easy a guess. Mind you, I also discovered demons utilizing glamour, pretending to be hunters. Not hard to imagine that it could be him and others being manipulated on Orphan's behalf. Either way, if we can find one, remove the hex that Orphan put on their tongues, and make them speak, we can get to the bottom of our problem."

"How do we go about that?" Kendra asked compulsively.

"Unfortunately? Luck—for now. Orphan's been very careful, and unless they slip up, we're playing twenty questions with a mute ghost." In the following silence, Zane glanced down at his hunter bracer, frowning for a moment as the indicator light flashed from it. He shook his head, slapping his knees before he stood.

"Welp, you guys should get going. Got my own side quest to attend to."

Eden straightened up, stretching as a yawn forced its way from him. With a shake of his head, he walked toward the door.

"We're meeting with Ethan shortly. Something secretive. We'll keep this conversation in mind going forward—guards up," Eden said, flashing Kendra a wary look. Kendra tightened her hold on the bag of syn-blood tablets, shoving them into the larger pouch on her leg and folding her arms.

"I'm not terribly confident about any of this," she admitted, slogging over to Eden.

"The only thing I can say is that you guys should be suspicious of anybody—everybody. Other than me, of course," Zane gave a cheeky smile. With a dismissive shake of his head, Eden grabbed the door handle and glanced at Zane.

"A part of me wishes it was you."

Kendra placed a hand on her hip and sighed. The reminder of their incessant feud spurred her irritation, and she smacked Eden's arm to chastise him. Zane was far from surprised at the animosity, brushing it off with a roll of his eyes. He teasingly winked at his former lieutenant, hand patting his chest.

"Love you too, Samurai."

Kendra stood with Eden in front of the barracks, inspecting her right palm. Her focus honed, fingers tensing as her claws formed while her image remained human. She breathed deeply, the strange juxtaposition of calmness and fury gnawing at her attention before she released it.

"Practicing?" Eden asked, his weary gaze fixed ahead. If not for his obvious grogginess, his tone would suggest disinterest. It wasn't that long ago that he had assisted in training her to use her abilities and energy irrespective of her demon aspect, which was more demanding of her energy. Being considered an expert on energy control, he had seen to her focus improving throughout her time as a cadet. As she eased her hand closed, she gave him a nod.

"Yeah. It's honestly harder than going full demon, but I'm not tired and starving after, at least," she muttered, looking at him with concern etching her face. "Still probably easier than your ability to sleep," she declared, but Eden stayed quiet.

Soon, a blacked-out sedan arrived, which Kendra found vaguely familiar. The dark tint kept her from seeing inside, and she assumed it was the kind of vehicle used for transporting high-profile personnel. As much as she'd bolstered her feats, she hardly felt as if she fit the bill, but she considered it apt for Eden.

The two approached, and the click of the lock disengaging prompted them to enter the back before Kendra shut the door. It was dark inside, snug and comfortable, with soft cushioning in the finely stitched pleather.

"Pleasure to see you again," Jessica spoke as she glanced back. Kendra stiffened, but Eden remained unbothered. Kendra glanced questioningly at Eden before recalling the same car had been in his garage when they were on vacation.

It was far from normal to be driven by any high-ranking hunter, let alone the general, and a pang ripped through her that revived the uneasiness from before. Upon noticing the subtle shift in Kendra's demeanor, Jessica offered a soft smile.

"I volunteered to drive you both. Nobody is in trouble," she assured and turned her attention to the road before driving from the curb in front of the barracks.

Kendra settled into her seat beside Eden, and the shared space reminded her how large Eden was. She was but a few inches shorter, but it was the entirety of his presence.

Eden had lived his entire life in a supernatural existence, whereas she was still glimpsing the more subtle and frightening aspects of it all. More than familiarity, he was cloaked in its umbrage. She once thought he was indomitable against it, and a part of her enjoyed believing he still was. However, seeing those tired eyes fight to stay open, she questioned her beliefs again.

He fell against her, asleep once more and breathing softly through the gentle drive. With his temple upon her shoulder, she relaxed and repositioned his head to nestle within the crook of her neck. It was the least she could offer, and she even felt useful being selected as a pillow. It was oddly humbling to serve as his respite in the uncertainty they approached.

Kendra knew Eden and Yuki spoke a lot about their pasts. There was a bond there she was never enlightened to understand. The stark differences between her and Yuki glared at her often. Yuki embodied empathy and compassion, whereas Kendra admittedly struggled to foster or inspire such empathy at times—perhaps due to her own leering shadows she had yet to conquer.

In that moment, it mattered little as he rested against her, and her lips twisted into a soft smile. Genuine relief washed over her, as did the wisps of his soft breathing.

"He's not this trusting, typically," Jessica suggested, her tone lighter than usual. "Thank you for being here for him."

Kendra's gaze shifted down again, admiring the peace in his expression—fragile and timid—she desired to protect that neglected peace. Her answer was obvious.

"Of course."

The rest of the ride was silent. As the landscape passed them by, they looped around to the southern entryway leading into the building—opposite the entrance she was accustomed to. It was heavily guarded, with several scanners, sentry turrets, and hunters stationed with high-powered rifles. Any unauthorized vehicles unfortunate enough to test the defenses would be shredded with ease.

Jessica came to the checkpoint, and a scanner shined over her face. The process was arduous, ironic since she was the general, but she drove through upon being cleared. Once inside the towering walls, they were funneled into a parking garage beneath the HQ building. When parked, she killed the engine and turned her head, and Kendra's attention returned to her.

Kendra gently shook Eden awake, and he rubbed his eyes as he came to. Noticing he had slept against Kendra, he muttered an apology, but she dismissed it quickly. They met Jessica's gaze, straightening up when she spoke.

"The elevator to your left will take you directly up to Ethan's office. Your hunter utility devices are temporarily tuned to access this elevator, which you will take back down once your business is over with. I shall be waiting to return you both to the barracks," Jessica explained to them, and they both nodded. Eden climbed out of the car, and Kendra fixed to do the same, but Jessica reached out, grabbing Kendra's shoulder. "A private word for a moment."

Kendra stopped, peering out of the car at Eden, who gave her a nod. She shut the door and turned her attention to Jessica, hesitant to meet her gaze directly.

"Yes, ma'am?"

"You are aware of the threat Orphan poses to us all. I can see it in your eyes, and while there is much fear ... I trust you entirely. I know what it means to be a homuntium, and to have overcome the alien sin that has wrapped around your body and soul." She offered a wry smile. "Kendra, you have done it, and you will continue to do it." She then reached into one of the pouches on her thigh. After a moment of digging, she removed a gem that resembled onyx, but it radiated gloom. A diminutive twinkle, a dying star within the void of space, flickered within its center.

When she placed it in Kendra's palm, it was strangely warm within her fingers. Paradoxically, an ethereal essence leached out, as if trying to bleed its heat to no avail. Jessica's hand then retreated, but her gaze lingered on the gem.

"This is a soul binder, one of very few. Your judgment may be what will illuminate the dark before us once more. It is the key to snuffing out Orphan. It is beyond selfish of me to ask, but will you shoulder this burden?" Jessica asked, her voice low.

Kendra was lost within the sole light thrumming inside of the soul binder as Jessica spoke. It had been an auspicious ask that Jessica gave her the rare item she had desired. As if it was a glimmer of hope, she dared not relinquish it, and her fingers curled tightly around it as she nodded.

"How do I use it?" she asked, her tone resolute.

"You feel it, yes? The essence that reaches through you?" she asked, and Kendra nodded. "You or whatever it is connected to act as a catalyst. Allow it to find another's essence, and as it grasps them, the light within it shall turn white. Once all the darkness of the gem has been erased, the once transient essence of your target is bound. For a voidling, it would destabilize their essence visibly. You've but to feel the cold for confirmation, but refrain from confronting. Report to me and me alone. Understood?" Jessica's eyes hardened, piercing Kendra's own.

"Yes, ma'am," Kendra confirmed.

Kendra left the vehicle, joining Eden at the elevator. They remained quiet while ascending, nor did they break it when emerging on the upper floor. Though the hallway was empty, it felt cramped. They assumed it was a mirror of their nerves. Each step they took was dampened between the carpet and thick walls. In the silence, palpable distrust slithered, roaring within the solitude. *It was just them.*

Kendra remembered the last time she had been alone with Ethan—when she had been held in confinement after her change. She had Eden for their current meeting, she knew that, but the ghost of that uneasiness still stirred within her. The threat he had made when she had mutated still loomed. She had overcome her hunger—her wrath—she knew that as well, but the intangible sting of crosshairs revived her anxiety anew.

Eden, having noticed her building tension, placed a hand on her shoulder. When her attention landed on him, he showed sympathy in his gaze.

"He was the one who decided against killing you when you first mutated. It was a decision that he and General Blackwell were on board with, and why you're still here today," Eden informed. The memory of that tumultuous meeting with the council was still bitter, even years later. In retrospect, he knew that Ethan had compromised to his wishes as best as possible, but there was always the lingering claim of nepotism levied against him. Commander Evans incessantly insinuated it.

"Really?" Kendra questioned quietly, her eyes drifting down as she sucked her lips in. "And who wanted me dead?" she asked, prompting Eden to pause.

"Almost everyone else," he answered.

Kendra went silent, taking note of the thought and tucking it away. More than anybody else, she trusted Eden's judgment. She determined that had to be enough, and it became her sole axiom in her responsibility.

They stopped before the door to Ethan's office, and Eden scanned in with the ID on his hunter bracer.

They entered, and Ethan gestured to the seats before his desk. Two folders were set before the seats, *classified* stamped in red ink atop them along with the number of a briefing room. The pair then took their seats and pensively eyed the folders.

"Thank you for joining me, Eden. Kendra," Ethan greeted, adjusting the collar of his suit. Unlike the usual gray suit he wore, he was wearing a black one, accompanied by a long wool coat that draped above his knees. With uncertainty in his smile, his gaze lingered with fondness, and he shifted his stance. "If I may be informal, I have watched your careers with great approval. This is of no surprise to Eden, I imagine, but you, Kendra, have exceeded my expectations since your time as a cadet. Your contributions have proven beyond auspicious, and your continued progress is something I would see prosper, even as these erosions persist." Ethan's smile faded, and he took his seat before them.

"I have dedicated my life to the Hunt, and I would give my very life to see its mission fulfilled, as I swore in my oath long ago." His brow furrowed, and he met Kendra's gaze. "My family was taken from me, and I would not see them taken again. Both of you, I consider as such.

"It is easy to become desensitized and detached from our work, and refusing to do so is integral in maintaining the human sentiment we strive to protect. To such an extent, I was willing to be hated by many—you included, Kendra—to protect others upon our first meeting. I had a younger sister once, as well. Aliza. Killed by a demon I dared to trust."

Ethan exhaled softly, pressing his closed fingers to his chest.

"Even if I considered myself justified in how I once chastised you, I give my sincere apology for any pain I undoubtedly contributed to."

Ethan bowed his head, eyes closed for several moments. Kendra watched, meeting his gaze with great trepidation. It all seemed performative—grim, even.

"Not to be callous, sir," Kendra began, "I'm not concerned with that time anymore, but I am concerned with the here and now. Your apology is noted and accepted, but can we know why we're here?" She looked to Eden, who still focused on the folders in front of them. She imagined he was closely acquainted with Ethan's history, having been raised by him and his mother. The information was intended for her, and she cared little to plunge her mind into a tangent.

"Forgive my long-winded preface, Kendra. I wished for you to better understand the gravity pertaining to both of us, as it is pertinent to what I will discuss with both of you." His eyes narrowed. "Orphan." They perked up at the name. "The voidling you two encountered is likely behind much—from Harvest, espionage, and the sickening fate of our comrades. I have to conclude that we have been infiltrated."

Kendra and Eden were quiet, expressions suppressed so as not to suggest speculation. Even stray glances were avoided. Ethan idly scraped the desk, his breathing low and steady to where even Kendra struggled to hear it. It was as if he, too, erased what his thoughts expressed. She hadn't paid it much mind before, but his heartbeat was irregular and slower than that of other humans. Having challenged his elusiveness, her attention recentered on the moment when he sharply tapped the desk and spoke.

"Due to this suspicion, much intel has been consolidated with additional security protocols, including information between myself and other high-ranking hunters being decentralized." Ethan pushed the folders toward Eden and Kendra, his gaze impervious to the insinuated fear of treachery.

"I have not reviewed the assignment in this folder, but I believe it necessary to advise that you both exercise crucial caution and trust no one. Not even me, should you deem it necessary. Assume there are lies and deceit waiting within all details being given to you. If there is *anything* in question, you may inform Jessica."

"Why not you?" Eden interjected, his tone softer than his words suggested.

"Would you trust me?" he asked, his eyes closing. "Tell me your answer when you have it. That is an order."

The two hunters tensed before Ethan. Eden's eyes refrained from deviating, but Kendra's own scrutiny dropped to her lap, wherein she idly reached into her pocket and grasped the soul binder within her palm. Her fingers trembled against it, and her other hand slid forward slowly. When she raised her gaze, she heard Eden's answer.

"No," Eden said, urging Kendra to pause. She glanced at him, believing he had been talking to her for a moment, but his staunch eyes were glued to Ethan.

"Then you have been trained well," Ethan spoke. When his eyes opened, he glanced down to see Kendra's hand hovering forward.

Kendra's heart stopped in her chest. Of the little Eden had allowed her to know, his insincerity was almost glaring. The neglected trust he once held in Ethan hadn't escaped her, and she could imagine the guilt clutching at his heart. As she met Ethan's gaze, she released the soul binder and raked the folder closer across the desk.

Ethan turned from them, settling with his hands joined behind him.

"You will review these documents away from my scrutiny and meet the commander in the room detailed upon dismissal. Understood?" The pair grabbed the folders and stood.

"Yes, sir," they spoke in unison.

"Dismissed."

Kendra and Eden turned, heading toward the door.

Releasing a heavy breath, Ethan bit his bottom lip, pushing away his hesitation.

"Eden?" he called, prompting Eden to stop. "For Jessica and me, please … be safe, my son."

Without further acknowledgment, Eden entered the hallway with Kendra.

Kendra exhaled heavily as she clutched her chest. Eden had been eyeing his folder when she peeked at him, his own breath steadying itself. After a moment, they made their way through the hallway to the elevator. They entered and set it to take them to a lower floor, as instructed beneath the security tag in the center of the folder.

When they emerged, they navigated the hall to the secured room. Eden held his hunter ID to the scanner, and the door opened. Immediately, the hairs on their bodies stood.

Commander Evans waited there at a long table, similar to the one Eden had sat at whenever he'd spoken with other high-ranking members. Much to both his and Kendra's surprise, Bonnie sat further down the table, her expression suggesting mutual surprise. They straightened when Commander Evans's gaze found them.

"Private Mallory, Captain Blackwell, take a seat and open to the synopsis of your missions. We will discuss the preface once you have both read it," Commander Evans spoke, his dark eyes idly scanning the room.

Despite the brewing wariness they were both possessed with, they did as they were instructed. The door shut behind them, locking as they took their seats across from one another.

They both tore the security seals on the folder and opened them to the brief. Who was overseeing the mission was printed on the top: *Com. Troy Evans.* That was the first time Kendra had seen his first name. *Doesn't look like a Troy*, she thought. The details they scanned were printed in a terribly bold font that was barely legible.

Their brows furrowed, the scope of the assignment settling on them. It had been just as Zane had warned them, evident in the mission's pertinent mention of Andrew. Kendra pushed her folder forward, and a moment later, Eden did as well. With confirmation, Commander Evans prepared to speak.

"I suspect you are all aware it has been a tumultuous period for the Hunters. Now, there is a disjointedness in communications to ensure we can precisely track operations from here on out. In our efforts to do so, we are monitoring all personnel closely. With reports we have garnered from several squads, we have cross-examined the information we received and identified data that is inconsistent. The intel here is top secret, and only I and a scarce few are aware of this mission. Your secrecy is mandatory, and these documents will be taken and stored within a SCIF upon this briefing's conclusion. Do you understand what I have just relayed to you?"

"Yes, sir," the three hunters of Seraph Seven spoke.

Commander Evans flipped the page on the paper in front of him, clearing his throat.

"As you have read, Angel Forty-Five was almost entirely wiped out during a mission that I had arranged two days ago. Two of the remaining hunters managed to take one of the assailants prisoner—an umbra demon by the name of Dahlia Noire, who we now believe to be associated with Fracti Alas. After searching her person and interrogating her, we discovered pertinent data that had been uncovered during your infiltration mission two weeks ago—data that, upon a deeper review Lieutenant Blair conducted, contained Private Carter's digital fingerprints. This falls in line with the timeline we have estimated."

As Commander Evans spoke, the hunters displayed disbelief and irritation, especially Kendra. Atop Andrew's implication, she knew the name of that demon. Her name crept from her memory and simmered into bitterness on her tongue, marring her expression. *Dahlia Noire.*

She had been affiliated with the Siegharts. She had attended the party Allen had invited her to—*Nox Invidia*, she recalled. For reasons beyond simple vanity, Dahlia had been overly hostile toward her. In retrospect, the passive-aggressive behavior from Allen's family was hardly surprising either; leaving early was the smartest thing she had done. She concluded that Dahlia's involvement couldn't have been a coincidence, but as much as she desired to volunteer her speculation, her distrust compelled her to abstain.

Commander Evans turned the page of his papers again and continued.

"Because of this, we have temporarily detained him, and he is being held in custody as we speak. While the investigation has yet to conclude, we hold in good faith that Private Carter is not a nefarious perpetrator working against our interests, but rather, a scapegoat being framed. To confirm this, General Blackwell and I have constructed a tandem secret assignment for you, which coincides with the mission Private Carter was briefed to embark on with Angel Forty-Seven tomorrow."

Commander Evans shifted, turning another page before looking to Bonnie.

"Lieutenant Blair has closely supervised the development of Private Carter as a hunter and understands him deeper than most would. Thus, she will impersonate and operate in his stead during this mission." Commander Evans broadened his attention, his expression grave. "I will be keyed in through a secret channel to monitor this mission. Should anything go awry, Captain Blackwell and Private Mallory, who will oversee Angel Forty-Seven in secret, will step in to handle any threats that arise. Should you engage any enemies, be they treasonous hunters or sapient demons, you will subdue them with reasonable force and bring them into custody for further questioning."

"And what exactly is this mission Angel Forty-Seven is engaging in? We should know should any abnormalities within their mission become apparent," Eden said, composed and unperturbed by Commander Evans's direness. His voice carried a hint of animosity, but that was far from atypical of him.

"For *certain* reasons, we have restricted some of the particulars of their mission to Lieutenant Blair alone," he said, causing Eden's gaze to narrow as Commander Evans continued. "None of Angel Forty-Seven, save for Lieutenant Blair, has been keyed into the true nature of your mission. Their own pertains to investigating suspicious rifts and a black-market deal, as was detailed to us by a demon Angel Forty-Five captured. We suspect the nature of Private Carter's involvement, knowing or otherwise, will present itself in this mission."

Bonnie raised her hand, and Commander Evans nodded at her.

"I assume that I will be receiving Private Carter's hunter gear. With your supervision, I'd like to key through it prior to placing it on to ensure there isn't a hidden failsafe upon detecting an unfamiliar pulse pattern or energy signature. It's best to disable it beforehand," Bonnie explained, although she winced at the insinuation of her own words.

"Of course, lieutenant. We will handle that with liberal time prior to your mission. Are there any questions from you, Mallory and Blackwell?" Commander Evans shifted his focus to them, and with a brief exchange of glances between the two, they shook their heads. "Good. You all know where to rendezvous. I will be storing these mission details in the SCIF. Should any pertinent details or rehashing be required, you will contact me solely through the secure communication tunnel you were each instructed to memorize. You are not to discuss these details in any way, shape, or form with any superior, up to and including General Blackwell, per her specific request with these decentralized mission plans. You are dismissed."

The hunters stood, and while Bonnie and Eden traveled to the door, Kendra straightened, her right hand tightly clenched around the soul binder she had secretly removed. She had planned how to go about testing her suspicions, even if it was haphazard.

"Sir?" Kendra called, approaching Commander Evans, who had been gathering the folders from the table.

"Private?" Commander Evans prompted in a flat tone, his eyes wary as she approached.

Kendra reached out for his hand as he grabbed the folder in front of her. Though it was for fleeting moments, her fingers had pressed into the back of his palm prior to his hand retreating. He gave her a bewildered look, his face scrunching up as his jaw tightened. If she knew Commander Evans, such a small gesture would invite chastising, but he was strangely without words, and the soul binder within her palm siphoned a small amount of warmth.

"Apologies, Commander," Kendra said, her voice low as she flipped the folder open and traced her finger across Dahlia's name. "Do we have any further details about this demon that can be shared?"

After a hesitant moment, Commander Evans reached up and gripped his jaw before shaking his head.

"This is impertinent to your mission. Consequently, I will not share any further details pertaining to her." Commander Evans's gaze narrowed skeptically, and his face twisted into something akin to a scowl. "Do be more mindful of your imprecision—especially with a superior hunter.

Understood?" he said, and Kendra straightened, her hand pressing to her sides as she pinched the siphon between her index finger and thumb.

"Yes, sir. My apologies," she said firmly, lowering her head and quickly taking to Eden's side by the door.

The three squad members left the room, unspeaking. Bonnie split off, leaving the other two to take the elevator down to meet Jessica.

However, composed she thought herself to be, her expression was knit with worry, evident in her deepening frown. She slipped the soul binder into her pouch again, and as they approached Jessica's car, dread resurrected within her. Her test had yielded a result that, while suspicious, was inconclusive.

As she glanced at Eden, their gazes met. She cursed the continued uncertainty, but she knew her trust in him was paramount, but that faith was shared between them, she felt. Within his fatigued crimson depths, she clung to her oaths.

To humanity and to him.

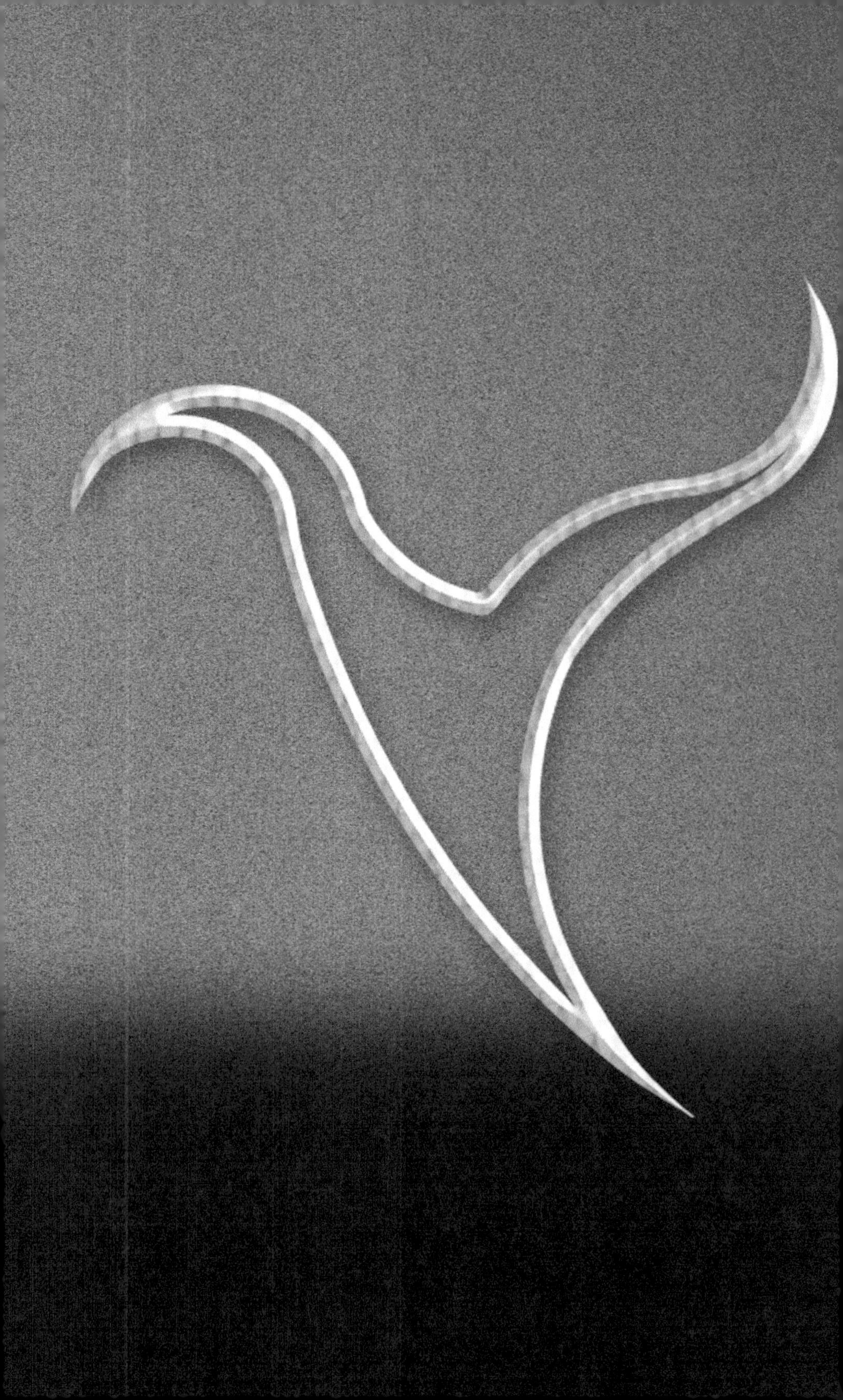

Nine

Oath of Chains

Jessica was the bastion of the Hunters—a paragon of the indomitable strength humanity offered against demons. She knew this, of course, but she had once relinquished her role as the Mistress of the Hunt. The turmoil of motherhood weighed heavily on many, but there were times she bore the burden of Atlas.

Failure.

A single sentiment roiled and invaded her expression each time she thought of the ones she loved. Her father, Desmond Blackwell, had given his life to save her and her sister's own when they were young bloods. Then there had been her change. They had become homuntiums, instilled with a terrible seed of wrath that perverted their very spirits. Her sister resigned, but she had been determined to maintain the oath she had taken with Ethan. Within the umbrage of her father's hat—his memory—the gravity of her promises was most bearable.

Should she have relented, she would have perished then. If the Blackwell bloodline was renowned for anything, it was their resilience. Perhaps she was the most of any before her, but she desperately wished Eden was the *invulnerable* one.

His crimson eyes were a beacon to her. From when she first saw them staring up at her, she discovered her strength's purpose: to prevent their embroilment in a world sharing their bloody hue. Such a prospect was forbidden, and she would rain every imaginable hell on anyone who would test it.

"General Blackwell, they will be departing shortly. I will monitor them with the greatest vigilance," Commander Evans spoke. The rugged man sat across from her, eyes showing a confidence she thought to be frivolous. However, that was mostly due to her impossible standards when it came to Eden's protection.

"Greatest?" Jessica questioned, peering from beneath the brim of her hat. "A stronger adjective is needed to placate me." Her tone snapped its jaws on Commander Evans, causing him to flinch before he nodded.

"Then with impervious vigilance," he offered, his gaze falling. "That's my promise," he said, dropping the formality. At this, Jessica lowered her head, and her fingers fell against the desk with a soft tap.

"That will do, Troy. You may leave." Without another word, Commander Evans stood and left the room.

Quietude pervaded, and with its frigid embrace, she surrendered to the tension in her muscles. Her nails raked the desk, her gaze receding to familiar memories—accursed and tender. How ill-prepared she had been for motherhood weighed heavily always, as did the guidance she had prayed for from Romanus. He never answered, chilling her through the warm union they once had. She was familiar with cold memories, but the way they rhymed weaved a bloody blizzard, swallowing her pleas.

She had watched Eden struggle in his recovery when he had been returned to her by one of Romanus's seraphim. The once vigorous boy, brimming with creativity and a yearning for life, had been whittled to a husk. He had no longer been the Eden she had raised—her son she so desired to see returned. Her remorse had meant little in the blossoming wrath and despair within him, and through its bloody lens, he couldn't see anything resembling a mother. She never faulted him for such a view—she agreed.

Nights of sobbing, nightmares blending with reality. He couldn't tell the difference even as she wept beside him. Even with his stature surpassing her own at the time, he was infinitely small in her arms—but his vitriol had grown feverishly. He lusted for vengeance, for freedom. Be it his own or for the girl he'd call for in the dark, she was uncertain. All the same, the ire in his eyes was directed toward her when she refused to see him become a hunter. However, her selfish desire was mutilated soon after.

It had been in the dead of night when his energy signature plummeted, and her voice shrieked through a waterfall of sobs. His body had been cold, unlike the blood that spilled through her fingers as she strangled his wounded neck. It had taken every ounce of her strength to keep him alive then, and she had damned the offending blade manifested from his ire. She despaired over giving in to his desires to hunt, but one too many times had she witnessed the retaliation to voicing opposition. In good conscience, she couldn't allow his vendetta to exist without preparing him to the best of her abilities.

While initially never having intended for him to become a hunter, she and Ethan had always ensured Eden could fight from when he was young. He was only five when the first demon had made an attempt on his life. Regardless of how capable she thought them of protecting him, she was not foolish enough to believe that would always be the case. No matter how many wards she'd crafted, there was always a looming cloud of danger that would follow him. Both before and after she had birthed him, she knew.

He knew.

Knocking roused her attention, and just by the feel of the energy, she knew who it was.

"Enter," she said after making herself presentable and stoic—as always.

Ethan entered the office and closed the door behind him. His long black coat was draped over his shoulder as he approached, coming to a stop beside her desk. He allowed the silence to persist a moment longer, waiting for her gaze to meet his before he kneeled beside the desk and took her hand.

"You're fretting," he alleged.

"I'm bad at pretending then?" Jessica inquired in a lighter voice than usual, finding it ironic.

"I know my Jess. Her eyes betray, even beneath the shadow of *his* hat."

Jessica suddenly removed her hat, flinging it across the room. Well-aimed and rehearsed, it landed on a hook next to her own coat, and she ran her taut fingers through her disheveled black tufts.

"Dissecting me like prey. You're truly irredeemable, my love," she spoke, her body seizing as a yawn fled from her. When she relaxed again, Ethan lifted her hand to his lips and kissed the top.

"I'd allow myself to be if it means staring into those jewels more often. No rest for the wicked, nor sleep for the damned."

Jessica's lips melted into a longing smile, and she stood slowly, careful to avoid prying her hand from his.

"Then I suppose we'll forever lounge in fire and brimstone," she suggested, slowly shutting her eyes. "Allow me a moment's weakness, if you will," she implored, stepping from behind her desk, and Ethan stood, staring down at her.

"I've allowed many, and I'd allow countless more."

Regardless of what he claimed, the guilt never fled. She was the General of the Hunters, but that was mostly ornamental, she thought. She hadn't truly done anything general-like in almost a decade. The official title truly belonged to Ethan, yet he had always declined it.

"Am I a bad mother? Was I mistaken in granting his wish?" she asked, her voice barely above a whisper, and even then, it cracked. Yet Ethan held firm, unflinching.

"The alternative was unthinkable."

It was. She knew that, but it resolved little to know the two choices were to let Eden hunt or—the other was no choice she'd dare entertain. Even then, the hollowness in Eden's heavy eyes bore through her, sundering the semblance of peace she wished for. That bitter memory stole her breath each time it flashed through her mind.

"Why must this world see him suffer so? I would do anything to see him live a normal life—drawing, making friends, and learning of love and levity. In the torments of what we endure, you and I can still see the beauty we would die to protect, and still ... he can't. I see it inside of him, buried deep, but he doesn't see me. How can I not think myself wretched for allowing that to happen?" she spoke. Jessica buried her face in Ethan's neck, inhaling through her clenched teeth before swallowing her reborn grief.

"He perseveres still, and I see he can wake to such sentiments with enough time. Can't you see that? His smile's returning, and he allows himself to be known by those who he is close with."

"And what of Onaga? Should he—"

"I would sooner die than allow him to take our son again," Ethan spoke firmly. As she focused on his steady heartbeat, unperturbed in his vow, she nestled into him further.

"Orphan cannot be allowed to persist then," she resolved. Jessica pried herself from his embrace but found herself unable to flee farther.

"Soon," he admitted, turning his head. "Our communication with one another has been sparse for too long. As much as I wish our efforts in uncovering them could be joined, this resolution of disjointed correspondence was necessary."

Jessica thought only of him in that moment. All else was submerged as she contemplated his dedication and undying devotion.

"I fear I'm playing pretend with this mantle as the head of the Hunters. You are far more suited to the role."

"You're stronger than you assume, Jess. You always were and always will be." He reached out, pushing her thin bangs from her eyes. "Perhaps I am more pragmatic and calculating, but that is not what leadership exclusively entails. It's human to desire a leader who embodies something we all aspire to, and for you, that is your unyielding strength. They would rally behind you, ready to die—but myself?" He pressed his hand to his heart. "I am unsure."

Jessica forced a smile, her eyes opening to meet his hazel depths. Searching deep, she pried into them to glimpse the unflinching truth they suggested.

"If only you weren't such a liar."

"You don't have to believe me."

Jessica took a deep breath, swallowing hard as she sat atop her desk. She briefly eyed the image on the wall of herself, Ethan, her sister, her mother, James, and Commander Evans. Once, long ago, they had been Seraph Eleven. Her mother, Izara, was a cannon who'd served as their captain. She and Ethan were her blades, Aisha their bastion, James their engineer, and Troy was another cannon—the best sniper of their time, she once professed.

Ethan had been the better swordsman and combatant than she was, and she suspected he still would be, if not for her mutations. Within the fleeting memories of their time as a squad, there was the sting of the grave ending. Her mother and father had died during the battle against the Alastair's former Lord of Wrath, Matthionne. His cruelty still permeated her blood, and she was reminded of his terrible eyes when she met with the current Alastair head—his daughter.

Jessica never forgave herself for her weakness, but Ethan always tried to convince her otherwise.

"Your silver tongue won't spare you," she teased, shifting on the desk as she puffed her chest out. Her eyes invited him, and he obliged by leaning in closer.

"I won't ever find redemption if you keep rewarding me like this." With a smirk, he glanced at the door. "We only have two hours until the command conference. That enough time?"

Jessica refrained from responding. Instead, she tugged Ethan's tie, pressing her chest to his to feel his heartbeat. She then kissed him deeply, not daring to allow space between them. But the kiss, unlike what she had hoped would liberate her nerves, offered no escape or reprieve. And his heart's cadence submerged her further, each beat an indictment.

Failure. Failure. Failure.

Its rhythm had become muscle memory in her, of which she paid far too much attention to, but no such welcomed memory surfaced. With only the feel of his lips and the thumps of his slow, drumming heart, that sentiment kept repeating in her head—no matter how she tried to convince herself otherwise.

Zane hadn't bothered to dress up. That day's off-the-record meeting with Asher was more abrupt than the last—nor was it facilitated by Jessica. Asher had texted him during his conversation with Eden and Kendra, requesting to meet as soon as possible. Not wanting to rouse suspicion, he waited until the next day—when many of the high-ranking hunters were busy with the conference—to sneak off.

"This has to be pretty important to call me here like this—especially so soon," Zane said, a hint of annoyance in his tone as Asher invited him inside. While he respected Asher, the timing was less than favorable. Zane was more than positive that Asher suspected that, but the unease in his expression suggested something grave.

"You know about the Venatums?" Asher asked, his body language tense. "Had some of them detain me a few days after our last meeting. Real scary shit," Asher spoke, leading Zane through the hall to the living room they sat in last time, only without nearly as much levity. Neither Asher's disheveled, sand-colored hair nor the turmoil embedded in his gaze wavered for a moment, speaking to the sincerity of his worry.

"Oh, shit ..." Zane spoke, and he glanced down at his wrist. "There was a jammer enacted on my hunter bracer. There's no way we were being listened to."

"They didn't suggest knowing what we talked about—just that there was a meeting with a hunter," Asher said, flicking his wrist dismissively. He backed against the wall, eyes locked on the floor. "Even threatened to use a void hex on Eva as a threat for me to talk."

Zane's eyes narrowed, and he turned his head with a deadpan expression.

"I risk sounding like an asshole right now, but what did you tell them?" he asked, and Asher met his gaze and flashed a wry smile.

"Not a damn thing—lucky for you. Didn't have to in the end."

"Is Eva okay?" Zane demanded, his scalding gaze damning the possibility of her having been harmed.

"She's shaken up a bit, but she'll be fine." Asher shifted, ushering Zane to follow him to the kitchen. The large open space had a white island in the center. Zane couldn't help but notice its emptiness for once. In the times he had been there in the past, it was always stacked with some dish or ingredients being prepared, but there was nothing this time.

"Caught a lucky break with some infernal intervention," he said, prompting Zane to cock his brow.

"Infernal?" Zane questioned.

"She said you'd know," Asher said and gestured to the patio.

Zane could think of plenty of women who could have intervened. He hoped it wasn't Eridianne, but he couldn't imagine she'd involve herself in matters she'd deem trivial. It certainly wasn't Tsubaki, the prospective heiress of the Xiao. He'd heard rumors of her animosity toward the Harbinger of Greed, but they had only met once, and she hadn't even learned his name.

Zane walked past Asher, his lips ajar as he stared outside at the patio, and he slid the door open. There was not a hint of malice, but there was an oddly warm body temperature nearby, and the density of blue omens suggested respite. It was almost performatively conciliatory, as to ease his wariness.

"I'll give you two some space," Asher said, turning on his heel and disappearing into the home.

Zane exited and shut the door behind him. The wooden deck beneath his feet was steady as he carefully crossed it, heading to the thick wooden rails. Below, the city was faintly visible through the morning fog creeping down the hills. It was one of the many things he enjoyed about Malibu.

He took a deep breath. The subtle ocean air almost disguised the undertones of something far more alluring. He knew the pheromones of succubi more than he cared to admit. Its gentle whisper could manufacture docility among the unassuming. Between the pervading calm among the omens and the scent, he confirmed without a doubt who he was speaking with.

"You didn't go through the trouble of getting me out here to kill me, I presume. Would be some twisted déjà vu if so." Zane turned to face the scarlet-haired woman as she landed on the deck without a sound, her large bat-like wings outstretched. "At least this time would be less harrowing for me." He met her pure red eyes, and they equally scrutinized each other.

"I've much dignity in my every action and reaction, Hunter. Should I have desired violence, I would have chosen to attack you when you breached that laboratory."

"But that's not your nature. I know the gaze of killers, and yours isn't one of them. I'm jarred, to be honest, but all is fun in theater." Zane breathed harshly through his nostrils, but he carefully bowed his head, feigning the drama in his gesture. "To what do I owe the pleasure, Princess Lucifina?" he asked.

The woman gripped the ruffles of her overskirt, shaking her head. Distaste painted her face briefly, but her expression calmed quickly before she curtsied with a flare of her wings.

"There is great urgency in this manufactured meeting. Still, I must implore," she began, her gaze hardening with a slight pout. "I would greatly appreciate it if you would forgo my formal title and refer to me as Lucy."

As she straightened her posture, her hair danced in the wind. The crimson waves swayed, resembling the weeping willows that guarded Zane's childhood home. And much like those trees, the mystique of her demeanor evoked an alien sorrow in his chest. Demon royalty, especially the primonium kind, were hardly casual. As he stared into the pools of her red depths, the faint emotion they emitted settled bittersweet, but their empathy was palpable.

The clothing she wore had a Victorian bend to it—a quaint form of attire even among demon nobility, but despite that, it complemented her flawless ashen complexion. Her incomparable beauty almost left him in awe.

"Before you speak, I have to know some things," Zane said, careful not to stumble on his words.

"Of course. It is only fair," she spoke.

"You've been bringing the fight to the Venatums, I hear. If this pacifist hunch I have about you is correct, killing off your father's loyal followers isn't the kind of thing you would willingly do."

Lucy flinched, sucking her lips in as she averted her gaze. Shame marred her flawless features, but she tepidly nodded.

"I deign to herald bloodshed or violence, truly. But my indolence would be far more egregious." She shifted, her wings folding in as she lowered her gaze. "They seek Eden—I cannot allow that."

Sensing the turmoil in her voice, Zane thought it callous to dig further into her relation to Eden. He dismissed that question and folded his arms, cocking his head expectantly.

"If that's true, then why a half measure? You could have sought us out long ago—helped General Blackwell find and put an end to Onaga."

Lucy raised her gaze, her eyes half-lidded. Her gaze became distant, and she composed her breathing.

"It would not be so simple. There are two primary reasons for this. While protecting Eden remains my primary prerogative, orchestrating a scheme of violence has been untenable." She exhaled shakily. "While it has proven fruitless, I ... naively held on to the hope of making my father see reason. I realize now this will never come to be in his living breaths." Lucy fell quiet for several moments.

The idea of raising a hand against a parent, no matter how vile one could find them to be, was a thought that Zane could understand. Even if his mother had secretly been a serial killer, disposing of her would have been inconceivable. When demons formed bonds, they were far more embroiled in the emotional entailments than humans tended to be. Even the most minuscule bonds were harrowing to sever.

"And the second reason?" Zane asked.

"You must already know this, but the voidling, Orphan, pervades your organization. They parade as one of you, and who that may be must be under the highest of scrutiny. Furthermore, the general would order my death on sight." She raised her gaze, shaking her head. "For this reason, that option would have proven vain. Speaking with you is the auspicious opportunity I have waited to present itself. It is not lost on me that you have acted antithetically to Orphan, so I can be sure the secrecy you have practiced assures you are not working with Orphan yourself. Also, it lends credibility that Asher assured me of your authenticity when I saved him and his wife."

"Sound reasoning," Zane said, needing not a moment longer to determine she was genuine. This was partially influenced by the fact that he only fully comprehended half of her vocabulary. "I'll hear you out."

Lucy's lips relaxed, the tension in her body easing. She pushed a long strand of hair behind her ear before approaching, the heels of her Egyptian-styled sandals soundless against the deck, and she held her hands out. She whispered softly under her breath, and a dark energy circled her palms as a large black tome manifested atop her slender fingers.

Zane knew what it was immediately, having studied demon alchemy his entire life. With Onaga as the progenitor of that infernal art, he knew of the history and genesis of it. In her hands was a Tome of Knowledge, one of several ancient tomes Onaga had penned. As Lucy held it, faint Indiox whispers carried from the enclosed pages, their professed knowledge almost overwhelming in his proximity to it.

"That's—"

"The Tome of Liminality, possessing knowledge of the means with which my father has evaded you hunters for so long," Lucy spoke, her deep voice low and unsteady. "I managed to steal it with the help of my younger brother." Hearing this, Zane cocked a brow.

"Brother? You're the only known kin of Onaga's I've heard of," Zane challenged, prompting a shy smile from her.

"It is not a siblingship declared by blood. Not many know of the half-demon boy born from a former prisoner in his labs. In his aptitude and curiosity, my father found it apt to adopt him."

Bewildered, Zane's lips were ajar once more. The idea of a child assisting in stealing an artifact possessing knowledge more ancient than existence itself was ludicrous. He considered it just preposterous enough to be something Onaga would never have anticipated. He could only wonder if the child taken from a prisoner was who he thought it to be. The looming gravity made his thought to ask the child's name irrelevant, however.

"You mean to sabotage him, then?" Zane's brow knit into a sorrowful one, considering the unquelled pain that undoubtedly brewed in her chest. "You realize ... we'll kill him?"

Lucy tucked the tome to her chest, her eyes lowering as she bit back a sob, and she nodded slowly.

"I'm ... making my peace with it. But if it means Eden may know a semblance of that ephemeral concept, it is necessary."

Zane took a step toward her. The silence was a melody of grief, and he understood the song all too well.

"I'm biased, but your decision is one I respect. Still, I condemn the circumstances that made it necessary. No one should ever have to desire the death of their parent." Zane took the tome, its weight making his knees buckle. It wasn't heavy in a physical sense, but his mind throbbed just holding it, let alone discerning it. The fact Lucy had shown no visible struggle in carrying it begged the boundlessness of her intelligence. "I will ensure General Blackwell receives it."

"However unlikely, can you be sure that Orphan has not assumed her likeness?" Lucy asked.

"Not a chance. It would be impossible for Orphan to mimic her, not to mention there is much that only she could know."

Lucy joined her hands, her fingers curling together tightly as she shook her head. What plagued them both was something far more perturbing than Zane could have anticipated. In his ignorance, there was a rift that was utilized by their common enemy, and the coming revelation was something Lucy dreaded to tell in fear of who Orphan was.

"The voidling is far more formidable than you may know. Should they have assimilated whomever they parade as, you would be none the wiser."

Again, there in the dark, Eden watched through crimson lenses as his hands tore chains asunder. No matter how often those shackles shattered, they reforged anew. With bloody hands that had paid their tithes, the voracious greed that subjugated them demanded more and more. He gave all that he could to that bereft, barren land.

Why? Eden thought again and again, but no answer resonated. He awoke in his bed, roused by the faint whispers of Cassiel's voice. And when he touched his cheeks, moisture saturated his cold fingertips. *Blood.* His eyes quivered as he stared at it, but he shook his head in refusal as he shot up. He reached for the orange bottle on his nightstand, but when he grabbed it, he realized it was empty.

He had forgotten he finished the last pill the night before. Long ago, it dulled the voice parading in his head—flames that forged sentiments he wished were damned—but the medication no longer extinguished them. He had told Yuki of its dwindling effects, and it was dangerous to up the dosage without risk of acute psychosis—something he learned the hard way once. That was all he needed, even with his growing desperation.

It took hours, but as the sun peered through his blinds, he finally composed himself, got ready, and left the barracks to rendezvous with Kendra. He knew he'd find her where she always visited before missions.

Eden was driven to the memorial stones, several monuments constructed southeast of the base. For generations, fallen hunters' names had been carved into the stone. Eden had known more than he'd wished, but Kendra only knew of one thus far: Vicente.

He adjusted the collar of his vest and navigated the several hedges of granite, whispering his condolences to the names he knew until he reached her. She crouched, hand resting atop the name. She had known he approached but still spoke silently.

"I wish I could tell you about it all, Vic. I bet I could lift more than you now, too, even though I don't look like I can. Zane went on and on about your feats, and I'm envious I couldn't see them, or that you couldn't see mine ..." Kendra droned on, and Eden listened silently.

He watched her reach into the pouch on her thigh, removing from it three tarot cards.

The Tower.

Six of Swords.

Death.

Kendra whispered a final prayer, standing slowly and shuffling the cards back into her pouch before turning to face Eden with a wry smile.

"Hey," she greeted, and Eden raised his hand.

"Hey," he replied in a quiet voice. He reached out and took her hand in his, then cupping his other hand atop it. "Ready?"

"Yeah," she said, and Eden released her before walking with her to the teleportation terminals. They were only half a mile from it, and several hunters were lined up on guard duty, with a few stationed atop outposts surrounding the area. Eden glanced at Kendra, nudging her to get her attention.

"Bonnie departed an hour ago. We'll know where to find and monitor her and Angel Forty-Seven through her tracker," Eden said, and Kendra nodded.

"Gotta stay quiet, so we'll use the major obscuring incantation when we arrive."

With no further exchange between them, they entered the zone. Though they checked in with the guards, the coordinates would be obscured from them.

Spotting Emily, Eden and Kendra waved goodbye, and she winked at them, maintaining a stoic expression as she held her rifle. Eden stepped onto the platform beneath the machine, similar to a node scanner if not slightly bulkier. The blood rune beneath their feet glowed as their energies interfaced with it, and the machine whirred to life, bathing both of them in shimmering light. In moments, their forms dematerialized.

When they reformed, they overlooked a grassy field on the far outskirts of a nearby town in Goiás, Brazil. The sky, while light blue, was assailed by teal creeping from the blurry horizon. The humidity quickly rendered them clammy, and Eden was thankful he had the foresight to refrain from wearing his coat. While Kendra's suit covered her entire body, the composition was breathable for such environments, but she was more acclimated to hot weather than he was.

"Gods, I hate the humidity in Brazil," Eden muttered, trekking through pebbly soil with soft crunches, holding his wrist up to look at the projected coordinates.

"Honestly beats Chicago right now, weather-wise. Not that I mind either, personally," Kendra claimed, following close behind him with careful steps. "Think there're snakes in this grass?" she joked, but Eden shook his head, sighing with contempt.

"Let's go dark," he said.

They then spoke in unison.

"Insenseilin."

Obvious benefits of the major obscurity stretched deeper than some assumed. It also manipulated the veil around their form, subliminally persuading less sapient creatures to shift from their path. It was especially useful when they were in the wilderness or pushing through dubious terrains.

As they made their way through the increasingly thick vegetation for several minutes, Kendra was reminded of their last mission and other reports before that.

"Say, do you find it odd that a lot of these laboratories are in South America?"

Eden mulled over the thought for a moment, then shrugged.

"It's weird, sure, but you can imagine that it's a lot easier to operate due to the remoteness and difficulty of hunter logistics. Not like the local authorities can do much either."

This reminded Kendra of how Chicago's police had been brought to their knees by a significantly less organized front of demons. An ancient network of laboratories headed by one of the first demons in existence was far more daunting.

"Guess so ..." she spoke, pushing the thought aside.

Soon, the lush green landscape became beige as they transitioned into a drier section of land connecting to a rocky canyon. Eden leaped across the cleaved ground and slid to a lower elevation, and Kendra followed. A snake nest filled with eggs rested close to the base, just feet away from them. However, the snake obliviously stared out, unaware of their presence as it curled its head into the burrow. Kendra shuddered at the sight, but Eden tapped her shoulder, directing her attention to a large cliff overlooking a forest more withered than the region they'd traveled from.

Between the changing climate and deforestation, she could only venture why it was so bereft. More pressing was the soft whisper of distortion within Ichor. The faint pulses carrying scarlet omens lingered like a stale odor, and she concluded there had to be a rift nearby.

"The rift is acting up," Eden said, his brows knitting before he dashed toward the cliff face. Kendra followed after, following his lead.

They had encountered something similar when they'd intruded upon the forest on their last mission. Oftentimes, there were hexes established around the labs to allow feral demons through from Inferos, but the purpose had never been confirmed by hunter intelligence. Seraph Seven had speculated it was a distraction, given there were usually well-trained demons much closer to the labs.

"Guess there really is a lab here then," Kendra spoke, clicking her tongue.

"Keep your guard up," Eden added.

Upon reaching the cliff face, they climbed it arduously, refraining from flashier or energy-based ascension methods to remain hidden. After several minutes, they reached the top of the cliff and marched to the opposite side to survey the location where the distortion had originated from. Screeches from the rift echoed in the distance, and from their earpieces, the signal from Bonnie's hunter bracer established, and Eden and Kendra tuned in to listen through it.

As they stared down at the land, the hunters were located through a thicket of dead branches that protruded from the dried earth. Bonnie, disguised as Andrew, was tucked away from the combat, and Sergeants Jacquelin Hopkins and Hyde Anderson stood guard by her. Jacquelin was a taller woman, staunch in her stance as she hovered her photon saber above the ground. Hyde was a stocky man of smaller stature with a shaved head and a shotgun tucked against his chest.

"All good, Carter?" Jacquelin's voice carried over, but her focus never waned from their comrades, who approached the pulsing rift.

"Oh, uh, yeah!" Bonnie called out, mimicking Andrew's speaking mannerisms as she adjusted the mobile tower. It appeared harder for her to work with while assuming Andrew's likeness with glamour, but the struggle, unintentionally, contributed to the accuracy of her performance.

"Probably best to wait a moment for that. We may be moving shortly," Jacquelin spoke, glancing across the terrain to where the rest of the squad gathered.

Like a scarlet eye peeking through reality, a slit undulated and contorted near the squad. Resembling the eye of a hellhound, it seeped with a malicious energy. Scarlet omens surged around it, swarming from the ground up. The distortion it wrought wrung the air itself, bringing about an intense pressure that pulsed across the area. Even from the distance they watched from, Eden and Kendra could feel its terrible presence emanating.

Kendra's eyes narrowed, watching with intrigue as the squad gathered and prepared to perform the rift-closing ritual—a joint effort that involved chanting Latin incantations. While she had been trained to do it, she never had the chance to before.

"This isn't right," Eden murmured, his eyes flickering as he eyed the rift.

"What?" She glanced at him.

"The rift only reacted when they neared it. Feels too contrived for your typical trap. It was located on loose intel, but if that were the case, it would have been more discreet," Eden explained, but Kendra cocked her brow.

"Not following you, Eden."

Eden crouched, frowning as his gaze intensified.

"When we closed rifts, you recall how much of a pain they can be to locate, yeah? They don't typically announce themselves unless something is stepping through. Yet ... this one is flaring, but nothing's invading," he declared.

Not a stray hellhound entered, but the rift pulsed ominously. Seeing the abnormality with Eden's explanation, her expression became grave, and they watched on with mounting urgency. With their focus divided, they listened back in on Bonnie's conversation as they watched.

"You're looking better every day. You've been putting a lot of effort into your exercise and diet, yeah?"

Bonnie gave a wry smile, only vaguely aware of what was alleged.

"Captain Larson helped me with a routine. Calorie counting to hit my macros and all. I've gotten a lot stronger since then!" she said, flexing her left arm with a bit of struggle due to the tower on her back.

"Soon enough, you'll be stealing hearts like ferali steal souls," she joked, flashing a teasing smirk that bordered on sardonic, and Bonnie gave a light laugh.

For a moment, Eden and Kendra could have sworn Jacquelin looked in their direction. Given the distance, they chalked it up to their nerves being strung tight, seeing as she immediately looked away.

As the rest of the squad focused on closing the rift, a glimmering streak of cool light darted from within its center, fleeing into the adjacent woods. Suddenly, the air near the hunters pulsed with an intense, malicious energy, and a growl tore through the woods. From deep within, something marched forward, trampling the infant trees and saplings that managed to survive whatever plagued the land. In an instant, a large quadrupedal beast lunged forward. The size of an adult hippopotamus, the avian talons attached to its rippling mammalian legs shredded the ground beneath.

A chimera.

Jacquelin quickly snatched Bonnie into her arms and drew back, and Hyde advanced forward, meeting the creature with gunfire. However, the bullets deflected from the quill-like fur that blazed on its face. With a pounce, it tackled Hyde, wrestling with his gun as it snapped its heavy jaws down at him. Its movements were imprecise, but its powerful maw quickly mangled the gun.

"Hyde!" Jacquelin let out, and she drew her pistol from her hip before unloading at the creature to no avail, the bullets unable to penetrate.

Eden stood immediately, drawing Avenger before glancing to Kendra.

"We're going!" he let out, leaping down from the cliff.

"Roger!" Kendra said, taking after him, using her claws to descend the cliff face since she couldn't safely jump from that kind of height the way he could yet.

Eden reached it first, his body flaring brightly as he channeled his energy, preparing to decapitate the demonic abomination. It would have been that simple if left unhindered. Just as he reached it, a red flash consumed his vision, and a wave of weakness coursed through him. As his form dimmed, Avenger sank into the back of the creature's neck but failed to cut through. Instead, it jammed into the tough hide and spine of the beast.

Now diverting its attention to him, the chimera shifted away, leaping back as it growled threateningly at him.

"Captain Blackwell? Mallory?" Bonnie let out, sighing in relief, although it was mostly an act since she had known they were there. While Hyde stood to his feet and backed away, his expression was stone-faced, and he took to Jacquelin's side.

"Great timing ..." he breathed out.

"Amazing timing," Jacquelin said, her hold on Bonnie tightening a bit.

Kendra landed beside Eden a moment later, and a red flash washed over her as well. With it, a similar and all-too-familiar wave of weakness quickly encumbered her.

"What the hell?" Kendra hissed, her eyes not daring to leave the chimera, and she glanced to Eden with concern. Intimate and accursed in her memory, her stomach churned with the sickening hex cast upon them. "Eden, keep your guard! This feeling ... it's—"

"Like you've been afflicted by the eye of Jugo?" Hyde interrupted.

Kendra spun around, and as if a wave of darkness circled her vision, she saw an envious green iris burning into her, indigo rivers stretching into the abyss it crawled from.

"It's been some time ..." Hyde continued, chuckling darkly as his form contorted. As if spilling out of clothing that was too tight, his form grew, and an ashen hue wrapped around his skin as his nails became black. From his head, curved black horns extended with the tips nearly joining as they pointed out, and waves of red hair spilled down his shoulders. His gaze then found Kendra, who immediately tensed.

"*You're supposed to be locked up!*" she hissed. Her fingers went rigid, an itch for vengeance gathering at the pointed tips of her claws. She was briefly confused as to why she hadn't smelled the sulfur blending with his normal scent. Glamour was superficial, only capable of fooling certain senses—her nose could detect demons easily. Seeing as the Sieghart were renowned for their powerful shadow magic, she assumed Oliver had used it to sell their disguise.

"Things were supposed to be a lot of ways, *girl*," Oliver hissed.

Eden glanced over his shoulder at the sound of his voice, but he quickly turned his attention back to the crouching chimera, which refrained from lunging.

Bonnie looked up at Jacquelin, her heart stopping when she saw remorseless black eyes and slit magenta hues staring down at her. Whispering a word in Indiox, light shimmered around Bonnie, stripping her form of the glamour that maintained Andrew's visage, and she took on her normal appearance again.

"Quite the convincing performance, but you were doomed from the start, little lady," spoke the woman parading as Jacquelin, her own glamour fading. Her stature grew to something far more imposing, taller than Eden even. Her complexion became leathery with a light gray hue, and pearl-white nails dug into Bonnie's neck as her slender fingers curled tightly around it. Her clothing hadn't significantly changed, akin to a hunter suit, minus the armored sections. It was pure black, utilizing a unique stitching pattern that also differed, and in the center of her chest was a twinkling reaper gem.

Eden's eyes widened, his heart racing for a moment before he composed himself. She was a ferali. He could never forget his encounter with Cecilia over a year ago—the unrelenting fury she had displayed. The resemblance was undeniable, but she was not the infamous lord he had witnessed his mother vanquish. Her long hair was a wild mixture of white and black instead of the pure white color of Cecilia's, but their eyes were the same.

"One of the daughters," Eden whispered, his dispersed attention dancing between her and the chimera. Cecilia had three daughters with Salem that he knew of. The one before them was the eldest, Salana. The fact she conspired with Orphan and Onaga hardly surprised him—vengeance was a motivator he understood intimately.

The OCN's trafficking of humans to Onaga was what originally led the Hunters to investigate them. Since interrogating the demon scientists, he had wondered about the resurgence in their activities, and Salana inspired a hypothesis within him. Suddenly, she chuckled darkly, the tip of her claw drawing blood from Bonnie's neck.

"Like that, you're ours, demigod. Pretty anticlimactic, but make no mistake, I will ensure you suffer for what you did to my father," Salana hissed, her eyes tracing to Oliver.

Petrified, Bonnie's fearful eyes met Kendra's and Eden's gazes.

"You have to leave me," she concluded with a sniffle, her voice strained under the pressure of Salana's fingers.

"Like hell I will!" Eden snapped. "We'll get you out of here!"

Oliver held his fingers out, darkness leaching from his palm and curling around his fingers menacingly, but he refrained from lashing out with them yet.

"You know why we're here. You're not stupid. Insolent, but not stupid," he spat coldly, his arm tensing as his black coat undulated with his festering energy.

"Captain ... you know they aren't going to spare me—even with your surrender. You two have to retreat!" she called out, her voice raspy as Salana squeezed the breath from her.

"Looks like she isn't stupid either," Salana hummed.

"Now!" Bonnie shouted. Her face contorted as a sharp pain spread from her back; as she lowered her head, a curved blade protruded through her chest. A light blue energy permeated the wound, siphoning into the blade.

Attached to Salana's right wrist, a pale blade jutted out from the metallic gauntlet on her free hand. Its surface glimmered with lilac energy, and in response, the gem in her chest gleamed brightly. She tore the blade from Bonnie's chest, the light from the wound surging into the gem. With a raspy groan, Bonnie fell to the ground, and her skin became taut and leathery. Soul torn from her body, its color quickly drained.

"Bonnie!" Kendra yelled, her chest tight as she thought to lunge, but Eden's hand shot out and caught her shoulder, firm but rumbling.

"*You scum ...*" Eden hissed. Rage swarmed his words, barely contained, and Oliver mirrored his displeasure, glaring at Salana.

"Are you *stupid*? She was a bargaining chip," Oliver spat.

"She was going to die anyway, and they knew that. I'd rather dispense with the dramatics and get this over with," she said coldly, the pale scythe-like blade on her wrist shimmering. Oliver shook his head and turned his attention to his prey.

"Even with my eye, you realize he would be a nuisance," he whispered, blissfully unaware of Kendra's hearing. With a snap of his fingers, several shadows manifested around them, where the rest of the *hunters* emerged. Their glamours melted to reveal the depths of Orphan's infiltration. Most of them were cloaked umbra demons—Siegharts that escaped with Oliver—and the other was a fleshy humanoid of lanky proportions. It lacked a proper face, with gaping holes for orifices and knife-like claws and teeth where its mouth was. A *legion*.

The two hunters were surrounded, and with their weakened connection to Ichor, their odds of escape were nearly impossible. The teleportation crystals given to them wouldn't bypass the pervasive distortion either. The drawbacks of teleportation through Ichor rendered it useless when distortion was great enough. While it was far from ideal, they concluded they would have to fight.

Kendra's nerves were more than tested, but as Eden's hand stopped quivering on her shoulder, a jolt of focus returned to her.

"Assume dire formation and stay close to me. We're at a disadvantage, but so are they. They have to pull their punches because of me," he whispered, his voice now tranquil. "First priority is to disable the chimera temporarily—don't waste your time trying to kill it. Don't engage that ferali alone. She's our biggest threat. Spread their focus; you only need a few seconds out of Oliver's eyesight for your connection to stabilize. I'll keep his attention while we thin their numbers. Understood?"

Kendra was beyond concerned. She was proficient, but without her flames, which were barely embers under Oliver's leer, she was relegated to basic combat. Eden's reliance upon her maintained her composure, and as she had done many times before, she placed her trust in him.

"Roger," she whispered, lowering her stance as to allow Eden the breadth of Avenger's reach—a wolf guarding his throat, positioned to retaliate. Oliver had barely noticed the shift while he and Salana bickered, an advantage for their rebellion. She stooped lower when Eden dug Avenger into the ground and swung it above her to scatter a cloud of dust in Oliver's direction.

The chimera lunged forward, but Eden leaped into the air, luring its gaze as he intended. It wasn't exceptionally intelligent, and she capitalized on that when she dashed past the chimera and cleaved through its ligaments with her claws. As it tumbled, its momentum carried it toward Oliver and Salana.

Shadows rose at Oliver's feet, lashing out and slowing the chimera before Salana slammed her hand into its side, stopping it before it hit them. Oliver was quick to return his right eye to Eden, who joined Kendra's side again.

Within the rush, the Sieghart demons surrounding them readied their magic, but mimicking Eden, she scattered dust and debris with her claws to create a smoke screen. With the demons' visions obscured, she and Eden advanced.

Oliver was unaware of Kendra as she lunged past the chimera toward him, but Salana met her approach, engaging her in close combat. The high-pitched sound of claws meeting metal prompted him to retreat into the shadows, reforming several yards away.

With the attrition fully ignited, Eden joined Kendra against Salana. He attacked high, and Kendra low. Salana reeled back, inhaling deeply while energy gathered in her throat, and Eden lunged in, snatching her face in his grasp and slamming her into the ground. With a yank, her jaw cracked in his grip.

"Go!" Eden ordered and pinned Salana's weapon arm down.

Kendra rushed toward Oliver, and several demons closed in on her. For reasons unapparent, the legion took to Oliver's side instead. A direct assault against Oliver would go poorly in her current state, even with her connection to Ichor minimally reestablished. Following Eden's suggestion, she aimed to thin their numbers.

Flames surged in her palms. By her estimate, she had enough energy for two attacks. With a flick, she sent a wall of fire curving in front of the demons, which Oliver's shadows immediately worked to stamp out. She condensed her remaining flames to her claws, her blue eyes brimming with embers.

Though they shot blasts of purple energy at her, she dodged, her agility greater than theirs. She closed in and cut two of their throats with swift swipes, embedding her claws into the back of the neck of another before hoisting him off the ground.

The umbra demons from the opposite side locked onto Kendra's energy signature, still unable to see her as the flames obscured their vision. They shot three bolts at her, but Kendra used the demon she held as a shield. When the bolts tore through him, she flung what was left of his body at one. She hurdled over the wall of flames and landed atop one of the several demons.

She twisted her core to yank him into their line of fire, then, as her teeth grew, she bit into his neck and tore a chunk out. The taste of demon blood was revolting, and it offered little in the way of power compared to a human's or her syn-blood, but it was good enough in a pinch.

Instilled with power, her scarlet irises cleaved the darkness pervading her sockets, and with a loud howl, fire exploded from her body, scorching the other demons. Immediate threats eliminated, she charged Oliver on all fours with her claws digging into the ground.

The familiar red flash assailed her when she met his gaze, and a large shadow tendril flicked from his feet, sending her tumbling back. Eden was there to catch her in his arms, pulling her to her feet before placing his back on hers. He had let go of Salana, and the chimera had fully regenerated now, marching to her side as its wounds steamed.

The legion beside Oliver approached them, and the only remaining umbra demon peeked from behind him. Surrounded again, Eden's eyes danced rapidly, and he held Avenger in front of him.

"Stay on me. I have a plan," he said, knowing Kendra would pick up on what he intended.

She nodded silently, glancing to see the black luster of Avenger as Eden directed its edge toward the legion. Crimson rivers climbed its edge, subtly pulsing with its appetite whetted. She then understood his intention.

The chimera charged, but it slowed in Eden's perception. He poised Avenger and stabbed it through the bottom of its bestial maw. Pushing it forward, he jerked its head to the side before driving Avenger deep into the ground. No matter how it'd writhe or pull, he knew it would be unable to lift the blade conventionally or break the ground, its thick bones working against it.

Eden turned to Kendra, gesturing his head toward Salana, who still held her dislocated jaw.

"Careful, she's seraph-classed," he said, and Kendra nodded. Unquestioningly, she then engaged Salana in vicious attrition.

Eden rushed the legion and sent a kick to its head. A sickening crack echoed, but it remained in place, cackling with an amalgamation of voices as its body contorted. It split into two, like a hydra's head—exactly as he intended. Blow after blow, its flesh distorted and split. Eden persisted in his relentless assault, maneuvering expertly between their increasing numbers and dodging the shadow tendrils Oliver conjured to assist the legion. With their numbers quickly increasing, Oliver's view became obscured, and he retracted direct assistance to reorient his sight of Eden and Kendra.

Eden leaped back, holding his hand out. Avenger suddenly tore through the jaws of the pinned chimera and shot into his palm before he stabbed through a row of legions.

With an audible pulse, Avenger flickered red as their blood widened the rivers along its surface. Avenger was immune to the leer of envy, and unlike Kendra, it relished the taste of demon blood. The blade thrummed in his grip, red veins of crimson energy streaking along it.

"Roar!" Eden called out as Avenger surged with red electricity, chirping like a thousand birds. Arcs of deadly energy branched to impale the legions, electrocuting them in unison before he withdrew and unleashed a volley of slashes. He turned in time to see the recovered chimera lunge at him. With a well-timed slash, the energy-filled blade sent the beast flying back again, and with the legions disabled, he had the path to Oliver he had planned for.

Eden spun and hurled Avenger at Oliver and his hiding ally. They raised their hands, and large shadow tendrils erected in an attempt to stop Avenger, but it sliced through the tendrils with ease. Oliver quickly ducked as it flew toward them, and the umbra demon at his side shrieked, doubling away. It had been a ploy, Oliver failing to see Eden approaching beneath Avenger's bright glare.

He punched Oliver, sending him tumbling back, and he closed in once more with the intention of ripping Oliver's accursed eye out. In that outstretched moment, Eden met his eyes, but Oliver gazed past Eden as shadows formed to shield his ears. Eden knew then that he had been too late.

A piercing shriek ruptured the air—Salana's voice—and wailing winds strangled all sound. Though Oliver fell to a knee and flinched, Eden, who hadn't been braced, fell to the ground, holding his ears while shouting in pain. In his debilitation, Oliver's shadows constricted his limbs and throat, pinning him.

Moments later, Kendra was tossed beside him, her ears bleeding and barely conscious as she gasped weakly. Salana approached, growling through her jagged teeth as she looked at Oliver.

"You seriously are useless, Oliver. You're more of a lord of cowards than envy," she hissed venomously, the muscles in her neck bulging as she exhaled heavily.

Oliver stood shakily, releasing his ears as he panted.

"You were the fool who thought this would be easy and gave away our leverage! My eye consumes more energy than you can understand!" he shot back, visible froth dripping down his scruffy beard. He stomped his foot down onto Eden's chest with a crack, but Eden barely reacted. The shadows continued constricting his neck as he ground his teeth, and he glared up at Oliver with a frightening focus that gave the demon pause.

As Kendra stirred, she tried to stand, but Salana kicked her onto her back and whistled. In the next moment, the chimera dashed over. Its talons pressed down around Kendra, one claw embedding itself into her left shoulder and jamming into the ground as she howled. It opened its mouth wide, its rancid breath washing over her as it prepared to take a bite.

"You will wait, beast!" Oliver hissed, making the chimera close its mouth, but it licked its serrated teeth impatiently as it eyed Kendra. "Dahlia, grab his weapon!" he called to the female umbra demon behind him.

Dahlia stood to her feet, rubbing her head with a soft moan as she lowered her hood. Brown curls spilled out, framed by shimmering, flawless black horns. She jogged over to where Avenger was and reached down before grabbing the hilt. When she tried to stand, however, the blade didn't budge. Something ethereal kept her from lifting it.

Eden's hand tensed, and his glare sharpened as he called Avenger back to his hand. It tore from the woman's hand, making her yelp as it flew toward Oliver fast, but before it could reach him, Salana deflected it with her wrist blade.

"Pay attention, you idiot! Have you ever been in a battle before? Either of you pathetic umbras?" she spat, crossing her arms expectantly. The legion waited on the outskirts of the circle that formed around the hunters, now fully healed from Eden's assault.

"We have," the legion spoke.

"Quiet," Salana spat, shooting the legion a glare. Despite their annoyed grumbles, they obeyed.

Oliver's shadows leached from his form and wrapped around Avenger to anchor it. Reminded once more of Eden's adamance, he glared at Eden's left arm—his dominant arm.

"Come to think of it ... I've yet to pay you back for what you did to me that night," he said, and the shadows around Eden's limbs quaked. The tendril slowly pulled his left arm up, constricting tighter around the limb as Eden's pained grunts grew in his resistance. Oliver raised his foot as the tendril twisted Eden's arm, and he brought his boot down onto the joint, snapping his arm with a sickening pop.

Eden howled as the tendrils further mangled his broken arm.

"If only we had that damned cinder too," he grumbled before kicking Eden's face to silence him.

"He shouldn't be able to resist now. Shouldn't we get going?" Dahlia suggested, shuffling to Oliver's side and gripping his arm.

Oliver's face contorted in dissatisfaction, and he met Salana's gaze. She scoffed at him dismissively, and he returned his attention to Kendra.

"Kendra Mallory," Oliver spoke, approaching her slowly. Their eyes met, and she growled at him through labored breaths. Her ears had healed mostly, but with her slowed regeneration, everything was still quiet. "You've caused me much trouble."

"I should have caused more," she spoke, breathing in a raspy breath as the talon in her shoulder shifted, making her whimper.

"You couldn't begin to understand!" he snapped, leaning down and snatching her face. "No matter how I bargain, beat, or berate him, my son refuses to see his potential—his destiny as the most powerful Lord of Envy to exist—and it's because of *you*," he hissed. As he spewed his venom, he raked her cheek and drew blood.

Dahlia snorted at the sight as she inspected Kendra.

"Wait, that's the girl from the Night of Envy? The tramp that was in the cheap dress? Fitting she's a mutt now," she chimed, smirking condescendingly at Kendra. "I can't believe Allen preferred you ... but it's okay, Ollie's better. And you'll be dying here, anyway."

"Shut up, both of you!" Salana spat, shooing Oliver away. "Your chimera can eat the bodies of the other demons that perished."

"Those demons were my kin, you bitch," Oliver growled.

"And they're better off as chimera shit," Salana said. She hovered above Kendra, the blade on her gauntlet glowing. "Get the demigod to that laboratory. I will inform my mother so Onaga may have my father returned to life, as per our agreement. I'm rather fatigued, so if you don't mind, I'll be taking the mutt's soul."

"No!" Eden gasped, his voice broken and barely audible. "You can have me. Leave Kendra out of this," he begged, his eyes wide as he gritted his bloody teeth through the pain.

"Oh, please. Have some dignity," Salana declared coldly, her face twisting. "You killed my father with no regard for how my family would feel, and yet you beg for clemency? No." She glared harshly. "I will tear this girl's soul out slowly and painfully. Then I will relieve her of her head—just as you had done to my father. Maybe then you'll understand!"

She pulled Kendra up by her collar, causing the talon to sunder her flesh further and draw an agonizing scream from her. Salana raised her blade, hovering it ominously over Kendra's chest. As she peered into Kendra's soul, her lips curled into a devilish smile.

"Two? What a treat ..."

None of the remaining assailants protested, watching on with mild intrigue. All the while, Eden writhed in his constraints, the pain thrumming in his body doing little to deter him as he brokenly pleaded.

"Ken, I promise I'll—I won't let them ..." Eden began, but Kendra's eyes greeted him with resignation. Palpable disbelief defined her expression, and her face twisted in pain as she gasped for a shallow breath.

Darkness stretched before Eden's vision, the pain overwhelming his consciousness, but he refused to pass out. The tears welling in his eyes finally spilled, and the scene before him faded.

He thought he had lost consciousness at last, but the darkness greeting him was different—*familiar*. He was submerged in its suffocating embrace, and cold whispers rose from within as dreaded eyes glowered at him. Windows peered through, arresting him once more. As if ready to cast him from his own body like it had done to Intico, the rebellion, staring him down, turned his limbs to lead.

"Once again, too weak. Once again ... you watch them take."

The voice boomed from within the darkness, and the palpable eyes before him pulsed with a bright red energy.

"Take. And take. And take. You watch helplessly in the name of holding onto her request—her light. But no such salvation will come."

The abyss surrounding them expanded, and despite his cries for Cassiel, it consumed all before it time and time again. Night after night. Day after day. All that remained dwindled, and when he dared to cherish another, they, too, were to be taken. Lucy, Cassiel, Kendra—everything he held dear ...

"Taken."

The voice's resolve prevailed once more, and his cheeks burned with a sentiment he abhorred, but he was powerless before its promise. No matter the sacrifice it demanded of him, he wouldn't allow fate to unfurl the same way.

"Would you allow them to continue to take?"

Eden's limbs glowed, banishing the shadows constraining him as he stood. With his eyes tightly clenched, his tears became blood, and he gave his answer.

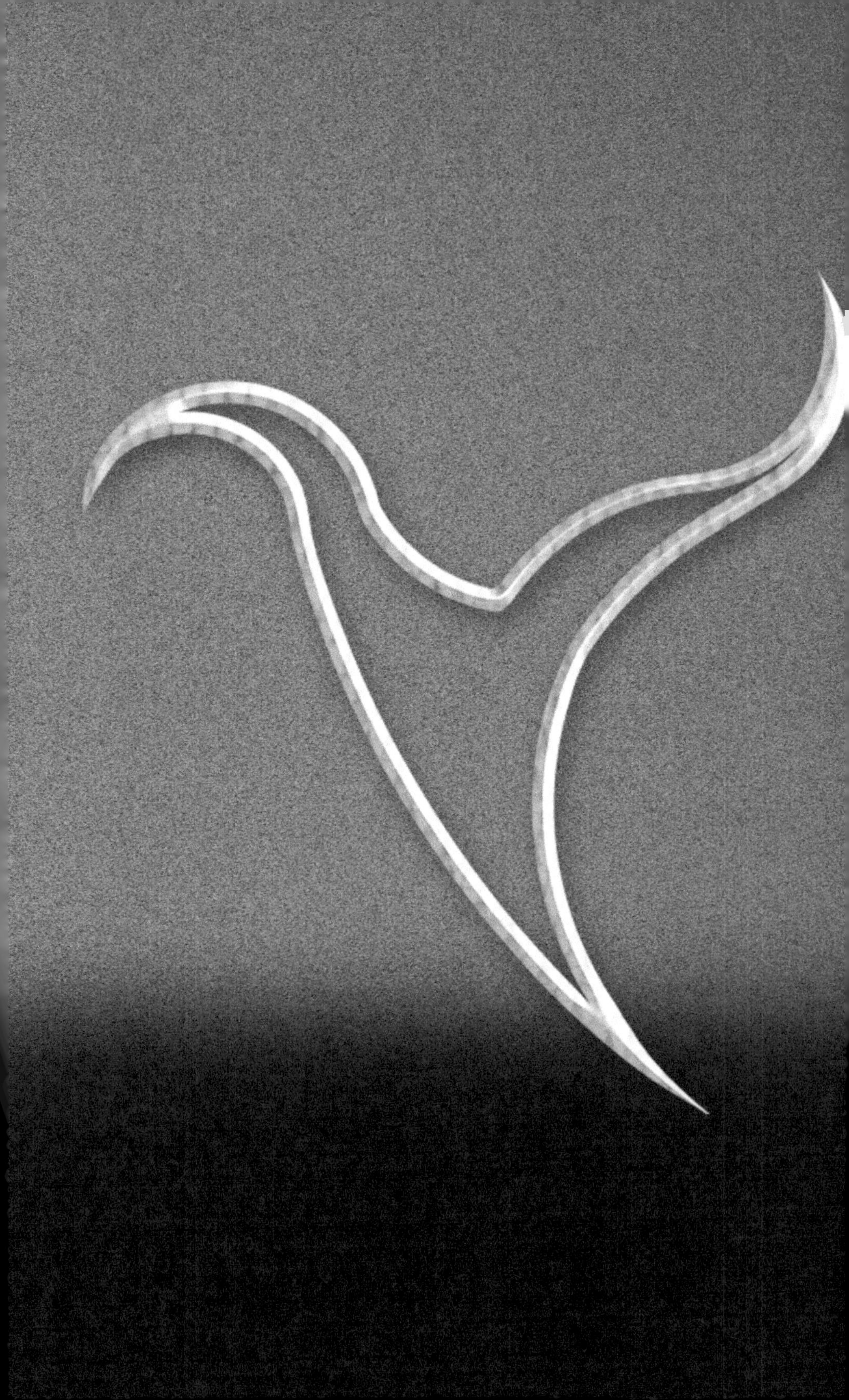

TEN

Near and Far

"No."

The air boiled bright red. Scarlet omens surged and quaked, shrieking and flickering with each silent release of his breath. His eyes glowed pure red, and blood trickled down his face. Burning and viscous, it formed into runes of vengeance atop his cheeks and continued to carve fissures down his body. The slow throb of his heart, intense enough to taste upon his tongue, compelled the air to thrum. *Blood and vengeance.* Time and time again, he unwillingly adopted those fruits. Consummated in ominous silence, his condemnation of their sweetness evanesced once more.

The demons stirred from their sadistic focus, looking back with perturbed expressions—save for Salana. She had pressed her blade against Kendra's chest, but the change of atmosphere prompted her to look in Eden's direction.

"You're too weak, Oliver. Hurry and restrain him," she commanded dismissively. She bared her jagged teeth as she dug the tip of her blade into Kendra's chest, but a tight constriction crushed her wrist.

They hadn't seen Eden move, but he was beside her with astounding speed. His tight fist easily snapped the bones within her limb, and his broken arm lashed out, separating her from the limb as she was sent tumbling across the terrain. Covered in her blood, his bruise-covered arm smoked as the limb corrected itself.

Eden's hand pierced the back of its mane, and he snatched it from atop Kendra, tightly gripping its spine. Although the creature thrashed and roared in his grip, he severed the spine with a squeeze and tossed the creature toward Oliver and Dahlia.

Oliver leaped to the side, but the less athletic demoness was hit by the large beast, and with a brief yelp, she was crushed beneath it. Oliver peered up, his wide eyes locked onto Eden as he focused his eye of Jugo on him, but Eden was unable to be subdued. The sentiment before him was a titan compared to his envy—eclipsed entirely. Even as his shadows lashed out toward Eden, the moment they neared him, they dissipated from the immense pressure of his being.

Barely conscious, Kendra peered up at Eden, her vision blurry as her head throbbed. Still, the pain lingered, even as she regenerated, and she remained motionless on the ground.

"Eden?" she called, but he didn't answer, his frightening focus refusing to break from the *purpose* before him.

Oliver shook from his paralysis and breathed a shallow breath, glancing at the legion. They appeared oblivious, barely roused to the danger before them.

"Restrain him!" Oliver called out, and the legion rushed in.

Eden inhaled, the world in his perception colored the same bright hue as his irises. Before him—*demons. One and all the same. To be vanquished.*

He hadn't bothered calling Avenger to his grip when he unleashed upon the legion again. Eden pummeled their vessels succinctly, repeatedly bathing the earth in their blood no matter how many rushed at him. Strikes faster than any of their eyes could see served as an impervious obstacle to their assault, but their fruitless attempts bought Oliver, Salana, and Dahlia time to recuperate.

Oliver rushed to Dahlia, prying the dead beast off her and pulling her still-healing body from beneath it. Even as Dahlia screamed at him, he stared on in dread. The brutality didn't faze him, but the thoughtlessness and ease did. Such fury he had only witnessed before from the Lady of

Wrath, Eridianne, and even she engaged in such violence with deliberate devotion. Eden's own was something beyond sentient consideration. *Primordial retribution.*

His attention then snapped to Salana, seeing her drag herself to her feet as her arm regenerated at an abnormally quick rate. Bone, muscle, then skin. Wiry strands of her hair then stitched around her arm, reforming her suit, but the blade that had been attached to the gauntlet shot from her forearm as she growled.

"Oliver, suppress him!" she shouted, unaware that he couldn't.

"He is suppressed!" Oliver called back, his green iris flaring brighter with his dormant envy. He thought of his son, the humiliation he'd endured for the past three years, and the expectations he had shouldered his entire life. Overwhelmed by all the envy he had conjured, his eye throbbed painfully and bled. It wasn't enough—*it was never enough.*

Eden held up the last vessel the legion possessed. No longer able to multiply, their cool-toned skin undulated as they gargled and spewed profanities using Indiox. Without hesitating, Eden swiped its head off and discarded the corpse. Then he returned his attention to Oliver and Dahlia, walking toward them as she cowered behind Oliver.

Salana rushed at Eden, drawing her weapon back. He caught her wrist when she went to stab him, squeezing it tightly. Through gritted teeth, she inhaled deeply, preparing to unleash another magic-fueled screech, but he slammed his fist into her throat, prompting her to reel back while grasping her throat.

Eden twisted her around, jabbing his hand through her chest, her reaper gem in his palm. Tears gathered in her eyes, her voice raspy and weak.

"Cecil ... Erena," she gasped, gurgling as her blood spilled from her lips.

Eden crushed the gem, its light scattering as it crumbled from his fist. As she went limp, he withdrew his arm with a flick and let her corpse crumple to the ground before turning back to the others.

Oliver trembled, his shadows latching at his feet in his attempt to retreat. The air quaked with Eden's scrutiny, and the shadows dissipated from the distortion Eden generated. Realizing the hopeless endeavor,

Dahlia shoved Oliver, turning on her heel as she began to dash away, running past Kendra, who looked up at the sheer horror her face spelled.

Dahlia gasped out as Eden caught her, hoisting her up by the back of her neck. She kicked and thrashed, begging for her life. Limb by limb, he tore her apart. Limb from limb, then her head. What remained of her once beautiful form was caked in blood as he dropped her, leaving Oliver.

Eden came to a stop before Oliver, eyes burning bright and unwavering. In the corner of his vision, Kendra stumbled to her feet, looking upon him with a mix of fear and concern. She approached hesitantly, her footsteps echoing in the raging calm. Oliver took trembling steps back, but Eden closed in.

His hand twitched, and Avenger shot toward him, the hilt snapping into his palm. The rivers of blood along it pulsed like a beating heart as the blood dripping from it disappeared.

"*On your knees,*" Eden said, his voice calm yet shuddering with power that subjugated the air. Be it defiance or fear, Oliver went still as their gazes met. When Eden saw Oliver's legs twitch, he swiped Avenger, severing them legs clean off.

Oliver fell, wailing in pain as blood pooled at the stumps of his calves. His fingers raked the ground, barely holding his body up as he writhed. He was only silenced when Eden slammed his boot into his face, making him tumble and slide. Gargled moans filled the silence, several teeth falling from his mouth.

Eden approached, methodical and slow as to stir urgency in his foe. He came to a stop above Oliver, unblinking and still. Though he was silent for several moments, the air thumped with pulses that rumbled in Kendra and Oliver's ears—his heartbeat.

"*You ...*" Eden began. "*I know you. Insatiable and wretched.*" His eyes narrowed with the harshest of indictments. "*Demon.*" Their eyes met, and Oliver coughed out several broken teeth and congealed blood.

"Wait ..." Oliver breathed out, and Eden obliged, expectant in the audience he granted. It was a well-known phenomenon: the demigod that escaped Onaga's lab. It was said very few survived the ordeal—he then knew why.

"*Speak*," Eden demanded after several seconds. Oliver gathered himself, the man's face contorting as his wounds sizzled.

"I—we were told to take you to Orphan. That man, woman ... or whatever the fuck it is, was to take you to Onaga's lab. I don't know where it is—I swear!" Oliver let out in a garbled voice, words slurred from his missing teeth.

"*Take me to Orphan*," Eden replied simply, but Oliver was silent, lost within the inferno in Eden's eyes. What Eden discerned within his gaze suggested direness—desperation. It sickened him.

"I can't," Oliver said. There was only a moment's silence, broken by a movement he hadn't even perceived. Eden stomped Oliver's arm, cracking the ground and leaving it hideously mangled—like Oliver had done to his arm.

Oliver screamed, making Kendra's ears twitch as she listened to the agonizing wails of the demon. She rushed toward Eden. Though odd, she wanted to protest in favor of bringing Oliver back to base for a productive interrogation, but with another beat of Eden's heart, she stopped. Something insidious petrified her as she neared him.

"Eden!" she called out in an unsteady voice, but *he* didn't hear her.

Oliver writhed beneath Eden, who pinned his chest with a bloodied boot. The gray hue of his skin peeled away, revealing the light human color beneath as his demonic features retreated. With all his energy going into regeneration, his demonic form was no longer sustainable.

"*Who is Orphan pretending to be?*" Eden asked.

"I can't tell—"

Eden snatched his mangled arm, tugging it from his body effortlessly.

Oliver nearly passed out from the pain as he cried and writhed. Eden crouched, snatching Oliver's face and glaring deep into his. Visions of agony assailed the pitiful demon, submerging him within ice and fire in tandem. This forced his bloodshot eyes open as blood dripped from them.

"I can't say it!" Oliver sobbed out.

Kendra shook her head, biting her tongue as she reached out and grabbed Eden's shoulder. Something hadn't settled with her. Oliver hadn't shown a great deal of resistance to interrogation, as Eden had once told her. Undoubtedly, Oliver would have spoken by then if that were true.

"There has to be a reason he isn't speaking. He would have already," she said unsteadily. Her hands quivered as his terrifying aura assailed her, nausea creeping through her veins. Its wrath—its agony—was indiscriminate. Insatiable fury that challenged all before it; she felt such a sentiment didn't belong to him. "Who are you?" she croaked out.

The silence peeled away what remained of her nerves, his heart still for too long. When he glanced back at her, who she stared at was not Eden.

"*What remains,*" it spoke through him. "*Untethered in his subjugation—eternally bound.*" Those chaotic eyes returned to Oliver, meeting his gaze. Oliver, with his remaining arm, reached up and grabbed Eden's leg, pleading unintelligibly. Without regard, he tore that arm off as well, tossing it to the side.

As Oliver screamed and heaved, Eden's heartbeat drowned it out, and his visage and sentiments scorned Kendra's vision.

"*Those who would see us suffer—those who would see us die. My wings become ash and serve as my throne in the dark. Upon these ephemeral feathers, bathed in blood, I become a despot of wrath—my reign bound in agony.*"

As Eden spoke, his voice, despite its calmness, drowned out Oliver's audacious cries. His eyes narrowed, expression suddenly marred. Hatred in the deepest sense revealed itself within his haunted depths. With that single show of emotion, Oliver's fate was sealed. Before the being above him, he was nothing but a disturbance to be removed.

"Please, no!" Oliver wailed, squirming in his final moments before Eden turned his head into mulch for the desecrated ground beneath. Gore dripped from his boot, and all semblance of emotion faded from his face.

It had all been too quick, and Kendra's hand slipped from his shoulder as she fell to her knees. She remembered to breathe, gagging as the suffocating pressure encumbered her. By the time she raised her gaze, Eden was walking away, sheathing Avenger on his hip as his once broken arm dangled loosely at his side. The healing factor in this state was not akin to a demon's, she surmised, but she had originally thought him incapable of accelerated healing.

"*Return*," Eden's voice echoed. Kendra stood, knees buckling as she resurrected her strength.

"Eden!" she called out, stumbling after him. He paused in his tracks and glanced back at her. "What—where are you going?" she breathed out, her heart pounding as if to escape from her chest the closer she was to him.

"*To Onaga. To end this once and for all.*"

"You don't even know where to find him, and if you did, you'd die all alone!" she gasped out, grasping her throat as she wrestled for oxygen within the hot air.

"*Forget me*," he spoke, continuing to walk away again.

"What the fuck, Eden? What kind of selfish bullshit is that? Forget you? I'm your friend. *I fucking love you.*" She breathed in. "You saved my life and think that's an option I'd accept? It isn't!" She panted heavily, marching after him before snatching his arm and turning him to look at her, and when she saw his face, she gasped in horror.

The blood that marked his skin undulated, the fissures along his body cracking and contorting as his face twisted.

"*Again, and again ...*" he said, and his voice lost its intensity as he exhaled. "They take everything. I can't lose what little I have left. If keeping you far away ensures you can remain, then ..." He gasped, his body trembling as his skin steamed, and he tried to step away from her. Instead, he crumpled to his knees, bloody tears spilling anew and widening the chasms along his body.

"Eden," Kendra whispered, her eyes quivering as she dropped to his level. "If you died, a piece of me would go with you. I wouldn't remain—not truly. Can't you see that? Don't"—she grabbed his face, wiping the tears streaming down his face away—"you want to live?"

Eden refused to answer. He finally met her gaze, perceiving her at last. At last, he had emerged from the abyss he was submerged within, and the light in his eyes faded. Before her, for the first time in a long time, his green eyes—the true color beneath his divinity—met hers.

Kendra's fingers tensed, his blood dripping down her fingers as she stared deep into those verdant depths. Though he didn't reply, she knew the answer—she always had.

His seclusion—his refusal to be known. Mirroring their battlefield, littered with desecration and death, his mind was no different. The countless times she saw him ruminating at that cliff, the times she saw him staring too deeply into Avenger with its edge toward himself—she knew deep down how he suffered. Orphan's declaration rang deep.

You will never be free.

Kendra failed to find words. Loss and grief were beyond familiar, but the despair in his eyes, she was a stranger to. She could endlessly espouse the value of life and living through adversity. She could profess the beauty of the world, but those forlorn green eyes would not discern it; for beauty was in the eye of the beholder, but jaded eyes could not glean jewels.

Eden gently pried himself from her, standing as he clutched his injured arm. He winced when he spotted Bonnie's lifeless form, and he inhaled with an agonizing wheeze through gritted teeth.

Fear. It always lingered in unsuspecting ways. Crescent white eyes that once pried him open and reminded him of everything he would never be free from. Shadows that mangled him tighter than Oliver's ever could. Intico's question from years ago fermented again—its answer he wouldn't have admitted before.

"I am broken," he breathed out, his voice low and cracking. Often, he struggled to speak clearly if he overused his voice—it had been that way since he escaped imprisonment.

Kendra stood, ready to testify—to admonish the sentiment he declared—but he growled deeply, shaking his head.

"We have to return to base and warn them."

Kendra pondered the thought, mulling over the tumult of their prior conversation a bit longer before she cleared her mind. She knew that he would shut down any attempt at further discussing it, but thwarting Orphan's ruse took priority.

"I know," she spoke quietly, her voice filled with regret, but she glanced to where the rift once was, seeing it closed following Oliver's demise. With it, the distortion was gone.

"If Orphan set us up, there is a chance that going back the conventional way is risky. Their moles may be guarding the terminals. That could rob us of the surprise we need."

"Evans ..." Eden spoke quietly, opening his eyes to face Kendra.

"Him ..." Kendra's teeth bared, thinking back to the tingling cold in her palm when she touched him. "He's Orphan?"

"The details of this assignment were classified to only him and General Blackwell. Either he's Orphan or a puppet. Whichever hardly matters right now."

"Right," Kendra said, swallowing hard. Something still didn't sit right with her about it. Orphan had made a critical mistake when they pretended to be Kendall. Calling her by the wrong nickname was an easy giveaway—one that betrayed the diligence she gleaned from the carefully woven conspiracy. Call signs weren't permitted, and Commander Evans was strict about keeping to last names; knowing her actual nickname would have been unlikely.

Eden shifted his gaze back to Bonnie's corpse, flinching again as his arm throbbed in his tight grasp of it.

"We'll need to sneak back in somehow. We'll have to come back for her body later."

"You're hurt," Kendra said, creeping toward him with an outstretched hand, but he shook his head.

"I'll keep. We need to think quick."

Kendra stirred for several seconds, biting her bottom lip until her canine broke through. The taste of her own blood somehow made it easier to quell her nerves and focus, as she had discovered when she inevitably bit herself.

Bonnie had never set up the communication array, meaning they hadn't been monitored over their hunter utility devices—a purposeful design, they both assumed. The terminals were their only timely option, Kendra determined. However, she knew they needed someone to assist them in reaching it discreetly—someone on guard duty.

"Emily is on terminal watch for about another hour," Kendra began, clenching her hands. "She'll help us get back unnoticed if I explain the situation to her," she said before reaching into her pouch.

"Orphan is likely monitoring the communications. The moment we set that tower up, we'll be discovered," Eden claimed.

"I have her direct number. We need to head back to town so I can send her a text to prompt her first, then call to explain." As she explained, his brow was knit with uncertainty.

"What if she doesn't answer?" Eden asked, but Kendra gave an assuring expression of certainty.

"She will."

"How many hunters have to shed their blood before we know who Orphan is?" Commander Trayvon Rigs spoke. With an expectant gaze, his dark eyes scanned the council of high-ranking hunters and Jessica alike.

Beside Jessica were Commander Evans and Ethan, both considering Trayvon's question. Commander Evans appeared more annoyed than anything, two fingers pressed to his ear as he received updates about Angel Forty-Seven from Command. Ethan's eyes roamed the room, but his gaze primarily resided on Commander Rigs.

"No more, if I can help it," Ethan replied.

"Then why the hell are we still authorizing missions while we *know* we've been compromised?" Commander Rigs challenged, and an older woman fixed her collar and cleared her throat.

"Ceasing our operations entirely is heavily disadvantageous. Germany did just that, and look where their hunters ended up. Every single one of them. Dead. We lie down now, we'll be the same. That's probably what *he* wants," she claimed sternly.

"So Orphan's a man then?" a younger major sitting beside her alleged, his face scrunching in disbelief.

"Considering General Blackwell and I are the only females on this council, yes." She tapped the table sharply. "And with my lack of involvement or knowledge of the assignment in which Angel Forty-Five was ambushed, it is safe to say I am not a culprit," she claimed. Major Rashon Carter rolled his eyes.

"Could still be an informant," Major Carter spoke. His gloved hand tightly gripped the table. Thin metallic frames lined his fingers, grime along his limbs as if pulled from a garage to be in the meeting. "If Private Carter is a suspect, any and all relevant intel is on the table, yeah?" he challenged with a snarky tone, echoing a sentiment she once espoused to him.

"You're out of line, Major Carter," she snapped.

Soon, the council was rife with raucous arguments and accusations. Different personnel tried poking holes in logic, asserting inconsistencies. A few seconds into the noise, Commander Rigs stood and slammed his hands on the table.

"Quiet!" he demanded, and the council obliged his command. Jessica's head was down, her hat's shadow looming over her face to disguise her expression and gaze, and soon, the council turned their attention to her.

"General?" a commander prompted, and Jessica slowly lifted her head, a scarily remorseless expression painting her face.

"Keep your friends close and enemies closer. That is the adage, yes?" Jessica began, her voice hovering at a low volume to ensure everybody actively listened. All the while, her fingers dug at the cracked sections of the table that had been crudely taped over—the spot Eden had damaged years ago. "Would you wager that Orphan understands this best? That tearing us apart and remaining embedded within the turmoil is advantageous?" Jessica stood, turning her back to the others.

They watched her with bated breath, none daring to interrupt. Ethan eyed the spot she had been sitting. It wasn't lost on him that she always sat at that spot during meetings. In that moment, as she prepared to speak again, he wished he could see her eyes.

"My son," Jessica began, her tone accusatory. "He has always been sought and hunted, and Onaga would see him taken again. If this is the case, an *upstart* such as Intico would never have been allowed to prosper. Taking the body of such a valuable target hardly makes sense if his vessel is needed for whatever that abominable fallen fiend is entertaining!" Her fists curled tightly, her dark energy boiling in her palms. "And yet … I must express I believe that was what Orphan intended. Eden being merged with would have rendered him easier to capture." She inhaled sharply. "Yes, that was the design, wasn't it, Orphan?"

Jessica turned, casting her glare over the room.

"To make me grieve again. To undo the thread that tethers our mission and goal. And now, you wage this corrosive campaign." She slammed her palms onto the table, splintering it at the same spot Eden had. As her fists rumbled with power, steam and particles of magic escaped her lips. "I will see you damned and sundered before I send you back to the pit you crawled from …"

A hand rested on her shoulder, and her glare snapped to the side. She half expected it to be Ethan, but instead, it was Commander Evans.

"Jess …" he spoke, his hand slowly slipping from her.

Ethan gently slipped his hand into Jessica's, tugging it softly as he firmly fixed his gaze on hers. Gently, her fingers traveled up his wrist, and she squeezed his wrist for several moments until he released her.

"Excuse my loss of composure," she stated, returning to her seat and hanging her head once more.

Following her speech, the discussion resumed, calmer than before. Ethan and Commander Evans remained quiet at her side, their solemn expressions burrowing deep when their pensive gazes met. An alarm sounded within the building as security announced a lockdown, and several commanders and majors stood from their seats, attentions on the door. Ethan's hunter bracer went off on his wrist, and he raised his sleeve. He tapped his earpiece.

"What's going on?" he asked.

"Sir, Captain Blackwell and Private Mallory have breached the building," the voice informed.

"What?" he gasped, his eyes darting between the door and Commander Evans.

Jessica gripped her hilt, her senses homing in until she detected the *intruders*, her eyes going wide.

Two hands tore through the thick wooden doors, black claws raking where the lock was. The commanders drew their guns, but Jessica held her hand up.

"Lower your weapons!" she demanded, breathing heavily.

Upon the locking mechanism being destroyed, Kendra kicked them in. Battered from the ambush, Kendra and Eden marched into the room. Eden held his arm, his green gaze finding Jessica, then both his and Kendra's glares shot to Commander Evans.

"Son, what happened?" Ethan demanded, voice panicked as he examined the two, but Kendra answered.

"You sent us to die!" she spat at Commander Evans, readying herself to lunge, but Ethan and Commander Rigs stepped between them.

"You guys ... what? Impossible. The updates never—what happened?" Commander Evans sputtered as he navigated his hunter gauntlet.

"Commander Evans is the mole!" Kendra said, pointing her claw at him ominously. "We were sent to look over Angel Forty-Five with Bonnie disguised as Andrew under suspicion of his involvement with Orphan." Kendra glanced at Major Carter, then turned to Jessica. "The Sieghart prisoners and other demons were parading as Angel Forty-Five and ambushed us." Kendra's teeth sharpened, her eyes threatening to become demonic. "They killed Bonnie, tried to kill me, and take Eden to Onaga," Kendra hissed breathlessly, her eyes challenging them all.

"The Siegharts escaped?" Jessica questioned, her eyes locking onto Commander Evans, who was desperately tapping away on the projection before he pressed his fingers to his earpiece.

"Command! Give me a report on Angel Forty-Five!" he demanded, and Ethan snatched his wrist, holding it up before pulling the earpiece from his ear and crushing it. The speaker on Commander Evans's hunter utility device then sounded.

"Yes, sir. Private Carter and Sergeant Hopkins reported in on the status of the rift ten minutes prior. All vitals of the squad are in the green," the operator spoke.

Ethan shoved Commander Evans away, holding his hand out.

"Religo!" he said, and Commander Evans's arms snapped behind his back as energy constricted his wrists. "You, Evans?" Ethan said, glowering down at him. "You're a traitor?" he questioned in disbelief.

The council was silent, watching as Commander Evans squirmed. The defiant man shook his head, teeth bared as his wide eyes danced between them.

"Of course not!" he stated, and Ethan gestured to Commander Rigs, who then grabbed Commander Evans, pressing his pistol against his back.

"Then you will explain this at once!" Ethan spoke, his eyes wide as he bared his teeth.

"I don't know what this is about! The operator—"

"Working with you guys? Seems that way."

Jessica was silent, her fists curled as she inspected the pleading commander.

"I have dedicated my life to the Hunt and would never engage in such treachery. Ethan, we trained together—hunted together!" Commander Evans argued.

"No. I hunted with Troy Evans." Ethan took a step forward, leering at him hard as he squirmed in Commander Rigs's tight hold. "You're Orphan, aren't you?"

Commander Evans went pale, eyes wide as his face contorted in discomfort. Kendra recognized that reaction—the same one he had when she touched his hand. Her eyes fell on Eden as he stared at Jessica.

The air was thicker than blood, and their breaths were arrested. Commander Evans's mouth barricaded, refusing to open to answer the question—almost as if magically bound. But the pervasive silence was ephemeral. Among their thumping hearts, Kendra heard the intensity of their anxiety—their grief.

Twelve thumping hearts were in the room. Then there was one less. Eyes shifted to the source of pained groans and pooling blood. The impervious face of the man embodying the conviction of all hunters was twisted, and within it, the dark truth revealed itself.

Beyond all expectations, the depths of treachery were realized with the dagger poking from Ethan's chest.

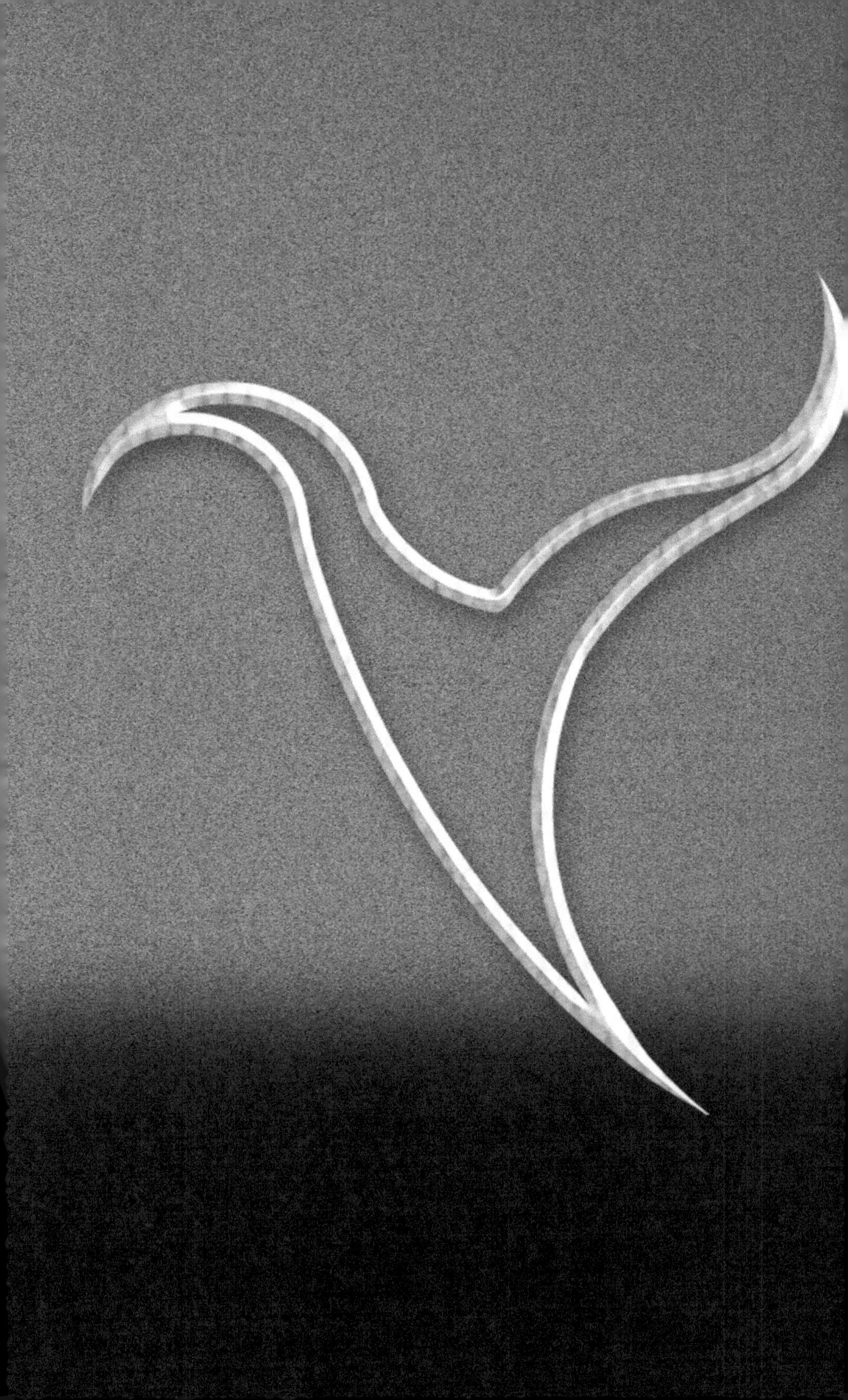

ELEVEN

SINS WE ABHOR

"JESS?" Ethan wheezed, turning his head as he trembled.

The hunters had been ready to draw their weapons, but they hesitated, unable to find their voices for an uproar. A low hum thrummed along the dagger Jessica had stabbed through Ethan, its length twinkling.

"That's quite enough, Orphan," Jessica hissed as she shoved the dagger deeper into *Ethan's* back.

Along the blade, the once crimson blood undulated and turned into a viscous black sludge, as did the pool of blood on the floor. The dagger pulsed with a subtle purple energy, white particles emanating around it as Ethan coughed up the same black sludge, his skin rippling. In the hilt was the soul binder, its inky hue retreating while white particles slowly expanded to the edge.

Tears welled in Jessica's eyes, forming an unsightly union with the wrath in her visage. Her knuckles crackled as her arm tightly constricted his throat. The mounting tension and twisting of the dagger were but a semblance of her barely contained fury.

"How long?" Jessica demanded in a fractured voice, but Ethan refrained from answering as he reached up for the blade jutting through his chest. It shrieked in response, making his hands drop as he lowered his head.

"How did you know?" Orphan's voice rang out, the sound of Ethan's own melting from it. Inhuman and lacking in defining traits, that remorseless voice was all too familiar to Eden and Kendra. The uncanny truth was now known.

Orphan had been Ethan.

Jessica twisted the dagger, causing Orphan to wince as their head raised.

"I know my Ethan more than he knows himself. It's one of those human things you would never understand," Jessica claimed. "You know the rhythm of his heart, but not why it beats." Jessica inhaled sharply, her grip on his neck tightening. "Again, I ask. How long!"

Orphan's expression melted, as did many of the defining features of their face—bleeding away into sludge. The hunters watched in shock, and Commander Rigs finally let Commander Evans go as Orphan began speaking.

"Six years," Orphan stated in a hushed tone. "Operation Gray-Matter—shortly after that seraphim returned Eden to you—I ambushed Seraph Eleven." A dark chuckle echoed from them.

"Ethan would never be so reckless as to let you get the best of him," Jessica accused, her grip on the dagger tightening.

"He wasn't ... or wouldn't have been under normal circumstances. In the report, I mentioned an encounter with Onaga's Venatum acolyte, Noell. He saw to my success," they said.

"You know much of him—beyond well-learned mimicry," Jessica shoved the blade in further, but instead of showing pain, a twisted smile formed from the melting flesh on their face.

"Because I assimilated him. We're now one and the same. Body—mind. Unsure of the soul—I don't get how those things work for humans. I wonder if it was sundered into a state not even Ichor could recognize." Orphan laughed softly. "I can only assimilate one at a time, and who better than the second-in-command? Practicality aside, I genuinely do like him—perhaps more than you do."

Jessica's grip loosened a bit. Her eyes widened as she ground her teeth, black aura flaring around her.

"*You* ..." she wheezed out. "I will fulfill my promise to annihilate you, but first, you will tell me of Onaga's whereabouts—where you intended to have *my* son taken." Her eyes flashed with intense power, an ominous chill filling the room.

"And why would I tell you that? I still have my failsafe."

"Failsafe?"

"The barrier around the base is quite energetic, lots of magnetic resonance that's volatile to those who don't match the safe frequency spectrum. Ever wondered what would happen if all of that energy was suddenly implosive? Could kill me and find out."

Jessica's aura retreated, and she let go of the dagger.

"*No,*" she gasped out, turning to Eden with frantic eyes.

"Wicked Witch of the West isn't so scary now, is she?" Orphan chuckled. "Five minutes. In only five minutes, the hexes will do just as I said. You can protect everybody in this room—the HQ building if you really tried—but everyone else? Well ... you can imagine."

The dagger slipped from Orphan's chest, clattering to the floor as their form slowly stabilized, albeit visibly undulating.

"Perhaps that can be evaded. You know my condition," Orphan said, slowly retaking Ethan's form and straightening their suit. "Don't you, Jess?"

"I won't allow it. You would just trigger it anyway," Jessica said, her eyes frantically dancing between Orphan and Eden. "We can't trust you."

"You can't," Orphan affirmed. "But you don't have much of a choice." They hummed lightly as the hunters racked their heads for a solution.

Eden lowered his head, hand tightly clenching his left arm. The moment given was scarce, but he searched deep to determine what to do. Eden knew resignation all too well—for himself. For others, he had always tried to set that aside. That moment was no different, and his gaze found Kendra. Her worried eyes quivered, and she slowly found his own. Within her royal-blue depths, he remembered her words faintly, even if they had been filtered through the ocean of hate he was surrounded by when his other self had emerged.

"Tick-tock," Orphan said, hands joining behind their back as they eyed the stunned hunters and even flashed Commander Evans a knowing smile. Eden steeled his nerves, focusing on the trust and conviction Kendra had shown. Though he knew not what he cherished most—what remained—there was an indomitable trust he harbored above all else.

"I said yesterday that I didn't trust you, and I know not to … but you know how we survived that encounter, don't you?" Eden quizzed.

"Ethan did train you well," Orphan suggested, eyes narrowing.

"You're not stupid enough to believe that's why. No. You know what I am capable of," Eden said, releasing his other arm before making a fist. "I would do it again the moment you trigger it. No suppression you could conjure would be effective enough, and you know it. Your plan falls apart."

Orphan was quiet for several moments, a smirk forming.

"Then we're at an impasse," they said, shrugging. "Whatever shall we do? Voidlings cannot make Ichor-bound oaths. Instead, I can assure you I'd leave the Hunters alone if you cooperated, but you don't trust me."

"I'd be a fool to, but … I trust Kendra," he said, his eyes glancing at her. With a subtle flash, Avenger appeared in its sheath before he removed it from his hip. "Avenger will find me should I ever drift too far from it, but what you didn't know is that it won't if it's being wielded," he said.

"Only you can wield it," Orphan declared.

Eden turned and approached Kendra as she stared in disbelief, and when he stopped in front of her, he placed Avenger in her palms. A soft pulse washed over the room, and Avenger rumbled with a low hum. Both the weightlessness and the implication of his gesture alike left her staggered, but Eden still showed certainty.

"The moment it leaves her possession—if she dies or wishes to inform me of you betraying your word—it will return to my spirit. You know what happens if it does …" Eden spoke in a dejected tone, his voice betraying his assertive claim.

A scowl formed on Orphan's face.

"You're just like him—sacrificial and annoying." Orphan clicked their tongue, shaking their head before turning away, facing Jessica. "These terms are agreeable. But you realize it is borrowed time, yes? They won't find the hexes, and once Onaga has you—not even the corrosion in your soul will be able to save you."

"I know," Eden replied, his eyes lowering. Kendra shook her head and tucked Avenger against her chest.

"Eden ... there has to be another way. This—I shouldn't—"

"I trust you entirely, Ken," Eden proclaimed, stepping toward her and pulling her into a hug. He breathed in deeply, trembling as he composed his nerves, and with trembling fingers, she embraced him back.

"We'll come for you. I swear," Kendra declared, pulling away slowly. When she met his gaze, her resolution cracked—discerning no such faith in his resigned gaze.

"Thank you, Ken—for everything," he said and spun to face Orphan but refused to meet their gaze as he walked toward them.

"Eden ..." Jessica whispered, breaking her silence, and for once, he looked at her. There were several moments when he thought of what to say, but each time he opened his mouth, his expression slipped to reveal his true feelings. She wanted to cry. She wanted to scream, but seeing such emotions brewing deep within him, she resolved herself not to fail him once again. And as Orphan took hold of him, she steeled her expression.

And with shadows that embraced them, they were gone within moments. No such resonance remained to be tracked—just as she expected of Orphan.

The room held silent, and Kendra collapsed to her knees, holding Avenger tightly against her chest. His promise had held, and her own now seemed out of reach. A deep sorrow wrenched her as she sobbed, and though her tears had been strong, their life was brief when Jessica's hand rested on her shoulder.

"Stand," Jessica spoke.

"What will we do? How can I?" Kendra croaked, and Jessica's grip tightened.

"If my son trusts you, then I trust you. *Now stand.*"

Kendra gathered her strength, pulling herself from the floor. Her gaze lifted, and she saw before her the same green eyes Eden possessed—determined and indicting the sorrow that once ruled them. Kendra's despair shrank before them, and she clamped her lips to cease their quivering.

"Are you ready to follow through on your oath?" Jessica questioned.

"Yes, ma'am," Kendra spoke, using her elbow to wipe the tears from her eyes. The weight Avenger bore was suddenly more significant, and she now understood the unspoken sentiment that Eden entrusted her with—*hope*. She exhaled sharply before clasping Avenger's sheath to her belt. Will renewed, the torn fabric on her suit ignited. When the flames burned away the blood-stained damage, the waistcloth frayed as their enchantment mended her suit.

She was ready, and she turned her gaze to Jessica, who spoke to the others.

"Troy, you bear that silencing hex on your tongue, do you not? Orphan invoked it when they were accusing you, I assume," Jessica said.

Commander Evans slowly nodded, opening his mouth and sticking his tongue out, and there, glowing red atop it, were the amalgamated runes of vengeance and blood.

"I suspect that if I were to remove it, that it would trigger an additional failsafe, yes?" she followed up, and Commander Evans nodded, casting his gaze down in frustration.

"Then how do we get the damn thing off? If he's got information on where those hexes are, then we need him talking!" Commander Rigs spat, finally breaking his silence.

"Is Oliver dead?" Jessica asked Kendra, who nodded.

"He was adamant about not speaking, and Eden ..." she said.

"He must have had a silencing hex as well. We need the eye of Jugo to disconnect him long enough for me to unbind and remove the hex safely," Jessica spat. Among her and the other high-ranking hunters, they threw out various suggestions—none useful. In disarray, they shuffled about, ready to resign themselves to evacuating, but Jessica rejected such a prospect. Should they have yielded, Eden would be lost forever.

Kendra thought back to the Siegharts they encountered, several having been present. Given the time constraints and the eye's rarity, it was unlikely they could reach out to the other branches of the family and convince them to help. The Kohen Treaty only compelled them to cooperate with their investigations. But Kendra remembered one who hadn't been among their attackers—someone with the eye of Jugo.

"General!" Kendra called, capturing Jessica's attention. "Allen is still in custody. He can—"

"Yes," Jessica gasped out, her eyes wide as she contemplated. "The heir—I forgot about him." Jessica paced over to Kendra while interfacing with her hunter gauntlet. "General Blackwell to Command. Put me through to Commander Baldwin in Archibald immediately." Jessica spent a few minutes prompting the man she spoke with, stressing the urgency. When she disconnected, her eyes landed on the others.

"Kendra, Troy—to me," Jessica commanded, holding her hands out. Once Kendra and Commander Evans approached, she grabbed their hands. "Rigs, initiate defense protocols and snuff out Orphan's moles."

"Yes, ma'am," Commander Rigs replied. Succinctly, he established order among the high-ranking hunters, barking orders among them and initiating defense protocols.

Jessica grasped Kendra's and Commander Evans's hands firmly, channeling her energy as a frigid white light engulfed them, and in a flash, they teleported.

Archibald Prison was situated in a remote region of Fresno—discreet and unassuming, given the surrounding military installations. One of a handful of facilities ran to hold demon prisoners, it served as a separate base equipped with many hunters as the primary staff, save for a scarce few government employees for administrative work.

A militarized fortress, the several acres it encompassed suggested the typical high-security compound many would recognize, but just as the Rosemary Fortress, a barrier subtly undulated around it.

Commander Baldwin served as its warden but had proven to be unaware of the breakout. With a brief investigation, they learned that their monitoring system had been compromised. In light of their chief security operator having gone missing after his shift several nights ago, it was quickly concluded that more of Orphan's moles resided inside. Jessica promptly called for their own defense protocols until they could siphon them out. She initially suspected that Orphan may have compromised their barrier too, but with how much smaller it was compared to the primary base, she quickly found no anomalies.

Afterward, they joined Commander Baldwin, who led them to the underground portion of the prison where Allen was held. Several hunters stood guard as they traversed those uninviting halls, only a bit less cramped than the laboratory Kendra had seen. Quickly, she grew suspicious of the heightened security measures. Offering clarity, Commander Baldwin eventually spoke to her festering questions.

"We put him under suicide watch. Kid refuses to eat most days, and we caught him talking to himself again. Usually, it's pretty grim," Commander Baldwin informed, adjusting his coat as he led the group.

"Solitary confinement?" Kendra questioned, her face scrunching.

"From the other, at least. Too dangerous to allow a demon of his caliber to conspire with them," he responded, and Kendra averted her gaze as she pondered that thought.

According to the hunters' speculations, Allen's increased surveillance had possibly saved him from being killed by his father or Orphan. Oliver's words had suggested that he didn't need Allen, but getting rid of him would have likely compromised their primary mission of capturing Eden. Commander Baldwin's caution with Allen proved auspicious in light of such speculation.

As much as she hated Allen, it seemed cruel, but she was of no mind to challenge their protocols. The last time she had fretted over him, it hadn't ended well. She had no pity to spare in that moment. Still, the irony was not lost on her that she was visiting his cell this time.

They came to a stop at the fortified cell door. The thick mesh comprising the door window allowed them to see the padded cell inside, complete with Allen being placed in a straitjacket. Several runes lined the back, leading up to a purple crystal at the base of the neck. No doubt suppression runes were somewhere on his restraints, lest he utilize his powers, but his sunken face suggested something far from hostility.

"We have stronger suppression hexes placed on him," Commander Baldwin added, and Jessica shook her head.

"We will be removing those for now. We need him for an urgent matter that you will be detailed upon later."

"General, his eye is beyond dangerous—even more so than Oliver's. He snapped at his father and overrode the standard suppression collar. Nearly killed him before we got him under control. I can't recommend removing those suppressions," he said, his hand holding the primary latch of the door. "He very well could lash out at us."

The thought of admonishing Commander Baldwin crossed Jessica's mind, but she composed herself, glancing at Kendra instead.

"He won't," Kendra asserted, her eyes softening as she peered through the door at him. The memory of Allen's words wormed its way through her head—his proclamations of not having had a choice. She had nothing but time to think about it, and with what Oliver and Dahlia said, she could imagine the extent of what he was forced to do for years.

She had known Allen since middle school, when his family had moved to Chicago. How effortlessly he had run through the linebackers at football tryouts made sense—as did the fact he hadn't even had a blemish when he was dogpiled. She had always thought he was tough, but her life over the past few years revealed how wrong she was. Before her was an emaciated version of his former self. His hair was long and unkempt, and his eyes were sunken beyond the despaired gazes of the somnium's victims.

Commander Baldwin hesitated, but he disengaged the locks and manually snapped the latches open. They entered promptly, but only Kendra approached. Allen's hollow gray irises narrowed, suddenly becoming avoidant. He had seen them. She knew that with the deliberate effort in casting his eyes elsewhere—even as she stood right in front of him. She hadn't known where to start, but it flowed from her without thought.

"You look rough," she said, her tone biting. "But you'd be happy to know that your dad is dead," she claimed, and suddenly, his gaze met hers again, his lips trembling.

"What?" he spoke in a low whisper.

"Did you know about Orphan? About his conspiring with Onaga?" she asked, searching his eyes for recognition, but no such familiarity stirred within them.

"He always kept me in the dark—said it'd be easier that way, but I suspected it wasn't that simple." He lowered his head, and Kendra crouched in front of him.

"He hurt you a lot, didn't he? You ... always deflected from talking about him, and now I know why. That wasn't fair."

Allen swallowed, breathing out shakily as he shook his head.

"I have no right ..." he claimed, his head lowering, but Kendra's finger lifted his chin, making him face her.

"You're right, but you can still feel. So, you're going to do what's right and help me," she said with bared teeth.

Allen stared, his eyes drifting to the torn hunter attire, the bloodstains on her form.

"Did he hurt you?" Allen croaked.

"Plenty, but he suffered in his final moments. Not nearly as much as he deserved ... but that isn't for me to determine, is it?" She watched him intently, seeing the tension snaking through his bound body.

"I've denounced all that I was," he spoke after several moments.

"Bullshit," Kendra hissed, snatching him by his collar. "You can't erase what you are just because it's tied to that oafish piece of shit, nor because you did the unthinkable." Kendra pulled him closer, her face close enough that her breath lashed against him. "You could tear yourself apart in a million and one ways. It doesn't change the fact that you're still Allen Sieghart!" she claimed, her eyes flickering, but never once did they shed their human visage. She then let him go with a huff, looking away.

Silence heralded the mounting tension, and Allen shut his eyes, biting his lip as he turned his head and choked up. With a heave, he sobbed out.

"I can't give her back."

"No, and because you can't, I could never possibly forgive you, but somewhere deep down—even with what you did—I know she'd suffer more seeing you like this."

"I have nothing left to live for," he spoke, meeting her gaze with teary eyes, but Kendra didn't flinch.

She had seen that same dejected gaze in Eden, and it sickened her to see it on Allen, but it wasn't for her to judge. For a moment, she heard Kendall's voice from when Kendra had shown a similar moment of despair—how she had snapped her out of it. In that moment, it was without shame that she'd borrow the sentiment Kendall had taught her to banish the foolish idea Allen held.

"It's never too late to change your story," Kendra said, her eyes narrowing as she challenged Allen's. "I found more that I need to fight for and protect. You can still do the same."

Allen was quiet, lips ajar. He bared his teeth, hanging his head once more in surrender.

"Whom must I cast my leer on?" he asked.

"Commander Evans," she called, and the other hunters joined them. Commander Baldwin and Jessica took to Allen's back, and Jessica channeled her power into the runes along his straitjacket. With a gentle shimmer, the crystal lost color.

Allen breathed in deeply, looking up at Commander Evans as he stepped forward hesitantly.

"You're the one that fiend wanted to spare ..." he mentioned in a low voice, and Commander Evans averted his gaze. "Something is holding your soul tightly. I'll need all of my demonic powers to sever it. You may feel weaker than usual, but I'll ensure it doesn't kill you," he informed. His skin slowly shed its human color, and his eyes became eclipsed by darkness. An envious green hue carved their center, and in his right eye, purple veins spread from the iris.

Commander Baldwin's hand tensed on Allen's shoulder while ram-like horns emerged from Allen's head, looping at the base before curving back. With a flash of red before Commander Evans's vision, he fell to his knees, choking up as his connection nearly severed.

"Show me your tongue," Jessica ordered, and Commander Evans carefully opened his mouth. In that moment, Jessica held two fingers up, palm toward him. "Enoch lazmos!" she chanted.

Jessica's black aura pulsed, meeting his form as a dark hand emerged from the floor, snatching his tongue. With a shriek, the runes etched into his soul were siphoned out into the black hand. It retreated into the puddle it had emerged from, and she lowered her hand, breathing out in relief.

Allen's demon form retreated, and he shut his eyes. As he breathed heavily, blood seeped from his right eye.

Commander Evans gasped for air, but he quickly regained himself as Ichor breathed into his soul once more.

"It's off?" Commander Evans asked, his eyes darting between Jessica and his hands.

"It is removed," Jessica confirmed, nodding.

"Shit, where to even begin …" Commander Evans said. "I got hexed right before I was sent to establish operations in Chicago. I was ambushed by Intico and Orphan, but Orphan wasn't pretending to be Ethan when they did. Didn't even know Orphan was pretending to be Ethan this entire time." Commander Evans breathed in deeply before continuing. "I was made to cooperate, mostly unwittingly, but I picked up some key intel throughout, and I know that Orphan colluded with the Covenant of Augury. I'm sure they lied to Intico as a means to Onaga's goal…" Commander Evans rambled on.

"Then why didn't you write it down or something?" Kendra questioned skeptically, but Jessica shook her head at Kendra.

"Hexes and pacts are tied to the sentiment of a thing rather than the technicality. It's not like genie rules. If he so much as betrayed the idea of what Orphan intended, he would be dead," Jessica paused, turning her attention back to Commander Evans. "Never mind the specifics. Do you know where the hexes are? Where they took Eden?" she asked, and Commander Evans nodded.

"I kept minor tabs, just in case—small things here and there, inconsistencies, personnel of concern. I did all I could to undermine Orphan's plans. Sussed them out months ago, but I couldn't say or do anything. As for Captain Blackwell, I don't have an exact location, but it can't be far from the mission coordinates where they were ambushed. They wouldn't have used conventional teleportation, likely."

"You will show me where the hexes are, then we will work to triangulate where they took Eden."

"At once," he said, and Jessica ushered for them to follow her.

"Our business here is done. Thank you again, Commander Baldwin," she said, and the commander nodded affirmatively in response.

"Of course, general."

Kendra was the last to make her way to the exit, but Allen's breath snatched her attention.

"Kendra," Allen called out. "Why did you let me live back then? It would have only been right for you to kill me. The human thing," he said, his voice dropping as he opened his left eye to look at her.

It was a question Kendra had considered plenty, but the answer wasn't obvious. She hated him, but a part of her still yearned for those years they spent together. The bond, as much as she strangled and maimed it, gasped for breath inside her. It was beyond chagrin, but she distilled what thoughts she could muster into her answer.

"I don't know," she said, her voice dropping as her fingers dug into her palms. "Human—demon—whatever you'd consider my decision to be ... I'm just Kendra."

In two short hours, the Hunters' base was finally secure. The hexes placed by Orphan were disabled, along with the barrier for a time—a counter-measure if things were more compromised than they could anticipate. All of Command had been detained and inspected for the hexes, of which Jessica discerned a handful of puppets within their ranks. It would have been impractical to use Allen for a thorough interrogation in that moment, but Jessica highly doubted they were aware of specifics. Many of them were only low-ranking humans with a handful of umbras.

The grains of sand within the hourglass grew heavy on the Hunters' conscience—Eden's gamble casting a shadow of expectation they would see illuminated. Their base was on strict lockdown, and everything was being monitored to the highest extent. Jessica and the council of high-ranking hunters worked to triangulate from the coordinates near Goiás that Kendra provided, but there was a large scope of coverage to pull from.

The labs they knew of were deemed unlikely candidates. The nature of Orphan's ruse required haste, and shadow teleportation was inherently slow and dangerous. Carried with it was the possibility of abstraction—the loss of one's being—a risk they wouldn't take with Eden.

The window of opportunity would have been short. Otherwise, the discrepancy would have been inviable without rousing suspicion. Jessica surmised that was why Ethan had called the meeting at the peak of Eden and Kendra's assignment—*a sickeningly careful distraction.*

Soon Jessica was alerted by the blinking light on her hunter bracer—a message from Zane. She hadn't expected it, but given their arrangement leading up to that moment, she knew it begged urgency. With a brief conversation, she placed the meeting on hold and quickly ordered him to be let through. Upon his arrival, his wary gaze scanned the room, but he took to Jessica's side, the Tome of Liminality tucked in his arms.

"Sorry I'm late. I was busy getting some important information. Anything I should know before I begin, madam?"

Jessica nodded, giving him a condensed explanation of what occurred. As she went on, his face twisted into a scowl, and he cursed himself silently.

"Shit ... if I had just met with Asher yesterday," he muttered, shaking his head. "Good news is that I have some important intel that'll come in handy," he said and hoisted the tome up. He then plopped it in front of Jessica, whose eyes widened the further she examined it.

"This is one of Onaga's tomes. How—"

"Later," Zane said, sighing as he gestured to the tome. "Point is that this one will allow us to find the Genesis Laboratory—where Eden was likely taken—and keep Onaga from shifting around. His study occupies a liminal reality and can be shifted from laboratory to laboratory at his whim. That's how he always evades us, and with you, we can crack down on that."

The hunters gaped at the tome with a mixture of dread and reverence the longer they stared. Many were forced to avert their gaze when the sight of it encumbered their minds. However, Jessica's eyes remained starkly fixed on it. Dauntless, she rested her fingertips on the black leathery cover.

"It exerts the weight of creation itself, and this is but a fraction, I'm sure," she whispered, her breath shallow. "The magic pervading this tome is complex beyond compare, and it would be incalculably arduous to understand its full breadth ... but I won't need to," she spoke aloud. From it, with its whispering knowledge, she was certain of the promise it offered to her seething desire.

However much Eden yearned for vengeance against Onaga, Jessica desired it tenfold. It burned in her blood—the same sentiment within him that had attracted the seraph that brought him home. Jessica had scoured the location he was found at, several miles for days at a time, but she had failed to locate Onaga's lab. She speculated on how far he had trekked, but Eden held no memory of his journey to say. She had given up hope of finding and destroying it, but now there was a chance to save him from Onaga's clutches, unlike last time. Conviction restored, her digits dragged to the edge of the tome before snatching it, wielding it more effortlessly than Zane had.

"I must prepare translations," she affirmed.

"I'll be with you to help decipher the alchemical aspects. I'm no expert ... but I'm rehearsed enough on Onaga's research to dig at it with you," Zane claimed, placing his hands behind his back. "If you can lock on to

Onaga's location, we can find Eden. Just have to know where to sift." His eyes met Jessica's, and she nodded at him.

"With haste, then," she began, standing up. "We will reconvene in two hours. Commander Rigs, continue drafting a breach operation utilizing a generic layout."

"Yes, ma'am," Commander Rigs said, and they dispersed.

Jessica led Zane to her office, where they studied the tome. It was inscribed in a mixture of Latin and Indiox—written in Onaga's blood. The symbols were of quaint familiarity to Jessica, learned in the days when she communed and studied with Izalin and her coven within the Middle East. Her fluency in Indiox and Latin was proficient, but the niche terms of demon alchemy and its equations were gibberish to her.

Zane facilitated her understanding of its principles enough for her to inscribe her own translations—which she considered adding to her grimoire once practiced. In that moment, she searched for what would best assist them—a means with which they could counter the liminality Onaga infused into his study and triangulate his position.

Jessica made quick work of scanning the contents, flipping through sections of his long-winded hypotheses. Eventually, she landed on the chapter he had dedicated to installing liminality onto locations. Admittedly, the philosophical language he had employed gave her a bigger headache than the most convoluted magic ever could.

Onaga's concepts of self and holistic embodiment were far removed from the ramblings of human philosophers. It would have been pretentious if not for the sincerity it commanded. She and Zane trekked through such dialogues and equations until she had mapped out a means with which she could translate it into a ninth circle spell. She carefully channeled her energy into the mixture of runes until she managed to peer into the *axes between,* as Onaga had dubbed them.

The tunnels were fathomless, close in proximity to one another within the mind's eye but physically far. She could imagine easily losing herself within them, but she composed herself and peered deeper. It was an infinite mesh of webs, but she scoured the countless paths until she discovered one that had been accessed recently. Its fabric ebbed with the cadence of sin—*greed*. She traced it carefully, took a deep breath, and peeked through. Diminutive, Eden's energy whispered its intimately familiar sentiments to her.

"Oshta ..." Jessica whispered. A light shimmered within the jewel on her belt, purple light twinkling within her eyes as her gaze slowly returned to reality. "The heart of the Amazon," Jessica stated, breathing hard as she turned her attention to Zane.

"All the way out there? Guess you wouldn't get many visitors," Zane said, but after a moment's thought, he shook his head. "Visitors that wouldn't be easily disposed of, I mean. Speaking of disposal, what are we going to do about Orphan? As much as I'd love to spend hours incinerating their forms, we'll be operating on a tight timer."

"Ah, yes ... that pitiful creature." She clicked her tongue. "I've a handful of reaper gems on hand—courtesy of Major Alahna's efforts against the ferali. I can make roughly nine soul binders—not counting the one I already possess," she explained, making Zane sigh.

"Looks like Drake's been busy, but we're going to need a lot more than ten for an operation this big. No telling who will encounter Orphan, and with how conniving they are, having extras on hand should be mandatory."

"Unless you possess a quick supply of duscillium crystals, we'll need to make do."

"Maybe ... ah, there's an idea. If you can siphon the ferali resonance from the gems, I can split the husk into smaller duscillium fragments using demon alchemy."

"That would reduce the potency quite significantly," Jessica argued.

"I think Confucius said a bowl is most useful when it's empty," Zane began. "Well, deriving from that, better we have a less lethal but equipped force than leave several squads as sitting ducks." Jessica sighed, shrugging in surrender.

"I suppose I cannot argue with that. Very well. You will have nine of them to split. How many will that make?"

"Around thirty, maybe, but give me the big one—it's best in my hands," he said with confidence, and Jessica sighed, nodding reluctantly.

"With that matter settled, all that is left is to block Onaga from the axes between. Not only would we rescue my son, but we might finally have an opportunity to end Onaga once and for all. Only then will Eden truly be free," Jessica said, her gaze turning back to the tome before she snapped it shut.

"Killing Onaga ..." Zane mulled over the thought. "I suppose that's not impossible," he mused, a smirk forming on his lips. "With the element of surprise and your might, we might just pull it off."

Jessica's expression soured, her eyes softening as she looked down at the desk in quiet contemplation. Zane cocked his brow at the gloom in her eyes.

"What's with the look? You're capable of taking him on. I mean ... he isn't going to be easy, but you're in a league of your own."

"I fear I will not be a combatant in this operation," she began. "Ninth circle magic of this magnitude will require every ounce of my focus, and the toll of that alone is extraordinary. If we're going to kill him here ... it will have to be you and the others."

Then it was Zane's turn to show hesitation. His mouth fell open, and his breath became shallow.

"I'm sorry ... me? I'm a pretty tough guy and all ... but taking down the Harbinger of Greed, the former seraphim whose hands crafted this realm, may be more than a tough ask." Zane held her gaze for several moments, releasing his breath as he turned around, fists clenching tightly. The seraphim were an order below the Primordials, but despite the fact Onaga had fallen, he speculated that the harbinger retained some degree of his former power. If it was as he suspected, Onaga was of a magnitude higher than he'd be able to contend against.

"You, Kendra, and Alicia should suffice. The measure of his power will be spread thin with my suppression of his liminal paths, and he knows better than to contend against our hunters outside while suppressed. I suspect he will maintain an interior position for an advantage, but you and Kendra are uniquely equipped against his feathers. With Alicia on auxiliary, you should be able to eliminate him with moderate difficulty," she claimed, her eyes firm.

"They're both still pretty new to all of this, talented or not. If it were Eden and me, sure, we could pull it off. But ..." he thought hard before snapping his fingers. "What about Drake? You able to call him out for this? He'd make it a cinch," Zane asked, enthusiasm in his tone, but it quickly faded when Jessica shook her head.

"Major Alahna is off the grid tracking the rest of the ferali, I'm afraid. He won't be checking in for another week, and this operation will begin as soon as possible. There isn't time to find or recall him, which I somehow suspect Orphan also planned for."

Zane let out a heavy sigh, running a hand through his hair as he racked his mind for another possibility, but he found none. Alicia would be valuable for engaging up close and controlling the terrain, but Kendra, who he considered remarkable, was hardly experienced enough for a foe like Onaga. The conflict permeated his face as he paced back and forth, but Jessica snatched his hand, holding it firmly.

"You fret, Zane, but even you know of her potential. The flames of chaos are powerful and would negate his regeneration to further debilitate him in a prolonged attrition. She was capable of defeating Intico, and that was before her training."

"And she had Eden, who—mind you—nearly slayed Intico on his own, according to the others. If she could control her flames better, those chaos flames would mean something," Zane said, and Jessica squeezed his hand harder.

"And she has you for that," she reminded, but Zane shook his head.

"I could guide her normal flames, maybe buy myself an extra minute or two in my demon form, but her chaos flames are too much for me to control. I already tried once when she was in training. They're more an imbuement of concentrated wrath than blistering fire, and I guess I can't overcome it like she did," he said, his gaze dropping to Jessica's hand.

"There were sentiments you had yet possessed and much you're just beginning to uncover about yourself—about your flame." Jessica slowly let his hand go.

Zane inspected his palm. His focus sharpened as he thought back to the warmth he once knew from his mother, a stark contrast to what Kendra's chaos flames had evoked from him. Fury beyond that which he could reasonably control—a fury he had kindled in the absence of his mother's warmth. But he grew uncertain when he thought back to her. She had always sung her praises and adoration for him, but she was not a liar. Her truths echoed still.

Zaikio, your flame, for which I gave you your name, is special—kindled from my own to stoke yours. It shall become whatever you allow it to be—you've but to discern those sentiments and understand how they would kindle it.

He always thought little of himself in that regard—a spark missing tinder and unable to reach its peak. He could burn brighter and brighter, but it would always pale in comparison to her memory. His trust in her wasn't gone, just forgotten.

"My trust is not given easily, but I trust Kendra, as did Eden." Jessica shifted, her fingers calmly settled into one another as her eyes pled. "I trust *you*, Zane. Time and time again, you have served the greater good since your alliance with us, and you decided to do so when you betrayed the Alastairs during the Athens incident. Your efforts are why we are able to plot my son's rescue and Onaga's demise."

She stood and removed her hat, sympathy in her eyes.

"I would not send you to your death. Not even for my own blood. I understand if my words do not resonate." Her eyes closed. "You may refuse to engage Onaga, if you believe your life would be in imminent peril."

Zane clenched his fists before shoving them in the pockets of his parka. He knew she wouldn't send him to certain death. Engaging Onaga was heavier a burden than any he dared carry before, but as he was discovering, the greatest uncertainty lay within himself. He soon came to the determination that if he couldn't believe in himself, he'd place his trust in her and his mother's belief in him. With that as his crutch, he had his answer.

"Mom always said to never doubt a woman's intuition, and I don't intend to start now."

"Attention!" Commander Rigs's voice boomed through the large auditorium from several speakers fixed to the room's crown. Several hunters stood before the stage he occupied. A few majors and commanders stood around him, and Andrew stood in front of Major Carter. Commander Rigs's knuckles bulged as he gripped the podium, and he leaned close to the microphone as he scanned the room. When it fell silent, he spoke.

"All of you who have been gathered are elite operatives, designated angel-classed or higher within your respective squads. Today, you are being called upon to fulfill your oaths as hunters in service of not only your comrades but of humanity as a whole.

"For centuries, Onaga has served as a blight to all who live and is responsible for the death of civilizations and many of our comrades of old. He has evaded us at every turn—until now. Orphan has worked with him, engaging in the most despicable of espionage by parading as Commander Ardon for years. Upon being discovered, they revealed that the Rosemary Fortress's barrier was weaponized against us.

"Captain Blackwell spared our lives by concocting a gamble that created an opportunity for us to disable the hexes that would have compelled the barrier to implode and kill us. Now we are encumbered with the duty of serving the trust he placed in his comrades. We will rescue Captain Blackwell and slay Onaga in one fell swoop!"

The hunters listened intently, worry knitting their expressions at the insinuations. Noticing their reactions, Commander Rigs quickly continued.

"This is a once-in-a-lifetime operation. Not only have we discovered the laboratory Eden is confined within, we now also have the means to prevent Onaga from fleeing. If we end Onaga, we decapitate their operations and can put an end to the demons who have long plagued humanity since their existence.

"General Blackwell will be serving as support by suppressing Onaga while we advance. Once we breach the laboratory, three of our finest will cooperate in slaying that winged fiend once and for all. Captain Zane Larson, Sergeant Alicia Romero, and Private Kendra Mallory, step forth." Commander Rigs spoke, and the three cut through the assembly and took to the stage, standing beside the podiums with their hands behind their backs. While they all adorned serious expressions and stiff stances, Zane stood out due to his casual clothing, while the others were in uniform. "These hunters will be at the helm of this operation. In this united front, we will prevail."

Kendra eyed the hunters through foggy lenses, hearing their whispers. The many reservations they suggested cast the greatest of doubts on the operation.

"What happened to Commander Ardon?" one hunter boldly questioned, but before it could be challenged, many others chimed in with their expressions of skepticism, doubt, and disbelief entirely.

Fear.

Pervasive, it soon fueled the raucous chatter and anxiety. The brewing tumult reminded Kendra of the police during Harvest. While there had been bliss within the ignorance of the police, there was no such release for the hunters.

For several months, their comrades were picked apart deliberately and by someone they were made to trust and rely upon. Ethan had been something of a folk hero among the organization. To suspect that he had not only perished but had also been usurped by an impostor to their detriment—that would breed the most impenetrable of skepticism.

Kendra's fists curled, and her stance loosened along with her composure. Commander Rigs failed to offer a rebuttal in his attempts to quell the noise. Declarations of death and comrades lost paraded. Raucous voices and deaf ears suggested a verdict she wouldn't allow.

"Enough!" Kendra shouted in a spew of flames whose heat washed over the auditorium. "We are hunters, damn it! It's because that Orphan bastard saw to the deaths of so many that we loved that we have to do this. Eden is waiting after laying *everything* on the line for us. Backing down after all he has done isn't an option!"

Zane and Alicia watched Kendra, their expressions softening before they turned their attention back to the crowd. A hunter then interrupted Kendra's chastising.

"You would say that, but you and Larson have demonic powers and can regenerate. It's easy for you to put your life on the line," the hunter alleged. "One of the first demons? Who the hell are we to challenge that?"

Kendra prepared to respond, but a firm hand on her shoulder froze the words in her throat, and a heavy stomp echoed through the room. In a Pavlovian response, the hunters' chatter froze.

Commander Evans stepped forward, releasing Kendra before walking over to the podium. Commander Rigs surrendered it to him without question, and even the sound of him clearing his throat snatched everybody's attention.

"You think them invincible? Shit, I wish they were. But you know who isn't invincible? Me," Commander Evans snapped, pointing his thumb at himself as he leaned closer to the microphone. "I was and still am scared. Orphan had me under their thumb for years—threatening to rip my soul apart—my family's souls apart. And they probably would have if not for Eden. I have a chance to do what is right by him—even though he has every reason to hate me."

Commander Evans stood tall, circling the podium to walk forward, eyes sharp with a tenacity he rarely showed.

"Chicago, three years ago, he saved us then. Rallied the forces we had, beat that damned somnium lord back, and before Mallory was even a trained hunter, he guided her to eliminate the threat of said demon lord. Eden is what it means to be a hunter, and a coward like me is willing to make a vow before all of you." Commander Evans slammed his fist to his chest, his eyes glowing as wind surged around him.

"A divine oath I declare upon Ichor: I will accompany *all* who attend into battle and lay my life down personally. Should I cower and run, should I commit to dereliction in leading the hunt against our great enemy, my soul will be sundered and condemned to darkness for that great sin!" With a high-pitched whistle following the wind, the thrum of a heartbeat rumbled from Commander Evans, his vow bound in the greatest of powers.

Silence fell upon the room. It was no mystery that Commander Evans and Eden were at odds. It had been apparent to anybody who had witnessed their interactions. A vow of the magnitude he made—no less to Ichor herself—carried every bit of the weight he claimed. Should he have betrayed it, much in the same way Orphan's hexes worked, his soul would be tattered and rejected by Ichor. They watched him shift, and in spite of the gravity of the soul-bound promise, his stark gaze held the same certainty and conviction as before.

"You may remain in cowardice and mistrust. I will not fault you for that. I *only* lead hunters, and my promise is to them and them alone. Should that be you ... that is your choice."

Kendra wished she could have heard applause. She wished the conviction carried through and spoke to them all, but several hunters fled from the auditorium. Of the thirty squads that had been present, only ten were left.

Of those that remained, reluctant faces watched on, eyes filled with fear. Terror in silence, those hunters stood nonetheless.

"Can you actually kill Onaga?" one squad captain asked.

Kendra and Alicia nodded assertively, and Zane gave a smirk that overshadowed his uncertainty.

"You really need to ask? This is me we're talkin' 'bout," Zane said calmly, his voice carrying as he held his hand up, extending his thumb to point at the roof. "We've got this," Zane said before returning to his stiff stance as Commander Evans reclaimed the microphone.

"All of you who remain, hunters, will follow me into battle," Commander Evans spoke. Silently, he returned to the line of commanders in wait.

Commander Rigs took to the podium again, scoffing as he stared intensely.

"Everyone will receive their specific formations and orders shortly. Engineers will meet at the terminals in an hour for recon assessment. The rest of you will rendezvous in two hours for deployment. Dismissed!"

Several squads convened, and Kendra stepped down from the stage with the others, glancing back at Commander Evans. There was much she could say about his vow, but she preferred to see him live up to it. It was ironic, in a way; a hex traded for a vow of even greater consequence. What was even more remarkable was the fact Ichor accepted it—a testament to the power behind his promise. If he had been insincere, ruin would have been immediate. As such, vows were held in the highest regard and greatly discouraged.

Seraph Seven joined her. Seeing them again, she was reminded of Eden and Bonnie's absence. She had heard they'd recovered Bonnie's corpse, and as she spoke with the squad, they mentioned attending the funeral service when all was said and done.

Andrew soon joined them. He had been released from holding, having been cleared of any involvement shortly following the defense protocols. Of higher consideration, they knew he was needed for the operation. Kendra was happy to see him, of course, but the air loomed with a tension even Andrew's signature grin couldn't cut through. Soon, he was called by Major Carter, and he sucked his lips in.

"I'll see you guys on the field," Andrew said, giving an assuring nod as he held his fist out to the squad. All at once, their fists connected in a circle, and Andrew left them.

Damion gestured with his thumb to the stage, where the commanders gathered and spoke with one another.

"Never imagined Commander Evans would outdo pops on a mic," he said, watching as Commander Rigs marched off the stage to speak with the hunters throughout the room.

"Honestly, he probably didn't even need the mic. You can hear that man from over the valley on a windy day," Kendra said, recalling her days as a cadet when Commander Rigs oversaw some of their exercises. Suddenly, her ears perked up when footsteps neared her squad, her nose twitching at the familiar scent approaching, and she huffed as her eyes rolled.

"Seven," Cassius's voice called. "Guess we're doing this," he said, folding his arms as he stopped in front of them. Behind him, the rest of Seraph Nine lingered, and Zane appeared, propping himself against the base of the stage as he eyed the converging squads.

"Honestly thought you'd have turned tail. I'm almost impressed," Kendra said, snorting.

"Yeah?" he scoffed, adjusting the collar of his jacket. "I'm sure you'd love to watch me walk away, but nah. Seraph Nine ain't letting this shit slip. Jack and Hyde were my teammates, treated me right." He frowned, glancing at the others when they took to his side, and Kendra spoke.

"Steiner too. What they've done to our comrades is unforgivable." Her expression dropped.

"Looks like we've all got scores to settle with Onaga and Orphan," Zane said, standing and approaching Cassius before slapping his shoulder and turning his attention to the rivaling squad. "Let's drop these double O's, Seven," he said and flashed them a grin.

Kendra held her hand out, meeting Cassius's gaze as her expression softened. He reached out, and their thumbs interlocked as their palms met.

"What Captain Doofus said. Show us what you got, Ken."

Hearing this, Zane feigned dramatics and grabbed at his heart.

"That's not very cash-money of you," Zane said, referencing Cassius's self-prescribed nickname.

"I'd pay not to hear your terrible references," Regina Byrd, Zane's lieutenant, said. The squads chuckled, and Zane clenched his chest more dramatically.

"Et tu, Reggie?" he asked before sighing and flicking his wrist. "Alright, Nine, go get geared up. I'll meet you all at the terminals for briefing."

"Not gonna rally up, Cap?" Cassius asked, cocking a brow at Zane as he backed toward his squad.

"Not yet. Gotta get some things prepped with Kendra."

Kendra's brow furrowed, watching as Seraph Nine left and her own squadmates spoke with one another behind her.

"What's up?" she asked.

"Hold the thought," Zane said. "Yuki?" he called out, and she turned her attention from Alicia. Their eyes held, and Zane ushered her to approach. When she did, he looked away, his lips pursing as he gathered his nerve. "You gonna be okay to lead Seven? There's a lot more riding on this than you know."

"Of course. I'm Eden's lieutenant. What's with the—" she froze, seeing the hesitation in his eyes.

"I just know how your nerves are about the labs," Zane said, and Alicia approached, placing an arm around Yuki.

"She's tougher than you think," Alicia said.

Kendra frowned, unaware of the unspoken understanding between them. Yuki never spoke much of her past, but the prompt for Kendra to inquire presented itself far less than it had with Eden. When she met Yuki's gaze, she cocked her head to the side.

"What's ... sorry, it's not my business to probe right now," Kendra said, but Yuki shook her head, a shaky sigh leaving her lips.

"I told you an incomplete version of how I became a hunter, but it wasn't entirely true," she said, pausing before continuing. "My parents were hunters, but I was only told when I was a teen. We were ... in Berlin," she explained, causing Kendra's eyes to widen.

Yuki composed her breath, swallowing hard and taking the water canteen Alicia shoved in her face. After a long swig, she held her chest and shook her head.

"I never intended to be a hunter originally, but for almost a year I was kept as a prisoner—more like a pet. And when Ethan and his squad raided the lab I was imprisoned in, I decided to join in hopes of finding my son I birthed in captivity."

Kendra listened quietly, nodding thoughtfully before glancing down. Her body language when they'd infiltrated the lab suddenly made sense to her then.

"My promise extends to him too, then," Kendra said, and Yuki offered a hesitant smile before returning the water can to Alicia.

"I will lead as I must precisely because of that," she affirmed, and Alicia grinned widely.

"That's my girl," she said.

Zane cleared his throat, circling to Kendra's side and nudging her. When her attention turned to him, he ushered for her to follow, and he led her outside of the auditorium.

The two navigated the rallying hunters and went outside, where Zane guided her away from the others. Soon, they were by themselves, and Kendra crossed her arms as Zane turned to face her. Before she could ask, he removed his jacket and flicked it across the pavement.

"What's going on?" Kendra asked.

"We need to prepare," he replied.

"Okay?" Kendra raised a brow, and Zane sighed.

"Last we left off, your flame control was still rough and imprecise. Strong, mind you, but pure might won't decide how this goes. If we're going to win, I'm going to need to confirm you can properly back me up."

"I've been practicing, and my control has improved. Add in my chaos flames, and we should be fine," she alleged, but Zane shook his head, his expression dropping.

"It's not that cut-and-dried, Ken. My flames are a part of me, an extension of my soul. To reach my proficiency, you'd need way more than just a few months. I'll need to guide your flames with my own. Think of it like … a magic chauffeur," he explained, hands clenching. "On top of that, when I go into my demon form, we'll have ten minutes tops—a little more if this impromptu training session pans out well."

"Huh? Wait, that's it? Why's it hard to maintain?" Kendra asked, and Zane sighed.

"I'm only half blaze, and on top of that, we never evolved to properly function in Mortale. Our biology is pretty unintuitive, being away from the wellsprings from which my kind arose. That's why I keep my serum on me—helps with that whole process, but I can only take it once every forty-eight hours. Unless I'm trying to consume a buffet three times a day, I've got stark limitations."

"Oh …" Kendra murmured, biting her bottom lip as she averted her eyes. "Honestly, I kind of thought you were just a fat ass. Didn't know it was a biology thing."

"Oh, I mean, I definitely am," Zane gave a sheepish smile. "But I'd be less of one and less lazy." Zane cleared his throat and wiped his expression. "Here's the idea. Given you can produce hot flames with greater power efficiency, I can conserve my power, and demon form, by guiding your flames. Understood?"

Kendra had never quite seen such direness in Zane's eyes before. He was always lackadaisical, something she suspected had been a veneer of sorts. It was ironically chilling, as if he had dropped an act.

"Yeah, I get it," she answered, and Zane reached out, palm facing the ground.

"Channel your flames into my palm here, and we'll try it out."

Kendra obliged, placing her hand against his. Embers flickered between their palms as bright fire erupted, washing off his hand harmlessly. After a moment, the flames flickered, melding with his own as he channeled them. Shortly, they lashed out around them in missiles of flames, forming a vortex.

"That's easy enough," Zane said, meeting Kendra's eyes. "There's just one more thing to check ..." Zane curled his hand in her palm. "Your chaos flames." When he said this, Kendra frowned, shaking her head.

"That isn't going to work. You looked ... constipated the last time you had me focus them on you."

"That was then. This is now," Zane argued.

Blazes and hellhounds were both immune to fire, but the scorn of chaos flames was different. They were embroiled in the sin of wrath, and that sentiment was beyond the physical threat of flames. It could easily consume, and from what he had learned from Eden, it could be fatal, even. Kendra was wary of that part, at least.

"You're really willing to risk yourself for Eden? I was under the impression you hated him," she said, and Zane shook his head.

"He's ... complicated, to put it lightly, and pretty rash. But I can deal with that. What grinds my gears is the way he treats his mom." He frowned. "Call me envious—maybe it's the demon in me, but I'd do anything to have mine back. General Blackwell frets day and night and tears herself apart for him, and you've seen how he reciprocates. I really wish he'd wise up to what he's got, but that can't happen if I don't pull out all the stops for this operation."

Kendra's gaze softened, her lips pursing as she thought back to the years without her mother present. She considered herself beyond lucky to have her back, but from within that absence, she could imagine how heavy it was for Zane.

With a brief staredown between them, she sighed.

"Let's do it," she said, relenting.

Still channeling her flames into him, she assumed her demonic aspect. Shortly, the scarlet glow replaced the warm orange, and Zane's hands became engulfed in the flames of wrath.

Hatred.

That scarlet-red sentiment burrowed into his being, anger snaking through his veins and digging its fangs into his soul. Its venom rendered him paradoxically frozen, and he growled as he wrestled with it. Like lifeless clay, all who lived were animated by the sentiments of Ichor, and that was where their power derived. Should he fail to know, understand, and coexist with the sin that entered him, it could consume him with lasting consequences.

Kendra and Lucy alike were known for wielding the flames, and he focused on how he differed. They knew loss and sacrifice. He knew loss. He knew sacrifice. But what he failed to know slowly became apparent: knowledge alone was insufficient. It needed a sentiment to counter the all-consuming rage.

Hope.

Zane hadn't been whole since his mother had been killed. Blazes' souls were kindled by their parents. For him, his mother. Her flame alone ignited his own, and in every way, she was forever a part of him. That was what made her death more harrowing. His flame felt like cinders in her absence—a sapling deprived of the nutrients it needed to grow strong.

Her absence, again and again, kindled that hatred. The scarlet eclipsed his flame, threatening to overwhelm him as his eyes went red. The contortions of his soul suggested he would explode, but something indisputably warm enraptured him. From within the swarm of red, a soft golden glow encompassed his being and liberated him.

"You've ... been here the entire time?" he whispered. Mind asunder, it came to a singular focus on that golden light, and a tear involuntarily dripped down his cheek.

"Zane?" Kendra called to him, moving to shift her hands away, but Zane gripped them, shaking his head.

"No, I'm ... fine," he declared through gritted teeth. The scarlet flames that licked the surrounding air soon emerged in a bright flurry, whipping around them with a degree of control Kendra had never successfully achieved. Zane's flames guided the wrathful sin within her own as he had done with her normal fire. She then understood what he meant more than if he had spoken it. The sentiments from which their power derived transcended the confines of language itself. Sorrow and jubilation alike.

Zaikio.

That name emerged within her mind, its significance elusive but profound. A smile emerged on Zane's face, genuine and sincere as she gazed into the depths of his true being. She returned it in kind, sharing in the joy he expressed. Finally, the flames receded. With an assertive nod, he affirmed his rekindled faith with honest words.

"*We'll* be fine."

"You seem ... different," Kendra said, a puzzled expression on her face as she examined the new certainty she saw within his eyes.

Zane's hands slipped from her own, and he stared at his palms. A flicker of gold light peeked through at the center of the fading scarlet, and the new sentiment burrowed into him. His hands crept closed, forming tight fists as he breathed in like he hadn't in a long time.

"I am," he said. Zane trusted what his mother had spoken of his flames, but at last, he understood what she had seen within him all along.

An impregnable inferno.

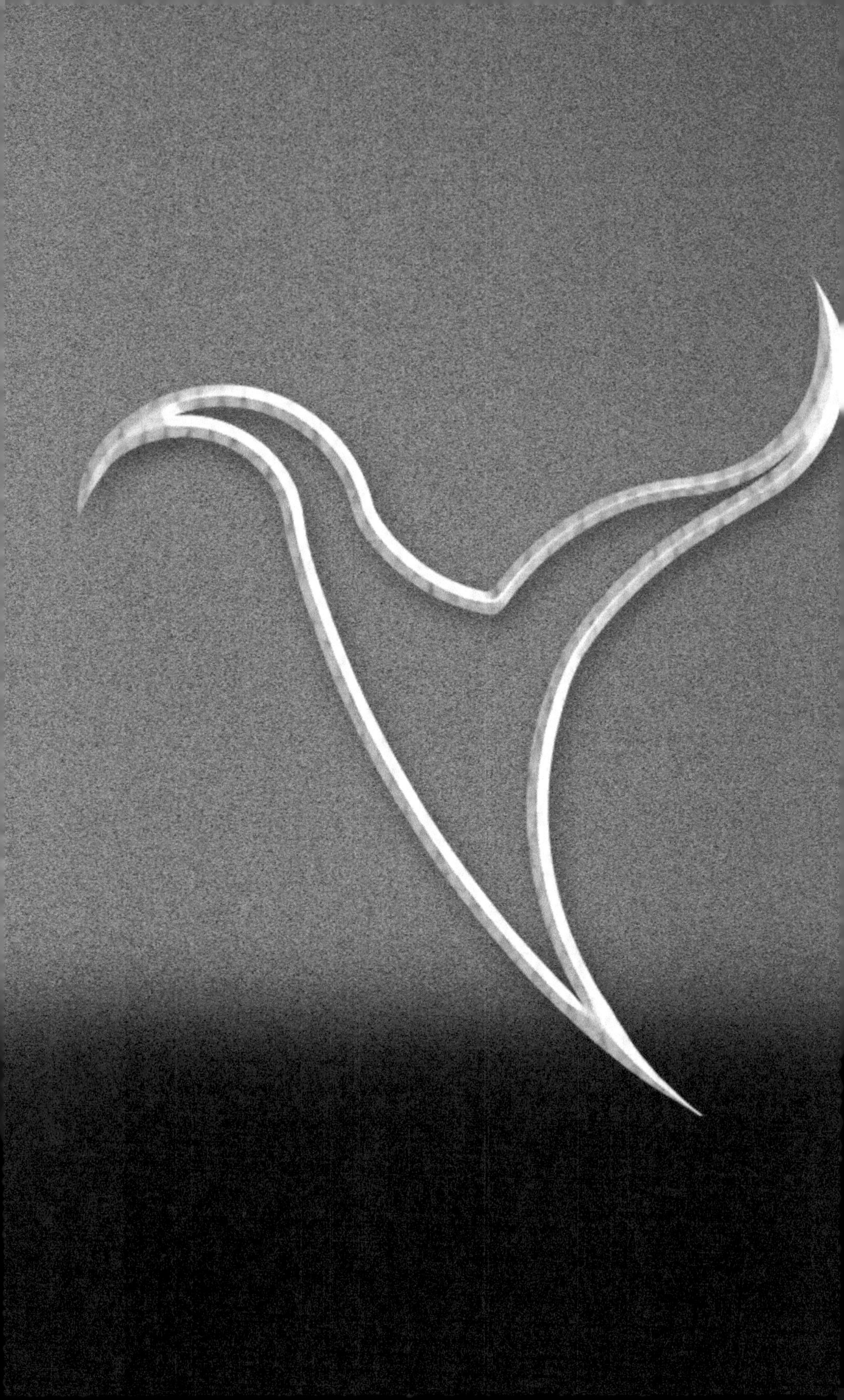

Twelve

Elegy of Sin and Sentiment

PENSIVE PURPLE EYES traced rows of flayed flesh. Within the large, well-lit room, black feathers danced. With perplexing precision, they incised several beings that lay at Onaga's feet: a vulcan, a demonic tiger, and a human—Zane's abducted comrade, Jaquelin Hopkins. Unconscious but breathing, a swarm of black feathers rent them, slicing away appendages and exposing nerves for melding. Piece by piece, they were torn and stitched together with fibers from the feathers, and other pieces were carefully attached. As Onaga weaved several diablo signs, the endings macerated and reformed as whole limbs.

The once-living creatures before him were successfully remade, their souls held in place by a blood rune that simmered in the chest of the mammal. Soon, the rift where their souls occupied would be supplanted, but first, he focused on the most arduous and mind-fraying aspect of the procedure. The head was peeled open, revealing its cranium. Removing its skull, he extracted the bestial brain with his feathers, leaving the nerves and stems intact. Carefully, he did the same to Jaquelin, elevating her mind and surgically implanting it into the cranium of the chimera. The nerves connected and fused, and the chimera was stitched into a complete entity.

Behind him, several demonic scientists waited, some sporting the typical umbra features—others possessed black wings, much like Onaga's. Hovering at his side was a wraith, its prismatic, reptilian form rattling while a long tail flicked behind it. A scythe-like appendage was fixed to the end, a dark blue energy seeping from it as it waited. After several minutes of the process, it clicked its sharp teeth, and Onaga grunted in response. One of his feathers smacked its snout, compelling it to refrain from further protest.

Onaga's eyes eclipsed in darkness, his glimmering irises peering from within at the abomination before them. Behind those eyes, doors opened, and his large wings unfurled as several slit purple pupils lined the feathers. The wings split into several smaller ones, intertwining into what appeared to be diablo signs, and his hands formed the ignis-diablo sign. With several pulses that thrummed, the chimera stirred, no longer bound to the tethers of its former beings.

Slowly, from where his wings met at the center of his back, several shadowy arms extended, grasping the space in front of his eyes before tearing open reality itself. A rift of pure darkness allowed a frigid energy to seep through, its tendrils licking the chimera's form before wrapping around it firmly. Carefully, an incorporeal essence was tugged free, displacing the souls from within it, and the wraith rushed forth. Its tail stabbed through the rune on the chimera's chest, and its pincer-like claws pried open the wound before it slithered in.

The chimera convulsed, the sounds of tearing and rattling soon dampening before it slowly opened its eyes—human in appearance. The veins stretching across the white sclera throbbed, and it turned its attention to Onaga before standing on unsteady feet with a snarl. With a few flaps of its wings, it briefly hovered before landing softly. Onaga's wings rejoined into two. His eyes returned to normal as he released his breath and spoke in Indiox.

"As I am rehearsed, I suspect each procedure would take longer for you all, but I expect you will be able to swiftly produce such specimens of a similar magnitude. Particulars will be edified with Zon Noell, as he will oversee production within the Daestrum facilities."

The scientists affirmed their understanding, several scrambling to retrieve materials. Before they could gather the remains of the corpses, the chimera summarily gobbled them up and waltzed down a large hall. None of the scientists expressed concern, however.

Noell took to Onaga's side. He was a fallen angel of similar imposing stature as Onaga, possessed of similar purple eyes, but younger in complexion and bearing long dreadlocks instead of smooth tufts. Rather than the black lab attire the scientists wore, he had donned archaic armor composed of an inscribed leather material stitched with several large black feathers decorating its gaps.

As they navigated to Onaga's study, Noell's wings folded tightly around him—a form of reservation in Onaga's presence. The stretch of halls before them was almost a maze—deliberate and intended to confuse in a mystique all too fitting of the fallen celestials. Yet they effortlessly navigated it.

"I surmise," Noell began, "we may yield a greater magnitude of formidability if we were to use angel wings instead of vulcans'," Noell said in his deep, gruff voice.

"Indubitably, but that also yields irksome scrutiny from the celestials. Should they send the guardians, our progress would be greatly impeded," Onaga claimed, rolling his shoulder as he turned through a narrower bend in the hall. Noell joined him, and their wings furled tighter, paying heed to a small demon woman who carried a thick journal. She passed beneath them, and Noell cleared his throat.

"Perhaps fallen angel wings would be apt. We are able to regenerate them, so we may be able to produce in excess," Noell suggested, but Onaga shook his head.

"The inviability of that option would make itself readily apparent. Our wings lose much of their potency once separated from the base while we are still living. Vulcan wings prove to retain their strength and utility even after death—they remain the suitable option for the current model of chimera production."

"Interesting ... I do wonder if this is because of the disjointedness of our celestial essence rather than a pure concentration in our wings."

"Pure celestials cannot regenerate, making their wings—the physical anchor of their beings—necessary rather than a vestigial remnant. While they are still intrinsic and retain formidability, when they are severed from us, the absence of our sentiments causes their power to wither. Grafting them to a new host would not restore their power, I assume."

"Ironic," Noell muttered, his wings shuddering as he pondered the thought. "Beings of shadow—both persistent and ephemeral." Noell clicked his tongue, shaking his head. "Perhaps we may find success in sequestering sentiments within our wings. Much in the same vein as preventing abstraction when leaping through the axes between. If successful, the prospective subjects granted these grafted appendages may retain their original potency." Noell mulled over the thought for several seconds, nodding to himself once he settled on it. "I will test this hypothesis and report the findings to you."

"Given your fruitful research of the Void, I anticipate comparable results." Onaga placed a clawed fingertip on his chin as he mused silently. "In light of the demigod's capture, what designation would you grant the Venatum?" he asked, glancing over his shoulder as the two walked.

"Our efforts are now strictly directed toward our dealings with the noble umbra houses," Noell said, his eyes narrowing as he peered hard at Onaga. "The Venatum's previous mission of capturing the demigod had rendered our forces thinner than before. Only half of us remain ..." Noell clenched his fists tightly. "Perhaps we may have captured him sooner if you had allowed me to deal with Kaal Lucifina. I suspect she is why the recent detachment I sent to interrogate those Kohens has yet to return. It bodes inauspiciously."

"Perhaps ..." Onaga spoke, his eyes fixed forward.

It perplexed him that she had interfered, suggesting a vested interest in protecting the umbra demons from the Venatum. The dealings with the noble demon houses had always vexed Lucy, he recalled. Her presence commanded the same reverence he and Lilith, as harbingers, bore, yet she rejected the weight of her lineage. The harbingers, as the original purveyors of sin, were held as idols among demonkind—the progenitors of their axioms. More vexing to him was the respect she commanded in spite of her self-effacement, as if the houses scorned the reverence typically demanded of them.

Through Asmodeus, he had ensured the heads of the families would still grant her an audience, despite their notarized disassociation from him and his faction. Such a compromise was needed with what was outlined in the Kohen Treaty they had penned with humankind. Auspiciously, neither that treaty nor the sentiments underlying it applied to Lucy.

Furthermore, Lilith was considered the matriarchal progenitor of the noble umbra demon houses, having birthed the Cardinal Sin Ordinances: Satan, Leviathan, Mammon, Beelzebub, Belphegor, and Asmodeus. From them, the noble umbra demon houses had emerged—barring Asmodeus. Given that Asmodeus, now the King of Avernus, embodied the sin of lust, it was considered ironic he forwent any biological offspring. While Lucy wasn't an ordinance herself, the differentiation was negligible to demonkind. The last he had spoken with Lucifer, it had bewildered him that his former colleague seemed oddly grateful for such a development.

Onaga could only speculate as to what conversations and brokering took place between her and the houses. The main branch of the Xiao regarded that she would only meet with one of the detached branches in Japan. That same branch scorned any dealing with him and the Venatum, going so far as to attack any Venatum who encroached into their territory. With Lucy having been reported meeting with them, Noell's speculation extended to such an observation as well.

Onaga was deathly curious to know more about her ruses, and he was reminded of such a desire when Noell killed the silence.

"She has evaded me personally thus far, but I suspect I may intercept her soon. When I do—"

"You will capture her. Alive and unharmed," Onaga's voice spoke from behind Noell, his image flickering with his brief disappearance. Point made, his order was final.

"Understood, Zakon Onaga," Noell confirmed. "I will also ensure the voidling adheres to this. In my studies of their kind and the void magics they practice, I have discovered their contingencies, should they deem you insincere. I have detailed it in the most recent report."

"I am aware. Your efforts are duly noted, Zon Noell."

Without further discussion, they walked until they reached their diverging paths. Onaga turned to face Noell, his quaint eyes unwavering.

"I will head to the Genesis Laboratory. Next we meet, Inferos and Mortale may very well be merged, and a new era will have commenced." Onaga turned, and Noell nodded, gesturing with his wings while bowing his head.

"I anticipate the advent of our answers," Noell said as Onaga left.

Onaga briskly navigated to a secluded section of the hall, where there was a dead end. Several feathers shot from his wings and assembled flat against the wall, forming an archway from which energy pulsed along its surface. Soon, a heavy black metal door appeared, and his feathers returned to his wings as he approached it and pulled it open.

Inside was an antiquated study consisting of several wooden desks, lit by sconces that decorated the thick beams lining the room. Piled atop the desks were several books, journals, and thick leathery tomes, caked in a light layer of dust that a flurry of his feathers easily cleaned off.

Suddenly, Onaga's wings split into multiple, crossing with one another to appear as diablo signs. As he shut his eyes, his hands clasped together, and darkness swallowed the study. From the wings, several purple-slit irises formed, eyes peering through the axes between. Infinite paths connected before the several eyes, and through each one, he saw where they led. Reality around him shuddered, and when he opened his eyes, it stabilized once more upon his arrival in the Genesis Laboratory.

Orphan was propped against the frigid stone walls, sporting Ethan's hazel eyes. Pensive and cold, he stared at Eden through the thick bars. Within the cell, he was bound in chains that bit into his bare skin. There was a collar on his neck and cuffs on his wrists, all connected by heavy chains that bolted to the ground. He had been stripped of the top he previously wore, a means of making his bindings more effective. The runes along them glowed ominously, casting an energy that undulated atop his skin. Despite this, Orphan dared not pry his eyes from him. The hexes, while powerful, were not nearly sufficient to contain the *other* part of him, should he dare to unleash it. The way in which he did so was unknown to Orphan, and that mystery was the bargaining chip Eden had gambled with.

The minutes turned to hours, and unblinking, they watched one another. The ire they shared for one another was palpable. Eden's—personal. Orphan's—pervasive. A hatred divorced of a targeted vendetta, Orphan's was perplexing, not that many bothered to inquire. Usually, most only knew of Orphan when they were to be made a puppet or perish.

It was all too silent when the black feather floated within Eden's cell. Both perked up when Onaga appeared, his dark visage bathed in a darkness that quickly faded, and Orphan flashed Eden a sardonic smile.

"Time's up," Orphan said flatly.

Onaga held two fingers out, and several feathers shot from his wings and sundered Eden precisely. Ligaments, joints, and the edges of his eyelids were slashed deliberately, with pulsing darkness left along the serrations. No blood spilled; tiny sutures remained atop the many wounds. Many of the injuries were left as irritants to disrupt focus.

It hadn't hurt as much as Eden would have expected, but the suppression hex left him debilitated, drained, and demoralized. By some miracle, if his other aspect could arise, the hexes Onaga placed on him would prove too difficult to overcome.

"With this, you will not escape again," Onaga said, his hand lowering as his wings retracted.

"If that was the worry ..." Eden said softly, lowering his head. "They've had enough time to evacuate."

"Oh, is that what you were worried about? I never intended to destroy them—at least, not once I brought you here. They're needed for the chimera experiments, after all."

Eden raised his head, eyes widening before the stinging forced him to shut them. He'd have dragged himself from the floor, but his legs refused to cooperate as the dark energy pulsed along his wounds. Seeing his helplessness, Orphan chuckled.

"What? Didn't think I was intent on letting them go unpunished, did you? Their acclimation and greater connection to Ichor is why they were suitable for the experiments. After all, binding flesh and nodes is easier with hunters compared to unconnected humans."

"You despicable monster," Eden hissed, growling as he glared at Onaga, whose remorseless eyes peered down at him. No such emotion spread across his visage, and Eden found that the most detestable. "A creature like you deserves damnation a thousand times over. I hate you with *every* fiber of my being."

"A minuscule price. There have been many before who have professed their hatred of me, and now, their progeny reap the rewards of my research," Onaga spoke in a low voice, then crouched before Eden. "Should your blood and hatred bring omniscience, it is meaningless."

Onaga held Eden's ireful eyes within his focus, studying them briefly before his own eyes narrowed.

"I do not hate you, demigod. I find you noble. Your suffering is a sacrifice that will pave the path to liberation from the tyranny of ignorance. Should we know all that plagues us, there is no bounty of uncertainty that will prosper, and perhaps all who would live will know peace at last. And should I discover how—I would see *both* of you returned."

"You don't know that!" Eden cried, shaking his head as tears gathered in his green eyes. "You sacrifice us on a prayer. She knew it more than either of us," Eden said, heaving as he inhaled. "Nothing will fill that cold, heartless pit inside of you!" Eden's eyes remained wide, forced open by sheer determination to see something stir within those voids that served as eyes. No such thing did.

"You lack the prerequisites to attempt fathoming an understanding. But the form you will take might," Onaga said. "Your suffering was admittedly wanton, and I saw to it that Modeo paid dearly for that. The sentiment of my apology is present, but I suspect it means little to you. I may understand your pain soon, as I hope you may understand gratitude," Onaga claimed, standing before turning his back to Eden.

"Did you ever even care for her?" Eden breathed out, his voice labored and broken when he deigned to ask the question. The tears in his eyes turned to blood, but no divine light emerged from within his depths—only despair. But Onaga was quiet for several moments, not even his breath discernible. Finally, he answered.

"There is no answer I could give to satisfy what you truly wish to know." Onaga's wings shuddered, and he appeared outside of the cell, his gaze finding Orphan before he beckoned him to follow.

The two left Eden to himself, no longer concerned with a phantom rebellion emerging. Orphan paced behind Onaga, stretching their neck as they cleared their throat to garner Onaga's attention.

"This is the second time I am delivering on my promise, in spite of your daughter's constant interference," Orphan began. "You have done adequate research into your Gates of Oblivion, or whatever you call it. You will deliver for me *now*," Orphan said, Ethan's voice cracking as Orphan's true nature spilled through their growing impatience.

"I did not forget, voidling. The nature of your kind begs mystique beyond compare, stretching further than even the axes between when not expelled from your Primordial. Your sibling lies outside within the stretches of conception—abstract beyond abstract."

"And you can bring her back," Orphan spat, expectant of Onaga's suggestion.

"Hypothetically. Through the Gates of Oblivion, the realms and reality itself are bisected. A sanctity forgone, all concepts can be manifested in exchange for something of equal magnitude—however one could gauge these things."

"I would sacrifice all if it means her return," Orphan coldly stated.

"I suspected as much, but it would hardly be necessary, I surmise. One soul would do, but—"

"No buts. You do it, or you will see your dreams of omniscience squandered."

"It is a complex process that I can and will endeavor, *Astrol* of the Void," Onaga claimed, stopping in his tracks in the middle of the hall. And their eyes met.

"That name …" Orphan muttered, and Onaga's wings spread.

"When peering through your mind long ago, I learned of that name you have since forsaken—intrinsically tied to this sister you call Astrea. When she perished, so too did your name, yes?" Onaga asked, prompting Orphan to glare. "Voidlings typically do without arbitrary constructs such as gender, to my understanding. Why would your sibling adopt such a thing?"

"Because *she* desired it. There need be no other reason," Orphan challenged. "Explain your machinations before I defect," Orphan demanded, and Onaga was all too eager to explain.

"Oblivion is the largest of infinities to conceptualize mathematically, let alone within practice. Concepts, concepts of concepts, and everything real and fake alike exist within a quantum state multiplying upon itself before, now, and forever. Vanquished from this realm, your sister resides within it, lost within a sea of concepts that I would peer within. I have viewed the infinite universe at its conception, and even I could not fathom Oblivion fully without abstracting."

"Suspend your lecture. I've no fascination in matters beyond my interest," Orphan said, the faint flicker of the fluorescent lights above casting dark shadows over their cold eyes.

"With the heart forged from the demigod and Cassiel, I will be able to do so without risk, for within the infinite expanse of knowledge I will bear, the concept of self cannot be lost. I can search beyond my initial attempts, and I *will* find her." They stared at one another, and Orphan's skepticism faded as they huffed.

"Even now … I can tell you aren't lying. Your honesty disgusts me, in a way. A little cynicism fits a villain."

"I am no villain, nor any such label bound by ethical considerations. Cynicism feeds a heart promises of reprieve from ignorance, but it does not abide by truth. It does not bring answers. Quite unproductive, but let me not pontificate. Keep your eye upon the demigod until we may summon Lord Paimon." Onaga's wings flicked out dismissively. "You will be given your due." With his promise, Onaga's wings closed, and he turned away from Orphan and continued down the hall toward the elevator.

Nerves eased, but not settled, Orphan shook their head.

"I expect you will, Harbinger."

Ryu's golden eyes danced across the jagged inscriptions along the page, written in Indiox, he struggled to comprehend intrinsically. Of the several languages he had been learning, it was the harshest to his mind. While he was alleged to comprehend it at a level beyond his years, such praise rang hollow when measured against Onaga and the texts they often reviewed together.

Comparing himself to Onaga was destined to cast his blossoming mind into umbrage—he knew as much, but that compulsion remained present, regardless. Ten years of age was young by human standards—even more by demon standards. His youth inspired awe at his progress. There was always something new he wondered about and investigated, and it was when he was able to resolve alchemical formulas as if they were intrinsic that Onaga granted his tutelage.

The door to Onaga's study soon opened, and Ryu peered up from the smaller desk he was able to comfortably occupy. Gold eyes met purple, both pensive and sharing in wonder. Ryu stood and gave Onaga a respectful bow of his head, gesturing with his arms much like Onaga did with his wings. His all-black attire of a blazer and shorts was woven with silvery seams and embroidered patterns resembling frayed feathers and the infernal insignia representing Onaga's creed. In that moment, Onaga remembered when Lucy wore a similar uniform for the academy years prior.

"Welcome back, Ku Onaga," Ryu spoke cordially using Indiox.

"Ku?" Onaga replied in the same language, clicking his tongue as he approached. "Perhaps many within the Academy in Avernus refer to me as such, but you will continue to use the honorific *Yokon*, since you are under my tutelage." Onaga crouched when he stood before Ryu, the candlelight casting a soft shadow on his stonelike visage. He peered down at the meek boy, as if seeing through the hesitant pout he gave him. "Who has instilled doubt within you?"

"The Xiao noble," Ryu replied after several moments.

"The minor branch—from Taiwan?" Onaga inquired.

Ryu silently rehearsed his tongue's position before responding. "Yes. Feng Xiao."

"Ah. There is much jealousy, perhaps, that a demonium of common birth would possess a talent I would see sufficiently nourished." Onaga reached out, the pearly nail of his finger lightly resting on Ryu's forehead. "You would doubt my intuition over their cynical words?"

Ryu shook his head, sucking his lips in while averting his gaze, and he breathed out a soft sigh when Onaga stood again.

"No matter your purported attainment, I know you would continue to reach higher and grasp that which is unseen to even trained eyes, and should your own be trained, you would reach further into the unknown and comprehend Oblivion itself. That is my suspicion," Onaga said, his eyes stern. "I would not be so cruel as to deny nurturing such potential," Onaga claimed, turning on his heel before approaching the adjacent desk. "Before you settle for your assignments, would you care to glimpse my divinations of origin and its subversions? I have long since prepared your axioms to grasp it, and it should be comprehensible now."

Ryu perked up, eyes shimmering as he sucked in a sharp breath through his nose. The candlelight was dull in comparison to the wonder that kindled within his golden depths—even illuminating the darkness that pervaded the voids of Onaga's moment the moment their gazes met. Onaga gestured with his hand to the desk, and Ryu jogged over as Onaga reached for one of his Tomes of Knowledge. He pulled it from a shelf installed in the wall. The Indiox word for *Genesis* was inscribed on the leathery face, the embossed letters undulating subtly against Onaga's fingertips.

"The very first of the Tomes of Knowledge I penned is here. Much like how demon alchemy subverted the will of creation and malformed it with infernal machinations, I did the same with Latin. Doing so was necessary in my deviation from the orthodoxy of creation I had been made to enforce for the plethora of my existence," Onaga said. The tapping of shoes on wood stirred him from his focus, and he glimpsed the top of Ryu's white head rising and falling out of his view.

With a wave of Onaga's hand, several feathers assembled where Ryu had been jumping, and the boy stepped atop them as if it were routine.

"Your indolent tongue neglects to alert me of my inattentiveness," Onaga spoke lightly, something akin to amusement pervading his tone.

"I did not wish to interrupt ..." Ryu protested quietly, peering down at the large tome in awe. "I always peered at them on the shelves, but their whispers deterred," Ryu murmured softly, several syllables and vowels stressed or missed as he spoke. His eyes squinted hard at the written symbols atop the tome, pupils dancing from line to line with a labored expression marring his pale features.

"You may interrupt with purpose and truth in your intention. It is easy to banish pertinent thoughts in favor of feigning understanding. Such farce is a cardinal violation within my creed," Onaga spoke, eyes pensive as they found Ryu, who nodded with his attention still firmly fixed on the tome.

"Yes, Yokon Onaga," he spoke.

Onaga opened the tome, flipping the weathered pages. The red ink inscribing them was indiscernible to Ryu, the text convoluted and above his grasp of Indiox. As Onaga recited pertinent terms and the history, Ryu's eyes fogged up, and he breathed with noticeable stress.

"Ryu?" Onaga called, interrupting his own explanations. "Would you find another tongue easier?" he asked. Ryu's noticeable struggle hadn't been lost on him, evident in his choppy, broken speech and discomfort when presented with the written language.

Ryu bit his lip, cheeks suddenly flushed as with the ink in the tome. He tore his eyes from the pages.

"Japanese," Ryu replied, chagrin in his voice.

"Admittedly, my fluency with that tongue is insufficient to convey the knowledge of creation," Onaga said with a whisper of shame painting him. "I will need to rehash the language again when my coming experiment is complete. Is there by chance another language you are comfortable with?"

Ryu's thoughts stirred, brow furrowing as he idly scraped the wood of the desk with his nail.

"English?" Ryu responded, and Onaga gave a nod.

"Ah, yes. It has become more common in recent centuries. Such an odd tongue, but its utility is ubiquitous in modern human cultures," Onaga said in English, and Ryu gave a small smile, reprieve spelled upon his rosy cheeks.

"My level with it is not as high as Japanese, but I speak it okay," Ryu said, his voice light and carrying a level of emotion he failed to convey previously.

"Again," Onaga said, finger tapping the top of the page. "The Empty—the first, inscrutable era—persisted. Then there was a sentiment, something which does not translate to spoken language or written text. The Resolution began, where these Primordial sentiments established order. Soon, by Izanagi's countless hands, the universe was given shape. Some of his hands were guided by myself, for I was granted a fraction of his immeasurable understanding of the world we would create. And when I gleaned the truths of reality, my own hands did the same. More complex, ripe with redundancies, Mortale was formed, and I became exalted ..." Onaga explained, finger landing on the last word of the page before carefully flipping to the next.

"Your hands made Mortale?" Ryu asked, skeptically eyeing Onaga's gray fingers.

"Not as you see them now," Onaga said. "This corporeal coil hardly encapsulates what I once was—what I can still be to a lesser extent."

"Was it because you fell?"

"Yes. When I fell, my hands were tethered, but my mind was freed." Onaga mulled over the fractured memories before he continued reading from the tome. He detailed the subsequent eras thoroughly to Ryu.

The Age of Ichor, where Ichor became the veins of life, and all who could observe and share sentiments. *The Broken Oath*, where the cracks of the Primordials' dissatisfaction permeated their chosen seraphim and where the first of humanity came to be. Following that, *The Great Division*, where angels formed factions in observation of Ichor's suffering due to the imbalances of sentiments among the Primordials.

"I dissected reality and molded it in my agonizing curiosity, and I soon fell asleep ..." Onaga's gaze turned to Ryu, peering hard at the innocent curiosity he knew all too well. Raw and unformed, he'd see it sated by all means necessary. "I awoke from my slumber, my skin as ash and feathers slick black. There in the dark, my eyes could see clearly that there was much unknown. My ignorance damned, I would mold a world without it." Onaga's eyes flickered, and his nails scraped the page, landing on harsh lines spelling a name Ryu did understand—a name all demons knew.

"*Lucifer*," Onaga spoke, the name itself commanding reverence. "The former Seraph of Light and Virtue, stole the heart of Ichor. Our interests converged for a time, and with the heart's power, my true hands were momentarily returned in their full breadth, and I created Inferos in the image of Mortale. But it was imperfect—incomplete."

"Encumbered by sin?" Ryu inquired with a wisp, stirring Onaga's attention.

"I see Lucifina shared with you her thesis," he said, and Ryu nodded.

"Big-sister Lucy told me all about the balance of sin and virtue, and how she believes it necessary—even if imperfect." Ryu's eyes drifted down suddenly. "I miss her."

Onaga shut his eyes, brows twitching momentarily as he sorted his thoughts.

"Dominance ... begets progress. Mindless indulgence breeds stagnation, but this ambition—*our* ambition—is anything but. Knowledge will liberate all from the tyranny of ignorance. Lucifina understood this, and while her thesis is sound, it lacks holistic consideration."

"Would you ... say balance is unnecessary?" Ryu inquired, his tone dropping as shame infiltrated his mind.

"It is wholly necessary—but its scope suggests itself too narrow. A tragedy and a thousand years of peace would ring balance the same as intermittent conflict in the same period. Death for progress, blood for sustenance. These things are subjective and arbitrary, but the sentiments they carry are not formulaic. We can create balance as easily as we disrupt it. That is my conclusion." Silence pervaded the two, countless words and thoughts brewing while Ryu absorbed the statement with hesitation written on his face.

Lucy had always been kind and understanding, wise beyond her years and expectations alike. His admiration couldn't be distilled into words, yet he couldn't speak a rebuttal on her behalf, even as he desired to find a way to challenge. That *daft* urge was banished quickly, a habit Onaga discouraged to avoid biases taking root.

"I've much to consider with your words, Mr. Onaga," Ryu said, breaking the silence.

"Excellent. I do not expect you to think of my pontifications as gospel. You will think and discover your understanding, rather than launder it," Onaga said, hand peeling from the tome and hovering above Ryu's head. He gently rested his palm atop, fingers lightly ruffling the silky white strands.

"Yes, Mr. Onaga," Ryu affirmed, and Onaga withdrew his fingers before he shut the tome.

"Soon, many questions will be replaced with concrete answers, and I would share in my divinations with you. Through Lord Paimon, we will see the worlds realized."

"Lord Paimon?" Ryu questioned, jumping down from the feathers he used as a stool, watching them silently shoot back into Onaga's wings. "For the divine heart? Will it work?"

"It should," Onaga suggested. "Lord Paimon, as Lucifer's progeny, is more than compatible with such an artifact. Whether he will survive or remain as he was, I cannot say, but his eagerness remains." Onaga grunted. "Noble—just as his father."

"Would it suffice? For you to learn with the time it will grant?" As Ryu's brimming curiosity peeked through the curtains of his gaze, something fanatical gazed back at him.

"It will. Dissecting reality as a whole and viewing its germination is far simpler than creating anew."

Eden opened his eyes to a melodic humming, having drifted off. He raised his head, despite how heavy it was to do so. The cool air stung his wounded lids, making it hard for him to focus on the lilac eyes staring at him through the cells. Unlike the warmth and joy they offered in his memory, these mimicries made the air scorching in comparison. Devoid of all one could call human or even demon, their cynicism indicted him—unblinking.

"Miss me?" Orphan asked, assuming Cassiel's voice and visage. Eden didn't respond. "I don't hate you—not specifically. You're ... a means to an end, as your kind are often keen to use for justification. I'm nowhere near as evil as you humans, all things considered. When I die—that's it. I cease to be. You get to frolic in your precious *Mother's* veins and be joyful. Death is hardly that bad when you think of it that way," she continued, pouting when Eden didn't respond.

There was no warmth between their eyes, and Eden lowered his head once more, refusing to open his eyes again.

"Nothing daunting, dear Captain?" Orphan said in Bonnie's voice, shifting to her form. "Couldn't protect me. Can't protect them. Can't protect yourself. Again and again ... it's poetic. Could rhyme, if I try," Orphan said, watching for a reaction that Eden refused to give.

"*You're no fun,*" Orphan said then, taking on Lucy's likeness. "I'm not your villain if you zoom out wide enough. I'm a victim like everybody else, reclaiming what was lost through coercion and violence—just like you humans do. Enemies, food … you kill everything if it's convenient or expedient. Resources that can be shared, petty squabbles over blood and creed. It's pathetic and despicable. Where's your vendetta against that?"

Finally, Eden raised his head, peering at Orphan with hollow, sunken eyes that burned with ire. With a delightful smile spreading, Orphan shifted to Kendall's image and spoke.

"Oh, right. Cecilia. She was a good example, wasn't she? You killed her beloved, claiming he was your enemy. Salem, yeah? I sent you after him, knowing you'd kill him, and you didn't even hesitate," Orphan chuckled. "Did you know she's still alive? And quite pissed, at that. You've another phantom nipping at your heels. It never ends … the suffering. I might as well stir the cycle if it's going to exist anyway."

"You're twisted," Eden spoke in a hushed, broken voice. With eerie quiet, Orphan gripped the bars, poking their head through as their lips twisted into a sinister smile, face shifting back to Cassiel's image.

"What's twisted is that you bitch and moan about what was taken from you, but you're the biggest thief of them all. If killing her husband wasn't enough, you even killed her daughter. Imagine how fucked up that is." Orphan chuckled darkly. "What's next? Who else will you take from someone else? Unfortunately, I'll be removing myself from the picture after this; reclaim what was taken from me by your kind."

At last, Eden's eyes teared up, falling down his stained cheeks as he shook his head in denial. He hiccupped as his lungs strangled the air inside of them, and he gritted his teeth.

"I know … how about a lullaby?" Orphan suggested, drawing back. "Or even better … how about I remind you of how she sounded when she was killed?"

"Stop …" Eden pleaded.

"Can't live with that guilt? Here, let me do an impression to set you at ease." Orphan cleared their throat. "All alone, I was waiting for you, but you kept running. It was so lonely without you … but we'll be together again soon. Thanks for coming back to me, Eden," Orphan sniffled out.

Eden growled, yanking his arm forward, hand outstretched as if he could reach Orphan. Seeing this, Orphan smirked before they stood up and morphed back into Ethan's form.

"She'd say something like that, I bet."

Orphan's eyes went wide all of a sudden, a red light flashing before their eyes as Avenger manifested in Eden's hand. The weight had proven too much for him to wield, and his arm fell. The weapon clattered against the stone floor, and Eden released the breath he had been holding, his expression mirroring Orphan's.

"Why?" Eden choked out.

Orphan was quiet, eyes dancing around the vacant hall, stillness stretching the intangible tension that fermented. And shortly, the alarm sounded within the laboratory. The grating screech bouncing off the walls made Orphan flinch, and they turned to see a shadow looming as Onaga manifested from a feather.

"Hunters," Onaga grumbled. "The demigod—we must prepare to move him to another laboratory. The process is arduous and sensitive to interference." His feathers began darting through the cell and slicing the chains from the ground as Orphan growled.

"How did they discover the location? There is no feasible ... your daughter. It had to be her. I pried my attention from her this past week in preparation," Orphan said, eyes narrowing. "Your Venatum proved insufficient, after all."

"*Eccen*," Onaga spoke, his deep voice booming off the walls. *Silence.* His use of the demon language with such disregard was far from common, conveying a gravity Orphan was forced to respect. Onaga threw the cell open and snatched Eden from the ground. Onaga took Orphan's hand, and a swarm of feathers swallowed them before they appeared within Onaga's liminal study.

Ryu was meekly tucked into the corner, eyes dancing with concern as Onaga and Orphan spoke their frustrations aloud. He briefly glanced at Eden before averting his gaze, face scrunching as he buried his face in his knees.

Onaga clasped his fingers together into the equilibrium-diablo sign, each finger connecting or crossing as they would when forming any of the four. His wings split, purple irises opening within the feathers before his darkness extended across the room. When Onaga peered into the axes between, seeking a path from which the study would leap, jade-green eyes glimmered within the dark at him. Several black hands then shot from their pupils and clamped each path before Onaga.

"Running again? Like a mouse with wings?" Jessica's voice echoed, causing the axes to shudder. "No, not this time. For centuries, your conquest—your greed—has seeded the soil of your grave."

Onaga's many eyes narrowed on her. Her hatred scorned him and his means of escape, but with only a moment's pause, Onaga grunted dismissively.

"I will know my truths, *Witch of Death*," Onaga claimed, and his physical eyes opened as his shadows retreated back to his form.

"The witch has accessed the axes between ..." Onaga stated, earning a wide-eyed stare from Orphan.

Eden slowly raised his head, his teeth grinding. His vision was intermittent, but those pensive purple eyes found him, and he was reminded again of what he feared the most. With the arrival of his comrades imminent, he silently begged for their lives in his broken voice.

Onaga raced to the bookshelf containing his tomes, eyes drifting over the various leather spines until they landed on the Tome of Liminality. The shelf shimmered, as if anchoring itself to reality the moment Onaga willed it. He pulled what he presumed was the tome from the shelf, but found the contents crudely forged in blood not his own.

"A forgery ..." Onaga whispered to himself, eyes briefly finding Ryu, but it was not the time for interrogation or questioning.

"Your damned daughter," Orphan spat, hand raising as the sludge of his being morphed into a black saber, ominously pulsing with white energy. "I'll have to go clean this mess up then. You're lucky I took additional precautions on the off chance they somehow did find this place. I can buy you enough time for the ritual, so bite the bullet and summon Paimon."

"With the current distortion, we would need a sacrifice of exceptional purity to give Paimon enough time for this ritual," Onaga claimed, eyes narrowing as Orphan glared.

"Are you a hypocrite, Harbinger?" Orphan asked, eyes drifting to Ryu. The boy winced at the harsh gaze, but the voidling turned and left the study.

Onaga knew Orphan was correct, but bitterness lingered on his tongue as his softening eyes found Ryu, whose concern had largely been unanswered. That, too, made the moment more unsavory. He set Eden on the floor, the wooden boards softly squeaking as Onaga approached Ryu, crouching before him.

"Dear Ryu, I spoke of a day where you would one day greet your human mother again. Such a day will be made reality, as per my promise to you, but I've one more thing to demand," he said. From his wings, he plucked a large feather from their abyss. The root was coated in his blood, and he gently tucked it into Ryu's small hands. For once, his face, usually devoid of expression, suggested a perturbance akin to melancholy. Ryu's eyes shimmered with glossy tears as Onaga gazed into them. The sentiments brewing between the two beings were bitter, but Onaga preferred that to the alternative. A betrayal of his principles arose, challenging him to commit to the highest order of his creed. In that moment, he had but one sentiment he could espouse to the boy he had nurtured knowledge within.

"Should I perish, I would have you make me a promise ..."

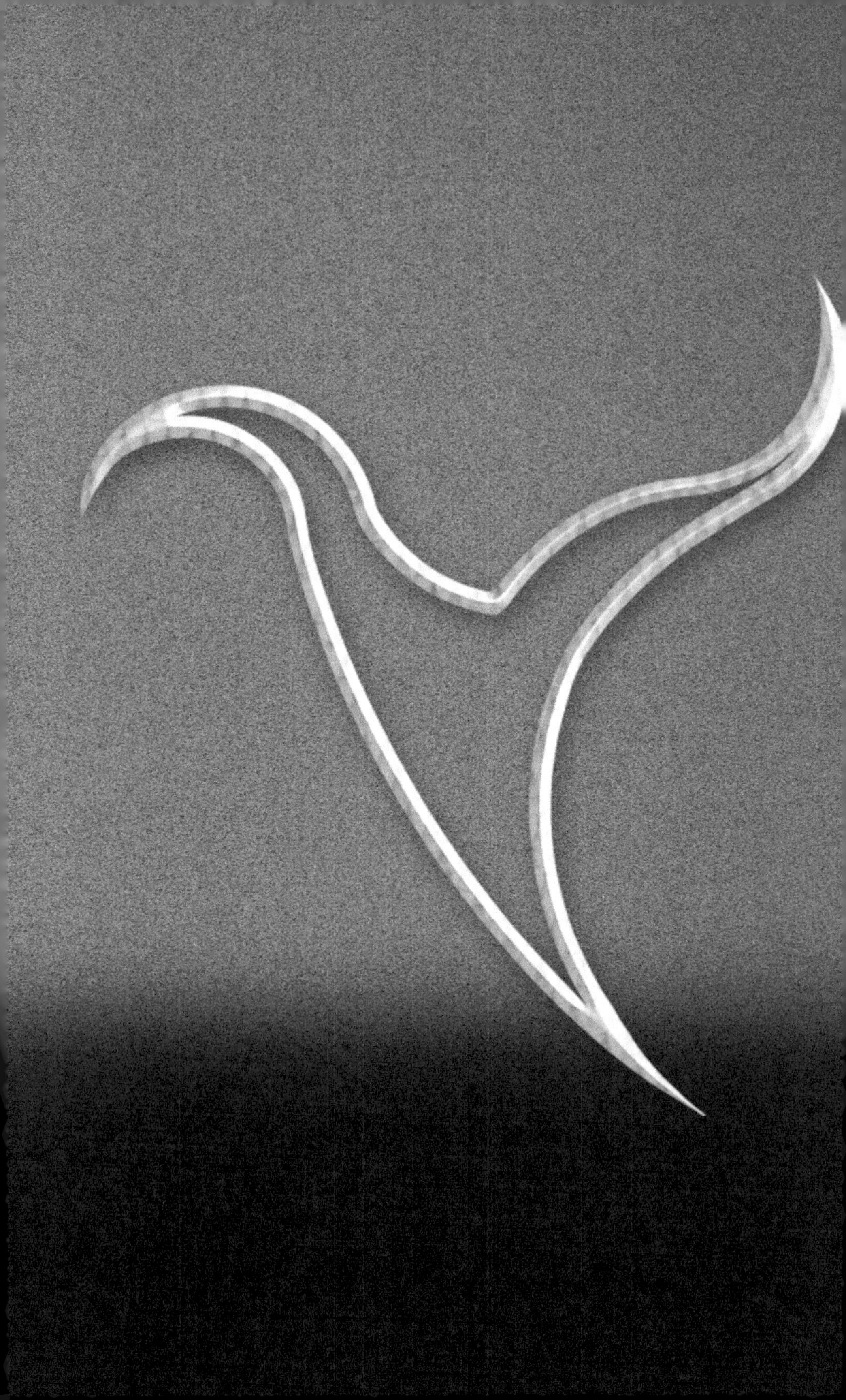

Thirteen

Rondo of Emptiness

KENDRA'S hands pressed together as she softly whispered a prayer. She stood at her dresser, a small picture of Kendall propped up with candles on each side. The scent of pumpkin drifted from the melting wax, and she ended the prayer with the soft tune Kendall had always hummed. She had always thought the song was more suited to Kendall's voice, her own being deeper and less fluid for such melodies.

Gradually, her fingers pushed away from one another, and her voice dropped.

"Sanguine ..." Kendra whispered. She opened her eyes and clapped, a gust of wind blowing the candles out. The aroma lingered with the humorous memory of Kendall's surprise clap at the door, both sweet and reminiscent of her visage.

Kendra wished she could visit Kendall's grave, another of her pre-mission traditions, but the protocol around travel was stricter leading up to the operation. Instead, she settled for a more symbolic ritual. Despite completing the prayer, a hollowness settled in her heart, the sundered pit where Eden was nestled. The despair he suggested before and during his gamble with Orphan was indigestible, something to be banished. Her oath to lay down her life for humankind had been solidified by his oath to defend her life with his own—an oath he made as both her captain and friend. That sentiment she shared reminded her of the despair she once knew—the despair he had rescued her from.

It's never too late to change your story.

Kendra wondered what cards Kendall would have drawn for him, but she knew what cards she could offer him in her absence.

The Tower.

Six of Swords.

Death.

She pulled each card from the drawer, studying each with due respect. The bond the living held with Ichor was bound in the sacrament of sentiments—their power proof of the love they shared as her children. But that bond, that love, extended with the sentiments between all who allowed it. She meant it when she said she loved Eden. Though he was hesitant to speak of the bonds he so feared losing, she knew where his heart resided. Each card, ripe with the power to overcome, she drew on his behalf.

To change his story.

With no further doubts, she slid the cards into the pouch on her thigh and clasped it shut before leaving the room.

The sun ascended the horizon, a chariot carrying the weight of the world itself—or at least the hunters felt it did. Engines hummed in the clamor of their assembly. Gadgets and communication towers were hoisted by squads and firmly attached to the engineers' backs. Others inspected their weapons. Blades and guns were readied, their edges and barrels cleaned with diligence. Working order ensured, they were fastened before the forces retrieved additional ammunition and various support equipment from the caches being offloaded from trucks.

Carefully, the hunters assembled, weapons safely in arms, barrels positioned high. Nerves were strung higher, but their stoic gazes remained staunch. The commanders waited in front of the largest of the teleportation terminals—the ones used for transporting large swaths of troops. Two fully staffed squads could be transported by a single terminal, of which there were three. The rest would be transported by the smaller terminals, a means of dispersing their forces efficiently.

Alicia and Zane waited at the front of the assembling hunters, turned toward them as a tactic of boosting morale and certainty. Zane's expression was sincere this time, eyes embedded with an indomitable presence he scarcely revealed—consciously or otherwise. And soon, all eyes landed on Kendra as she pushed through the crowd, not a hint of hesitation in her staunch demeanor.

She stopped in front of Alicia and Zane, and she nodded. A puzzling muse flashed in Zane's eyes before he gestured to his unoccupied side. Kendra rolled her eyes before positioning herself there, giving him the center of the three of them. She returned her gaze to the hunters, reassured by their preparedness. Unlike when they performed drills, they all had some form of headgear—hoods and helmets based on their roles. She never wore one on account of it being a potential fire hazard.

The hunters went silent, and Jessica stepped forward, standing in front of the three as several commanders stood at the sides.

"Hunters!" she declared, her voice booming with power that made the air ripple.

"Ma'am!" the hunters responded in unison, taking straight-legged stances with a stomp.

"Today ... is a once-in-a-lifetime hunt," Jessica announced. "Securing Captain Blackwell is our primary objective, as is slaying the Harbinger of Greed, but our survival is paramount to those goals. You watch each other, and you stay sharp at all times. Your coordinates have been given, and we will guide you with the recon data we have garnered. Our comrades have readied our spawn points, and an initial anti-demon vacuum bomb is being deployed against the region shortly before engagement. Be sure to maintain your barriers around your respiratory systems and orifices. This goes for Mallory and Larson especially. With the enemy forces hindered, we will penetrate the laboratory defenses."

Jessica paused, her eyes flashing as she firmly gripped the hilt of her sheathed saber.

"The voidling known as Orphan is virtually guaranteed to be present, and our countermeasures have been developed. Each squad will be given two soul binders, a means by which Orphan can be eliminated. While we would ideally give one to each hunter, they are scarce. One is to be held by the senior engineer, and the other by your most accomplished cannon or bastion. This is to ensure they can be eliminated effectively, along with having a backup."

As Jessica explained, Major Carter handed out soul binders to the squads. The predetermined *accomplished* bastion or cannon in question was the one with the highest number of demons eliminated—assists included. For Seraph Seven, that was Alicia, who held the gem up to Kendra and winked before snapping it into the slot on her belt buckle. Zane then held his own up, and Kendra huffed, realizing it was rehearsed between them to tease her. They would be operating with their own squads when the speech ended—she had to trust Alicia would handle Orphan if they appeared.

"Given Orphan can take on all forms, remain vigilant of *everyone*. You will coordinate two passwords with one another. To access channels for communication, you will need to enter the passphrase, *ashed wings will be vanquished*.'" Jessica's eyes narrowed. "You will also coordinate a squad passphrase with one another to avoid espionage among your own. Orphan cannot maintain their form when afflicted by the soul binder—nor can they directly touch it. Remember this should doubts arise." Her eyes dropped for a moment.

"I will be auxiliary for this operation, suppressing both Onaga's means of escape and the full thrust of his power. Seraph Seven and Nine are to converge at the laboratory entrance, and Captain Larson, Sergeant Romero, and Private Mallory will carve forward. Units are to locate and recover Captain Blackwell, and our chosen personnel will then converge to engage Onaga. You were all given the compendium details pertaining to Onaga, and should he appear, you are to report his location immediately and disengage. I repeat, do *not* engage him in combat."

Jessica turned on her heel, gaze fixed to the ground as she walked past Kendra, Zane, and Alicia. She stopped in front of the terminal, grip tightening on the hilt of her blade. She drew it with a chime ringing through the area, its gunmetal hue glimmering brightly. The guard on the hilt was entwined, thorny, as if two rebellious rose stems—*the Thorn of Twilight*, a blade gifted to her by Izalin of her former coven.

"As is tradition for a hunt of this magnitude, I, Mistress of the Hunt, will engage first. I stake my life on the line, as you do yours." Jessica's form shimmered, her eyes glowing as she held her blade up to the sky. As she ascended high for all to see, its luster practically carved the rising sun.

The hunters readied themselves as Kendra, Zane, and Alicia turned. They marched to their respective terminals, and the hunters followed, converging with their respective squads or groups. With a bright light shimmering across Jessica's form, she called out for all hunters to hear,

"Let the hunt begin!"

Aerosolized rosemary pervaded the thick vegetation of the Amazon, its scent marching through it. Firmly fixed in its center, the Genesis Laboratory sat, the air surrounding it undulating with dark energy—a barrier. Soon, the earth quaked, and a large purple arm with monstrous digits tore through the soil. The sharp digits cleaved the air, sundering the barrier while their ferocious force wafted the rosemary into its umbrage. No longer an asylum for the demons, many of the guards standing duty were debilitated by the irritant and forced to retreat or engage in countermeasures.

Flocks of vulcans took high to the sky, their shadows looming over the forest as their several demonic eyes searched for the interlopers. The wind whistled with bullets, sniper fire raining on the unsuspecting demons.

Blood rained from the skies as the demons were methodically eliminated or forced to return to the ground, where they were disadvantaged. Come their landing, half of the vulcans had been shot down.

Demonic screeches filtered through the foliage, and with their cries, the hunters advanced. From their camps, several squads traversed the largely unknown terrain, guided by the direction of their main camp, Roost. Enemy positions were called out from the predator drones operated by the engineers, and more perceptive demons were summarily eliminated by the advancing squads led by Commander Rigs.

"Angel Eleven breaching the halfway mark," a hunter spoke over the radio.

"Seraph Nine closing in on position K-22, preparing a blaze to drive clusters into the sky. Ready your fire on my mark," Zane's voice called through the radio, and several snipers took their positions from the large cargo drones they were suspended from. Flames erupted from the northern quadrant of the forest, driving several vulcans into the sky. "Targets ascending. Fire at will." With prompt speed, most of the vulcans were quickly shot from the sky, screeching as they crashed back into the waiting flames beneath. With their targets eliminated, the flames ceased, leaving little damage to the surrounding forest thanks to Zane's precise control.

"Roost to Seraph Seven, do you copy?" an operator spoke, but for over a minute, there was no response. All units' locations were supposed to appear on the base-camp terminals upon the squad engineers setting up their communication array. Seraph Seven's didn't appear.

Loud sirens soon filled the forest, and malformed growls and howls echoed throughout. Surrounded by her comrades in the far base camp, Jessica meditated with a soft purple and black shimmer around her form. Eyes shut, peering within the axes between, her focus manifested staunchly. The trust in her comrades centered her entirely, allowing her to fulfill her role without concern.

Elsewhere in the forest, Seraph Seven had emerged. Andrew scanned the environment in confusion while inspecting the coordinates on his hunter gauntlet. He immediately began setting up the tower on his back, and the rest of the squad looked on in concern.

"What's wrong?" Yuki asked, her visor flicking up.

"This isn't where we were supposed to be," Andrew announced, and the squad's faces twisted in confusion.

Kendra watched as Andrew snapped open the port where the antenna extended high into the air. Once he entered the passphrase to connect the array to the central system, Yuki wasted no time contacting their comrades once it was ready.

"Schaefer to Roost. We've been transported to an unintended location. Requesting a ping of our coordinates," Yuki's voice sounded over the radio.

"Seven? What was the delay? You're six kilometers west of your designated location," an operator from Roost broadcasted to the squad.

Yuki cursed under her breath, turning to face the rest of her squad.

"Standby," Yuki said into her earpiece, then dropped her hand. "How the hell did we end up here? The terminals were programmed individually for each squad," Yuki inquired, and Andrew's brow furrowed. After several seconds, he lifted his wrist and navigated his hunter gauntlet.

"The teleportation terminal was synced to my rig, and I had checked it before our deployment. Something must ... oh," he spoke, going pale as he eyed the diagnostic he ran. "A scrambler? When did—Orphan." Andrew sucked sharply through his teeth. "Fuck! It must have been when I met with Ethan before that mission."

"They thought that far ahead?" Valeria mumbled, tugging on her helmet before shaking her head. "Why didn't it set off a warning before we ported?"

"The threshold of location varied enough for this operation that the position it keyed in for us didn't flag as an anomaly. Clever way of splitting us off," Andrew said, shifting on his feet. He lowered his wrist and quickly turned to face the communication array. "Orphan probably suspected that Alicia and Ken would be important to a potential operation—thus using my rig to hinder that."

Both Alicia and Kendra scoffed, but they turned their attention back to Yuki, awaiting her orders. Yuki held a finger up to them and touched her earpiece again.

"Assuming no obstacles, ETA to the original point is four minutes. We'll meet with Nine thereafter."

"Copy. Make haste and exercise caution, Seven," the operator spoke. "The laboratory has released several chimeras. Seraph Nine recommends aiming for the inner mouth and joints with high-caliber weaponry."

Yuki held her fist up, the squad taking attention and preparing to head out. Damion insisted on carrying the tower so Andrew could focus on running. He didn't protest, and once the tower was collapsed, the squad quickly dashed east through thick vegetation.

The squad ran into trouble quickly—packs of hellhounds and vulcans that had waited away from the others.

"Pack formation!" Yuki shouted. She and Alicia stayed close to Andrew in defensive positions, and the squad's cannons opened fire, making quick work of most of the hellhounds. Others dodged, then expelled waves of flames from their mouths.

"Enoch Lazmos!" Alicia called, and several purple-hued arms shot from the ground, and as her palms glowed, she twisted them in conjunction to swat the flames away. The sharp-tipped fingers dug into the hellhounds as they snatched the fiends, and with them held firmly in place, the barrage of gunfire easily killed the rest. As the vulcans dove with their weapons, Kendra flung fireballs to scorch them, the hellish flames melting the flesh from their slender frames.

It hadn't ended there. Once they advanced further, the ground thrummed with the raucous footfalls of several chimeras closing in on them. Kendra lunged forward to meet them, weaving through their formation as flaming claws slashed through their tendons to slow their approach. With another incantation, Alicia wrenched their mouths open, revealing their vulnerable spots to the squad. One was put down by well-placed shots from Joseph; the other's cranium was atomized from the inside when Damion shot it point-blank in the mouth with his shotgun.

"This had to be a planned ambush," Damion growled, drawing his gun back and using the grass to clean the barrel at the end.

"We've got company!" Kendra said, her nose detecting a faint scent reminiscent of rain, but the faint energy signature was infernal—another kind of demon.

Several black feathers darted through the trees toward them, and Kendra fanned flames from her palms to keep them from harming her comrades. Emerging from the tree, a shadowy figure darted toward them, shooting past Kendra entirely. Fallen angel wings slashed at Yuki, Alicia, and Andrew, but Alicia's magic arms managed to deflect it at the expense of them being overwhelmed and shattering right after. Yuki followed up, the hilt of her photon saber flashing bright to blind the demon assailant before she lunged and drove her blade through both of the demon's wings at once.

The fallen angel pushed back midair, retreating from the bunch and attempting to take to the air. Alicia quickly spoke aloud the same incantation as before, the arms shooting from the ground to snatch the wings, holding the fallen angel in place. In the next moment, his chest gaped as a bullet tore through from the spot between his wings, and Emily's hood fell from the recoil as she huffed. When Alicia let the fallen angel drop to the ground, Emily examined the distinct sigil on its armor and nodded in approval.

"One of the Venatum on my record," Emily said, tucking her rifle against her form before wiping the sweat from her face.

"Clean shot," Joseph complimented, lowering his rifle. "Stole my kill," he alleged, making her roll her eyes.

"Stay focused," she said, pushing past him to rejoin the squad.

"Seven, we're moving," Yuki commanded, sheathing her photon saber. With minimal protest, the squad readied themselves and continued through the thick forest. If it had been level, dry terrain, they would have arrived minutes sooner. Boots muddied and fabric ripe with stray foliage that snagged on them, they endured the arduous hike. Eventually, they arrived at the small outpost of hunters and engineers waiting at the spot they were originally intended for.

Damion set the tower down, and Andrew quickly got to work deploying it again. They wouldn't have to move it again—or so he hoped. Once they were synced up to it, Yuki touched her earpiece again.

"Schaefer to Roost. Do you copy?"

"Loud and clear," the operator responded.

"We've arrived at our designated anchor point. Private Carter is established for continued communications. What's Seraph Nine's twenty?"

"Seraph Nine's tower went offline, along with other squads. It appears many have been targeted. We are working to manually relink transmission to Roost instead. Angel Thirteen was just ambushed, presumably by Orphan, and now their tower is offline. Remain on guard and cautiously proceed toward the laboratory to rendezvous with Seraph Nine."

"Copy," Yuki said and relayed the orders to her squad, then turned to Andrew. "Drew, stay put here. Em and Damion, keep watch over him and the others," she declared, flashing them a small smile. Andrew bit his lip and held out his left fist.

"See you guys soon. Be safe," Andrew said, and the squad connected their fists to his before dashing into the thick of the forest.

Kendra idly swatted at the swarms of insects, making a note to flare her flames intermittently to *cleanse* her skin or anything that latched on. Even with the advent of her discovering demons' existence, bugs still terrified her more than anything. The knowledge of the demonic insects she had glimpsed within the demon compendium was even more harrowing to imagine.

The sounds of gunfire echoed through the woods, followed by updates from Commander Rigs, who instructed the personnel's further movements and positioning.

"Seraph Seven, come in!" Commander Rigs's voice spoke through their radio. "Angel Eleven needs immediate backup. They have made contact with Orphan. I repeat, they have made contact with Orphan."

Yuki held her fist up, stopping Seraph Seven as she skidded to a stop in front of a tangle of overgrown trees tucked against a shallow pool.

"Schaefer to Commander Rigs. Ready to report to Angel Eleven upon receipt of coordinates."

"Coordinates en route. Make haste."

The squad's hunter utility devices buzzed with the coordinates of their comrades under attack, and Yuki gestured for the squad to follow her.

"We have to play this safe," Yuki said, her eyes narrowing. "Alicia, on me. Survey for traps and anomalies."

"Roger," Alicia said, her eyes glimmering with a mix of purple and green as they homed in on the world around her. The pervading omens became more pronounced before her, and the veins of Ichor flickered between them. When the squad drew close, she dashed forward and raised her fist, gesturing for the others to stop.

"Warp trap ahead," Alicia barked as they came into a tangled glade of grass, bushes, and dead roots—crimson staining all of it. Rotting corpses, dripping with a black and purple substance, littered the ground. *Angel Eleven.*

"We were too late," Kendra muttered, her eyes twitching as she bared her sharp teeth. The scent of decay stung, a grisly glare of blood and melted flesh like a serrated knife dragging across their nerves. "What happened? This is fucked."

"Accelerated cellular corrosion, a form of void magic. Like a cancer that rapidly melts your flesh," Alicia explained, stooping to a knee. "Abigo ..." she whispered, and the terrain undulated as energy dispelled into the air harmlessly. "We're clear," Alicia said, standing straight as her pensive green eyes examined the three distinct corpses, wary as the squad examined them.

"That seemed too easy," Yuki suggested to Alicia, who nodded and tugged on her hood.

"Yeah, and it's the only thing amiss here. Stay on guard," she said, glancing at Kendra and gesturing for her to keep watch.

As Yuki called in with an update to Roost, Kendra turned, staring deep into the forest. Eden was so close, but the grave implications fermented with the revolting scent of sacrifice. She was thankful the pervading rosemary from the vacuum bomb had faded, allowing her to disperse her focus from the barrier she kept around her face.

The rustling of leaves drew their attention. A flock of macaws peered down from the trees, loudly vocalizing their distress from the gunfire and distortion brought by the battle. Animals, while not necessarily connected in the strictest sense, did exhibit a greater awareness of the supernatural than standard humans typically did.

The birds squawked, their eyes fixed on the hunters below with passive interest, which Kendra found strange, but she detected nothing odd about them. Alicia, however, showed immediate skepticism.

"Guess they're hungry ..." she speculated, glancing at their comrades' corpses. "Not happening. Enoch Lazmos," she spoke, and a purple hand sprung forth from her, swatting at the macaws. Deterred, they took to the air—all but one.

The bird shot toward Alicia, its form growing and twisting into a humanoid figure. Orphan manifested from it into Ethan's form, a black blade forming within their palm before they swiped at her. She narrowly dodged, but Orphan took aim with a pistol and fired directly into the soul binder on her belt. When the bullet connected, the gem shattered.

"Shit!" Alicia hissed, flinching as she doubled back.

Yuki was first to react, lunging past Alicia at Orphan and locking blades before kicking them back several feet. Joseph took aim with his rifle and fired several rounds, but Orphan lurched to the side, evading with exceptional speed. They flung their hand, scattering a wave of dark energy at them, but Kendra erected a wall of flames to dispel it before meeting Orphan head-on. In their brief tangle, she evaded their pistol fire and sent them back with a flaming kick to the face.

"Pack formation!" Yuki called, and the squad quickly dispersed, positioning around Orphan in a crescent shape with their weapons trained.

Orphan stood slowly, dusting their black coat off as they waved the stygian blade ominously, eyes flicking between the squad.

"Hello, Seven. I see the squad's lighter than usual. Here for your captain?" Orphan taunted. Gunfire sounded as Joseph and Valeria opened fire on them, but with a swipe of Orphan's blade, a white rift in reality swallowed the bullets. With another swipe, Orphan returned them from that rift, and Alicia quickly raised her hands.

"Enoch Lazmos!" she shouted as the purple hands rose before the squad, blocking the bullets. "Hold fire!" Alicia stated, realizing the magnitude of the void magic Orphan employed against them. "Danger-ous game there, Orphan. Extended use of void magic will attract the guardians from Caelum—eventually the angels too," she claimed.

"And? Eden should be assimilating into the divine heart as we speak. It'll be too late for them to do anything, but I invite their sacrifice." Orphan laughed sardonically as the rift closed before them.

"Bullshit!" Kendra hissed, flames flickering to life along her jagged claws.

"Stay calm. They're lying," Yuki whispered to Kendra, poising her blade as her visor lowered. "You're stalling for time," Yuki alleged, eyeing the stygian blade Orphan held.

"You'd bet on that?" Orphan replied, their burned face undulating as it reformed anew.

"You're a snake in the shadows; confrontation isn't your style, especially given we hold the key to your demise," Yuki said, prompting Orphan's lips to curl into a smirk.

"Held," they corrected. "You know ... it would be unbecoming if I didn't mention how all of these additional deaths are your fault," Orphan glared at Kendra. "If you hadn't interfered, that somnium would have taken Eden's body and none of this would have needed to happen."

"What the hell are you on about?" Kendra hissed, defensively rais-ing her claws, flames dancing along her fingertips.

"You know what I mean. These deaths fall squarely on your hands," they said, staring deep into Kendra's eyes as a burning white twinkle simmered in her depths.

"You talk too much," she hissed, readying herself, but Yuki grabbed her shoulder to stop her.

"Wait ..." she said and lowered her stance. Her eyes narrowed on Orphan as they played on the brewing tension. They didn't make a move yet, and she planned to use the moment wisely. Yuki gave a nod to Alicia, who quickly placed a finger on her earpiece.

"Romero to Roost. We've made contact with Orphan—requesting immediate support to bring another soul binder," Alicia whispered.

"Roost to Romero. Private Carter is the closest with a siphon. You're now connected," the operator spoke.

"Romero to Carter, you read me? Need you to bring that soul binder, *stat*." In response, Andrew's voice came through.

"I read you! We're under attack at the nest. Once the threats are dealt with, I'll rush over!" Andrew said.

"Do you have a time estimate?" There was a long pause, and Alicia dared not tear her gaze away from Orphan with the standoff underway.

"About ... ten minutes," Andrew said, making Alicia curse.

"As quickly as possible. We'll hold them off until your arrival." Alicia lowered her hand, glancing at Yuki and then the squad. "Don't let that blade touch you. It contains the magic that killed Angel Eleven."

"We'll buy time," Yuki muttered, glancing at the desecrated corpses. "Kendra, on me. We keep Orphan off the others. Alicia, take auxiliary. Valeria and Joseph, cover the outer perimeter but hold fire until it is safe to shoot," Yuki said, eyes fixed on Orphan through her black visor.

"Roger!" the squad confirmed.

"Trouble at home?" Orphan questioned. "Don't fret. I know exactly what's going through your heads right now," Orphan said, readying their blade. In a blink, Orphan propelled toward them, and both Kendra and Yuki engaged.

Their clashes caused the air to shriek. Blades and claws met, and Kendra's flames seared the air where she swiped, a gaping maw of fire threatening to swallow Orphan. Yuki coordinated to avoid them, having practiced such drills several times with Kendra to know how she utilized them.

Orphan was quick, their strikes proving difficult for either of the women to keep up with. Their method of movement was controlled and deceptive, measured by both guile and skill. When they took aim with their gun, Kendra was quick to melt the bullet and disable the gun with intense flames once her comrade was out of its path. The gun dropped to the ground, half melted and glowing hot. It was a normal weapon, leaving Orphan to their other means of attack.

Yuki quickly caught on that Orphan had inherited their combat skill from Ethan. She remembered such movements when he had trained her long ago, while Kendra recognized it from Eden's swordplay.

Kendra ducked under a swipe, but within the flurry, tendrils latched onto both her and Yuki, constraining them suddenly. Before Orphan could deliver a decisive blow, a shimmering light undulated across their skins, and their bolstered barriers caused the blade to deflect. After, the arms of Alicia's most prominent spells grasped Orphan, and a well-placed bullet from Joseph tore through their head.

Orphan's form melted and reformed several feet away, attention then drawn to Alicia. With a flick of their hand, dark energy flung into the air, forming several spikes of magic that then rained down on the hunters. When Alicia conjured a barrier above them to defend, Orphan charged at her, but Valeria stepped forward, aiming her shotgun. Orphan raised their blade to deflect, but she instead shot at their feet, making them jump to avoid it. Joseph leaped over Alicia and kicked Orphan away, making them tumble and stab their blade into the ground to catch themself.

The attrition persisted in a similar sequence as before. Yuki and Kendra took to combating Orphan up close, and Orphan worked to advance on Alicia. As Orphan danced around the squad, they slashed the air at random, opening several rifts that surrounded them. With the rifts established, Orphan shifted between them, creating difficulty in predicting where they would emerge.

Kendra hurled a wave of fire, and as the flames tore through them, the force tossed them into one of the rifts. Emerging from the rift behind the squad, Orphan twisted and lunged right for their cannons. Joseph quickly blocked the first swipe of their blade, the barrel of his gun carved through before Orphan pounced atop both him and Valeria. They then dropped their blade and snatched their necks, dark energy undulating as hexes burned into their skin.

Alicia kicked Orphan away, but her comrades writhed on the ground as the hex transmuted their energy against itself.

"Stop! That thing will destroy your node network if you try to channel your energy," Alicia informed them.

"Clever witch," Orphan quipped, charging at Alicia again.

Bright light shined onto Orphan from Yuki's hilt guard, momentarily blinding them before she drove her saber through their neck and slashed their legs. The blade tore their form apart as they met the ground, and the puddle reformed several feet away. Orphan was still, taking a defensive position as they eyed the hunters with a barbed smirk.

"Tick-tock," Orphan spoke melodically.

Kendra immediately took back to Yuki's side, her eyes suddenly bathed in darkness as burning slits emerged, and she glanced behind her to the rest of the squad. The surrounding rifts pulsed ominously, and she considered how Orphan used them to both traverse and deflect their projectiles. Secretly, she had documented which ones were portals and which ones would deflect.

"Yuki. Dire formation," Kendra said, raising her claw above her head as embers boiled in her palm. Yuki nodded in confirmation before lowering her stance. Her saber then tilted to guard Kendra's legs.

In that singular moment, in the void of Orphan's eyes, a burning revelation shined onto Kendra. Everything about Orphan was borrowed rather than embodied, and she recalled what Eden had said to her when she was training. *The truest measure of a hunter is not in skill, but in the ability to adapt to the challenges before them.*

Orphan's moves were similar enough to Eden's for her to keep up with if she used her demonic aspect, but most importantly, she could see the flaw in Orphan's focus. That flaw birthed a plan she would use to buy time.

Kendra flung a fireball at Orphan, drawing their focus in dispelling it. Once the voidling was occupied, she hurled several others at the rifts closest to the ground, flames rising to impede them.

"On me," Kendra said to Yuki, rushing forward with her to engage Orphan in another clash. She lurched forward into their slashes, carefully timing a parry, like Eden had taught her. Her claws scraped the metallic substance of the blade and sent Orphan's arm back with it before spinning into a repelling kick.

Orphan was sent tumbling into one of their rifts, and Kendra twisted to her left, bolting toward the rift she knew they would tumble out of.

She greeted them in their trajectory and sent them through another rift. In a volley of kicks and tosses, she weaponized Orphan's own rifts to keep them in constant motion from her attacks. The rapid ricocheting and bombarding blows rendered Orphan immobile, all of Kendra's attacks deliberately non-lethal to ensure they couldn't shed their form and break from the combination.

The rifts finally faded, and Orphan was sent into a tree, their form convulsing as they slid to the ground. Kendra panted heavily from exertion, the flames she conjured growing as they burned the surrounding vegetation. The wild flickers of their glow shined on Orphan, reflecting Kendra's resolve as her gaze incinerated the blasphemous voidling.

"You seem winded. How long can you keep this up?" Orphan taunted.

Yuki stepped forward, flicking her blade to slant in front of Kendra. Her visor lifted, and she glared at Orphan as she trained her pistol on them. Orphan's attention turned to her, and their form twisted, shifting visages. They visibly shrunk, manifesting the same white hair as hers, but their face was filled with youth—eyes gold and shimmering with feigned innocence.

Orphan could practically hear Yuki's heart stop as the color drained from her face, her eyes quivering. The hand gripping her gun shook unsteadily, and she inhaled with a wheeze as she eyed the form of her son.

"Ryu ..." she whispered out breathlessly.

"Wait, Yuki!" Alicia called out, but Orphan had already flung dark magic at her.

The unstable energy exploded, sending Yuki tumbling toward Alicia, who caught her. Orphan then rushed at them, form twisting back into Ethan's likeness as they shot past Kendra, who had been stunned by the magic. Alicia wouldn't have been able to respond in time, and Orphan poised their murky blade to cut through them.

A round object suddenly collided with Orphan's forehead, stunning them as a shockwave erupted, sending them sliding back. The air distorted as energy rippled and convulsed from the shockwave grenade Andrew had chucked, and he rushed into the clearing, skidding to a stop beside his comrades.

"Kendra, get out of the way!" Andrew called out, taking a wide stance with his dominant leg arched back, and the mechanical whirrs from the bulky attachment on his calves shot heavy anchors into the earth. He raised his arms, and long hexagonal speakers rose from his wrists before clicking into place. He aimed them at Orphan, his body locking as his suit engaged itself for structural stability.

A massive consolidation of energy formed within Andrew's body, the speakers engaging at a frequency only Kendra could detect. She quickly leaped to the side, covering her ears when Andrew closed his fists.

"Sonic cannons, *fire*!"

The air surged as energy exploded from the speakers, compounding upon itself with reverberating power. The region rumbled as thunderous energy slammed into Orphan, propelling them through thin trees and into the trunk of a much larger one. The energy sundered their form, the power of the soul binder in Andrew's grasp embedding into the energy pinning them.

Orphan let out a distorted yell, skin peeling to reveal the black mass beneath, and they opened their eyes as the weapon tore away at their form. Seraph Seven covered their ears, the frequency and vibrations disturbing even less sensitive ears. The wind blared around Andrew as he chipped away at Orphan. As his hair flicked behind him, his determined blue eyes remained focused through the thick goggles on his face.

As Orphan's arms swung back, they held the black blade tightly. With precious moments, the blade swung back, slicing a rift into the air that it then flung into when they released the hilt of the blade. The continuous force pushing it created a loop of momentum, pulsing with compounding speed until it shot the blade toward Andrew quicker than he could react. It sliced clean through the side of his hand, inflicting its hex upon him.

Andrew registered the pain a moment after the blade hit, his form recoiling before he tumbled across the ground from the abrupt imbalance, the cannons and anchors disengaging. As Andrew tumbled to the ground, the soul binder flew off into the foliage as he gripped his hand. The wound bled, only the side sliced open, but that changed quickly.

"Andrew!" Kendra called, quickly rushing to his side as the noise dissipated. She skidded to a stop before him, crouching to see his hand change into a sickly purple hue. The fingertips quickly drained of color, blood, and even flesh. The bones and nerves frayed and cracked, and the decay set on quickly, even with the initial wound being small.

Andrew howled, chest rapidly pumping as he tried to catch his breath. The pain assailed him, and he cried as the abysmal magic ate away at him.

"What's happening!" Andrew cried, blue eyes wide in panic as he writhed in the dirt.

"Hold still!" Kendra shouted frantically.

She snatched his arm, her own eyes frantic as she inspected it. When she tore his sleeve off, she saw the corrosion traveling up his wrists, and the flesh began to discolor. With no time to consider alternatives, Kendra swallowed hard and clenched Andrew's forearm, her other hand's claws extending as she focused. Those fearful blue eyes made her dread what she'd need to do. A quick glance at Alicia was enough for the two to communicate their plan.

Kendra squeezed his biceps tightly, pinching it to cut off the circulation. She drew her arm back and brought it down quickly, her claws cutting clean through Andrew's forearm and severing it entirely. Before he could even register it, she grabbed the bleeding stump and seared it shut with intense flames.

"Somnin!" Alicia called, palm facing Andrew, and a surge of purple energy flashed through his eyes. He was unconscious in moments, barely a squeak leaving his lips. With how fast everything had occurred, it was too quick to process.

Kendra was relieved to see the hex had been severed along with his arm, her eyes then returning to Orphan as they stood to their feet. As the soul binder's effect waned, their corporeal form flickered.

"So close," Orphan mocked, their indistinct voice transitioning to Ethan's as they reformed in his image. Before Kendra, Orphan's black eyes shifted, the voids within them showing a fathomless depth of suffering. The voidling drew from the bodies they had slain over their lifetime, and however many they had killed, there were countless more. Those voids were supplanted by stolen eyes, but in the brief glimpse Kendra got, the slain hordes within them chilled her beyond compare.

Orphan lunged, blade arched to impale Kendra through. Their path was impeded by Alicia's magical arms she had conjured, but Orphan evaded their grasp, drawing close to Kendra. In those pertinent moments, their glares met, and Kendra readied herself to deflect their attacks, her arm shimmering with burning energy.

A pop and a bright streak slammed into Orphan's chest, punching a gaping hole through it as it pushed them back. They tumbled hard, and the wound oozed black. The sludge painted the ground as white particles ascended from the injury, skin evacuating to reveal the indistinct form beneath their facade.

Stepping into the clearing, Zane's hand clenched tightly around his soul binder, and the other, his gunblade. The muzzle was trained on Orphan, burning hot and smoking in its focus-fire configuration. Rather than making a quip, he was silent, eyes coldly fixed on the voidling as they dragged themself back and pushed against a tree.

Zane glanced at Seraph Seven, briefly seeing the stump of Andrew's arm before he exhaled roughly and turned back to Orphan. He flicked his wrist, and the gunblade returned to its blade configuration, heat still smoldering from the barrel.

"You've been a nuisance," Zane said, auburn eyes narrowed as Orphan's visage dripped. Slowly, they shrunk to a form more recognizable. Voidlings, when not parading as others, were childlike in their stature, small and diminutive as their ephemeral position in Mortale. Orphan was no different.

"That was the intention," Orphan spoke, with no further distinction or charade within their voice. Now, it reverberated in reality and was light—like a child's voice. No such innocence existed within it, however, and Zane was not one to be fooled by it.

"Could end this now—put a bullet in your head like you did to me all those years ago," Zane said, mulling over the idea before shaking his head. "How many have you killed? How many civilizations?" he spoke, pressing the tip of his blade to their neck.

"Not enough," Orphan said emotionlessly.

"Too many ..." Zane declared as Kendra and her squad recuperated. Once on their feet, they closed in on Orphan.

"Finish them off, Zane. We—" Kendra began, but Yuki snatched her shoulder, eyes glistening. Kendra clamped her lips and granted respect to the moment, tucking Andrew's unconscious form against herself instead. Though urgency plagued her, it eased at the surrender Orphan suggested in their true form.

"Is it ever enough, Zaikio?" Orphan spoke, their voice taking on a feminine tinge that mimicked Zane's mother. "The blood paid to know reprieve from loss? She'd have wanted this. She'd be proud you're finally getting your revenge."

"Nope," Zane said, dipping the blade tip into Orphan's neck threateningly. "*I* wanted revenge. My mom is different."

"Such human sentimentality. Or should I say demon? You demonic lot are cheap with your love. Oh, but when you give it"—Orphan chuckled darkly—"I can only imagine how cold your heart still is, knowing she's eternally adrift in the shadows."

Zane held his free hand up, palm hovering in front of his chest as he inhaled deeply. When he released his breath, a soft golden flame flickered to life above his heart, the brilliant glow illuminating his face and eyes alike with a serenity foreign to Orphan.

"I know where she is, and I know what she'd have wanted. As much as I think you deserve to suffer ... even with the atrocities you've committed against us, she'd desire you to know peace." Zane smiled softly, shutting his eyes. "And I don't intend to start disagreeing with her now."

Orphan was quiet, a soft laugh echoing from them as they leaned into the tree, holding the hole in their chest as white light shimmered from their form.

"Peace?" Orphan questioned. "I came from nothing—I will return to nothing. There is no peace awaiting me. There is no afterlife or reprieve. In the end ... I'm nothing without my sister."

Kendra understood that sentiment, but it was far from uncommon among many humans. Unlike the complicated and poetic nature of that sentiment pervasive in the children of Ichor, Orphan lacked an understanding of how they were wrong. She knew, and Zane did as well.

His expression never strayed as he stared at Orphan, a serene smile that perturbed the fading voidling more than any wrath they had ever known, and it infuriated them.

"Why aren't you angry?" Orphan demanded with a hiss, like a child throwing a tantrum.

"Quiet," Zane mumbled, carefully grabbing the golden ember atop his chest and placing it within the cavity of Orphan's. And when he opened his eyes, that glow spread through Orphan, supplanting the darkness of their form and consuming them slowly.

In Orphan's final moments, there was no pain or discomfort, slowly drifting away as the world ceased to be around them. The nothingness consumed, but there was a sentiment adrift within the mysterious embrace.

Astrol.

That forlorn name—the anchor to all they could call their own—embedded itself within Void. Orphan had discarded that name: Astrol, sibling to Astrea. *My sister*, Orphan thought. They wept softly as the golden flames absconded their being from Mortale, but a familiar hand reached forward to grasp their own when they thought they would fall into nothing. With that palm holding to theirs, the infinite nothing suddenly gave an unexpected welcome.

Orphan was no more, Astrol of the Void once again. And as their eyes fixed on the sister they long thought to be gone, they found the sentiment long absent from their time as a tormented vagrant. And with serenity and closure finding the once-orphaned voidling, they gave their final cry within Mortale.

"Astrea?"

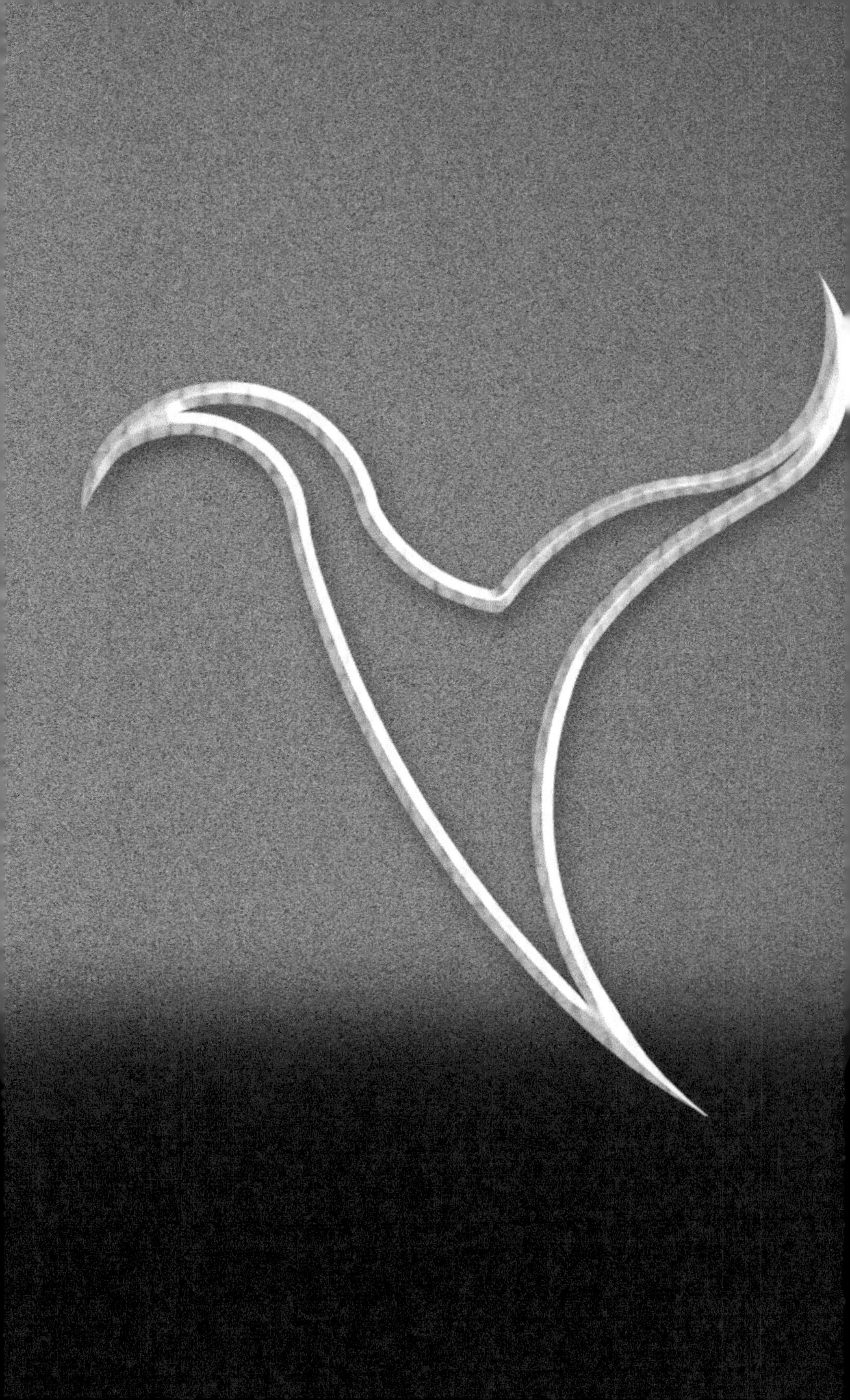

Fourteen

Oblivion's Call

KENDRA STARED DOWN at the tear-stained face of Andrew's unconscious form, eyes flickering as her human visage returned. Her eyes fixed on the stump of his left arm, the blood caked on his suit, and the crudely burned flesh that stopped the worst of the bleeding. Though he was asleep, the anguish of his mutilation settled bitterly on her nerves.

"I'm sorry, Drew ..." she whispered as Alicia crouched down next to them.

"Let me see his arm," she requested, carefully lifting the stump and examining it pensively. She bit her bottom lip and ran a finger around the unmaimed edges. "All things considered, he got off lucky. That quick thinking saved him," she said, a reluctant smile finding her.

"But—"

"None of that right now," Alicia interjected. She channeled her energy into her hands, a soft blue light shimmering in her palm. "Medeorko," she whispered, and the light spread through Andrew. Akin to the light that had once relieved Kendra following her attack, it visibly alleviated Andrew, as evident in his relaxing face and softer breathing. "He'll be okay—because of you," Alicia said, slowly releasing his stump, which no longer bled nor appeared burned.

Zane stood from the tree Orphan had perished against, turning to face them before stepping forward.

"I would have gotten here sooner, but these security protocols were a double-edged sword. Mind calling in Orphan's death so we can get moving?" Zane asked, and Yuki turned to call the base camp. With Orphan no longer a threat, they could relax their security protocols to communicate freely between the squads.

Alicia turned to the rest of Seraph Seven, relieved to see Joseph and Valeria were doing well once the hex had dissipated.

"He's stable, but we need to get him back to camp for further treatment. I pretty much put a band-aid on it for now," Alicia explained, and Valeria stepped forward, crouching next to Kendra.

"I can take him back to Roost," she said, reaching out and taking Andrew's hand. Kendra nodded in response, slowly shifting him into Valeria's arms.

"Joe, can you go with her? If you're not hurt, I mean," Kendra asked, standing.

"Nodes are a bit tender after that hex, but I'll be good to go," Joseph said, rolling his shoulder before slinging his rifle over it. He looked to Valeria as she stood with Andrew, her form subtly shimmering white as she channeled her energy to carry him without hindrance.

Yuki lowered her hand, having finished delivering her update over the radio.

"Are you and Alicia okay? You both expended a lot of energy," Yuki asked, taking to Kendra and Alicia's side.

"I'm good," Kendra said. "I'll take some syn-blood prior to breaching the lab." Kendra then glanced at Alicia, who cracked her neck and knuckles.

"Peachy. I was mostly defensive with my spells," she asserted, and Zane walked past them.

"Seraph Nine is waiting by the lab. Danny is running some echo scans of the compound before we breach," Zane said, ushering for them to follow. "Let's get moving."

"Right," Yuki affirmed. "Joe, Val, rendezvous with us after you get Andrew to Roost. Travel with the auxiliary squads when you come back."

"Roger," they spoke in unison, and they left with Andrew.

Kendra clenched her fist, taking her flask and mixing in the syn-blood capsule before downing it quickly. A flare lit in her eyes, and a surge of energy coursed through her veins. Her muscles briefly tensed as if she had consumed fresh blood, a welcome change courtesy of Zane's recent improvements to the formula.

Seraph Seven and Zane trekked through the forest. The terrain was more amenable the closer they ventured to the lab, but Kendra imagined there was a purpose to the deceptively clear path.

"Should have seen all the traps," Zane said, breaking the silence. He glanced back at Kendra, meeting her gaze. "Reed took care of them on our way there. Made getting to you a lot quicker." He returned his gaze to the environment, eyes locking on the several tangled trees, of which many black feathers were scattered in pools of blood. Fallen angels were strewn across the floor past it, appearing crispier than their already dark complexions would have otherwise suggested.

"With all the distortion, how did you find us? Or even know we were fighting Orphan?" Kendra asked, and the others looked at Zane expectantly, interested in his answer.

"A part of the forest got stupid hot, and I knew that had to be you, Ken. The rest was guesswork after Nine's communication array was taken despite Orphan not attacking us. Apparently, they showed up, destroyed the tower, and bounced. Makes me think they especially didn't want me to find out you guys were under attack, but I'm not *that* conceited."

"No, it's a good observation, considering how easily you took them out," Alicia said.

"Would have been harder if they had known I was there. Made it a point to lie low when I approached. I would have been quicker, but I had to focus to ensure I didn't inhale rosemary," Zane said, clicking his tongue. "Anyway, we're almost there. Stay sharp."

Zane held his fist up, coming to a stop by a narrow ravine. He exchanged glances with Alicia, who nodded and channeled her energy to focus hard before she clasped her hands together. A wave of energy shined over the ravine, and she held her palm out.

"Abiko!" she called out, and a mass of scarlet energy dissipated from the hidden hex, scattering into the air in a dazzling display.

They continued without further incident or obstacles, coming to a stop by a mountain face where Seraph Nine stood. Zane approached one of his engineers, Daniella Abrams. The squad gathered by a cliff face, and embedded within the stone, there was a three-meter-tall arch-shaped door. It was composed of a roughly shaped black metal akin to wrought iron. Kendra could tell she wouldn't be able to cut it with her claws. It was imposing, with demonic etching she could barely make out, less legible than the Herculaneum scrolls she briefly studied. Of the few Indiox characters, the ones center top read, *Wings of Beginning*.

"Captain," Sergeant Abrams called, "I've mapped out the entryway and corridor into the lab, but we're going to need help getting the door open. It's a lot stronger than Reed anticipated," she said, glancing at their bastion, Reed Jenkins. Her attention turned to Alicia when she marched past her.

"It's fine, leave it to Lieutenant Jenkins and me," Alicia said, taking to the lieutenant's side.

"It's a tough one," Reed informed, eyes fixed on the edges where he had scrawled several runes. Each of them showed subtle burns—a sign magic had flowed through them in a previous attempt.

"No kidding," Alicia muttered, examining the runes, eyes then turning to the glyphs. "I think ... it's because of a lack of equilibrium. You are fixated on the technical symmetry of runes as opposed to the nominal value of their sentiments. It's the kind of stuff you learn with seventh-circle magic and really dig into with eighth-circle rituals." Alicia ran her fingers along the runes, magic flowing through her fingers as she traced the rune of descension, comprising down-facing wings that intersected and three eyes. She carefully erased it, then replaced it with a rune of equity—an eye surrounded by an M-shaped shell with two prongs that crossed over the iris.

"Whoa, never considered it that way," Lieutenant Jenkins said, pushing his dark hair back as he held his chin.

"You have to when dealing with forces that powerful, and this door is in that category," Alicia huffed.

While all hunters were expected to know basic incantations to varying degrees, magic at a more fundamental level applied differently. Most couldn't use it like Jessica or Alicia—given their demonic genetics. Even in the Seraph-ranked squads, most bastions were lucky to reach sixth-circle magic.

"We ready to breach then?" Zane asked.

"As ever," Alicia said, taking several steps back with Reed.

"On my twenty, Seven and Nine. Cannons, take aim. Blades, beneath them," Zane instructed.

"Roger!" the squad said, taking their positions, guns trained and blades drawn. Their forms faintly shimmered, barriers readied, and embers crackled in Kendra's palms. With a nod to Lieutenant Jenkins, Alicia turned back to the door.

"On my cue, Lieutenant," she prompted.

After a brief countdown, the two clasped their hands in unison.

"Enoch Lazmos!" they both spoke, and magical hands, blue and purple, clasped the runes at the top center, and the door cracked, crumbling. As the dust rose, Zane formed the ventus-diablo sign to cause the gases in the air to condense before dispersing, creating a powerful gust of wind that cleared inward.

Both Alicia's and Lieutenant Jenkins's magical arms formed a protective barrier. The several umbra demons within fired various projectile magics at them, but they were deflected by the barrier. Cassius tossed an anti-demon aerosol and fired his gunblade to detonate it prematurely. The rosemary immediately filled the room, causing them to collapse or focus on defensive measures. Zane tossed a fireball to illuminate the demons' positions within the entry hall.

Of the demons who stood with their barriers, the hunters shot and eliminated them with ease. As they crept inside, the demons on the ground blistered and swelled as the rosemary took hold in their systems.

"Religo!" the hunters called out, and the demons' limbs snapped behind their backs, bound by energy. The squads advanced inside, carefully examining the branching hallways from the main corridor. Zane stood before one of the branching paths, waiting as the bastions surveyed for traps. With quick determination, they concluded it was the largest of laboratories the Hunters had encountered—perhaps by Orphan's design.

"Larson to Roost, we've successfully breached and detained initial combatants. Send reinforcements when applicable," Zane said, turning to face the hunters. "We're to search for security access. Intel from the staff, server rooms, terminals—anything that can be used to streamline finding Eden's location. Blades are to escort other members. Cannons, watch the sixes," he said, suppressing a scowl of disdain for the military lingo. "I'll work on making these bozos talk," Zane said, ominously leering at the demons who managed to remain awake.

"Roger!" the hunters spoke, breaking up into four separate detachments before venturing into the corridors.

Within the snaking paths, the hunters uncovered several rooms used for research experiments. The deeper they entered—the more grotesque. It was of old construction, with eroded stonework and unfamiliar architectural styles. The rooms, while sanitized, pulsed with ominous frequencies denoting the disturbance within Ichor. Scarlet omens, disparate and sparse, pulsed with echoes of the sin they emerged from. Fear and anguish alike stained the air.

Kendra and her team entered one such room within the lower levels of the laboratory, and her eyes landed on a glowing vat. Eerie and familiar, it brought her back to the one at the last laboratory she had infiltrated. Instead of masses of flesh, within the center of the tank was an object in the shape of a blood rune. The material was alien, comparable to living crystal. It glimmered red, pulsing with golden veins inside of it.

While it was only the size of a hand, the energy permeating it forewarned them of the potential it harbored. Joseph, perturbed by the sight, readied his hunter gauntlet and approached.

"What is that?" he asked, holding up his gauntlet. The hunter utility device shined a green laser scanner that slowly descended across the object inside. As the hologram sitting in front of his face flickered with several values being calculated, his fierce hazel eyes studied the list. As several elements displayed, their database parsed what it was. Glass for the tank, plasma for the liquid, but the blood rune-shaped object was unknown entirely. Kendra beheld it with a phantom anxiety all the same.

"Something feels off about this. There's something I can't describe inside that thing. Alive? I don't know how to put it," Kendra said, her face scrunching before she whipped around and marched past Joseph, but Cassius, who stood by the door, stopped her.

"Real quick," he said. "You said it felt alive. I assume you mean an energy signature, right? Hellhounds are sensitive to soul resonance—can you tell if there is a soul in there?" he asked, adjusting his helmet.

Kendra mulled over the thought, her eyes widening as she glanced back at it, and slowly she stirred with a realization. The thrumming inside it was familiar but incomplete compared to the way she knew it. She had briefly convened with Kendall's soul years ago, and while the specifics were lost, she knew there was more to Kendall's soul—both the consciousness and sentiments within it.

The object suspended within the vat possessed what she could tell were the sentiments of something that once lived, or at least some of them. As Kendra thought about it, Joseph took several steps back.

"Cover your ears," he warned.

Kendra saw him raise his rifle and immediately covered her ears along with Cassius before he shot the tank, shattering it.

"Hey, what the hell, Joe?" Kendra hissed, lowering her hands as the crystalline object fell, clacking against the floor and undulating with a familiar crimson energy. The golden veins within it throbbed, the Ichor within them suddenly dissipating into the air before the glow died. The scent hit her, and while certainly diluted, she knew the scent well. "Eden..." she muttered, her teeth grinding as she glared. While it wasn't apparent, she knew it made little sense for it to be a recent development.

The higher levels of the laboratory suggested an order of magnitude. The higher levels they had searched were less kept—less recent. The documents she glanced through in the room they occupied, while drafted in Indiox, were dated weeks prior. The blood had to be several years old, she presumed. However, the sentiments within it were more recent.

"The divine heart Orphan mentioned," Kendra said, meeting Joseph's gaze, "this has to be it, right? Or the concept of it. His blood is inside that thing, and it was here long before they captured him again." As she spoke, Joseph huffed, shifting his weight before shrugging.

"Let's make this speculation irrelevant by finding him," Joseph said before marching past her. The three entered the hallway again, and Kendra took the lead once she had gathered her nerves.

Once she composed herself, she touched her earpiece.

"Mallory to Larson, do you copy?"

"Loud and clear," Zane spoke.

"We found some strange crystal object shaped like a blood rune. Appears like some research wing for this artifact that Onaga is trying to make. Find any intel on your end for where Eden is being held?"

"Maybe. Got Abrams working on cracking into a terminal we found. Should have some floor plans soon."

"Copy," Kendra muttered, and the group continued their advance. As they trekked through the corridors, they cleared several rooms. The scientists they came across posed little threat to them, easily surrendering themselves. The ones who attempted to act were eliminated. Kendra found no qualms in bloodying her claws or burning them alive—she found it cathartic, almost. With each encounter, they informed Roost for the descending reinforcements to address as necessary.

Shortly, they secured another room toward the end of the hall. The initial demons were pinned beneath the sliding metal doors that Kendra tore from their sockets, and the rest were quickly apprehended thereafter. As she stood above the demons, the others searched the room. Among the computers and vials that filled the lab, several camera feeds were present with similar vats encapsulating the crystalline objects.

Kendra eyed the feed warily, flames flickering in her palms as she turned to face the group of bound demons.

"Explain what those are," she demanded, but the group showed visible confusion, their eyes flickering before they spoke Indiox.

Before she reacted, Joseph stepped forward, patting her shoulder before he stooped before them. Seamlessly, they had an exchange with a fluency Joseph possessed. Once finished, Joseph stood and turned to Kendra.

"It's as we speculated before. That thing Onaga is trying to make—these are the trials from over the years."

"And why are there remnants of souls in these things? Whose souls are they? Where is Onaga?" Kendra snapped, flashing her sharp teeth at them. Joseph translated the question to them, waiting for their response.

"Human subjects—demon subjects. They're being held at the lower levels," he said, watching as Kendra's hands clenched into fists.

"And Eden?" she asked them directly, glaring into their souls.

Before they could answer, she heard a voice through her earpiece.

"Abrams of Seraph Nine to all units. Be advised, map data has been sent to your hunter utility devices. Levels are opposite. Floor numbers go up the further we go down." Sergeant Abrams's voice rang out. Following right after, another voice came through.

"Larson to Romero and Mallory, do you copy?" Zane chirped. Both Kendra and Alicia confirmed, and Zane continued, "The subject ward appears to be positioned on the eighth floor. Eden is likely on floor eight, or the ninth floor below. I'm going to instruct everybody to rally on floor seven. Once we're together, we'll retrieve Eden before we hunt Onaga down. He has to be hiding somewhere in here."

Kendra touched her earpiece before responding.

"Roger. We're heading down now," Kendra said, ushering Joseph and Cassius. "We're going to meet with the others now. You can put these guys to sleep," she said, spinning around and marching toward the doorway. The pair sighed and held their palms out toward the group of demons.

"Somnis," they spoke, and their energies washed over the demons with each iteration of the incantation. Once they were all bound and asleep, they joined Kendra before following her to the elevator lobby.

They tucked themselves inside, and Kendra hit the button for the seventh floor and propped herself against the wall. Joseph and Cassius occupied the adjacent walls, silently pondering the state of the operation.

"You think he'll show?" Cassius asked Kendra.

"Onaga? Probably holding Eden hostage is my guess," Kendra said in a low voice. "Was supposed to be a lot quicker, but Orphan set everything back."

"It's not like his security force is doing much to stall," Joseph muttered, pursing his lips. "He's got something up his sleeve for sure..."

Kendra frowned, sighing as she propelled from the wall, watching as the elevator opened to another hallway.

"We'll have to be extra cautious. The fact that he hasn't appeared yet means he's waiting," she speculated as they left the elevator. The three walked through the hall, the fluorescent lights above them subtly flickering. The floor they traveled through was far more barren—lacking energy signatures beyond the hunters.

Kendra led her team into the large room comprising several terminals, desks, and amenities befitting demon scientists. Hardly anything could serve as a hiding spot or security retreat, much to their preference. The open layout explained why the upper floors were more occupied but also begged the question as to the conditions of the remaining floors.

Gathered by the terminals, the rest of the squads waited. Once they rejoined, Zane ushered Kendra to the side with him and Alicia while the others convened.

"Things here aren't exactly confidence-inspiring. The place would be a carnival for OSHA inspectors on the best of days, and I'm willing to bet the final floors are worse. We need to find Eden before we go searching for Onaga, or before he comes searching for us," Zane spoke, scanning the room warily.

"Any of the demons you caught talk? None offered any useful information to us," Kendra responded.

"Nada," Alicia said, clicking her tongue as she folded her arms, and Zane sighed before giving his response.

"I was looking over the floor plans more. Interestingly enough, the seventh and ninth floors have a room marked as his study, but we didn't find any room like that during our sweep. Like it was never there to begin with."

"Think it's that liminality bullshit he uses?" Alicia asked, glancing at the lobby where the elevators were.

"Probably," Zane said and began walking. The two then took after him. "Our units are going to bust out the big guns and triangulate his energy. Luckily, the tome had plenty of reference data for us to work with. He's definitely waiting for the right time to strike."

"And why wouldn't he confront us if we're so close to fucking up his schemes? We were kind of betting on that since he can't escape with Eden while General Blackwell blocks his paths," Kendra said, making Alicia sigh.

"He's probably not stupid enough to take the obvious bait, but it's not like he has much of a choice at this rate," Alicia muttered.

The three stepped onto the elevator, taking it down to the eighth floor, nerves wound tightly as the elevator's sounds indicated their descent.

"If I didn't know better, I'd guess he was doing the cliché thing and waiting on the final floor like some mafia don," Kendra said. She dismissed the idea with a shake of her head as the elevator opened, revealing the murkiest of the floors they had seen yet. All of them were pensive, staring into the darkened corridors and absorbing the musty air they would soon breathe.

"Or maybe somewhere he thinks he stands a chance in..." Zane muttered, stepping out of the elevator.

The faint flickers of light throughout the prisoner floor did little for their vision. Dissatisfied, Zane held a fist up, conjuring a flame atop it to use as a torch. Within the halls, prison cells lined the walls on either side of them, and they crept slowly to glimpse any signs of life—but there were none.

Remnants of skeletons were chained in a few of the cages, some of their bones splintered or showing gaping holes that had been picked at. Kendra could venture a guess as to *what* had done it, and snarls from within an enclosed door told her what she needed to know.

"Hounds..." she muttered softly, her fists tightening against her sides.

"The hell they need those for?" Zane questioned, his auburn gaze hesitantly eyeing the door before he focused ahead. Alicia then stepped ahead as they came to a bend, stopping them to scan for traps.

"Probably for soul extraction without fracturing. Even ferali can't extract a soul without bisecting it. This heart of divinity thing probably requires a soul intact, and no better than hounds for that. Similar to how Harvest unfurled," Alicia said, her eyes glimmering in the dark before fading. "All clear to proceed."

Kendra stepped ahead, inhaling deeply as she focused. While she never found much of a reason to do it, she discovered she could trace scents like a bloodhound if she focused her energy into her nose. The process was more deliberate but significantly more effective than tracing energy signatures. She half expected Eden's scent to be dulled, but remarkably, it seeped from further in on the eighth floor.

"He's here," Kendra gasped, gesturing for them to follow before she broke into a dash. Although foolish, her mind focused solely on his scent and navigating to it—even as Zane and Alicia called out and struggled to run after her. Kendra could see in the dark, making for an easier traversal through the hall, which darkened the further she went.

As she drew closer, it became apparent that he was fixed at the end of the hall, something that seemed too convenient to all of them. Despite her suspicion, Kendra fanned her flames, testing to see if what was before her was a thin-veiled illusion. No such magical deterrence suggested itself, and she skidded to a stop before the cell, spotting Eden inside it.

His scarred body was on display, fixed upright with his back against the wall. His head was slumped, several shallow wounds lining his form as thick shackles bore down on his wrists. Though his eyes were shut, his shallow breath served as proof of his consciousness—as if he was dissociated rather than slumbering.

"Eden!" Kendra called out, grabbing the thick bars, taking a moment to eye the locked mechanism before jamming a burning claw inside and melting it. She bashed the door open and rushed in, scooping him into her arms. Lifting his head, those jaded green eyes that enshrined her vow slowly focused on her, recognition flashing within them soon after.

"No…" he whispered, lips trembling as his body tensed in her grasp. He flinched away and took a raspy breath, coughing out as she tucked him closer.

"We're here to take you home—Onaga won't be able to hurt you again," Kendra said, barely containing the sorrow in her own voice. His treasured eyes, pillaged of all semblance of hope and luster, were unable to see the brimming hope before them. That tragic reminder slowly became kindling that reignited her burning hatred toward Onaga.

"You shouldn't charge ahead!" Zane said as he came to a stop in front of the cell, marching in and grabbing her shoulder. "Is he okay?" he asked, much to his chagrin the moment he inspected Eden. The dejection, the scars, and wounds signifying his torment—the entirety of his visage suddenly cast shame over his underlying annoyance with him. "Shit..." he muttered, his lips pursing tightly.

Kendra glanced at him before lifting Eden's chains, thinking of how to cut him free given the fathomless magic that rested upon them. "He needs medical attention," she croaked, tucking Eden against her chest. Though he had protested, his vision drifted in and out, his eyes struggling to stay open for more than a few seconds.

Zane reached out and gripped Eden's shoulder, snapping his fingers.

"Wake up, Samurai. We're taking you home," he said, turning his head as Alicia came to a stop in front of the cell door.

"That was stupid, Ken. Could have been a trap," Alicia scoffed, then touched her earpiece. "Romero to Roost, we've secured Eden. Requesting exfiltration team on the eighth floor."

"Copy that, Romero. Sending hunters for extraction," a dispatcher said over their earpieces.

"Romero of Seraph Seven to infiltration units, do you read? Do we have Onaga's location triangulated yet?" Alicia continued, watching Kendra cut through Eden's shackles. For several moments, there was radio silence, and she frowned. "Romero to all units, do you read?" she barked but still received no answer.

"Is our signal cut off down here or something?" Zane asked, and both looked back, a chill running down their spines as a single black feather, silent and carrying only a semblance of energy, descended in front of Alicia.

Alicia leaped back the moment she sensed it, eyes wide as Onaga emerged. His wings had barely missed her, unfurling to slice the air in their path.

"Watch out!" Alicia called. She dashed toward Onaga, hands crackling with green and purple energy.

Kendra and Zane held their hands out, shooting vicious flames at Onaga from up close, but his wings folded in front of him to dispel them. The clap of his hands echoed through the cell, causing it to become awash in dark energy.

"*Umbra consumxo,*" he spoke, and reality itself shuddered.

The space before Kendra and Zane became a dizzying flash of images, as if physical reality had become disjointed. The cell quaked, wind hissing in their ears. In that brief stretch, dark wings consumed both the cell and their vision, and several twinkling purple irises in the dark scrutinized them within its umbrage.

Kendra's fingers reached in the dark for Eden, but he was absent. She hadn't remembered him leaving her grasp, but all too swiftly, he was snatched from her. She stood to her feet, shaking her senses back into place. Her head swam as she turned to face the exit of the cell.

Zane was crouched in front of it, glaring out into the large, stretched tunnel. Onaga's silhouette loomed in the center, and in his grasp, he held Eden by the back of his neck with a dim amber light peeking from behind him. That damning purple leer beckoned them as he hovered back.

She was worried for a moment that Alicia had been buried beneath the rubble, but as she focused to find her, Kendra glanced above, sensing the energy signatures of her comrades above them, along with Alicia's. Her attention snapped back to Zane when his labored grunts filled the cell.

"Get up!" Zane commanded, his hands pulsing with orange energy and flames as his fingertips dug into the ground. The cell cracked around them, barely contained by Zane's demon alchemy. "Hurry before this becomes our tomb—I'll be right behind you."

"You'd better be," Kendra said and leaped over him and gave chase.

Kendra's demonic visage surfaced with a burning gaze to challenge Onaga's, and her claws sharpened, flames fanning with her every step. Her body quivered with the energy surging through her muscles, and she took to all fours in a rapid acceleration of her speed. She quickly gained on Onaga as he retreated, reaching out to strike him as she closed in. Just as her claws would have grazed him, Onaga tossed Eden into the chamber and liminally shifted out of Kendra's reach. Reemerging further within, he caught Eden by the back of his neck again and slowly descended.

In the large chamber, located on the wall across from Kendra, was a giant tank with glowing amber liquid inside. It was tranquil and unstirred, but there, fixed in the center, a large blood rune-shaped crystal floated. Both gold and red, the center thrummed with a heart that didn't beat—no veins stretching from it like the others.

The stale air hugged her, and despite the size of the chamber, the dark surfaces threatened to strangle her the longer she observed its emptiness. Pervading the room, Onaga's black feathers hovered ominously, but they refrained from shifting toward her. Soon, her eyes found Onaga again, and she glowered.

"Release him," Kendra warned, snarling as she took a lower position, threatening to lunge again. Her feet spread, boots digging into the rigid tiles beneath.

Unexpectedly, Onaga tossed Eden into the air, his feathers carrying him to a high corner of the room. The feathers then impaled his hands, anchoring him to the wall. He could scarcely yelp in pain, his labored breathing echoing through the chamber.

"You motherfucker!" Kendra shouted, hurling a fireball at him. Before it reached, Onaga disappeared again, appearing at her side where a feather had been hovering.

"You are too hasty, Kendra Mallory," Onaga spoke, disappearing once more when Kendra swatted at him. "Orphan spoke of your infernal divergence. You, who knows the reaches of both sin and sacrament"—Kendra hurled flames where he had been—"should understand what there is to gain," he continued.

"Shut your damned mouth!" Kendra spat, whipping around to see Onaga hovering in front of the suspended crystal.

"The powers of divinity are scarcely measured in might—but in the divinations they offer. Sentiments so narrow are selfish, and in their ignorance, they rob us of what could be. We would know if not for such obliviousness..." Onaga spoke, softly landing on the floor as his wings folded in.

"I don't care about the bullshit you have to say, or whatever promises you can make," Kendra said, her claws flickering as she flashed her sharp teeth. An explosion of flames shot from the tunnel as the cell she had been in collapsed, and Zane skidded to her side, exhaling heavily as he stood.

"What she said," Zane quipped, standing up as he cracked his neck. "Forty acres and a mule, or whatever other shitty elevator pitch you've got." His eyes flicked to Eden before he drew his gunblade from the holster on his back, flicking it open into its blade configuration.

"Such ignorance prevails. A shame," Onaga spoke, his hand raising as the crystal within the tank pulsed with energy, a light shriek echoing from the walls. "Before your demise, you should know what your deaths will herald."

Darkness undulated through the room, a radiant light twinkling from the heart of the large crystal. *Her* voice reached them, the soft weeping rousing their attention—including Eden's, who peered at it with half-lidded eyes.

"Cassie..." Eden softly spoke, his eyes tearful and quivering before he was forced to shut them again.

"The Heart of Virtue, a divine artifact that will soon be completed. With it, the tyranny of ignorance will come to an end, and I may liberate this world from its umbrage." The heart pulsed with power, wisps of white energy reaching out toward Eden, falling short of grasping him as it reeled back in with a clap of Onaga's hands. Silence pervaded once more, and only the harbinger's leer remained.

Zane glowered at Onaga, searching his unfathomable depths. Though Onaga represented his least favorite kind of *villain*—the ones who never shut up—he used the opportunity to assess their situation.

His fingers raised and touched his earpiece, but the static coming through it signified that the distortion coming from Onaga blocked their signal. He clicked his tongue.

"This must be the ninth floor. It had no discernible entry when I checked, so looks like we're cut off." His eyes narrowed as he scowled. "Cliché to say, but it's just us now."

"It'll have to be enough," Kendra whispered, her eyes refocusing on Onaga and his feathers.

"Stay close. I'll initiate when he's done yapping," Zane warned in a whisper, and Kendra nodded. Once they finished whispering, Onaga cleared his throat, beckoning their attention in a way that they both deemed desperate.

"This world, though bathed in light, was never free from the darkness, and this aversion to the dark is what maintains the veneer unseen. The Primordials are cruel to deny us such a yearning—to forbid us from knowing these ubiquitous machinations. All before us I was allowed to create, but not fathom. This very ground you stand on—molded by hands I once possessed. The hands I forwent in the hopes of sating my fascination."

"So what?" Kendra spat, taking a tentative step forward as her eyes danced between him and the Heart of Virtue. "You're here pissing and moaning about a shortcut to knowing shit, and you expect what? Sympathy? You're an immortal, fallen celestial, and you expect me to feel sorry for that childish complaint?" Kendra said, her form shuddering as scarlet flames rose on her limbs. With a blink, her body was engulfed in the same power of wrath she once used to challenge a demon lord—a power Onaga knew intimately.

"Your impudence does not deter me," Onaga said, his eyes narrowing. "You wield the flames of wrath, the same as my daughter. Yet you would neglect the extent of their sentiment—the grasp of what they would allow you to see." Onaga's face twisted into something akin to a scowl. "Such ignorance is detestable."

Onaga closed his eyes, feathers shooting from his wings and drifting behind him. Seeing this, Zane reached into his vest, removing his demon serum and holding it closer.

Mulling over his statement, she projected her response. "And sacrificing Eden isn't?" she asked, watching as his eyes sharpened on her.

"Eden Blackwell shall free this world. And with omniscience, such trivial plights: pain, sorrow, *ignorance*"—his voice dripped with malice at the mention of the last term—"all of these concepts will abscond, and your blood will give me these precious answers I have long sought."

"That's it?" Kendra questioned, pressing her claws to her chest as flames surged in her palm, forming a spinning multi-pronged star. "That's why you're playing god? Your greed won't liberate anything!" she said, her eyes darting to Eden as if to channel his lament.

"Foolishness," Onaga spat in his thickening accent, his feathers shifting and spinning into a cyclone. Those dancing knives of greed whistled with an ominous hum, and feather-shaped shadows danced over the room in an ensemble. Their song heralded Onaga's dying patience.

"Like legends proclaim Prometheus gave man fire, I, Onaga, gave you knowledge. I have granted all of your greatest minds the revelations that extricated you. I informed the Greeks of constellations; I taught the Egyptians secrets of agriculture and engineering, allowing them to stave off famine and build great monuments; I dropped the apple on Newton and revealed the constraints of our corporeal realm; I delivered unto Einstein the insights with which he uncovered the formulas of unfathomable power.

"All of your greatest minds found the genesis of their prestige within the influence of my tutelage. The revelations that allow man to prosper would be condemned without the dominion of my sin." His eyes narrowed, feathers obscuring his face in darkness. "If you cannot bear the weight of truth, then instead, I will educate you on Oblivion."

Just as Onaga finished, his feathers swarmed his form, swallowing it almost entirely. Mirroring his descent into darkness, his eyes became abysses, only the remorseless purple slits shining from within to illuminate. And as the swarming feathers reached their crescendo, Zane stepped forward and jammed his demon serum into his chest before tossing the empty injector aside.

"Thanks for the unskippable cutscene," Zane scoffed. "Tyranny of ignorance? You beat yourself off like a professor who didn't receive tenure. Gods, you're pretentious, but I don't know what I was expecting from the scholar of the first sin," Zane said, his form shuddering before erupting into furious flames.

His skin darkened and became as stone. Fissures lined his skin, and his hair flared and flailed like a torch's flame. Jagged horns curved from his skull as he erupted into a white-hot effigy of his demonic form. Standing next to Kendra, their respective furies formed a marriage of white and red. Flames and embers scored the air as their sentiments converged into one, their challenge for the unyielding sin before them.

"Since you want to educate us, I have a question, professor," Zane began, his voice filled with the brimming sin that crept through him. His gunblade boiled with flames within its etching as he took aim, the barrel radiating intense heat. He didn't fire yet, the moment dispersing its tensions as he waited for the opportune moment to attack. And as the feathers of greed cloaked Onaga's face, Zane's finger tensed. The single eye peering back at him announced where their dance would commence.

"Did you know angels can fall twice?"

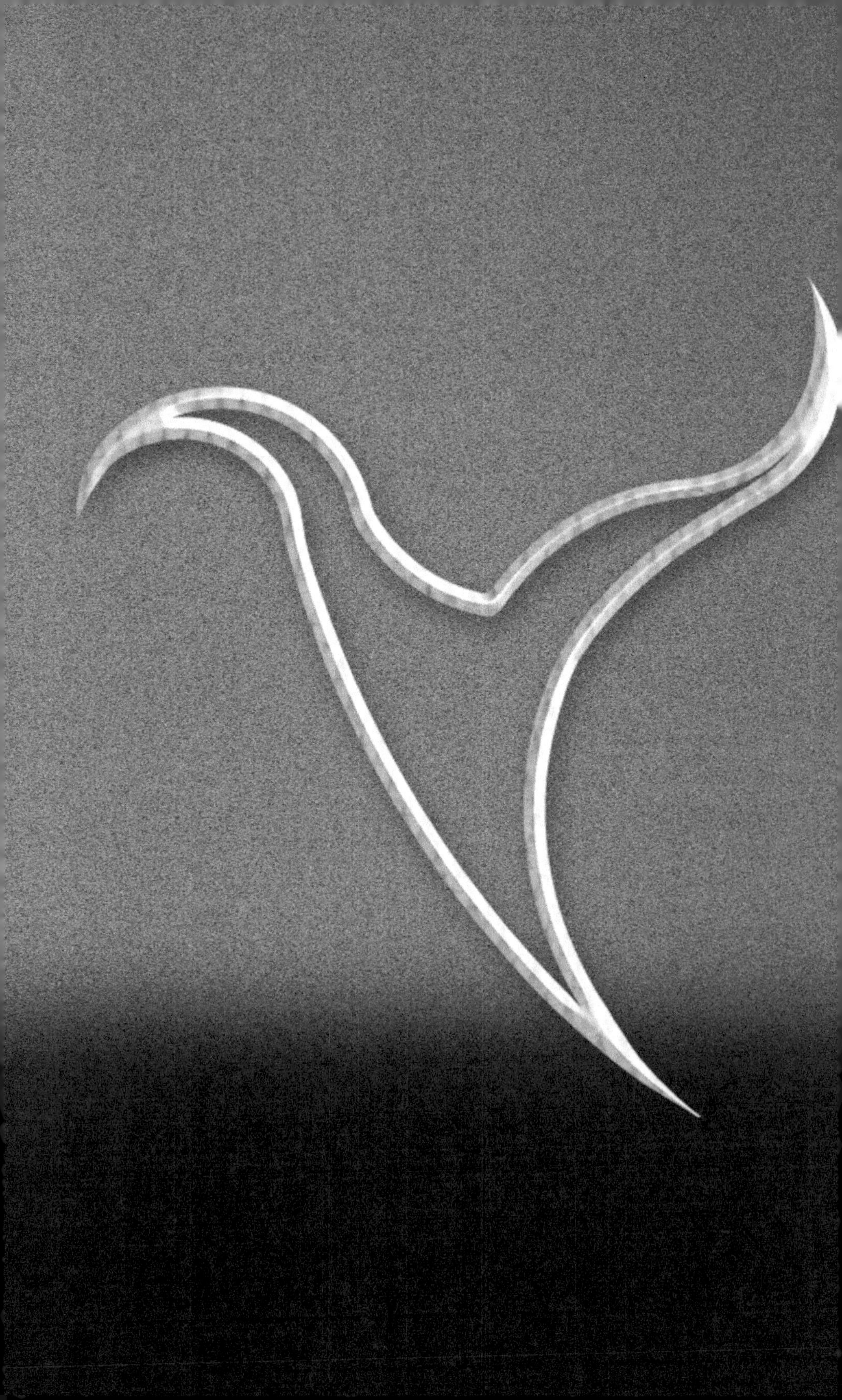

Fifteen

Dance of Greed

"PLEASE DON'T DO THIS … DON'T HURT THEM," Eden's voice echoed within the umbrages of his fatigue. The weight of his eyelids bore a sharp throbbing in his mind when he deigned to open his eyes. Kendra and Zane had stood before Onaga, their voices incomprehensibly far, but he feared his voice was even further. The words refused to escape his lips.

His fingers twitched, and the feathers impaling his palms were impervious to any such rebellion he could dream of. The pain didn't register for long, as he soon sank back into the darkness he failed to crawl from. Onaga's wings were spread before him once more, fanatical monologues and a transcendent disregard of his pleas. It was always the same.

Timeless—in memoriam of all he foolishly dared to cherish—they would always be taken.

The wisps of Cassiel's voice called to him, and a radiant light reached for him in the dark. Her cries of remorse and eternal lament echoed raucously—blending with his tainted memories. He wanted to reach back, to apologize, to call for her with his pilfered voice, but in the famine of his breath, he could only bring himself to regurgitate the same statement.

"Stop …" he begged. He wanted it to stop, but that would impede the *truth* Onaga insatiably desired. No *selfish* yearning for reprieve would deprive his avarice.

The darkness swallowed Eden's vision again, and hope once more absconded as the fear of oblivion loomed over who Onaga would take next. But a single rebellion pealed below, and he opened his eyes briefly once more when a bang jostled him from his resignation.

A bullet, streaking with bright white flames, flew toward Onaga's eye. In the next moment, Onaga appeared from the feather hovering behind them.

With their backs to him, the dance began. Soundless, Onaga's wing cleaved the air, meeting the flat of Zane's burning blade as he turned. Deflecting it, he attempted to kick Onaga away, but he was gone again.

Onaga's shifting through liminal space would prove beyond difficult to contend against. Kendra barely realized where Onaga had been. When she turned, he had disappeared again. Zane nudged her, and they rushed forward to where Onaga materialized next.

Kendra closed in quickly, but her claws only met the air where he had been. The fibers of the feathers crumbled within her hand as they rushed around her in a flurry. They stung against her skin, creating shallow wounds that pulsed with remnants of dark energy. With a flare of her chaos flames, they were banished from the cuts, but they didn't heal as they usually would. The danger of his feathers dawned on her, and she spun on her heel to face him again.

Despite their best efforts, neither of them could even graze the harbinger, instead finding only deadly feathers in the advancing swarm. Making matters worse, Zane barely followed the feather swarm that closed in, but he still managed to burn them before they could hit.

Onaga rapidly shifted, feather to feather, deceptively directing their eyes before he hovered in the air before the glowing tank. His fingers lightly intersected, weaving into the equilibrium-diablo sign as his wings split into four parts each. Purple-slit pupils glowered at them atop the feathers, and the wings curved to form their own diablo signs.

Onaga's long, dark, tendril-like arms of greed stretched forth from between his wings, their claws gripping the fibers of reality and stretching it open to reveal a black blot. Its expanse, a concept beyond concepts, was impossible to stare into, but Zane knew what awaited should they remain idle—should they bear witness to the opening of the Gates of Oblivion.

"*Heed the music of Oblivion's call,*" Onaga's voice rumbled through the room.

"Disrupt him!" Zane called to Kendra, clasping his hands in the ignis-diablo sign as a spark shot from his horns, supplanting itself into the blot and stretching to its corners. The blot pulsed, tugging in conflict as the spark simmered within it. In response, some of the arms relinquished the darkness and rushed at both of them with outstretched fingers.

Kendra charged forward, meeting the arms head-on. Claws and flame tore through their lengths, and she managed to vanquish a few. One other caught her forearm in a tight, frigid grip that sapped her of energy akin to the wound his feather inflicted. She incinerated it just as quickly, leaving only the holes it left in her sleeve. Once she got close enough, she leaped through the air at Onaga and slashed at his face.

As expected, he disappeared from the spot, and the blot in reality stitched shut. Kendra came to a stop against the tank with a thud, cushioning her collision with her arms. While she slid toward the floor with a loud screech, her claws left no marks on the glass. She propelled from it.

Zane took to her side, gunblade smoking as he aimed where Onaga appeared. A wall of feathers challenged him to shoot, but Zane refrained. Instead, he took the moment to assess the threat before them. In his vigilance, he glimpsed slit purple eyes peering from within the storm of feathers.

"You see those larger feathers floating around in the swarm? The ones with eyes on them?" Zane asked, and Kendra traced the flying feathers with his question in mind. When she spotted them, she frowned.

"Yeah ... what are those?" she asked.

"Not sure exactly, but they look important. Try to target them. He'll tire us out if we don't wear him down soon." Zane kept his gunblade trained on Onaga, glanced at the flames of wrath coursing across Kendra's limbs. "Place your hand on the base of my weapon and channel some of your flames into it. We can't have him regenerating if we hope to win. Keep his attention while I find an opening."

"Roger," Kendra affirmed, her eyes flaring brightly before she pressed her palm to Zane's gunblade, and the scarlet fire filled the etching in the weapon, causing it to glow brightly. In the next breath, she broke into a zigzag sprint toward Onaga and juked. From her limbs, lashes of flames burned away some of the feathers lunging at her, and she leaped back to dodge an incoming wave of them that homed in on her.

The feathers were unnaturally quick, and the tiny fibers composing them were fine-edged scalpels. With her regeneration hindered, she had to curb her aggressive style in favor of hit-and-run tactics. Though she targeted the feathers with slit eyes, lesser ones always took the blow as they shifted out of range.

She dug her claws into the ground, dashing low until she enclosed Onaga in a ring. With hard focus, she willed the flames to rush toward Onaga all at once—a feat that challenged the apex of her control.

When Onaga liminally shifted to the area above, Zane fired a bullet at him, streaking red with Kendra's chaos flames. He shifted once more to another spot out of the way but raised a brow when the bullet instead hit one of his feathers possessing a glowing slit pupil. He grunted dismissively, his arms rising before clasping them together, and several feathers shot from his wings as a cyclone closed in on the hunters.

"On me!" Zane called, rushing to the center of the cyclone and holding his arms out. Kendra quickly rushed to him, pressing her back to his as the feathers' shadows threatened to consume them. With her flames joining his, they snaked around them with rapid, precise movements that fanned out from their forms and created both a sword and shield, defending and thinning their numbers alike for several seconds.

The brewing security, however, was short-lived, and Zane watched pensively for the moment the cyclone would break. With their arms occupied, channeling the flames to keep from being turned into ribbons, they were effectively immobilized. One wall of feathers was breached, and dark wings cleaved through like an axe, threatening to sever both of their heads, but Zane's eyes and horns alike flared brightly. A flash of flames forced Onaga to retreat, but Zane gave chase.

"Let's go!" he called, and Kendra followed. As Onaga shifted to avoid their attacks, their tenacity allowed them to glean an important insight. The successive shifts grew negligibly slower—just enough to show his cautious movements the more the hunters nipped at his heels. Zane's eyes narrowed, and he leaped back, firing at Onaga to create space.

Kendra returned to him, panting heavily as her fingers twitched and her eyes flickered with sporadic light within their embers.

"He's slower," she said. "Not that it'll matter at this rate."

"He's using those feathers to shift," Zane surmised, glancing at the ones possessing eyes again. "Create two walls of your chaos flames around me. I'm going to make some obstacles, and I need you to break toward the center once they're up. Keep the crux of his attention while I make it happen."

"I don't know how long I can do that. Would be easier to do an all-out explosive flash or something," she claimed, her eyes following Onaga as he shifted around.

"That'd cook Eden, but trust me. Just buy me time," he said, his hands weaving into the terra-diablo sign and glowing with power.

Kendra growled and erected two protective walls of flames around Zane before she engaged Onaga again. The strain on her spirit compounded, and her limbs became heavier with the successive maneuvers, repelling Onaga and dodging his slashes whenever he appeared.

Once they were in the center of the room, the ground quaked, and several pillars of stone erected from the ground. They surrounded her and Onaga, limiting both his ground and aerial mobility within their confines. His feathers shifted once more, surrounding the pillars and collapsing in. She dashed through, evading the feathers and swinging from the pillars to break eyesight from Onaga. As she glanced up, she saw the slit-eyed feathers shifting from within the flurry, casting their leer on her and revealing her location to Onaga. Instantly, he appeared before her, slashing through the pillars and aggressively pursuing her when she retreated.

With another quake within the room, several spikes shot from the ceiling. The precision commanding them was palpable, their tips impaling most of the slit-eyed feathers that hovered in the air. Flames coated the stone, carried from the walls of chaos flames Kendra left. With that single move, most of Onaga's more troublesome feathers had burned away.

When the harbinger manifested from within the rows of pillars, his gaze shifted to Zane, using his wings to block the initial slash before they exchanged clashes. Blazing metal scorned his dark wings blow by blow, forcing Onaga to shift within the refuge of the pillars to escape the onslaught.

Kendra, spotting him, immediately lunged forward, and he raised his wings in time to block her foot, albeit he was sent sliding across the floor back into Zane's path. And with a decisive slash, his burning blade carved Onaga's chest, drawing blood and slicing open the dress vest he wore.

Onaga shifted several feet away, fingers tracing the wound with labored breath escaping his lips. Blood dripped from the wound, and Onaga grunted. Kendra emerged from within the pillars, her form flickering slowly between scarlet and orange as her energy waned.

"Knew you could bleed," Zane jeered, smirking sardonically even as his demonic visage waned. "Focus on thinning his feathers," Zane instructed Kendra before grinning at Onaga.

Usually, he quelled the chaotic sentiments within him, but the more he tasted wrath—the more his flames burned a man so worthy of it—the less he could bring himself to suppress it.

"You wanted music? Then let's rock!" he called, and the two hunters rushed at Onaga in tandem.

Blade and claws shrieked with each clash against Onaga's wings, and the harbinger's liminal shifts slowed further. Kendra broke away and dashed around the outskirts of their radius, flinging flames at stray feathers in a dare for Onaga to shift with his reduced dodging capabilities. The tenacity of the hunters pressured him to break when Zane shot his wings with his gunblade's focus-fire, repelling them from protecting his form.

Zane lunged and snatched the harbinger's face. An explosive flame erupted from his feet, and they propelled into a wall with an explosion. Blazing, sharpened fingertips gripped Onaga's face and scalp, flames flaring along the palms. He dragged Onaga across the wall in the next breath, shredding the stone and bathing him in burning fury.

When Onaga shifted away, his wings were tattered and frayed as embers fell from the wilting feathers. His face was charred and bleeding, and he heaved while regenerating from the damage. His wings shook loose ashes as he hovered backward in retreat. When Zane continued his attacks, he could only evade for a short duration before Zane gripped and tossed him into one of the remaining pillars.

With his hands weaving into the terra-diablo symbol, Zane slammed his palms into the ground. He willed the remaining pillars to form a jagged tomb that strangled Onaga and crucified him, wings splayed. Though the demon lord writhed, flames coalesced and crawled from beneath—a furnace. And with a reverberating growl from Zane, they exploded in a blazing geyser.

Zane exhaled heavily, rising from the ground as he watched the inferno, and Kendra stumbled toward him as the flames evanesced, the room dimming. The scarlet glow around her faded, and she gasped as the tension released in her all at once, causing her to stumble.

"Is it over?" she asked, peering up at Zane's visage with bated breath.

"Looks like it ..." Zane said. The stone prison became molten stone, and a single severed wing rested aflame atop the burning floor. He raised his gunblade, examining the drum briefly. "And I was on my last bullet too. Was kind of hoping to put it through his head," he sneered, eyeing the sizzling remnants.

Kendra turned her attention to Eden, but her eyes widened when Eden fell to the floor. One of his palm wounds was gaping—the other held up by a black feather that slowed his fall. Kendra gasped, whipping her head around to see the dreaded dark silhouette manifest behind Zane.

She called out to him in alarm, and though she lunged and kicked Onaga away, his remaining wing had already cleaved through Zane's back. As if a candle had been snuffed, the light in Zane's demonic eyes faded, and his form contorted into its human visage as he fell into her arms. Blood splattered along the floor and spilled from his back as he yelled in pain.

Kendra held him close, turning him over as she examined the diagonal slash that nearly sliced through to his spine. The wound oozed with the pilfering energy Onaga's feathers carried, and it was evident his wound was unable to regenerate as it fed on his dwindling reserves of power.

His raspy breathing filled her ears, eyes glazing as he trembled in her arms.

"*Shit, shit, shit* ... please hold on," she pleaded, voice strained as her eyes darted between him and Onaga. She feared the damage and shock alike would have killed him immediately, but he sharply sucked air in through his teeth, trembling as he grabbed her hand.

"Hold ... him ... off," he breathed out between grunts. She was reluctant to let him go, knowing he would bleed out in mere seconds. She surmised that if Onaga was dead, the energy would be dispelled and allow him to heal, but the haste that demanded seemed impossible by herself.

"You better not fucking die," she snapped at Zane, carefully setting him down before stepping forward.

Though she herself was running on fumes, Onaga looked worse. The smoke cleared, revealing injuries along his body that sizzled as they regenerated. Though tattered, his ash-covered blouse and pants had endured the flames. Only one wing remained, littered with burns and several claw marks from her earlier assault. She could only hope its defensiveness was diminished.

With a shake of her head, she rekindled the flames across her form. The scarlet fire had been all but exhausted, and she surmised she only had enough energy to hold it for a single claw swipe. Her form shimmered, and she let her tenacity guide her as she lunged at him again.

Onaga danced out of range of her attacks, leaping back and weaving between each of her efforts. Air boiled around her arms and legs, but his wing kept extinguishing her weakened fire. Despite that, her claws managed to rake the wing several times. Peeled and patchy, the flesh beneath peeked out at her.

She dropped low and slammed her foot into his chest, sending him tumbling back onto the ground. *Now,* she thought, and her claws sizzled with her scarlet flames as she dashed at him. Her arm reeled back, and the scarlet slit in her eyes undulated.

Onaga's body shuddered, and the feather from Eden's other palm floated behind him. His form liminally shifted to it, putting several feet between them as the energy in his wing rippled.

With their eyes meeting, his gaze damned her. She gasped, the momentum of her lunge suddenly weaponized. Time slowed, and with wide eyes, darkness consumed her vision as his wing cleaved her in two.

Silky shadows stretched before Kendra, caressing her in something akin to comfort, but she hadn't remembered entering them. Her eyes were no longer bathed by the Heart of Virtue's light nor the flaring flames of her fury. Numb and mute, she could only gaze into the darkness.

Even the floor comprised shadows, rolling softly like waves on a shore, but they were solid under the soles of her boots. Despite the lack of light, her hands were visible as she gazed down at them, but she dropped them in surrender. The embrace became cold, inviting memories of the moment before she awoke within it. Upon recollection, her lips twisted into a scowl, and her eyelids became dams that held back her tears.

"Eden ... Zane ..." she choked out, her breath shallow and uneven. "I'm not strong like either of you. I couldn't change—"

A chorus of wispy jeers filled her ears, and she flinched as her eyes snapped open, staring into ghastly white crescents that leered at her from afar. Coming into view slowly, a damned, dreaded figure emerged in a sitting position. Despite the stillness of the air, *its* cape flapped as if assailed by winds. Long, slender fingers, the same color as the shadows they imposed upon, adjusted a tie. With its other hand, its lanky arm jutted out toward her, thumb down while the entity booed her.

"You're dead," Kendra alleged in disbelief, taking a defensive stance as she conjured flames along her palms, her claws extending threateningly.

"If I could die again, your performance surely would have despaired me into the grave," Intico spoke, flashing her a wide, glowing grin. "What a terrible finale this would be—I was on the edge of my seat too," it scoffed, uncrossing its legs and standing.

"I killed you!" Kendra called, defensively taking a step back.

"You did. And in a much more impressive display than you're showing me now," it purred, adjusting its hat. "Contrary to what you are currently thinking, I am indeed ... *dead*."

Kendra's eyes widened, and she glanced around for a moment as the implication settled on her, and she then stared at her hands.

"Dispense with the melancholy, Mallory. You are still very much alive," Intico said, flicking its hand dismissively at her.

"What?" Kendra questioned, raising a brow. "I saw him—I was cut in half."

"You *thought* you saw him cut you in half. The eyes are so very unreliable in inauspicious ways, but this time, it's quite favorable for you," Intico said, approaching her slowly.

"Cut the baiting bullshit and tell me what the hell is going on," Kendra hissed, taking another step back. "If I'm not dead, how are you here?" she asked, and Intico paused, its finger thoughtfully tapping the corner of its mouth.

"An apt question, but I may only speculate," Intico answered, mimicking the sound of clearing its throat. "Those chaos flames, or whatever wacky name you call them, killed me. While I expected the traditional demon afterlife of becoming an oblivious gloom within the twilight gardens, here I am instead. Alone. With the one demonic being more clueless than I," Intico spoke, its tone suggesting annoyance at her urging its explanation. "Your urgency is spoiling my mood. Gods forbid a demon act mysteriously when we've much time to pontificate within *your* shadow."

"My shadow?"

"Prove my point, won't you?" Intico sighed, shaking its head. "Hellhounds are such useful creatures. The Siegharts summoned plenty to make Harvest possible. They harvested souls, and I harvested them. So much harvesting a farmer would blush." Intico chuckled, then continued,

"Typically, hellhounds assimilate the sentiments of the soul soon after and expel the consciousness. I surmise this is a more conscious effort, however. Seeing as I am here, and you are oblivious," Intico said, circling her ominously. When it had drifted too close for her comfort, she hurled flames into it, causing its form to erupt in flames. However, Intico didn't visibly react. "Oh no, I'm burning again. Forget me not, mon amour," Intico wailed performatively.

Kendra growled, watching as her flames faded from an unperturbed Intico, and it dusted its tattered suit before snapping its fingers. Before them, the darkness molded itself, and several buildings and high-rises erected before them. The smoking streets of a desolate Chicago pervaded. In her perplexity, Intico circled her again.

"As I was saying, I believe you consumed my soul with those scarlet flames. In a word, you've yet to ... *digest*."

"And I don't plan to. Nightmare demons aren't a part of my diet," Kendra spat, eyeing it warily.

"While I am jubilated to hear this, we are at quite the impasse in this place of time dilation. The moment you leave, you will most certainly die—even with my brief interference," Intico claimed.

"Interference?" Kendra questioned.

"The illusion I compelled you to perform," Intico clarified.

"Wait ... you controlled me?" she growled, her eyes narrowing as she clenched her jaw.

"Nothing of the sort, Mallory. Think of it as ... tickling your nose to make you sneeze," Intico said and chuckled. It paced toward the smoldering building—the place Intico had perished. "You have a once-in-a-lifetime opportunity to utilize a power not your own with full volition—the power of a demon lord. And while it is but a vestige sequestered within your soul, you may kindle its potential within your corporeal form," Intico mused, turning to face her again.

"*Your* power?" She scoffed. "You orchestrated so many deaths. Vicente ... my sister ..."

"All very tragic, yes. I could play therapist and let you lament for weeks, but time is not infinite in this place. Eventually, that wing will cleave you in two, and then we will both enter the shadows of the twilight gardens. And worse … the deaths of both that zany demonium and Blackwell alike will be guaranteed."

Kendra scowled, turning away from Intico as she clenched her fists at her sides. As much as the thought disgusted her, she knew she had no other option. After several seconds of pensive silence, she exhaled.

"Then I'll make an exception this once and consume you for real this time," Kendra said. She marched over to Intico, who suddenly removed its hat.

"Mercy, Mallory. Allow me to toss my hat into the ring of this negotiation," Intico said.

"Negotiation? I'm not bargaining with you," she said, coming to a stop in front of it. Though she was once fearful of Intico, at that moment, her burning eyes were dauntless as she stared up at the fiend.

"You may wish to, for you wouldn't benefit much by digesting me. One: As I am now, I am but a shadow, lacking my former prominence and agency. In other words, empty calories. Two: You wouldn't acquire my abilities—just a small measure of temporary energy," Intico spoke, earning a puzzled look from her.

"Then … what the fuck is the point?"

"To make a pact as the umbra would," it cooed, grin widening. "We would tether our souls, cementing my place here in your shadow and giving you a fighting chance."

"First, I need you to tell me why you're bothering to offer helping me. As much as I hate you, you've got an angle to this," Kendra said, and Intico reeled back while clutching its chest.

"Your cynicism could make me weep, Mallory! Can't a demon act out of the kindness of its ethereal ooze where a heart should be?" it asked, but Kendra stared, deadpan. Intico scoffed, folding its arms as it glanced away. Its face formed something akin to a pout, its grin melting away. "That voidling known as Orphan *really* ticked me off," Intico hissed. "They had me believing I was a king when, woefully, I was but a pawn to that winged snake. Blasphemous! Even you could agree I would at least be a bishop—or a rook!" Intico yelled, its voice reverberating through the empty city as its cape flailed.

"Orphan and you were working together then? So that's what they meant ..." Kendra muttered and shrugged. "Kingpin was actually a goon and now gets a chance at revenge. Typical demon." Kendra clicked her tongue. "One more question. You could have just gathered souls on your own to remain in a physical form for as long as you wanted. Why did you want to merge with someone so badly?"

Intico stared deep into her eyes, its crescents shrinking as it mulled over the question. It tepidly placed its hat back on, fists clenching tightly as they fell to its side.

"You and I ... were one. You should know the answer to that," Intico said flatly.

Kendra sighed, staring down at her palms for a moment as she considered the grave implications of making a pact—something she thought she'd never do officially. When she remembered the jade eyes she sought to liberate and her duty to save Zane, she finally relented.

"What are the terms of this pact?" she asked.

"Simple," Intico began. "I've but two conditions. One, you will allow me to see those light shows we witnessed days prior when applicable."

Kendra cocked her brow.

"The fireworks?" she quizzed, giggling at the absurdity of the demand. "And what's the second? Want me to take you to the circus?" She folded her arms, raising her brow skeptically.

"What a grand and intoxicating innocence!" Intico said, laughing. "Our desires are more aligned than you may suspect, dear Mallory. You see ... I grow bored within this purgatory."

She watched Intico's eyes light up, the sinister grin she knew it for reforming with a resolve she found to be oddly inspiring.

"I do enjoy your own light shows and wish to see you use them for a grand finale to this epic saga of sin and tragedy. Put on a show neither he nor we will forget. That is my final condition." With its conditions proposed, Intico held its hand out, shadowy energy undulating from its digits. She stared at it with the same skepticism as before, hesitation awash in her tense body language. "Now … take my hand, Mallory. It's not like you're making a deal with the devil."

Kendra reached out, her hand glimmering with the scarlet red of her soul. When their hands joined, a radiant flash of scarlet and black illuminated before them. The city was awash in their combined energy as the scenery before her began melting away. In the final moments, the darkness consumed her vision, and she stared into those crescent eyes until they became the only thing she could see. The vision within her shadow evanesced, and with a dark chuckle, Intico spoke.

"The stage is yours. Break a leg, Mallory. Preferably his."

Onaga's wing tore through Kendra's *body*, her torso severed from her lower half and her white eyes flickering as their light faded. As the tip of Onaga's wing scraped the ground, he watched the remnants of her form tumble. He frowned, his wing dry with only fading embers dripping from his feathers.

"*Where are you aiming?*" the unified voices of Kendra and Intico rang out. The bisected body combusted, and from the lower half beside Onaga's unguarded side, Kendra emerged, claws flaring bright red as she slashed upward with the last of her power. The black claws impaled Onaga's chin and raked his face in a clean arc. The scarlet flames dancing on her palms sundered his flesh, leaving several jagged marks that took half of Onaga's face off along with his eye.

The harbinger doubled back, howling as he reflexively grabbed his torn face. Coagulating blood dripped from his chin, and he reeled back to retreat, but she snatched his wing and pulled him close.

"*You want blood?*" Kendra growled, her claws tearing through the wing. Onaga twisted from her hold, his wing swatting her away. She remained tenacious, keeping low to the floor and dashing to his blind side.

He pivoted to keep away from her, but she closed in, twisting as she slammed her foot down onto his femur, snapping it before yanking him close by his arm. Her face hovered inches from his, her slit pupils flickering a mix of red and white. Her sweltering breath scorned him as she glared deep into the void of his being. *"Me too."*

Kendra's other claw dug into his shoulder before she mounted his back. Not a hint of hesitation marred her wrathful expression as she dragged her claws and jerked his head to the side. Her jaws then snapped on his neck, teeth gouging him deeply.

Zane watched from the floor as Onaga wrestled against Kendra's hold, taking the moment to tear the split remnants of his shirt and vest from his body. Out of focus and dizzy, his vision waned as he reached for the smoldering gunblade in front of him. Though it had lost a significant portion of Kendra's chaos flames, scarlet cinders still glowed within the etching.

Keep your eyes open, he thought, his teeth gritted as he wrenched it with his uncoordinated fingers. He lifted it with the one arm he could move and braced himself. Biting down on the hem of his vest, he pressed the blade to his wound. While normally impervious to fire of all kinds, in his current state, Zane was vulnerable to the malforming wrath of the chaos flames. It was unfamiliar—akin to freezer burn to him—but the pain assailed him to tears.

Auspiciously, it shocked him into alertness, his consciousness anchored by it. Once the wound had melded closed, he found he was unable to stand. He glanced at Kendra as she held onto Onaga. His gaze then flicked to Eden, eyes narrowing as he slowly switched the gunblade to its focus-fire configuration.

Onaga's wing, now regenerated from the recent damage, pried Kendra from his back, surging with energy before flinging her away. She twisted in the air and landed on all fours, her claws scraping the floor until they anchored her. As she looked up, a wicked glint returned to her eyes. Scarlet flames coalesced around her form once more, and she reluctantly licked the blood from the corners of her mouth and channeled her renewed strength.

She rushed in, reprising their dance as the two clashed and spun with critical regard. As Onaga's wing flung against her form, it burst into flames—an illusion—and she resurfaced beside him. With his guard up, he watched for her illusions, sweeping his wing and blocking her follow-ups. Each of his attacks met one of her illusions, but soon he spotted her real form and readied his wing. When he dared to slash her, she parried it the same way Eden had taught her, and his wing sprung back as he tumbled.

With his defenses removed, she delivered bone-crushing blows and kicks in rapid succession. Her claws tore his flesh, burning him all the while. Much like the namesake of the scarlet flames' infamy, she embodied their wrathful sentiment entirely. She leaped, spinning several times before her leg slammed into Onaga's neck. Nearly snapping it, he was sent tumbling back from the force.

This is it, Kendra thought, and she charged after him, her body glowing brightly. With no further feathers to escape to, she intended to turn him into an ashen corpse. His eyes narrowed, his sunken face showing little reaction even as doom approached. Their eyes met, but something ancient was unearthed, glowering at her. Within those voids, several slit eyes manifested, and from within, a transcendent voice spoke.

"The witch relents ..."

Fresh feathers and several wings shot from his back while shadows crawled along his skin, and as Kendra struck, his form shifted through reality to stand upright several feet away. His many wings weaved into diablo signs, and he clasped his hands together into the equilibrium-diablo sign, a clap echoing throughout the room. Arms of greed shot from his back at Kendra, snatching her by her wrists and neck before slamming her into the adjacent wall.

Their hands tightened on her form as several slit eyes formed along his wings, boring into her with a terrifying reticence. In the dark, the depraved manifestation of greed reared an endless avarice, heralded by countless eyes that opened. His remaining arms lurched in front of him, grabbing the hems of reality and wrenching it open to reveal the inky blot Zane had dreaded.

"Be not afraid ... in the advent of Oblivion and its revelations." Onaga's voice thrummed throughout the chamber.

As the blot expanded, incomprehensible concepts flooded Kendra's mind, threatening to devour everything she was. Sight, sound, scent, and sensation were robbed—only the legions of greedy eyes remaining in their absence.

The Gates of Oblivion.

The resolve anchoring her was all that tethered her to reality the more it grew. The wrathful flames quickly absconded from her limbs and heart as if she would abstract, but an invisible claw clutched the sentiment pervading her heart. Scarlet flames spilled from her mouth while she forced air into her lungs, and she fiercely met those eyes.

Within the all-consuming dark, a bang ruptured, and the world around her returned briefly. The hand holding her neck fell, and she wrenched the oxygen back into her lungs. Onaga fell to his knees, his wings wilting to the ground as the floor molded around them to anchor him. His back smoked as blood spilled from the wound where his wings connected. Behind him, Zane lowered his gunblade, his other hand on the floor.

Stone undulated beneath Zane's fingertips, and his eyes met Kendra's as he breathed frantically.

"Finish him!" Zane called out, the stone then erecting into a shield over his and Eden's bodies.

Kendra tugged at the hands still holding onto her wrists, but their tight grip refused to relent, even with Onaga's weakened state from the bullet in his weak spot. She grunted, her claws digging into the wall as she pulled herself forward. Her limbs cracked as she dislocated her arms, her head drooping.

The breath in her lungs compounded, the last of her scarlet flames sweltering within. She knew exactly how to erase the harbinger before her. With a burning indictment in her eyes, she met Onaga's gaze as he turned to face her, the Gates of Oblivion snapping shut.

"Here's your revelation ..." she growled.

The breath inside her reached its apex, and she remembered what Eden had said just a week prior. Both she and Onaga were bound in place, creating the most opportune of circumstances for her signature attack. With the flames taking away her ability to speak, she loathed that she couldn't grant Onaga its name.

Allow me to assist, Intico's voice rang in her head, and white crept through the abysses of her eyes, spilling from the edges of her sockets to form undulating crescents. They flickered with her scarlet glow, and their respective voices echoed through the room despite her not speaking the words physically.

"Hell flash!"

Wild scarlet light exploded before Kendra as she expelled the flames. Onaga's face illuminated, his hair and feathers flailing in the wind. He was bathed in the scorching scarlet, flesh, feathers, and feeling alike devoured by its wrath. He was silent in his final moments, pensive to the last second his body existed to know.

As the flames cleared, she realized the hands of greed had vanished. Kendra pried herself from the wall and rolled her shoulders, popping them back into place. Her form smoked as the fabric of her suit crumbled around her forearms, and the cloth on her waist had been consumed by her power. Once she had regenerated from her injuries, her demonic aspect faded. Stumbling forward, she readjusted her glasses to be snug against her face again. The fact they had survived was a testament to Zane's resourcefulness with flame-proofing her accessories—she just hoped he'd live to continue helping her in that regard.

Nothing remained where Onaga had been. The ground smoked against her boots, and she approached where Zane was prone. The stone shield had melted away almost entirely, but from behind it, he groaned as he dragged himself to his feet. With Onaga dead, his wounds regenerated slowly, save for the remaining scar on his back.

Kendra turned her attention to the other side of the room, meeting the lusterless glint of green eyes peering from behind the shield Zane placed around him. Eden reached out, his voice faint beneath his labored breaths, and Kendra's eyes shifted away. Her trembling fingers touched her hunter bracer. Atop the small screen, she saw the connection had reestablished in the absence of Onaga's distortion. She inhaled before touching one of the analog buttons on the side and raising it to her lips.

"Kendra to all units," she gasped out, taking a moment to recapture her breath. "Onaga is slain—Eden is secured." Her hand dropped, and Zane gave her a thumbs-up.

He limped over to his vest, and though tattered, he plopped himself on the floor and dug a crystal from one of the pouches. With a flash of light, he summoned a beige parka, placing it over his shirtless form.

"Damn, that hurt," he muttered. "Good thing I always keep at least one bullet." He groaned and fished a juice box from his coat pocket, using the tiny straw attached to drink it. He turned to face Kendra as she approached Eden, his expression softening. Once finished, he crumpled the juice box and tossed it to the side, snapping his lips shut to refrain from further commentary.

Kendra stopped, standing above Eden, and she carefully scooped him from the ground. Though she attempted to hoist him onto her back, Eden shook his head, slipping from her hold to stand on shaky feet. Instead, she leaned him against her for support.

"We're going home for real this time," she said. Eden didn't protest that time, and as he leaned on her, she glanced back at Zane. "Zane, do you have any teleportation crystals for us to get out of here?" Kendra asked, but Zane shook his head.

"Negative. Didn't think we'd need them, to be honest."

"But a juice box was so important ..." Kendra muttered, shaking her head as she raised her hunter bracer. "Mallory to Roost. Need our twenty." A moment later, the speaker sounded, her earpiece having melted away in the fight.

"Roost to Mallory. You and Larson are reading as on the ninth floor of the laboratory. No known entry point. General Blackwell is en route to extract you both."

The group's attention turned to the Heart of Virtue within the tank, the mostly undamaged glass glimmering as a white light pervaded from the heart. Within its vestige, soft cries echoed upon the omens.

"Cassie …" Eden whispered, his eyes quivering as he stared up at the heart within the tank. As Kendra turned her attention to him, she slowly nodded.

"Zane … we need to free her."

Zane rubbed his chin, carefully approaching the tank and examining its surface pensively.

"Tough ask. This thing is barely damaged, and I'm positive at least one of my bullets hit it." He mulled over the thought, pursing his lips. "Also, there's a lot of that liquid in there. Not a good idea to flood this place with an unknown substance."

"We can't just leave her," Kendra said, staring hard at the heart as its light pulsed.

"Unless we know where the control panel is, we won't have much luck as we are now," Zane said.

Kendra's attention suddenly snapped to the tunnel they had come from, her ears twitching as soft taps echoed. She reflexively tucked Eden close against her, jaw tightening. Zane turned to face it, and soon a small, pale boy came into view. His golden eyes, stark and glimmering in the dim chamber, landed on them. And in Ryu's arms, he carried a dark tome.

Zane eyed it warily before studying his appearance in his tepid approach. He had demon blood, of that he was certain, but there was something more to him that he was curious about. When Ryu came to a stop, he tucked the book close and peered up at the tank.

"This room is controlled by a mix of demon alchemy and magic," Ryu said.

"Do you know how to control it?" Zane asked, stepping forward.

"Yes," Ryu answered simply, his eyes scanning the torn room. His gaze narrowed as he searched the chamber for several seconds. He frowned but slowly approached, carefully skipping over the grooves and breaks in the floor.

While Eden's focus was removed from what was going on, both Kendra and Zane came to a realization about Ryu's appearance as he drew closer. Orphan had briefly taken on the boy's appearance, and Kendra knew it had to be Ryu. His pale skin, Asian features, and silky white hair were indisputably reminiscent of Yuki.

Zane crouched as Ryu drew near, cocking his head.

"Are you ... Ryu?" he asked.

Ryu defensively tucked the tome to his chest, stopping several feet shy of Zane.

"How do you know my name?" he asked, eyes wide with curiosity. "Did Mr. Onaga speak of me?"

Both Kendra and Zane appeared puzzled, but Zane cleared his throat.

"No," he said truthfully, wary of lying to the boy. "Someone close to me knows you, though."

"Someone close?" he mused, glancing around once again as his fingers dug into the tome. "Is ... Mr. Onaga gone?" he asked, eyes glued to the floor. Zane exchanged glances with Kendra in response, who was far too confounded to chime in.

"Yeah. He went away, and we could use your help to get out of here," Zane said.

"Then ... I've to fulfill my promise," Ryu said, looking up. The statement astonished them, and Zane stood straight as Ryu approached dauntlessly. "He instructed me to give the Tome of Genesis to the hunters and to destroy the Heart of Virtue—should he perish." Ryu then hoisted the book carefully, holding it out to Zane. "I will assist in escorting you out."

"Why would Onaga have you make a promise like that?" Zane asked, and Ryu pursed his lips.

"He said that in his death, the heart would yield no knowledge or truth to warrant the soul within it suffering further," Ryu said tepidly, fidgeting with the book.

Zane reached out, carefully lifting the book. It was far heavier than the previous tome he had held. Its weight and Ryu's own ability to hold it inspired many questions, but Zane offered Ryu a soft smile, standing and tucking the book beneath his arm.

Ryu walked past them, approaching the tank before weaving the terra-diablo sign and touching the floor. Several pillars possessing glowing runes extended from the ground, and energy flowed through them in a combination that then caused the tank to glow brighter. From the center of the room, the floor opened as a pedestal raised, and a glowing light atop it twinkled in correspondence with the Heart of Virtue. In a flash, the heart appeared atop the pedestal, human-sized, as they quickly realized.

"Geez, that's big," Zane muttered. They were all exalted, and even Eden had looked up, staring at it with a pained expression. Ryu approached them again, hands joined in front of him as he stared at the heart, watching the three tips of it slowly fade into the light within it.

"The soul within it is untethering. It will be released shortly. Nothing else is required for it to become obsolete," Ryu spoke, prompting Eden to stir from Kendra's grasp and stumble toward it.

"Wait!" he choked out with the remnants of his voice, but Kendra caught him before he could fall.

"I'll take you," Kendra said, understanding his desire immediately. Carefully, she led him closer, and the white light within it permeated the area, wisps of its brilliance reaching out in response to Eden's presence.

As they neared it, Eden reached out, his arm heavy as his trembling fingers spread. His green eyes flickered, and he took a deep breath as the serene energy entered him, whisking him away within its gentle reprieve.

"You've grown so much ..." Cassiel spoke, her lilac eyes glistening as she gazed upon Eden. Both of them occupied the ephemeral space sequestered within the Heart of Charity, both of their souls naked and freed from the impurities of their respective physical states.

"I'm sorry," Eden said, swallowing hard as his fists tensed. "That you were alone—waiting." The light shimmering from Cassiel's radiant form shone over him, but her unexpected smile was far more glaring. He looked down, unperturbed by their nakedness. They had seen one another as such several times before, but the sensibility had never concerned him.

"Don't be silly, Eden," she said, her eyes softening as her fingers knit together and rested atop her chest. "I'm glad you're alive—and that I get to spend my last moments with you before I return to Mother," she spoke, her voice swelling with joy. Adoration filled her lilac eyes, and she approached slowly. Her bare feet sank into the fluffy light surrounding them, and her white wings spread wide along with her arms.

Eden raised his head. Her pristine form, whole and unmarred, urged him to hold back his tears, but before they could spill, she embraced him close. Her wings wrapped around him gently, her cheek pressing into his chest to feel his heartbeat.

"We've never touched before," Cassiel voiced lightly, betraying her lament.

"Just your feathers," Eden affirmed shakily, his hands raised, free from the weight of his corporeal injuries. However, he refrained from embracing her. "And now ... your light."

"It'll be enough," she promised, nuzzling into him as her fingers pushed through his hair. "If you can keep the promise I asked of you ... even better."

Eden surrendered, embracing her tightly, afraid to let go as the light dimmed, and he was left desperately clinging to her own.

"I don't know if I can. If I enter that place again—if I wake up in that cell without you ..." he whispered breathlessly, her form fading from his arms.

Her lips curled into a knowing smile, and soon, only the twinkle of her light remained, a single feather resting securely in his palm.

"I know you can," Cassiel said. "And no matter what, remember ..." her voice faded along with her feather, and though her light diminished, her sentiment remained. As soft as she had been, warm and comforting beyond anything he had known, it wrapped around him.

"You'll never be alone."

Eden's eyes opened, his hand falling. The Heart of Virtue dimmed of any semblance of brilliance, now no more than a crystalline object that crumbled atop the pedestal. His lips were agape, eyes wide and distant. Finally, he hung his head, resigning himself to the weakness he had ignored.

Kendra tugged him closer to her.

"We're going home," Kendra affirmed, her eyes finding Ryu as he stood with his fingers fidgeting while interlocked. Zane cleared his throat, gesturing with his thumb toward the tunnel.

"How do we get out of here?" Zane asked.

"The liminal study," Ryu replied, walking past him. "I will lead you out."

As they followed, the amber light from the chamber faded, and Zane created a small flame atop his thumb as Ryu led them. When they came to the end of the tunnel, rather than the collapsed cell from before being present, there was a blank wall. With a clasp of his hands, Ryu focused hard, his form shimmering with radiant energy. With a grunt, his energy shot out and formed an arch against the wall, and from within its outline, a large metal door formed.

"Woah ... that's so cool, Ryu," Zane cooed, earning a shy nod from the boy as he pulled the door open with a hefty tug. They then entered.

Though Zane thought to look around, he remained respectful. Ryu shut the door, holding onto the handle as he glanced back at them.

"I ask you to refrain from touching anything while we shift. I am unsure of what everything in here does still," he warned, seeing Zane had been inspecting the bookshelves with intrigue.

"Right ... just noticing a lot of the books I studied, and the ones I've yet to," he admitted sheepishly.

Ryu's hands glided down the door's surface as he focused. The room throbbed, shadows washing over the candlelight that emitted from the sconces upon the wall. When things settled a moment later, Ryu carefully opened the door, revealing a corridor on the seventh floor.

Kendra took Eden from the room, but Zane stopped at the door, glancing back at Ryu, who seemed reluctant to join them.

"Go on ahead. I'll catch up," Zane said, and Kendra nodded before walking off with Eden. He turned his attention back to Ryu. "Something on your mind?" Zane asked, crouching down.

"Onaga gave no further instruction, and I am forbidden from exploring the labs without his approval. I worry if I will be permitted to return to Avernus Academy without his sponsor," Ryu admitted, his eyes quivering.

"Sounds like he really cared for you. Like a father, even," Zane said, thinking back to his foggy memory of his own father. While poisoned by Orphan's meddling, he thought back fondly on learning of his father's research. He had always been eager to share with him. He saw himself as he stared upon the demonium boy.

"He wished to 'see my curiosity nurtured,' he said. He adores the curious, and thinked me to be extra curious," he said, and Zane chuckled lightly at his speech gaffe.

"You know demon alchemy, right? Since you're so curious, what say you come with us? I'll even teach you everything I know to thank you for giving me this tome," Zane said, holding the book up and waving it playfully. Ryu watched with curious eyes, seeing how Zane could lift the book as well.

"You, too, possess the requisites to hold it. You must know a lot to hold it in such a way," Ryu said, mouth agape as Zane flipped it in his grasp.

"You bet yah I do," he chirped, standing tall. "Oh, and by the way, I'm Zane. You're a bright kid, so what do you say?" Zane sang, intentionally rhyming as he held his hand out to Ryu, grinning.

Ryu giggled, stepping forward and taking Zane's larger hand with both of his, nodding eagerly.

"I would be privileged, Mr. Zane," Ryu said, his cheeks coloring pink as excitement coursed through his glimmering golden irises.

"Then it's a deal, little man. You'll be the best demon alchemist there is in no time," he said, standing tall and gesturing for Ryu to follow him. As Zane stepped out of the study, Ryu did too, shutting the door behind him. They then marched through the stale, white-tinted halls until they reached the open floor where the hunters congregated.

Within the rows of terminals and desks, they were gathered. The original teams present were laid out and slowly stirring back to consciousness. As Zane and Kendra learned, they had become unresponsive due to Onaga having shown up, or so Joseph explained in his groggy state.

Kendra spoke with a frantic Alicia while Commander Rigs barked orders to the conscious hunters who occupied the room. Zane tucked Ryu close to him, noticing how nervous he became during the chaos. He cleared his throat, garnering Alicia's attention, who then approached.

"You're so lucky—" She froze. Her green eyes studied Ryu, then flicked to where the unconscious hunters were still waking up—where Yuki held her head while propped against the wall.

"Hey, Ryu, meet my friend Alicia. There is someone here you're going to want to meet, and she's going to take you to her. I'll be with you again shortly, though. Promise," he said, and flashed Alicia a knowing look.

"Yeah," Alicia said, watching as Ryu's tepid eyes followed along to where she had been staring, and he observed Yuki for several seconds. Her soft, silky voice echoed in his mind as she spoke to the medic, urging an exalted recollection. Nervously, his fingers tugged at his blazer as he took a step toward Alicia.

"*Okāsan*," he whispered, his memories stirring. From his infancy, though slightly hazy, her spirit resonated with his own; an ethereal, maternal sentiment that nestled him. As he began to walk toward her without guidance, Alicia gave Zane a nod before following Ryu.

Across the room, Kendra held Eden close. While Alicia had provided a modicum of healing to him a minute prior, she had claimed his physical injuries weren't terrible. However, his node network was beyond what she could tend to on the field. Kendra waited with him, his waning focus on reality concerning, but she understood it all too well.

When Jessica appeared from the elevator lobby, she rushed over with frantic eyes, examining both her and Eden.

"Are you—I—forgive me for not being here sooner. Blocking the liminal paths was far more taxing than I anticipated. I came when I was no longer able to maintain it," she said, swallowing hard as her worried gaze found Eden. Though their eyes met, she knew he didn't see her. She knew he didn't see his mother. She opened her mouth to speak, but as she saw the all-too-familiar forlorn sentiment within his green depths, she went quiet.

"Madam," Zane called, approaching her and taking to the others' sides. "I'll explain what happened. Both of them need rest." He glanced at Kendra, nodding to her. Jessica reached out, touching Zane's arm with concern in her eyes.

"Only if you're okay," she said, but Zane smirked.

"A little light-headed and ravenous, but I'll live," he informed her, and Jessica sighed in relief, whispering her catharsis in Latin. She lowered her hand and touched her chest.

"I'll have units take you back to Roost so you can seek proper medical attention," Jessica said, but Kendra adjusted Eden against her side, shaking her head.

"If I may ... I want to take him alone," Kendra said, her eyes lowering. Though she had exhausted her rebellion, what compelled her was something less selfish.

"I've no objection," Jessica spoke, tearing her eyes from Eden as she walked past them. She paused, the words in her throat turning to concrete, but they never arose. In silence, she marched away, beckoning Zane to follow. With one last glance, Zane took after her.

The trek through the facility was quiet. The elevator, while tranquil, ebbed with phantom reminders in Eden's head. The blending halls, ripe with must and blood, loomed from within and without hauntingly. Ghosts of his pain walked alongside him with each room passed. The prick of feathers that tore and sutured him—the sting of fangs and needles impaling his veins—the mangling grasp of shackles that bit into him. With every step, its bitter vestige raked through him, and soon, he sank once more.

His world went dark, and the air fled his lungs, strangled within the cold, familiar chains he writhed in. Endlessly, he thrashed. All light from within was suffocated once more, and he sank deeper into that sea of despair.

He begged and pleaded with his broken voice, his words suffocated and swallowed. *They take. They take. They take.* It repeated endlessly, and he knew what invited him. The cold was replaced by a burning flame. *Wrath.* All that it invited grasped him and dragged him closer, threatening to take him again. He knew its promise—a promise that would betray the one he suffered to hold dear.

Cassie! he called desperately, heavy limbs shoveling through the murky darkness. He searched and begged for her voice—her light. Its memory wilted in his mind, the hollow remains of its pillar impossible to see as the heat scorched his back and crawled up his neck. Again, he was dragged toward it. *They take*, it repeated, and he cried once more. *Please… I want—*

"Eden," Kendra's voice called, snatching him from the fiery grips of wrath, and he opened his eyes.

The sun glared down at him through the trees, as if he had awakened outside once more. Its warmth threatened him—that slippery reprieve could flee again. That he might blink and be within that cell once again. As he looked around at the forest, the fresh breeze cooled his skin and tossed his matted black hair.

His cheeks were saturated with blood, having spilled from his eyes. He nestled into the even more comforting warmth holding him subconsciously, and he lowered his gaze to meet Kendra's royal-blue eyes behind her lenses. Suddenly, they were alone.

He dared to remember her own tears as she cried over what had been taken from her. He dared to remember how she desperately sifted through the ashes of tragedy to find what remained to cherish. He dared to remember how forsaken she had been—how forsaken he was. But within the corpse of his wallowing, he was pulled from beneath the shadow and into her illuminating embrace. She tucked his face into her neck, her fingers coursing through his hair.

"It's over," she whispered, and he remembered it all again until all that was left before him was her. And he finally believed what Cassie had begged of him.

With his heavy arms summoning the strength to bear it all again, he wrapped them around her, holding her close in fear of her disappearing. Even with that fear, he knew he wasn't alone.

And the silent forest echoed with the quiet weeping of his broken voice.

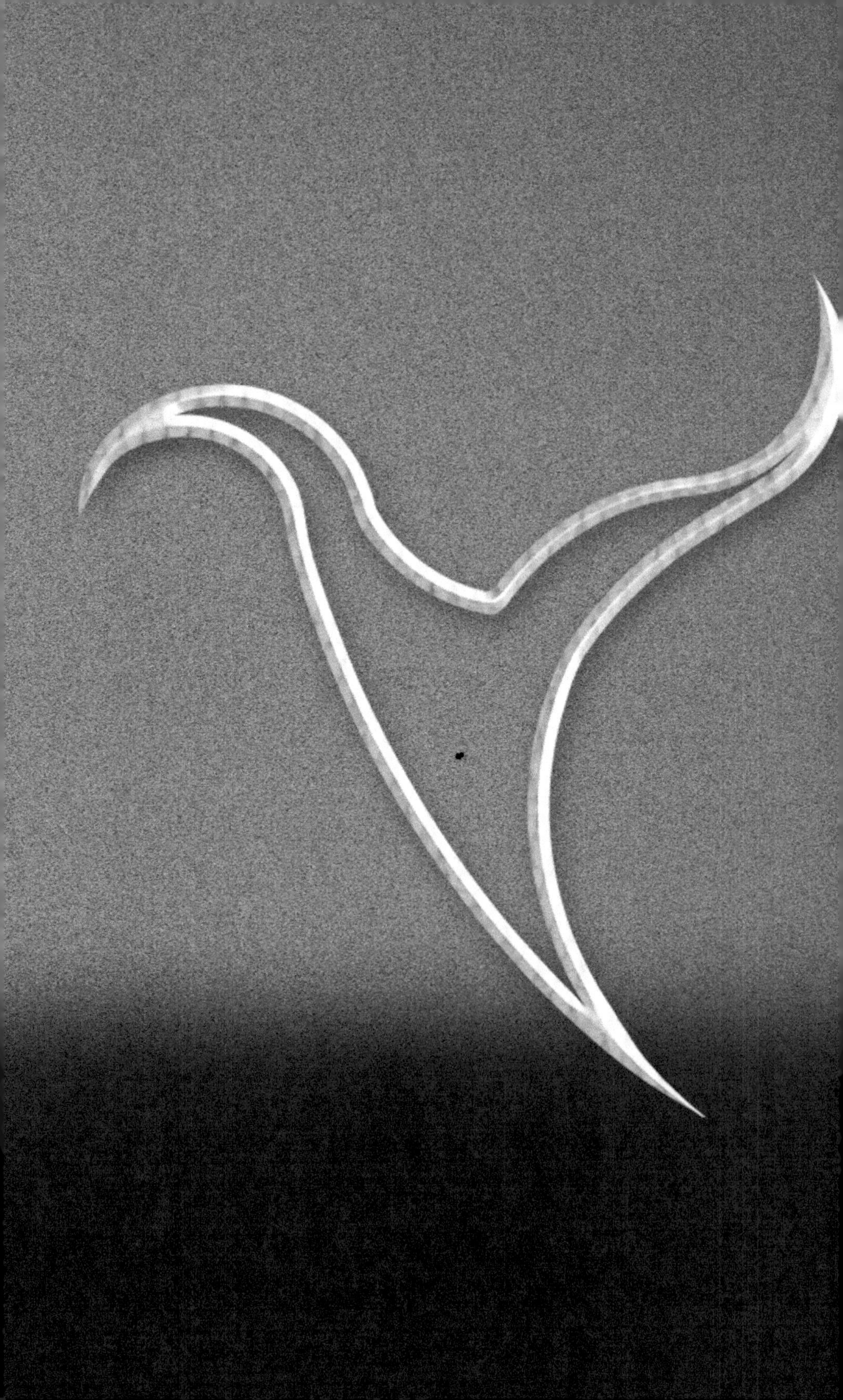

SIXTEEN

EVANESCENCE
OF
CONDEMNATION

CHIMES COAXED KENDRA from her afternoon slumber, and she stirred beneath her blanket, slowly coming to. Across from her, Yuki's tidy bed was illuminated by the sun glaring through white curtains. For a moment, the amber hue reminded her of the chamber she had killed Onaga within. She had never pushed herself that hard before, which was partly why she was napping more frequently after.

As the chime thrummed through the room again, she groaned, pulling her hair back as she dragged herself from the bed and placed her glasses on. Tension compounded in her arms and legs, and she stretched with such ferocity she almost tripped back into bed. Once steady, her feet pressed into the wooden floor, and she crept over to her drawer.

"Impeccable timing," she muttered, throwing the drawer open and pulling the ice mirror from within it. When she focused on it, the familiar image of Azazel flashed across it, the cyan blue hue stirring along the magical feed as he came into view. "You've reached the voicemail box of Kendra Mallory. Unfortunately, you will have to call back when she is not taking a nap," Kendra said groggily, prompting Azazel to cock his head.

"Voicemail? Perhaps a message recording feature would be in order if I can work the method out. I am certain Dhaka would know a book with a potential solution," Azazel mused.

"The hell's a Dhaka?" she questioned but quickly shook her head. "Never mind. Don't wanna know. What's up, Zel?" she questioned, clearing her throat as she retreated back to her bed and fell into it.

"Forgive my inopportune timing. I've just settled for the evening in Avernus and have been receiving odd reports you may find interesting."

"Reports?"

"My scouts have been tracking some of the activity around the Fracti Alas laboratories of Onaga. Unusual activity—relatively speaking, I must clarify. Disarray and less meticulous network oversight. Atop that, Onaga has refrained from visiting his estate within Avernus. All this after additional reports of the Hunters' raids."

Kendra put on a poker face as she listened, nodding along as she pursed her lips.

"Funny," she said.

"I just desired telling you that I commend whoever disposed of him. I have known of his daughter's crusade against his Venatum, but I never suspected his death would arrive," he spoke with a smirk, and Kendra cocked an eyebrow.

"Lucy? Why would she be attacking her own father's lackeys? That doesn't make sense."

"Your bewilderment mirrors my own. Perhaps it's demon politics—not uncommon for children to usurp their parents to claim power, prestige, or whatever other desire humans would write parables about."

"Probably one of those." Kendra shook her head and sighed. "Well … I hope whoever did Onaga in really put the hurt on him."

"I'd thank them personally," Azazel agreed. "If not for my position as a knight of King Asmodeus and my adherence to the Code of Satan, I'd have taken the task upon myself."

"Ooh. Big words from Zel," Kendra teased, snorting as she sat up.

"Hardly," Azazel affirmed. "But I'm certain that whoever killed him was plenty capable, nonetheless."

As Kendra stared into the mirror, she noticed that Azazel wore a more casual blouse compared to the outfit or armor she usually saw whenever they'd interacted.

"Evening plans?" Kendra inquired, and Azazel snickered.

"I do have a pretty romantic evening planned with my pillow," Azazel claimed, making Kendra chortle.

"Lucky girl." She clicked her tongue. "How ironic. Waking me up from my nap to tell me you're heading to bed? Have you no shame?"

Azazel chuckled, his environment shifting to that of an arched door, which he opened to step onto what appeared to be a balcony. The image in the mirror didn't display precise detail, but she saw a large bird land behind Azazel, hooting at him with a demonic tinge to its voice.

"It would be odd if a demon didn't go to bed with a wicked misdeed," he asserted, the corner of his mouth tugging into a hooked smile. "Forgive the audaciousness of my vulcan compatriot, Cinnel. She is quite feisty when I have been gone for long."

"You have a pet vulcan?"

"Of the owl variety, yes. She was watching us in secret the last time we met, but she's rather shy with others." Staring into the several black eyes peering from behind Azazel, Kendra chuckled nervously.

"Shy ... sure," she muttered. "I'm sure she's also upset that you're calling me so late. I'm sure it be-*hoo*-ves her how inconsiderate you are," she said, making Azazel chuckle.

"Perhaps I am considerate of something else I wish to ask you, now that I have stolen your attention," he said. Meanwhile, Kendra twisted her lips with his lack of a reaction to the pun she deigned to make.

"Okay, phantom thief. Shoot," Kendra urged, cocking a brow.

"Do you feel strong yet?" he asked, and Kendra's expression softened. A thoughtful glimmer entered her eyes. The answer that came to mind mulled into sweet wine, and she gave her own devilish smirk.

"Maybe I'll tell you the next time I see you."

"And deprive me of self-aggrandizing satisfaction before my slumber?"

"Consider it my wicked misdeed for interrupting mine," she said, and Azazel laughed heartily, gifting her the satisfaction he previously deprived her of.

"The symmetry offered in these banters pleases me so. I'll have to bring the duskberry wine I last spoke of when we meet again. Perhaps the bloom of spring in your region would be apt?"

"I can make time mid-April, and that duskberry wine better be as good as you've hyped it up to be. I'm ashamed to admit I'm becoming a bit of a wine mom," she said, thinking back to the last brand she had tried. The thought of it made her face scrunch. As she had discovered, more expensive did not mean it was better.

"Then I anticipate your elation," Azazel spoke dramatically, and the feed faded along with the light within the mirror.

Kendra huffed, standing before she tossed the mirror back inside of the drawer. When she glanced at Yuki's dresser, she eyed the violin perched on its stand and a stack of cards next to it. They had played blackjack together a few times, and she always found herself impressed with how Yuki shuffled the cards. In truth, she was more entertained watching her weave them like a waterfall than actually playing.

Remembering what Intico had told her, she recalled it had mentioned passing the time with cards. It further spoke of a surprise the next time she'd visit, of which her skepticism had run amok since. Contrary to her hesitation, she was more than aware it was harmless within the recesses of her shadow. Even then, the concept of its presence did peeve her enough to make her less inclined to inspect her own body in fear of its prying eyes. While it declared it had no interest in such things, she wasn't inclined to take its word.

"I'll need to start charging it rent," she muttered, running a hand through her wavy brown hair, tossing it over her shoulder before plopping onto her bed. She crossed her legs, humming a tune to herself as she focused with her eyes closed. Meditation was beyond boring for her, but she channeled her focus and slowly retreated into her shadow.

When she opened her eyes, she was sitting on a stool before a dainty wooden bar, of which her fingers pressed into idly. The sensations within her shadow were duller than reality, but despite that, she scowled at the bare wood. The idea of a soul splinter sounded more painful than a real one, somehow.

Soft jazz played from an unknown source, but it was oddly relaxing and of good volume. The perfect ambience, by Kendra's sensibilities. She spun around within the plush leather seat and studied the saloon-styled room lined with several counters and game tables reminiscent of a vintage casino. As she scrutinized the exact composition, she felt as if she had stumbled into one of Chicago's dive bars—complete with the scent of whiskey and cigars. How Intico knew to replicate such a scent was beyond her. More concerning was how an entire realm of darkness was juxtaposed where a wall should have been.

"You've been busy," Kendra said, standing as she found the impossible-to-miss ten-foot-tall demon lord. It had been changing a lightbulb within one of the hanging light fixtures, and the sight of its spindly digits dwarfing the bulb amused her.

"I so do believe in the protestant work ethic," Intico mused. "Cleanliness is close to unholiness, I say."

"You say a lot of things," she affirmed, clicking her tongue before jumping from the seat. "But I like what you've done with the place, even if the idea you can do this inside of me is more than disturbing."

"If it didn't possess a hint of horror, I'd hang my hat up in shame and ask to be digested," Intico said, screwing the bulb in. Once finished, it walked across the room and stood in front of a blackjack table, where its crescent eyes inspected her. One eye widened as if it were raising a brow. "The rare bedhead Mallory, I see."

"I was woken up from my nap and randomly thought to pop on by, but if you're going to make me self-conscious, I'll leave."

"Apologies," Intico said, leaning down as it picked up a deck of black cards with glimmering white illustrations that undulated the same as its eyes. "I was quite bored without *good* company. I was secretly hoping a discerning matron would appear to give her opinion of my decorating. I am thinking of calling it ... Den of Mallory." As it spoke, it spread the cards out within its fingers, flicking them into the air before swiping its cape over them. When the smoky tresses covered them, the cards were gone, and Intico gestured to the room.

"Name sucks," she said, rolling her eyes. "I'm not an interior designer, but my two contentions right now are the poor choice of surfaces. The rough wood is too rustic for this whole casino dealer thing you're going for, and also, not a big fan of the scent. Something less ... suggestive of old dudes playing poker with revolvers on their hips." As she stared at Intico, it thoughtfully tapped its chin while its other hand drummed the table.

"Duly noted. In honesty, the wood feels nice against my talons and fingers, but this is a place for the weary souls of damned demons. I must not be so selfish—or I should be more," it mused, shrugging.

"Oh, and one more thing," Kendra interjected, her face scrunching as she glanced to the side where she peeked out into the endless darkness. "You've kind of got a whole wall missing. Not entirely certain that gazing into the abyss is a part of the whole experience you're trying to curtail here."

"Ah, yes, *that*," Intico said, grinning widely as it peered into it. "The winged snake insisted on having his own space." Intico chuckled darkly, flicking its hand. "The geezer destroyed the pool table in the process too. He's no fun."

Kendra peered hard into the darkness at the mention, her lips pursing as her eyes drifted down to where the floor faded into the shadows. There, resting atop the weathered wood, was a black feather.

"Right," she murmured. Thinking about it, she recalled seeing the ominous purple light for a moment when she first spotted the darkness, but she had no desire to go trekking through it. "At least he's quieter than when he was alive. Seemed the type who'd yap your ear off if you got him started, and not in the endearing way." Kendra sighed heavily, shaking her head. "Still not sure how this whole soul-eating thing works."

"For such a pedantic gentleman, he is remarkably mute now, but in fairness ... so was I for a while." Intico flicked its hand to shoot the deck of cards from its sleeves, which it splayed through its long fingers.

"I could probably make a fortune off all the salt I'm detecting in here," Kendra mused. Intico gave a fake laugh as it shuffled the cards in the same way Yuki had.

"Care to show how much salt *you're* worth in a game of blackjack?" Intico challenged, one of its eyes widening theatrically.

"As much as I'd love to indulge you in a game of cards in the shadow realm, I'm going back to bed. Also, stop peeking at what I'm doing without permission, perv," Kendra chastised.

"You wound me as if to slay me twice," Intico said performatively, pulling a handkerchief from its suit jacket and pretending to wipe its eyes. "His company urges me to seek entertainment through your daily ventures."

"As long as you guys aren't fighting, I don't really care. Don't need to be a mom to two dead demon lords." Kendra sighed, and she clapped her hands together as she focused on leaving. "Make things easy for me, and I'll take you to see some holographic fireworks next month."

As Kendra's form began to dissipate, Intico tossed the handkerchief. It removed its hat and bowed with the accessory gestured across its chest, snickering as she disappeared.

"Fret not, I'll behave."

The incandescent blue skies kissed the valley below, and the clouds garrisoned within it diffused the brimming sun. It was a moderately cool day—a break within the cold spells and snow. Ripe with muck, the land below was peppered with piles of congealed, melting snow. Yet the hill Kendra marched up had been undisturbed. While the grass and gravel were moist, its traction still allowed her to ascend the cliff.

When she reached the top, Eden came into view. There, by the edge, he stared down at the valley. The reflection of the blue sky married his crimson irises, and a purple hue was born as he stared upon the drifting omens.

Despite the frigid air, he was dressed in only a gray long-sleeved shirt, where the front collar was undone to reveal the ruby hanging from his neck. His sleeves were rolled up, smears of blue and white paint streaking down his wrists and hands. Next to him, a black easel stood, a paint-covered apron draped on one of its protrusions. Atop the canvas was the painting he had been working on moments before Kendra had arrived.

As she approached him, he stared down at the valley and the omens dancing across his hands. Like dew adrift, the sentiments they conveyed tingled against his palms, and his ambiguous expression beckoned Kendra to drift closer. Though her steps were hesitant, she drew nearer under the assumption he was already aware of her. Her eyes flicked to the basket containing the bottles of pastel paint, but she didn't look at the painting yet.

"How'd you know I'd be here?" he asked, his low voice tranquil as the still winds.

"Lucky guess," Kendra lied, smirking sheepishly as she stopped by his side. She smoothed her white sweater minidress before placing her hands behind her back.

They stood quietly, and Eden continued to stare down at his hands with a hard expression, but unlike the many times before, the distance within his depths was notably shorter. She hadn't seen him much since the rescue, and while concerned, she respected his solitude.

"Honk, honk. Watcha thinkin' 'bout?" she asked, and Eden's hands slowly closed.

"What to call the painting," Eden replied, glancing back over at the painting, and he met her gaze at last. Holding it for several moments, he gestured to the painting, nodding.

With his permission, Kendra turned to look at it finally. She took a step closer to inspect it, leaning in to see the wet smears of cyan blue, lilac, and royal blue—like her eyes. Those tones captured the valley below. Its color was lighter than reality suggested, with the darker blue defining the trees and ground. At first, she thought that snowflakes dotted the scenery, but upon closer inspection, she saw they were small feathers adrift, descending from the heavenly light that pierced the curtains of clouds.

"It's ... my first time working with pastel palettes. I wasn't confident. My blending is definitely off, and I'm pretty sure I messed up—"

"You know how precious you are to me, right?" Kendra asked, turning to face him with a wide smile.

Eden blushed and turned his head. Though he tried to maintain his stoicism, his lips curled into a small smile. Then he began to chuckle heartily, crossing his arms.

"Not sure I'd be able to forget," he managed to say between his bouts of soft laughter.

"Good," Kendra affirmed, nodding triumphantly as she stepped toward the painting, then peered down at the basket. A book was tucked between the bottles of acrylic paint, and she leaned down and carefully pulled it up to examine the cover.

"Bookworm," Kendra accused as she ran her thumb across the title. A giggle escaped upon seeing the illustration of turtles adrift in a cloud-filled sky. The pages were weathered but remarkably maintained for an older title.

"Recently," Eden admitted, rubbing his fingers together before he approached the easel and used his apron to wipe his hands clean. "I just started it. Ethan gave it to me when I was a kid, and I found it while going through my stuff. Thought I'd see why he liked the book so much," Eden said, his lips tightening. He released a heavy breath and shook his head. "I'm liking it."

"Lathe of Heaven ..." Kendra whispered, tilting her head before she slid the book back into place. "The cover is kind of funny, but turtles are cool."

Eden grabbed the thin brush that rested in a groove of the stand, pausing as he scrutinized the painting. Finally, he carefully raised it to add a white streak to one of the feathers he spotted in the painting. His eyes continued dissecting it for several seconds, but he finally set the brush down, his lips clamping tightly.

"Liberation," Eden said, and Kendra stood, cocking her head. "That's what I'm calling the painting."

Kendra turned to the painting again, and she peered at one of the feathers, disheveled yet floating within the serene sky all the same.

"You've got the Mallory stamp of approval," she said, winking at him before patting his arm.

Eden turned and carefully approached the edge of the cliff again, but rather than peering out over the valley, he stared down at his feet. As his boots dug into the damp grass, he clenched his fists tightly as his smile faded.

"I've thought about it a lot," he said. He bit his bottom lip, spinning to face her, but his eyes were still fixed on the ground. "If I'd wake up in that cell again when I fall asleep. What would be waiting for me if I did. But recently, each time I have slept, I haven't dreamed. It's weird, but I almost miss seeing it, as if ... I'm leaving something behind in spite of the suffering it brought."

Kendra approached him, her fingers clenching her long sleeves as she peered behind him. There, atop the branch of a sapling, she saw a dove tucked along the branch. Its black eyes were fixed on Eden, she was sure, but it was too far to tell. She returned her attention to him, seeing his head slowly rise. And with her being his captive audience, he continued.

"What was left of me had been dedicated to putting an end to Onaga. It's been so long, but now that he's gone, I don't know what to make of it all," Eden admitted, his eyes quivering. "I don't think ... I'll ever truly be free from that place or Onaga's looming wings in my memory, but the more I think about what lies ahead—the life I want to live"—he took a deep breath, his fists unclenching as he met her gaze—"I think I'm ready to move forward again."

His crimson eyes glistened with an unfamiliar resolve. Within the tatters of tragedy replaying in those bloody depths, Kendra saw the silver lining gleam at last. She lifted her glasses and approached, but the moment her boot crunched against the gravel, the dove flew away from the sapling. They were alone again. The phantoms lingering and the ghosts of trauma were quiet, and the silence was theirs to fill.

She stopped in front of him and took his hands in hers. As her fingers ran over his, she conjured a smile—genuine and brimming. With the silence no longer welcome, Kendra found the sentiment she'd recite to usher him from the darkness.

"And I'll be right here with you. I promise."

The memorial stones cast their shadows over Kendra as she prayed before the newest engravement. *Bonnie Blair*. She opened her eyes, taking several steps back across the gray brick pavement, her eyes sinking as she turned from it.

"Be at peace, Bon-Bon," she whispered, joining her hands behind her back. She had already prayed at Steiner's name, and suddenly, she thought back to their days as cadets and Bonnie lecturing both of them about taking care of their hunter suits. She had burned hers plenty, but Steiner, experimenting with incantations, had left his thrashed possibly more. She chose to hold that memory close.

She journeyed back through the maze, making her way to the ATV that waited to take her to the Engineering Center. She had received her new suit weeks prior, albeit she still had to wait for a new waistcloth for when her suit inevitably got burned by her own flames again. However, she had gotten better at regulating them since the battle against Onaga.

When Kendra turned, she met the gaze of another hunter wearing a black suit—Donovan. She'd met him a handful of times, and from their limited interactions, she had come to know why he was considered many people's favorite driver. In his older age, he had resigned to less physically taxing roles, and as her senior, she respected his persistence to grow old in the profession.

"Hey, Don," Kendra greeted, and he tipped his hat as he approached.

"Not many your age pay heed to the value of life as they should," he said in a low voice. "Always see you here. Praying and remembering."

"Vic gave his life for me, Steiner lost his far too soon, and Bonnie lost hers in front of me. I cherished all of them," she said, approaching Donovan as he flashed her a wry smile.

"I fought alongside and drove many of these fine people around. You never do get over not seeing their faces in the rearview or blurred in inebriation as you laugh and exchange stories. I gotta remember why I'm still alive, so every day I'm here. Don't go home till I've paid respects."

Kendra gave a sad smile, shuffling to stand at his side.

"It's heavy. But I think it's heavier if I don't. If I don't try to remember how easily it can all be wrenched away. Really makes me want to try hard to keep more names off these stones."

"Hunters like you come along only once a generation. Maybe twice—not sure how they count these things anymore." Donovan wiped his eyes, readjusting his hat before he nodded at her, walking past her with a labored gait.

"Then I guess I'm the chosen one," Kendra mused, drawing a hearty laugh from Donovan as he raised two fingers.

"Keep on keepin' on, kid."

Kendra turned on her feet, a soft smile spreading on her lips as she navigated back to the ATV.

The ride was quiet. Her braid caressed her cheeks, carried by the wind, and she stared ahead past the armored vehicles and jogging cadets. Their squad hadn't gathered often since the operation, but Eden had been absent, as had Andrew until their last meeting.

As they came to the dirt road, the garages came into view, and she gripped a support bar as she leaned out, searching for garage F-19. With each of the bold red-lettered signs they passed, she counted down beneath her breath. She lost track when she saw Seraph Nine assembled inside the open garage. While they congregated peacefully, she couldn't help but remember the losses they incurred as well—Jack and Hyde, whose visages had been stolen for the ruse against her and Eden.

She spotted Cassius, who still wore the bold shades that hid eyes she rarely saw, but she could tell he had spotted her. Rather than flipping him off, she raised two fingers, pressed them to her temple, then gestured them at him. In response, he smirked and flashed her devil horns.

She knew that Andrew preferred the large door closed when he worked—a sensory preference for him. As such, it was closed when they approached, but she saw shadows peeking from the sides where two vehicles were parked. When the ATV stopped in the front, she patted Devon on the shoulder and twisted to face him.

"By the way, Devon. Birthday is on May nineteenth. You got a few months to pick something out for me," she mused, her other hand gripping the outside roof of the ATV.

"I'll get you an Arby's gift card and the cheapest wine I can find at the discount market," Devon joked, brushing Kendra off.

"You'd be my new favorite person," she said and leaped from the ATV before sending him off. As Devon drove away, she circled to the corner, eyeing the two cars parked alongside the garage. One was a navy-green cargo van she didn't recognize, and the other was a white beat-up Humvee she recognized.

"No way ..." she muttered before jogging to the garage and entering through the side door. She sprinted through the hall, coming into the open center.

The squad congregated as they usually would. Alicia stood beside Yuki, who had Ryu on her lap while he played an old fighting game on her handheld gaming console. Emily, Joseph, and Damion were bickering about firearms—again. At the largest workbench, Valeria and Andrew stood next to James and Major Carter. For some reason, Zane was there too.

"J-man? What are you doing here?" Kendra asked, earning the attention of James and her squad.

James set down the pencil he held, letting it roll across the blueprints they had hovered over.

"Just here putting my expertise to use with my former fetch-monkey," James said, adjusting the goggles on his head before Major Carter nudged him defiantly. "What? I said former," James scoffed, shaking his head. "Speaking of which, Sal is making a good recovery. Told him I'd be seeing you today—he says howdy." Hearing that, Kendra smiled and crossed her arms, thinking of Azazel's involvement.

"Guess I'll have to make a call. A lot of people have been waking up," she mused, shaking her head. "So, you and Major Carter go back then, huh?"

"My rigor is in audio-resonance technology and drone systems. James here mentored me before he took on a passive role with the Hunt. Real good with prosthetics," Major Carter complimented before gesturing his thumb to James. "Considering you worked with him once, you're more than aware of how much of an overachiever he is." The statement caused Andrew to pout, huffing in defiance.

"My dad is the one who helped me design those awesome sonic cannons that I got to unveil—the equations and system specifics especially. He's got way cooler stuff he's drafted up," Andrew said, as if chastising his father. "Next time, I'll update the frequency firmware of your earplugs so you can block out the sound. Dad is working with me on it, and we should be done with it sooner than later. He's the best!"

"He's the best at what he *does*, but so am I," James chimed in, snorting at Andrew. Kendra then sneered playfully at James.

"James can disassemble and reassemble just about anything, but if what his missus said is true, he still can't cook rice in a rice cooker," Kendra teased as she marched forward.

"He can't!" Joseph called out, prying away from his conversation to corroborate Kendra's claim.

"And why the hell would I need to?" James argued sheepishly, wiggling his eyebrow before snatching the pencil up. "Making the kid's new arm is more useful than some damned rice, anyway."

"I could kill an entire pot of rice after a long mission," Zane said, breaking his silence.

"They ain't paying ya enough to get takeout or something?" James spat.

As they went back and forth, Major Carter smirked, patting the top of Andrew's head.

"Looks like we won't be putting the rice-cooking module in there after all," Major Carter joked, making Andrew crack up with that impervious grin everyone knew him for.

Kendra spun to Valeria, flashing a smirk at her as she hovered behind Andrew with an adoring smile.

"Maybe at least a mini-oven for the nugs," she suggested, and Andrew perked up.

"That would be awesome! But ... I get enough heat as it is from getting hugged by Kendra and Zane," he said, making both the girls laugh.

"Kendra's a hottie, yeah," Valeria affirmed, winking at Kendra.

"What can I say?" Kendra began, gesturing her hand down her form. "Hot girl summer year-round."

"That apply to me too?" Zane said, having finished bickering with James. He stopped in front of her, his arms crossed.

"I can think of a few girls you're cattier than," Kendra alleged, and Zane scratched the air in response.

"Speaking of catty, you guys should have seen Kendra tearing Onaga up. Gave him the thrashing of a lifetime. Even finished him off by yelling out her signature move—*Hell Flash!*" Zane projected, using his hands as a megaphone, causing the room to crack up as Kendra's cheeks flushed.

"That's so cool!" Andrew called out, breaking from the pattern of amusement with genuine wonder.

"And this is why you'll be spared in my manifesto," Kendra said, scrunching her face as she fist-bumped Andrew. She spun on her heel, facing the others with a hand on her hip. "Beating Onaga means I'm not such a rookie like Damion claims."

"You had Zane's help," Joseph challenged, folding his arms as he removed the upper half of his suit, revealing the black compression shirt underneath as the suit hung at his waist.

"Easy mode," Valeria chirped.

"And what about Orphan? You two were on the ground while I kicked them around in a game of four-D soccer," Kendra affirmed, and Zane gave them a thumbs-down.

"I'll give you your praise where you've earned it. Nice work, Ken," Damion chimed in, waving at their jeering comrades. As the team continued speaking, Kendra turned to face Andrew again, leaning close.

"By the way—sonic cannons fire? Top-tier unveiling of your own attack," Kendra said. Zane snorted and leaned in with his arms around the two.

"I never thought to go shouting my attack, but I'm thinking of calling that furnace thingy I did *Hell Raiser*. Whatcha think of that?"

"Sounds about Zane," Kendra affirmed, and Andrew tapped his chin, idly glancing to the blueprint his father and James talked over.

"I like it. But what about that thing you did against that Magenta weirdo?" he asked. Zane's eyes widened, and he considered it as he released both of them. He snapped his fingers, pointing to the ceiling.

"Supernova!" he declared, nodding triumphantly. "While I'm thinking about it, I should totally name my demon form too." He tapped his chin, pacing for a few moments. "Thinking ... Super Zane, or maybe Devil Trigger?" As he postulated, Alicia booed and gave a thumbs-down.

"You're just jealous that the hottest people in the room stole all the glory," Zane shot back, winking mockingly at Alicia.

"I would have made it too easy, is all. The fates didn't want me knocking either of your egos down," she bolstered, and Yuki tugged her arm playfully.

"You still did wonderfully," Yuki praised, her eyes shimmering up at Alicia.

"Your praise is all I care about," Alicia said, grinning down at her.

"Mother," Ryu chimed, snatching Yuki and Alicia's attention. "I prefer playing the pretty lady in blue than the guy sharing my name," he said. His golden eyes then flicked from the screen to her face, and Yuki smiled brightly.

"She's such a fun character to play. Good to know both of us think she's pretty," Yuki said, brushing his white hair from his face. "Kawaii," she shrieked as she gazed down at him, and Ryu blushed as he handed her the console.

"Mr. Zane?" Ryu began, jumping from Yuki's lap and carefully walking across the garage. "Can we practice demon alchemy now?"

Zane tapped his chin, smirking as he met Yuki's gaze, who flashed him a kind smile.

"Tell you what, if you can recite the three principles of demon alchemy without your notebooks, we can go to my lab for the afternoon."

Ryu's eyes perked, and he held his hand up.

"Principle one is knowledge. Principle two is ambition. And principle three is equilibrium," Ryu said, and Zane crouched, tilting his head.

"Hm ... and why are those important?"

"Knowledge is needed to understand the physical and spiritual elements of reality, ambition is necessary to will it to your desires, and equilibrium is needed to govern the balance that must be maintained."

The hunters' jaws dropped, and Yuki couldn't help but give a small clap as Zane rubbed his head nervously.

"Smart kid," James grumbled, peeking up from working on the blueprint.

"He knows five languages already," Yuki said dotingly.

"I am only good with two, though," he said, a hint of shame in his voice. Kendra then crouched next to them, flashing a grin at him.

"And that's two more than Mr. Zane, including his English," she said, and Zane shot her a frown.

"Hey ... I know words. I have the best words," Zane complained, sighing. "Alright, Ryu. Go get your journal, and we'll get started." As he said that, Ryu squealed and ran over to Yuki, who was already rummaging through the bag next to her for his journal.

The room went quiet as the door opened from down the hall, and they watched as Eden stepped into the room, dressed in his usual combat attire. He hesitantly looked around at the faces of his comrades, but when he saw Andrew, he pursed his lips.

"Captain," Kendra called with a smile. Their eyes met, her expression beckoning him.

Eden swallowed his hesitation, clenching his fists as he tepidly approached Andrew. When he stopped at the workbench, he met his young comrade's wide blue eyes, but briefly, he glanced at the tied sleeve of his missing arm.

"I owe you an arm," Eden declared, and Andrew's lips went ajar as James gawked.

"That's one way to say hi," James muttered.

"Given we're both left-handed, and that's the arm I happen to be missing, you'll have a lot more lifting to do," Andrew said, offering a small smile as he held his hand out. Eden nodded and took it in his left hand with a squeeze.

"I promise," Eden alleged, and in the solemn solidarity they shared, Eden cracked a smile when Andrew grinned at him.

"He's not gonna be a burden, you know," Major Carter said, placing a hand on Andrew's head and ruffling his hair. "By the time James and I are done, his new arm will be so amazing that nobody will miss the old one." Andrew snorted and snatched his father's hand from his head.

"It'll be amazing because *you* made it, not because of any fancy gadgets we'll be attaching to it," Andrew alleged.

"Taking parenting notes, Dad?" Joseph called out to James, who shook his head.

"Arms and legs I gave you are workin', ain't they?" James huffed out.

"No thanks to your cooking," Joseph shot back, making the squad chuckle. "But they're awesome enough, regardless."

Zane cleared his throat loudly, beckoning Eden's attention as he approached him.

"You know, I got a pretty gnarly scar on my back fighting for you," Zane prompted, folding his arms. Eden turned to face him, his expression elusive.

"Want me to kiss it better?" Eden retorted, and collectively, the women cooed, hearing that.

"I'd pay to see that," Alicia mused, and Yuki laughed softly.

"Not with Ryu here, please," Yuki chastised. She carefully placed a textbook and journal in his hands, whispering before releasing him.

Zane shifted on his feet as Ryu came rushing back, hoisting the large textbook written in Indiox and a smaller black journal atop it.

"You'll just have to kiss my boo-boos another day, Samurai. You can thank me by buying more dino nuggies for Andrew. Kind of finished the box this morning."

"*Zane ...*" Andrew groaned, glaring at him, and Zane sheepishly smiled before ushering Ryu to follow him as he spun and waltzed out of the room.

"Later, Seven and the old-heads," Zane said, waving goodbye.

"Have Ryu back by sundown, please," Yuki reminded him as the two disappeared down the hall.

Kendra felt a tap on her shoulder, and she turned to face Eden, whose eyes danced nervously.

"What's up?" she asked.

"I'm meeting with General Blackwell at the end of the week, now that I'm officially cleared to return for duty."

"Yeah?" she asked, puzzled by where he was leading. She had always known him to be aloof about his mother, but uncertainty was riddled in his gaze. As she watched him hesitate to speak, he reached out, taking her hand and squeezing it for comfort.

"I ... have a favor to ask," Eden finally admitted. He averted his eyes, but Kendra squeezed his hand, urging him to meet her gaze again as she spoke. "Of course."

"I am unsure of how I will pay back the debt I have incurred with you," Jessica spoke, staring across her desk at Zane. "My selfishness is my burden, and I thrust you into harm's way to see it remedied."

"I had my reasons for agreeing when all is said and done," Zane insisted, drumming his fingers along her desk before glancing at the picture of Jessica's former squad. He then focused on Ethan's face with fond recollection. "Orphan really did a number on us. Their damage is probably deeper than

I'd care to dig, but I'm sure it'll eventually surface even if I didn't." Zane stopped his drumming, peering up as he thoughtfully mulled over the idea.

"I wouldn't ask you to again," she said, and Zane sighed in relief.

"Good. I'm done playing detective for a while—starting when I leave this office."

"Then you have something on your mind while you're still here?" Jessica asked, perking up as she reached across her desk, resting her palm atop her hat.

"More than I'd care to pontificate about," Zane said, clicking his tongue. "Geez... pontificate? Gods, I'm sounding like Onaga now," Zane whined in dismay, shaking his head. "Anyway, before I dig into the meat, I wanted to say your insight is a lot keener than I gave you credit for. Kendra kicked serious ass when shit hit the fan, and she even used illusion magic all of a sudden. Still don't know what that was about, but I'm alive."

"Illusion magic?" Jessica questioned, cocking her head as her eyes flicked around as she considered it. "I wonder if Alicia has been teaching her..." Jessica muttered but shrugged. "However, her proficiency wouldn't fool Onaga, I imagine."

"Maybe she's got a knack for it? She refused to tell me about it when I asked."

"Just another auspicious mystery, as are the tomes that were gifted to you," Jessica claimed. Her hands balled into fists, and her attention fell onto the Tome of Genesis that was opened in front of her. "When I entered his study, the tomes appeared locked within liminal access paths—only illusions of sight outside of the specific laboratories where their blood is present. In the absence of Onaga's blood, we'll have to find the other laboratories each book is bound to in order to take possession of them. If only it were as simple as peering through the axes between—he seemed to patch that loophole prior to dying."

"That was another thing on my mind. The Tomes of Knowledge," Zane said, clearing his throat as he leaned forward, tapping the tome in front of her. "They appear to operate in a similar way to this one, such that only those possessed with the prerequisite knowledge, or a foundation, can hold them. Blood enchantment and all. Well... Yuki's son could hold the one you're reading." Jessica perked up at his statement.

"The boy is capable of such a thing? He must have been taught well."

"By Onaga," Zane confirmed, his eyes narrowing. "Lucy mentioned that Ryu had been taken under his wing, pun intended. He and Lucy were close, from what I was told. Thinks highly of her... but—"

"She betrayed my son—shattered his heart. I am under the assumption that whatever angle she is operating from, it is with cynicism and deceit," Jessica spoke bitterly.

"I know... or so that's the story," Zane said, holding Jessica's glower with firm regard, and he bit his lip before crossing his arms. "A story of subterfuge and deceit for Onaga's benefit. Sound familiar?" Zane questioned.

In that instance, their fingers fled the page, and Jessica diverted her gaze. Though she hadn't the capacity to entertain the insinuation, she knew what Zane was suggesting. She snapped the tome shut before shaking her head.

"I am done studying for today. These fanatical scribbles make my brain tremble," Jessica said.

"Should have heard the author. Worst kind of yapper," Zane mused, cringing at the memory.

"Onaga has taken much from this world, but his greed shall not harm another soul," she declared, leaning forward and resting her chin on her knuckles. "If only I could say it wouldn't haunt another soul..."

"Lots of pain, blood, and loss." Zane sighed. "While we could sit here moping for hours, I wanted to push back on this sentiment of yours you've been suggesting, if I can be personal for a second," Zane said.

Jessica's expression stirred in response.

"And what is that?"

"This fixation on lambasting your *selfishness*, madam. I kept doing the same for a long time after Ethan recruited me, and at one point he told me the same thing I'm about to tell you." Zane cleared his throat, tapping the desk sharply. "The world is give and take, and if you spend all your time feeling sorry for what you've taken, you'll never bring yourself to give instead."

"Oh, Zane," Jessica chuckled, leaning forward. "You aren't the only one who he has spoken those words to. He was big into his books and always had some fancy, philosophical quote to give when he saw others struggling."

"Then you know what he'd say to you now," Zane retorted. Jessica's shoulders sank, and she sighed as he shifted to cup her cheek.

"I try to remember where Ethan began and Orphan ended, reflecting upon these several years. It's one of the few falsehoods I can say makes my skin crawl—but while I understand his heart... I can't say I believe all of what it declares. He chose to love me after all—wouldn't be the last sentiment of his I was skeptical of."

"Hm. Hard for me to come up with a retort to that one, so I'll just play my trump card," Zane said.

He took a tranquil breath, hand hovering over his chest. With a calm focus, the golden embers within him brewed into a soft, flowing golden flame that colored his face in its serenity.

"Using my own big-boy words, if you keep focusing on what you lost, you'll never find it again," Zane said, smiling softly. He lowered his hand, and the flame faded. "It's ironic, really. Best hiding spot was the one nobody knew about, but she trusted me to find her when I needed her the most. Now that's poetry," Zane said, snickering with a grin.

"You truly are remarkable," Jessica mused, her eyes falling again as she scooped her hat up. She glanced back to the squad photo, and as her fingers tensed along the hat's brim, she released the fermenting breath that threatened to burn through her. "I'm unsure how you've adopted such peace within all of this chaos."

"I didn't," Zane corrected, snapping his fingers before a scarlet flame flickered on the end of his index finger. "It's a balancing act." Zane blew the flame out. With a yawn, he turned from a dumbfounded Jessica and patted his stomach. "It's late. So, before this turns into another philosophy session, I'm gonna head out—end this detective saga the way the gods intended."

As Zane walked away, Jessica placed her hat back on, shaking her head with a sigh.

"You're too much," she muttered. "Enlighten me on how the saga of Detective Larson ends?"

Zane looked back over his shoulder, winking.

"A boatload of tacos."

As Kendra and Eden occupied the elevator leading up to Jessica's office, they were both silent. Much like before, when they went to see Orphan, there was a silent tension.

The maternal bond had ceased long ago—their tapestry bathed in bitterness and tragedy. It had been an alien thing to Kendra. She had contacted her mother every day since she had awakened. Even the days of hell prior to Onaga's death hadn't been a roadblock to that burning desire of hers. The dinner Eden had with her and her father proved that much, yet it wasn't until recently that he had truly witnessed what it meant.

Kendra was the one person alive he could trust completely. They understood one another in a way unseen—barely articulable. He had once staked his life for her, and she had done the same in turn. Waking from his slumber in the night, ears rattled by the echoes of what once was, he could imagine what she'd say to every daft fear he could espouse. Every stray insecurity, she'd swat aside and attack the root. And while the weeds were deep, her claws dared to dig deeper.

"It's funny, isn't it?" Kendra asked, breaking the silence. "In a way, it feels scarier than last time." Her acknowledgment pulled a bittersweet smile from him, and he shrugged.

"It is scarier," he confessed, pursing his lips tightly when the elevator opened. With tepid steps, they quietly treaded the halls. As they came to a bend, they were greeted by opposing footsteps, and they stopped upon spotting Commander Evans.

Their paths had intersected unintentionally, but the air was heavy nonetheless. The pair straightened their posture and saluted, as was custom, but Commander Evans came to a stop. Before they could speak, he reached out and pushed their hands down, shaking his head.

As his stern eyes met theirs, he found himself hesitating for a moment. His tongue twisted in his closed lips, and he swallowed.

"Twenty-two and six," he said. "Those were the number of confirmed kills I made in Operation Avarice and the number of losses we incurred during Harvest. Six good hunters, paid back threefold, but I wish it had been four."

Eden watched him quietly, letting him finish speaking. His hands fell to his sides, and he glanced down at Commander Evans's trembling hands.

"I thought I would die when that somnium showed its head. Orphan suggested as much—said I'd be sacrificed when I wasn't needed any longer. I think about that night. How I froze. How I could have saved my subordinates who had relied upon me for clarity and guidance in the darkness. Then you... you reminded me of what it meant to be a hunter. That despite the adversity towering above us, we ignite with hope."

Kendra shifted to Eden's side, and as she lowered her gaze, it dawned on her—the gravity that had weighed on their superior. She saw nothing but genuine human regard in Commander Evans as he spoke. Fear and pride alike joined into one resolve that both she and Eden came to admire as he went on.

"When Ethan—Orphan—suggested promoting you, as much as I tried finding a reason to spare General Blackwell the anxiety of thrusting you into the jaws of hell, I knew that our comrades would be safest led by you. There is no perilous night I could find in any nightmare you wouldn't stand to push through. And for that, Eden... you have my eternal gratitude." Commander Evans saluted them.

As much as Eden searched for words to say, he wouldn't get the chance. Commander Evans marched off without another word, and Kendra tugged Eden's sleeve, smiling at him.

"Never thought I'd see the day Commander Evans smoked himself instead of us." Eden chuckled lowly, nodding in agreement. Without letting the moment simmer further, they continued through the hall until they reached Jessica's door. And Eden took a deep, shaky breath, his fingers extending as he shifted his hand. Kendra's own finger found his, and she gave them a squeeze before they entered the office together.

Across from them, Jessica sat, hat in lap as she stared up at them with fond eyes. Quickly, she tore her eyes from Eden and cast them on her desk.

"Private Mallory, you have the deepest stretches of my gratitude and admiration. And while I am certain you suspect that is already the case, it bears repeating with sincere words in privacy rather than in a public spectacle," Jessica said. She bowed her head for several seconds, making Kendra stir with sheepish chagrin.

"I would do it a thousand times," Kendra said simply, unable to think of anything else to add. They took their seats across from Jessica, who nodded in understanding.

"I pray my selfishness would make no such demand of you for that sake." Jessica reached out, pulling a small picture frame across from her closer, and she sighed. "While I want to pretend that this won't be the case, no doubt there are many more Fracti Alas laboratories yet discovered, likely being maintained by the Venatum. This presents the pertinent task of both snuffing out their schemes and locating the remaining Tomes of Knowledge. I haven't even touched on the troubling news of Cecilia's persistence. I'd be daft to assume she and her OCN vermin will remain dormant."

"And I'll gladly be a loyal foot soldier to bring hell to them all," Kendra said, glancing to meet Eden's shy gaze. A smile tugged at his lips before he spoke.

"I want to see a world completely free from the whims of those accursed labs. Until every one of them comes down, I'll be restless," Eden declared, and Jessica stirred uncomfortably.

"I understand your wishes, and I will refrain from working against them," she said after a few moments. "Ethan would have wanted that, I believe. To see me relinquish my fears for the greater good." Eden placed his hands on the desk, his eyes falling as hers had.

"I wonder if the ends justify the means—the sacrifices we make for dreams. But if the means consume us whole, would we see an end we could even recognize?" Eden pondered aloud, and both Jessica and Kendra watched him with thoughtful stares, and Jessica couldn't help but offer a bittersweet smile before tugging the picture closer to herself.

As she stared at it, she allowed herself to feel the weight of each word, compounding with the resonance of a familiar voice.

"You sound like him," Jessica accused. "He loved that book. Said he wished he could have turtle dreams and settle down one day, but I couldn't say yes with the condition he made." She slowly rolled the silver ring on her finger with her thumb. "I wonder if he knew... but I shouldn't get lost wondering about such things. He'd chastise me."

Eden went quiet. He lowered his head, hands clenched, but he released the building tension when Kendra touched his arm. Jessica then tucked her hat against her chest. Her eyes met both of theirs directly and claimed their unwavering attention.

"I apologize for the pain I failed to prevent. A part of me became numb." She pursed her lips. "I didn't feel his heart prior to that meeting, but I couldn't bring myself to believe such a cruel reality. Not again. In fear of losing what remained, I allowed you all to suffer in my unending selfishness. As Mistress of the Hunt, that is a sin far graver than the greed purveyed by Onaga. And for that, I offer you both my sincerest apologies," Jessica said, her composed tone betraying the nature of her words. And as she bowed her head, they watched silently.

The respect Kendra harbored for Jessica had never wavered or ceased. She knew the promises that loomed in Orphan's wake—the fear of what could have been if they had persisted. These two polarizing sentiments resonated in a way she wouldn't deign to admonish.

While Eden closed his eyes, he remembered what it was that he refused to let go for the longest time, and what he would have done if he had been where Jessica sat. If it had been Cassiel or Kendra who had been assimilated and assumed by Orphan, it was unthinkable, and as he damned himself in searching for a viable answer, he came back to the conclusion of the impossible position his mother had been forced into. His heart ached deeply at the thought.

Soon, Jessica cleared her throat and carefully placed her hat atop her head.

"Forgive my moment of weakness. I've no further reason to hold either of you. The year is still young, and there is much work to do. Please be safe," Jessica said, dismissing them. But as Eden hesitated, Kendra squeezed his hand, gesturing her head toward Jessica.

As Jessica stared at them, she was greeted by Eden's eyes. They bored into her like the dagger she had used on Orphan, but rather than condemning her or shying away, a light glimmered from within. With it, a sentiment she had long thought to have been taken from him. Once more, she was greeted by the red apples she remembered fondly from when she'd birthed him.

She was speechless even in that moment, despite him not speaking those sentiments into words. She feared for her heart when he opened his lips to speak.

"Mom..." he called.

The breath in her lungs froze, and the world that had stretched between suddenly became small. The condemnation that was within those precious eyes of his had all but disappeared, and both she and Kendra waited with bated breath.

"Do you think you can make apple pie for me again?"

There was much pain present within the world. Though light lost its way within the suffocating shadows, it was those moments of remembrance that tethered them to the sentiments that gave them both life and purpose. However often that light was taken, they found the strength to kindle anew with its wisps. And those sentiments transcended all arbitrary boundaries of those who would live, be it blood or creed.

Though Eden's quiet voice had been sundered by the finest of glass, its clarity could split the heavens like the book Ethan had so cherished. At its advent, she tilted her hat to conceal her face. Unlike the insidious eyes of greed that stalked Eden from the dark, the only thing peering at him from the shade was a brimming smile. That shade fled when she removed the hat and tucked it to her chest, but her smile was no less dim.

In remembrance of what was taken, at last, Jessica was given hope. And with her quivering voice, she gave her answer.

"*Of course.*"

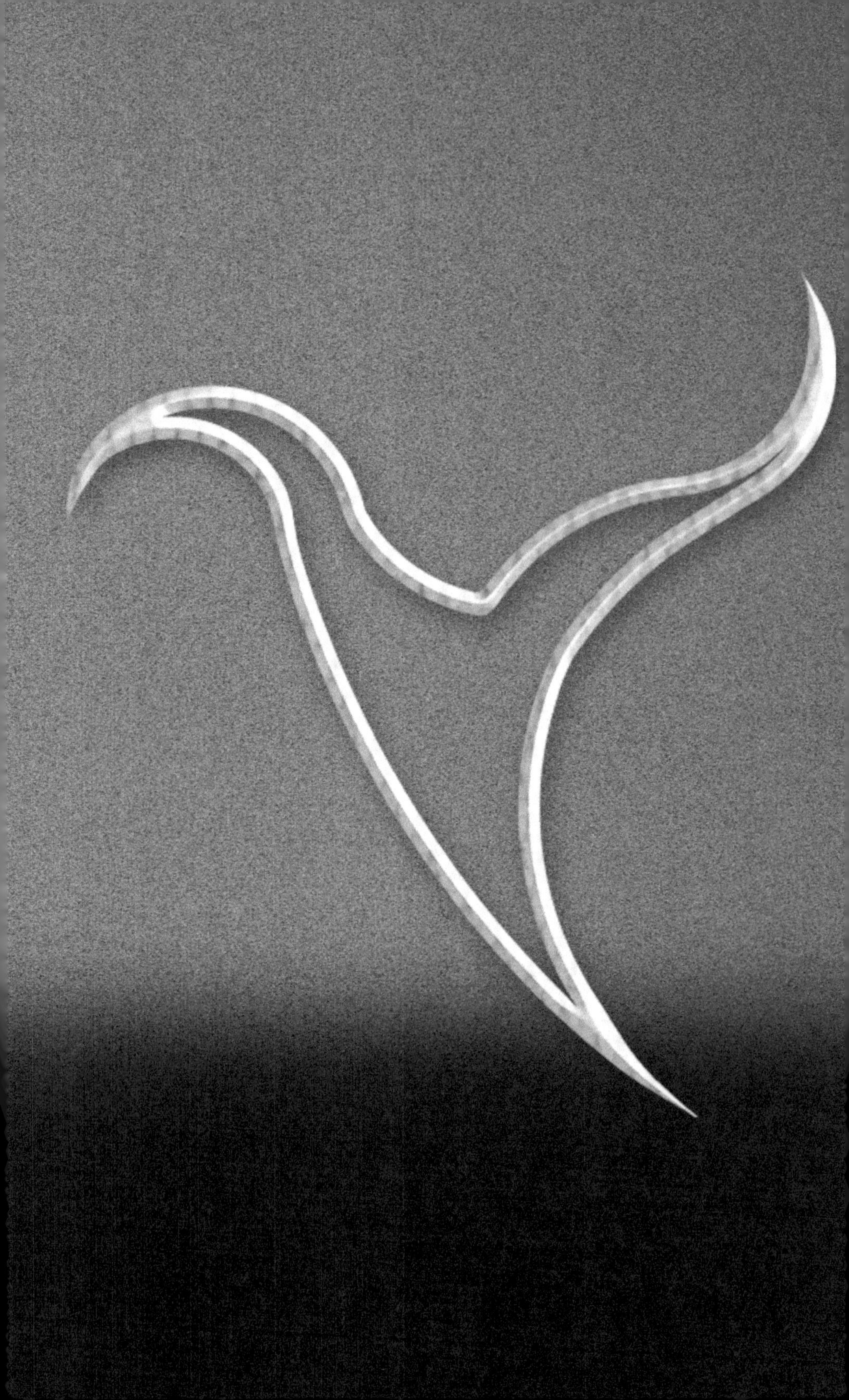

THE END

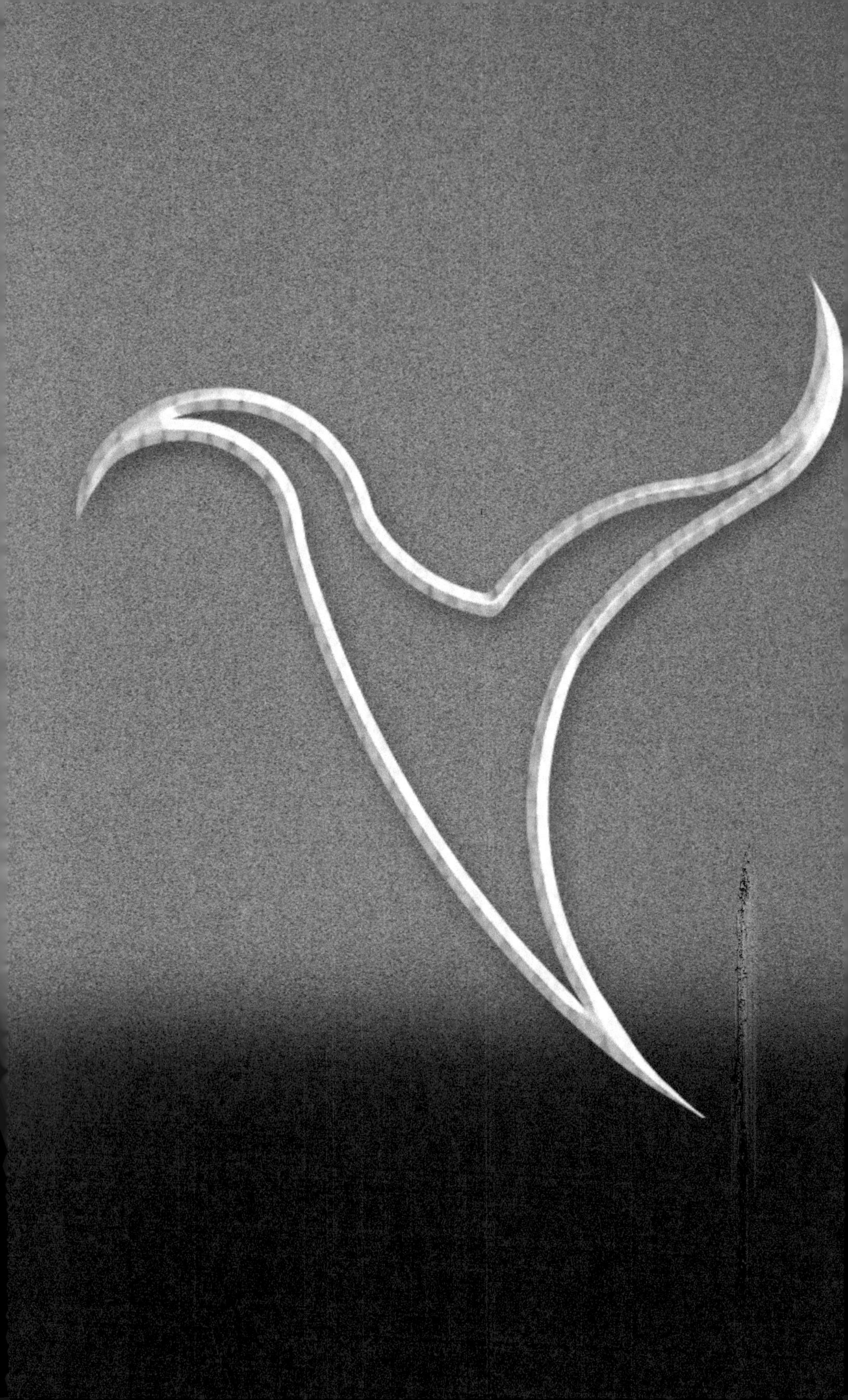

Thank you for reading!

Blood Creed will return

RETRIBUTION

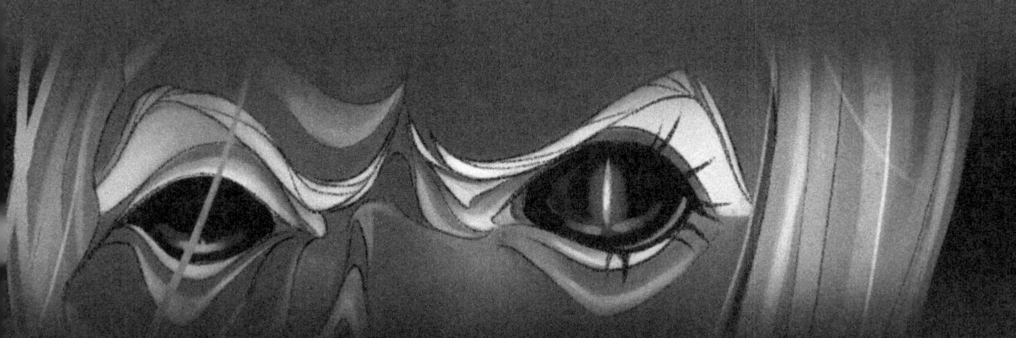

Tributes

I commemorate my eternal appreciation of my friends, artists, and beta readers: Skylar, Elijah, Philip, Devon, and Anna.

I thank Sky, both for all the art they've done for me and for sensitivity reading chapter six to ensure I tackled the themes responsibly.

Elijah, as always, deserves a special place here, due to how he continues to encourage me along my journey as an author! I appreciate you to the moon and back, brother!

I thank my dear friend, Philip, who, atop continuing to provide me art, still endures my long rants about Blood Creed's lore. They also designed the blood rune with me! Also, I publicly thank you again for being a mad lad who drew over 100 eyes for Onaga's true form. Still can't believe they did that. (I didn't ask for that many. I swear. Artists are just built different)

I thank Devon a million times for continuously providing both input and support to elements of this series. She drew up 8 of the nine runes for this book when I needed it most. Fun fact, she also helped design the book title! I appreciate you so much for all you've done for me and this series!

Lastly, I once again pay tribute to my artist, Anna. She continues to provide amazing art and helpful advice along my journey. Thanks again, my friend!

If you would like to follow Eric or subscribe to his newsletter, scan the QR code below!

About the author

Eric Still is a dark fantasy and horror author based out of Los Angeles, California. Most wouldn't know it upon first meeting him, but Eric is autistic, and he is quite proud of the tribulations he has overcome. In fact, he has turned it into his super power, channeling his hyper-fixation in order to craft his stories and efficiently utilize his creativity! Eric decided to become an author due to his  natural love for writing and poetry, and his deep desire to tell stories around lore he has created for over a decade. His love for all that is dark and macabre naturally spurred his desire to write within a genre that combined fantastical and horrifying machinations alike.

His hobbies include playing video games, reading (obviously), hiking, going to concert, attending goth venues (was it mentioned he's goth? Did his black cat make it obvious?), and spending time with his friends in general. He greatly enjoys meaningful conversations covering philosophy and can monologue for hours on a topic he's passionate and cares about!

He draws inspiration from several sources, from the dark world of Marvel's Blade to the Young Adult mythologies of Percy Jackson, video games like Skyrim, God of War, and Dead Space, and anime such as Re:Zero, Dragon Ball, and Full Metal Alchemist. He is certain that, if one is so discerning to catch them, they can glean several references throughout his books!